*For Dana—*

# Rules and Secrets

*The story on page 48 was my first story. Enjoy!*

stories by

## Ruth Moose

*Ruth Moose*

PURE HEART PRESS
Main Street Rag Publishing Company
Charlotte, North Carolina

Copyright ©2007 Ruth Moose

All rights reserved. This book, or parts thereof may not be reproduced in any form without permission

Cover by: Miriam Sagasti

Library of Congress Control Number: 2007922832

ISBN: 978-1-59948-066-4
ISBN: 1-59948-066-2

Produced in the United States of America

Pure Heart Press
Main Street Rag Publishing Company
PO BOX 690100
Charlotte, NC 28227-7001
**www.MainStreetRag.com**

# Acknowledgments

"Biography in Seven Lives" was first published in *Atlantic Monthly*.
"To Banbury Cross" was first published in the *Roanoke Review*.
"The Vinegar Jug" was first published in *Sing Heavenly Muse*.
"Summer Kitchen" first appeared in *Redbook*.
"The Swing" was published in the *Uwharrie Review*.
"The Wreath Ribbon Quilt" first appeared in *the new renaissance*.
"Eyes of Argus" was first published in *The South Carolina Review*.
"Knotty" first appeared in *Southern California Review*.
"Sisters" was published first in *Cotton Boll/Atlanta Review*.
"Pieces of Crow" was previously published in *St. Anthony's Messenger*.

"Daisy Wars" was first published as "The Marigold Wars and Therma Ann" in *Cardinal: An Anthology of North Carolina Writers*.
"Friends and Oranges" was first published in *New Delta Review*.
"The Green Car" was first published in *Crop Dust*.
"He Holds a Black Umbrella" was first published as "Jesus Christ and Other Salesmen" in *Ohio Review*.
"King of the Comics" first appeared in *Crucible*.

The following stories: "Biography in Seven Lives," "Moon Over Magnolias," "To Banbury Cross," "The Vinegar Jug," "The Summer Kitchen," "The Swing," "The Wreath-Ribbon Quilt," "The Eyes of Argus," "Knotty," "Sisters under the Skin," "Pieces of Crow," and "Green Lightning and the Tablecloth Bride" were published in the book *The Wreath Ribbon Quilt* published by St. Andrews Press in 1987, ISBN 0-932662-66-8.

The following stories: "Peanut Dreams and the Blue-Eyed Jesus," "The Women's Club," "The Girl Who Looked like Irma Budd's Little Sister," "The Pink Bed," "Daisy Wars," "Wooden Apples," "Across the Bridge," "Happy Birthday, Billy Boy," "The Green Car," "Rules and Secrets," "Who Cooks for You?," "King of the Comics," "The Silver Crescent," "He Holds a Black Umbrella," "Cows, Coathangers, and the K-Mart Kid," "The Blue Bonnet Bug," "Judas at the Table," "Even the Bees in Denmark," and "Friends and Oranges" were published in the book *Dreaming in Color* by August House Publishing in 1989, ISBN 0-87483-078-8.

*To Talmadge*

# Contents

Biography in Seven Lives. . . . . . . . . . . . . . . . . . . . . . . . . . . 1
Moon Over Magnolias. . . . . . . . . . . . . . . . . . . . . . . . . . . . . 8
To Banbury Cross . . . . . . . . . . . . . . . . . . . . . . . . . . . . . . . 18
The Vinegar Jug . . . . . . . . . . . . . . . . . . . . . . . . . . . . . . . . 24
The Summer Kitchen . . . . . . . . . . . . . . . . . . . . . . . . . . . . 41
The Swing. . . . . . . . . . . . . . . . . . . . . . . . . . . . . . . . . . . . 48
The Wreath-Ribbon Quilt . . . . . . . . . . . . . . . . . . . . . . . . 65
The Eyes of Argus . . . . . . . . . . . . . . . . . . . . . . . . . . . . . 72
Knotty . . . . . . . . . . . . . . . . . . . . . . . . . . . . . . . . . . . . . . 90
Sisters under the Skin . . . . . . . . . . . . . . . . . . . . . . . . . . 99
Pieces of Crow . . . . . . . . . . . . . . . . . . . . . . . . . . . . . . 106
Green Lightning and the Tablecloth Bride . . . . . . . . . . 115
Peanut Dreams and the Blue-Eyed Jesus . . . . . . . . . . . 146
The Women's Club . . . . . . . . . . . . . . . . . . . . . . . . . . . 160
The Girl Who Looked like Irma Budd's Little Sister . . . 168
The Pink Bed . . . . . . . . . . . . . . . . . . . . . . . . . . . . . . . 174
Daisy Wars . . . . . . . . . . . . . . . . . . . . . . . . . . . . . . . . 182
Wooden Apples . . . . . . . . . . . . . . . . . . . . . . . . . . . . . 189
Across the Bridge . . . . . . . . . . . . . . . . . . . . . . . . . . . 196
Happy Birthday, Billy Boy . . . . . . . . . . . . . . . . . . . . . 204
The Green Car . . . . . . . . . . . . . . . . . . . . . . . . . . . . . 218
Rules and Secrets . . . . . . . . . . . . . . . . . . . . . . . . . . . 227
Who Cooks for You? . . . . . . . . . . . . . . . . . . . . . . . . . 239
King of the Comics . . . . . . . . . . . . . . . . . . . . . . . . . . 246
The Silver Crescent . . . . . . . . . . . . . . . . . . . . . . . . . . 255
He Holds a Black Umbrella . . . . . . . . . . . . . . . . . . . . 270
Cows, Coathangers, and the K-Mart Kid . . . . . . . . . . . 275
The Blue Bonnet Bug . . . . . . . . . . . . . . . . . . . . . . . . 288
Judas at the Table . . . . . . . . . . . . . . . . . . . . . . . . . . . 294
Even the Bees in Denmark . . . . . . . . . . . . . . . . . . . . 303
Friends and Oranges . . . . . . . . . . . . . . . . . . . . . . . . . 314

# Biography in Seven Lives

## I Am Fifteen

THE BOY I hold would like to do other things, but he is the wrong sign in the wrong moon. However, we kiss a lot. He has not discovered breath mints and his tongue tastes of salt and burlap. The next time he calls, I say I'm busy. Then I stop answering the phone. Later I drive past his house at strange hours with strange friends. We honk the horn. Who lives there? they ask. I tell them I don't know. His father stands in the doorway in an undershirt. He wears a hat, black, round as a chocolate cake. He waves his fist. We sail away, folded in laughter.

## At Seventeen

Someone has given me an ankle bracelet. I wear it in a green ring around my foot. I paint my toenails purple, smoke cigarettes in bathrooms and back seats. I drink gin from paper cups, throw up beside the lake where lovers park.

## At Nineteen

I marry in a white lace dress. It has a train six yards long. My mother tells her friends, Six yards. Her voice in all caps. To me she says, Are you sure this is what you want? I am not sure, but she has given me all the advice I can take.

*Ruth Moose*

Does it have to be him? I don't know. He likes my laugh, the way I say things when I'm mad, how I look with moonlight washing my face and hair.

We drive a car decorated with words and streamers. Honeymoon Special. Rocks rattle in our hubcaps. We don't care. We'll have one night in a motel. I undress in the bathroom. He undresses in the bathroom. All my clothes are new. The labels scratch. I miss my old robe with its soft, sagging pockets. I miss my room where even in darkness I knew what hung on the walls. I miss the books I read in bed, left stacked like a ladder on each side.

We brush our teeth together, make faces in the mirror. Look, Ma. We read aloud from the one book we brought, an illustrated blue paperback; it tells all we need to know. This is what the doctor said, the one who gave us blood tests, sold us this book from his bottom drawer. He wanted me to take off my blouse so he could take my blood. I pushed up my sleeve, very high, very tight.

In bed, we study all the pages, words under the pictures. Are you sure? we say. We touch and giggle. What is this? How is it spelled?

After we turn out the lights, we tell ghost stories, play "the dead man game" His scrotum feels heavy and cool as a bunch of refrigerated grapes. Later he sleeps. I listen to trains in the night, a soft rain.

Next morning there is a stain where we slept. We leave holding hands, sharing secrets.

## At Twenty-One

I have a job in a brown bank building without windows. I make roads of winding tapes for that great corporation. The numbers are a language all their own. I cannot speak it and all day must listen to their screams. At lunch, I escape. I run eight blocks to the steamy cafeteria, eat quickly, drift slowly back. I memorize department store windows, all the prices on drugstore specials. I let it rain on my face, snow on my nose, anything I can feel. Anything but the brown bank that sucks away my life.

A fruit vendor sits in an alley. I buy oranges, apples, grapes, one day a pear. He speaks no English, polishes perfect fruit shiny enough for a painting. One day he says, We mekka beautiful baby, no? I no longer buy the fruit but walk two blocks to avoid his alley.

When the baby is born, my mother says, Why couldn't you have waited? Did you do this to stop working?

My husband wanted a girl. I love my son, take him for long walks, show him the sky, trees, birds in many colors.

My husband hates his job. He comes home and yells things, pounds the table, rocks coffee in his cup, makes the baby cry. His sleep is a mix of snores and angry phrases. One day he wrecks the car. After, he has to take the bus to work. We try to save.

I push the baby in his stroller everywhere. We walk in rain and snow. If I stopped, we'd be statues. Pigeons would find us frozen, frost masks on our faces. Headlines herald Mother and Child Frozen in Park. Human popsicles. Eggs in my market basket turned to marble. I learn to knit. A friend teaches me over tea. Camomile. We share the same bag. She likes lime juice, but I eat the wedge from lemon rind. I learn to heel perfectly, make a matching pair. I knit all the time; my goal, a pair of socks. Blue, wool, size Men's. The first time he wears them, he says they itch. I wash the socks in very lovely hot water, spin them dry, and they are mine. I deserved them from the first.

I learn to make good spaghetti. And fruitcakes. I make shining wreaths of them The baby grows. On his second birthday he reaches for the cake, breathes out the candles that sputter in the wind.

My husband sits on the floor, asks, Are you happy?

*Ruth Moose*

I cry at the sink, dishes stacked gray as oysters' shells beside my salty sea.

Would you like another baby?

I cry louder. Great rocking waves.

He goes out, comes home with a cactus in a red plastic pot. He puts it in the bedroom. The plant hates me. It sprays stickers when I get near. One day, in counterattack, I spray it with sweet and flower-smelling starch. Pffft. It coughs. A year later, dies.

I do not get pregnant. No one has invented the Pill, but someone thought of other things. I thank them with all my heart and soul and with all my other things.

My husband puts a fence around the backyard. I plant a garden. Lettuce and onions. Also mint, thyme, radishes, roses. I lean my face into them, inhale their air, crush them between my fingers, tuck sprigs in my pillow for dreams. A morning glory grows around my doorstep, climbs gutters, blooms in my face. Its blue trumpets say things only I know are true. When frost blackens it, I cry, hold the dead hearts in my hand, curl the dry vines like hair around my fingers.

In summer we sit on the porch, cut the baby's hair. He looks like a young midget, sad and scared. His eyes are dark, deep, absorbing as a priest.

Silly, my husband says, it will grow back.

## At Twenty-Four

My husband gets another job in another town and we move. Every night we put the baby to bed, then walk around boxes. We pack and pack. I say goodbye to neighbors I never knew. We'll miss you, they sing. I'll miss morning glories, the silent, wise sayings. They will be back, but not me. I leave aphids on the rosebushes. They will have to be taught to trellis by someone else. Will she know? Will she call them by name? Learn their special ways? I want to leave instructions, a list. Don't, my husband says, it will only get lost. I tape it inside a cabinet door, shut tight.

In the new town, I join clubs, go to meetings, play dress-up, guess who I am.

We have another baby. This time I do not cry. She is a happy child. Fat as a pumpkin, smiling like a jack-o'-lantern.

I walk her in sunshine. We make valentines together, cut out cookies, plan parties, play games. I Spy and Animal, Vegetable, or Man?

We join Brownie Scouts, learn things. Where man began, why dinosaurs died, how woman was made. We ask questions of the plastic parts, study the fine wire tuning, the empty head.

## At Thirty-Five

I go back to school, sit in a class with long-haired boys who wear leather bracelets, smell of soap and spice, collect sugar in their beards. I paint large canvases I must have help to carry to the car, to our apartment with no one home but the cat, Arthur.

One weekend I join a group of sisters, a pajama party, a one-day boarding school. I wake in a row of beds, we eat crackers, drink ginger ale, juice. Practice walking the line until we are steady enough to leave. For a week I bleed babies, my egg basket empty. Coward, I call my husband, a vasectomy is so simple.

Simple to you, he says, not so simple to me.

He is forty-five and hates his job. It isn't going anywhere. He isn't going anywhere. Do you want to be like this when you are sixty-five? he asks. His friends from the rat race drop by the wayside. We wire flowers, send job résumés by mail.

Teaching, he says, is the answer. He has never taught before, but an overzealous administrator thinks he can. They give him chalk, a roll book and pen. He whistles in the shower. After three months of teaching, they reprimand. Conduct unbecoming a man of the faculty. A student shed her woes on his shoulder four noons in a row.

## At Forty

We move to the woods, build a house on ten acres of rock. No one in his right mind would live here, a forest ranger claims. At last we found the place, my husband says.

A creek tumbles by our doorstep, but we drill 465 granite feet to find water. The bit churns gray grit like a core to the middle of the earth. We pay by the foot. I expect oil, or at least vintage champagne.

The water, when it comes, is urine-yellow, tastes of rust and month-old eggs. Minerals, my husband says, we can bottle and sell it.

I cut trees, grow strong, a Paula Bunyan. My daughter and I clear Wonder Woman Corner. She says a woman should not be forced to work this way. It is not becoming. Her friends ride in cars, go to dances, eat pizza. She runs away with the lightning rod salesman. No rod he sold has ever been hit. He gives no guarantees. Drives a red Mustang with dice dancing above the dash.

I find my son in the closet kissing the Avon lady. She is fifteen, dressed in blue. Her hat and satchel match. Her legs in fringed short jeans match. It's our latest shade, she says. Would you care for a sample?

Are you sure? I ask my son. Is she the one?

One? he says. What is one? They leave in a van with double bumper stickers. The front says, "Opera Lives" and "Save Our Ballet." The rear reads, "Preserve Wildlife. Kill Hunters."

They cross the bridge, don't look back.

I wave. My hand feels hinged at the wrist.

*Ruth Moose*

Do you know what it's like, my husband says, to go in cold? To ask for work from strangers? Make appointments? To write these letters no one ever answers?

The game warden drives a green car. He has a red beard that shines like sunset, smells of fields, tickles like moss. The hair on his arms and chest is fine gold wire. I curl it in my fingers, kiss it in my sleep. While my husband hunts for work, the game warden comes. I let down my hair. We swim in the lake. Are you in charge of fish? I ask. He laughs like the mating call of some rare bird, chases me through woods to a pine-needle bed. Won't someone see? I ask. Who? He breathes sweet into my neck. Who? An owl during the day. I am filled with clouds and sky and leaves of green, green, green. An old song, a tune I've hummed along the years. Today I shout my name.

*Ruth Moose*

# Moon Over Magnolias

SOME WOMEN, WHEN they were pregnant, went to museums and art galleries; Annabelle Givens went to church. In her seventh month, for some unknown reason, she began to be drawn to churches: brick colonial churches, graystone red-doored cathedrals, a blue-domed mosque, white-steepled clapboards. Every time she passed a church, Annabelle imagined herself sitting in the congregation, preferably under a stained glass window, the sun streaming through a radiant madonna with child. The background was always blue with both clouds and stars.

Annabelle first tried a church two blocks from their apartment. One Sunday morning she put on her pink gingham, combed her long, dark hair and tied it back with a pink scarf. She felt like a six-year-old going to school the first day and that perhaps she ought to skip her feet, but that would bounce this basketball she wore where her stomach used to be. She brushed her hair, pulled two tendrils over her ears and thought wistfully of a straw hat she'd worn as a child. A wide sailor with navy velvet ribbon that streamed down the back, held on with a thin rubber band that cut into her chin. She'd chewed it in two once listening to her grandfather, black-suited and white-shirted in the pulpit, holding his gold watch on a chain and calling on God to "lead them in the paths of righteousness!" Annabelle thought that was the longest hour in the world. It was a week long-forever, but she sat quietly in that garden of hats and flowers.

*Ruth Moose*

Her grandmother's hats had veils and silk roses. She sat quietly as prayer in that small Southern church of blue-green windows where piano notes drifted out and a yellow jacket or bee drifted in to be blessed. Somehow Annabelle felt she ought to wear gloves or at least carry them, but they went out with hats. Besides it was too hot. She snapped shut her flat leather purse and started out.

Richard lifted an eyebrow over his newspaper as she walked past.

"I'm going to church," she said. "The white one on the corner."

"Okay," he said, refolding the sports section, then stopped and looked at her. "Are you all right?"

"I'm fine," she said. "I'm just going to church."

He shook his head and gave her a little corner of a smile that said she was subject to whims "in her condition." That Victorian phrase. She read it in his eyes. "Her condition" was her own choice and she'd waited a long time for it and she was enjoying it—most of the time. She didn't enjoy the twinges in her back, nor feeling like Humpty Dumpty, not being able to see her toes...but she did like feeling for the first time that her body could do wonderful things, she was a special person doing something only she could do. Which wasn't altogether true. She had to give Richard a little credit. But after that the rest had been up to her—body and mind.

She walked slowly, sunshine on her forehead, warm on her shoulders, past two blocks of apartments identical to theirs except for an occasional plant in a window, watching cat, bird cage, or twirling mobile of gulls or boats or shells.

Still she was early. There were only two elderly men inside the darkened vestibule. The tall one reminded her of Richard's Uncle Harry. The other had a bald spot the size of a quarter that shined as he bent to hand her a bulletin.

She eased into a rear pew. The organist started chimes and bells, "Sweet Hour of Prayer," and a few people drifted in, seated themselves. Annabelle was surprised she recognized the music. And pleased. She admired the polished wooden pews, the altar arrangement of orange spiked flowers and white chrysanthemums big as salad plates.

Two women took seats in front of her, continued their conversation. The younger one in black linen, too-red hair and thick makeup wore a heavy perfume that reminded Annabelle of the time she was three and poured her mother's perfume down the front of her dress, emptying the whole bottle. She had been promptly popped in the tub and scrubbed, soaked, and shampooed. Annabelle coughed. Magnolias. She hated them. "Dusky Magnolias" had been the perfume. Her mother never wore it again and even the word became a family joke. Anyone put down was said to have been "magnoliaed." Her father, dousing the neighbor's persistent dog on the boxwoods with the garden hose, laughed that he "magnoliaed Pee Wee."

The woman in black said to her friend, "I've only been there once. I don't care for that kind of music, but I'm forty-seven and still single so I think it's about time I started looking seriously—don't you?"

The woman nodded.

"Even though I don't think I look it—forty-seven, I mean. Do you?"

She went on without waiting for an answer. "No one would know if I didn't tell them." She fanned with one of the hymnals, flapping its cover with a slapping sound. "This is the hottest place in the church. I've told that sexton the air conditioner doesn't reach back here and I don't think he's even tried."

She swiveled in her seat, said to Annabelle, "Are you a member here? Who are you?"

Annabelle opened her mouth but the woman went on. "I've been here over thirty years and I've never seen you before."

Annabelle felt herself being inspected like a cake in a bakery window, sides, top, and all around the edges.

"I'm—" she started, but the organ swelled suddenly and the choir filed in. She almost said "Magnolia."

After the service, Annabelle signed the Friendship Register: name, address, member of this church. She checked No. Would like a visit from the minister. She checked No!

Next Sunday she tried the graystone church. No one there asked her name, but the minister looked like Robert Redford in a black robe with yellow satin cowl. She put him in a cowboy hat on a prairie with a changing sunset behind, then a canyon and a river. He had great flowing sleeves and dramatic movements with his arms that seemed to Annabelle he might scoop up all the congregation and suddenly lift off toward the skies. He preached sermons on responsibilities to earth, keepers of the here and now, caretakers for the future, our children's children's children. She liked that and that was the church she chose.

Richard didn't understand, but each Sunday he cleared away the breakfast clutter, grapefruit shells, waffle batter, and honey pitcher. When she returned, he had things marinating for dinner. One Sunday he made sourdough bread from starter his brother had given them. Annabelle might be concerned about spirit, but Richard wanted to make sure there was bread.

"If you're worried about something," Richard said one Sunday, kneading the dough with both hands, rocking it back and forth, "we can talk about it."

"No." She untied her hair, fluffed it out. "I'm fine. Really."

He kissed the back of her neck smelling of wheat and earth, left a flour smudge on her cheek.

She was a little tired. For the past several nights she hadn't been sleeping well. The baby woke her in the early morning hours, restless, kicking, thumping inside like an acrobat. He (she'd called the baby that since the first hard kick—future quarterback's toe, she was sure) wasn't going to be the sleeper his father was. Richard lay beside her sleeping deep as a rock. She rose and walked to the window, gazed across the back lawn. Everything was silver, softly dusted in powdered silver. Moonlight. Too beautiful to waste on sleep. She'd always felt that way. As a child she often walked the house at night, listening, looking out, touching things. Everything was different at night. Her mother called her a moon child, a night-blooming cereus. A flower that bloomed at night. One summer Annabelle stayed up all night in her mother's garden watching the cereus open, her sleeping bag in the swing, with a flashlight and her Raggedy Ann, whose button eyes saw everything Annabelle did.

Annabelle wondered now if her baby would be another moon child? She thought of him now swimming in darkness, eyes shut tightly as a kitten's, swimming and kicking.

She drank a glass of cold milk standing in the light from the refrigerator. Richard stood in the doorway, rubbed his sleep-twisted hair. "What's wrong?"

"Nothing," Annabelle said, "the baby woke me. Kicking." Richard rubbed her stomach. "I'm sorry," he said.

"I'm not," she said. "I'm excited and happy and exhilarated and everything but sleepy." She reached both arms around his waist, buried her head against his warm chest, listened to the steady knock of his heart. They walked back to bed, arms around each other.

"I used to carry you," Richard said.

"Give me a rain check on that," she said and was asleep within minutes after slipping between the sheets.

Two weeks before her due date—it almost glowed in neon on the calendar to Annabelle—she decided to give herself a home permanent. The instructions on the box sounded so simple. Ten Easy Steps to a New You and a Lot of Body

Without Curl. Or curls galore. She had a lot of body—oh boy, did she—what she'd like was a little curl.

While Richard watched Monday night football, Annabelle got out scissors, timer, towels, cotton, curlers—a rainbow-hued box of them in six different sizes. She shampooed and started winding. No odor, no mess, the box promised, but her fingers kept slipping and her eyes smarted. She wore a pair of old black maternity shorts and one of Richard's holey T-shirts. "Make Love, Not War" printed on the back, but the "War" was almost faded off.

When she finished she was a walking beachball with a wreath of curlers, her crown of plastic. She twisted on the plastic turban, waded past towels and cotton and misspent end papers, timer in hand, to the screened porch.

There she sat cooling herself amid plants and record jackets, books and milk-carton crate furniture. At this point, Annabelle had discovered the only comfortable chair in the house was a folding canvas one. She fitted into it as if the chair had been made to fit—there wasn't an inch wasted. She was reading "Introduction to Motherhood" and didn't hear the bell. Only voices. Close. She looked up from her magazine to see Richard and the two women from church, who stared at her. "We're from the visiting committee," one said.

"What?" Annabelle, startled, tried to get up, only to find she'd outgrown this chair and it wasn't going to let her go. The chair rose a few inches with her, before she sank back down.

"Church," the woman said. "St. Mark's." "But I checked"—Annabelle started.

Richard offered the ladies seats on the daybed they used for a sofa. He gave them pillows from the stack on the floor and they accepted them eagerly, tucked and pummeled them behind their backs. Then he disappeared after they said a glass of iced tea would "just save their lives at this moment." They were "perishing."

*Ruth Moose*

"We usually call first," the woman in a blue print polyester said. "But we were in the neighborhood and saw your lights and I said, Carolina, let's just drop in. We won't stay but a second. Just to say we've been and can put it on our card."

I'll kill Richard, Annabelle thought. How could he do this? She struggled to make her lips form even a tight little smile. Of all the times…she tugged down her T-shirt, reached toward her plastic-wrapped head.

"We've been out since four this afternoon," Mrs. Green Shirtwaist said, running her fingers inside her belt. "And we haven't even introduced ourselves," she giggled. "I'm Carolina Stout and this is Evelyn Love. I bring you love, I tell people." She poked Evelyn, who beamed.

"I'm in the middle—" Annabelle held out her timer.

"Of course you are, dear," said Carolina, "and my, don't you look cool? That's important at a time like this. I planned my babies so they'd be born in the winter and I wouldn't have to suffer so during the hot weather. I do suffer so with the heat, don't you, Evelyn?" She turned to her friend, who had pinched off the tops of four avocado pits Annabelle sprouted.

"If you don't do that, honey," Evelyn said, "they just run to the ceiling and you have nothing but stalk. I know. I used to run a nursery, didn't I, Carolina?"

"She's done the flowers for St. Mark's for over twenty years. You ought to see her cross of white lilies at Easter," Carolina said. "With little lights and all."

When Annabelle's timer rang both women jumped, put their hands to their chest. "Goodness gracious, that startled me."

"I have to do the next step," Annabelle stood, this time without the chair. "Now if you'll excuse me." She'd planned to check a test curl in thirty minutes, now it had been forty. She had to hurry. Where was Richard? She yelled, louder than she meant to—and noticed the women exchange glances.

*Ruth Moose*

Richard came from the kitchen balancing a tray with two tall glasses, napkins, a dish of sliced lemons, even a sprig of the mint that had overtaken her salad garden. "I couldn't find the iced tea spoons," he said.

She dashed to the bathroom, unwinding curlers as she went. Who cared if all the curls came out—it would be better than a tangled Brillo-pad mass of them.

She heard Richard showing the ladies out as she worked the neutralizer through her hair. Curls. She had thousands of curls, each demanding to stand up—out—in an individual way. But she wasn't going to cry. Maybe it was supposed to look like this. She rinsed until the water ran cold, then reached for her rollers. Surely when she took it down, she would look like the picture in the folder. Easy. One, two, three, for the beauty shop look at home prices.

Richard was propped in bed reading when she finished. She had decided never to speak to him again. Their child would have to learn to talk early to tell Richard all she wanted to say. How could he have done such a thing?

"I couldn't help it," Richard said. "They just came in."
"You could have told them I was indisposed," she hissed.
"I've got a feeling typhoid wouldn't keep those two out," he mumbled.

She slept in his arms, not waking once. He left for the office without waking her.

The first thing she did was take down her hair, trembling. What if the permanent hadn't worked? All her work and worry for nothing. Each curl tumbled off its roller, squiggled out like a corkscrew, danced, looked alive. And she looked like Orphan Annie—a very pregnant Orphan Annie. Which wouldn't do at all. Maybe for another face at another time and place, but not her, not now. Her own baby wouldn't know her with all these curls that had curls. Magnoliaed, she saluted with her hairbrush, and a sigh.

*Ruth Moose*

Annabelle drove to the drop-in beauty salon where slim-hipped girls and guys in jeans snipped and aimed blowdryers. "Cut." She made scissor motions with her fingers. "Off."

"Is this your first?" the beauty shop operator asked. "How much longer you got?" She measured Annabelle's girth, the chair, with her eyes.

"Permanent?" Annabelle said. "I hope not." Then the scissors flashed around her like a swarm of minnows. When she looked her hair lay like wood shavings on the floor and she felt pounds lighter. Someone with large eyes, bangs, and a gamin grin looked back from the mirror.

"It's you," the operator said. "The real you that's been inside trying to get out."

Annabelle laughed. Inside her was a real little person trying to get out.

She paid the girl, had brunch at the snack bar of an oldfashioned drugstore with a whirling wooden-bladed paddle fan.

Too early for her doctor's appointment, she walked through the park, sat on a shady green bench. Pigeons with purple and green necks strutted around her feet, pecked. She had nothing to feed them, not even a stale cracker in the far corners of her bag.

"That's okay." A bag lady of a woman wobbled up. "I bring bread every day. That's what they want."

The pigeons cooed and fluttered around her. Some sat on her head, shoulders, arms, as she pulled bread scraps from brown bags and fed them, called them by name. "June Bug, Pretty Boy, Dancing Girl...Lillie Marlane ...Gigi ...they know me," the old woman said.

Annabelle wanted to move but she was afraid she would hurt the woman's feelings. She wore a wool hat and sweater with the elbows out. It wasn't buttoned in front and you could see her slip, the color of burlap.

"When you due, honey?" the woman asked, petting a

pigeon on her lap. She stroked its head like a cat and it gave purring coos.

"Two weeks," Annabelle said. "On the seventeenth."

"You won't go until the thirty-first," the woman said. "That's the full moon. I used to work in a hospital. I know." She folded her bag and tucked it inside her sweater, shuffled away.

A woman with a blonde ponytail and green slacks walked by pushing twins in a stroller. She smiled at Annabelle. The toddlers in matching sun hats clutched sand shovels and pails that rattled and clanked.

"One or two?" she asked Annabelle, who found she was cuddling her stomach.

"One," Annabelle said.

The woman laughed. "My mother always said I never did things the easy way. Good luck." She aimed the stroller toward the play area and started up again, the twins singing.

Annabelle followed and chose an empty swing, watched the congregation of mothers—and children, fathers and children, a grandfather and children. In the distance she heard a carillon—or was it the ice cream vendor? Through the trees sun filtered like stained glass. Annabelle relaxed. She felt suddenly happy enough to shout, and inside, her moon child kicked and jumped.

*Ruth Moose*

# To Banbury Cross

RILLA SAW HERSELF in the toes of her Sunday shoes: her saucer face, her long blonde hair, and Mama brushing. She wiggled her feet, the pictures blurred, disappeared.

"Sit still." Mama's hand capped Rilla's head. The brush smoothed down, scratched her neck and tickled.

"Let me do it." Rilla reached around.

"Not this time." Mama drew back the brush. "We're in a hurry."

"You hurt," Rilla said.

"I have to get the tangles out," Mama said, lifting Rilla's hair. The air was cool on her neck. "You don't want Daddy to see you with tangles in your hair."

"If you don't sit still"—Grandma spraddled like an old sawhorse before the tall dresser mirror—"and let your mama get the tangles out, birds will come build nests in your hair."

"I wish they would." Rilla cupped her hands, made a round place in her lap.

"Pshaaaa." Grandma made an ugly noise with her lips, took a hat from a square gray box.

Birds nests in my hair, Rilla sang under her breath. Red birds, blue birds, squat. Birds would lay eggs and I can take them to the hospital. A present for Daddy. To make him feel better. Get well.

Grandma jammed the black knob of a hat on her head, jerked it off, pushed it on again.

*Ruth Moose*

Mama's fingers moved gently in Rilla's hair, the brush singing low noises. Whispers. Last night there were whispers after the patrolman left on his motorcycle. Daddy had a motorcycle that made loud hissing and popping sounds. The patrolman's motorcycle was quiet like his voice when he said Daddy was unconscious and nobody could find Mama. She was here with me, Rilla thought, here all the time. When Daddy came to, the patrolman said, he told them where Mama was. Came to what? The hospital? Unconscious was asleep, Mama said later, and not to worry, Daddy was fine. Rilla didn't go back to sleep for a long time after that. She dreamed Daddy rode a bucking black horse, a wild horse. He kicked his sides and made him paw the air, blow smoke and fire from his nose. Daddy fell off and lay on the ground. Unconscious. Un-con-scious. Rilla puffed the word under her breath.

"Be still." Mama brushed a tangle.

"Ouch." Rilla's eyes stung.

Grandma jabbed a pearl-headed hat pin in her hat. "I've never in my life seen a youngun so tenderheaded." She made a face at the mirror.

Mama brushed harder. "We've got to hurry."

"If I was you, Merle"—Grandma powdered her neck and throat—"I'd cut that child's hair. Not put up with that fuss." Her powder puff made soft slaps, fluttered like something caught in her dress front. "If you'd cut her hair it would thicken up. I cut yours when you was little." She closed the powder box. "And you've had thick hair ever since. Thick as a horse's tail." .

Rilla stuck out her tongue. "I don't want a horse's tail for hair."

Grandma picked up her purse, swung around.

Rilla quick-licked her lips with the angry tongue.

"I'd not lick my lips and go out in this wind." Grandma peered into her purse. "They'll chap quick."

*Ruth Moose*

The metal feet of Rilla's hairclasp scratched as Mama slid it into place, snapped it shut. Daddy liked her white bow hairclasps. Bows in her hair, he'd sing, bells on her toes. He said rhymes, made her laugh.

"You've got some natural curl." Mama patted Rilla's hair. "Not as much as your Daddy's, but some." She smoothed the back of her dress. "I wanted your hair to be black like his, not blonde and stringy like mine."

Rilla played with Daddy's hair when he slept on the couch, sometimes. Curling it over and under her fingers, ruffling it up and laying kisses in it.

"The baby's hair . . ." Mama started, then stopped, turned away.

Grandma's purse clicked shut. "Better hurry. I heard Mr. Ellis turn off the highway. He'll be here in a minute. He's mighty good to take us and we mustn't make him wait."

Rilla flung on her coat, started past Grandma.

"Wait," Mama called above the coat-hanger clatter. "You need your cap. Wait."

Rilla tried to dodge Grandma in the doorway.

"We'll put it on easy and not mess up your hair," Mama said.

"No." Rilla tried to go around the other side.

"Better put it on." Grandma grabbed her shoulder. "I don't want you keeping me awake half the night with another earache. I don't like to get up and heat sweet oil for little girls who won't wear their caps when they ought."

Please. Mama formed the word with her lips, please. Her fingers fumbled under Rilla's chin as they heard Mr. Ellis's car brakes squawk. Mr. Ellis parked his car in the barn, chickens roosted on it. He used it like a truck, the back seat out, drove out to the fields. Rilla had seen the car often on the hill, its trunk open like a hungry mouth and Mr. Ellis feeding it bale after bale of hay.

*Ruth Moose*

Mr. Ellis held the seat for Mama and Rilla to climb in back. "Cold enough for you?" He chewed, shifted the pouch in his jaw. "There was ice in my hog troughs this morning."

He had put a wooden chair in the car for Mama. Rilla stood until the car reached the highway, then climbed onto her mother's lap. It was good to sit on Mama's lap and not have Grandma say she was too big, that her mother wasn't strong and Rilla would break her down.

Mr. Ellis shot a brown stream, rolled up his window. "It looked like this winter was never going to get cold enough to do any hog killing. Craziest weather I've ever seen. Them hogs got fat and meaner every day." He shot again and brown dribbled the glass.

Through a hole in the floor, silver dollar-sized, Rilla watched the road flow under them. Sometimes there was a sparkle of glass, a bit of white.

Grandma droned in the front seat, "...fool on a motorsicle. I knowed before it happened. I said a hundred times when him and Merle was living with me, he was going to get himself killed. Bless pat, if he didn't near do it. I'll never know why the Lord saw fit to spare the likes of him"—she lowered her voice—"and him riding with . . ."

"That's enough, Ma," Mama said so sharply Rilla jumped, almost slid off her lap. "I don't want to hear another word."

Grandma sniffed, straightened her shoulders.

Rilla reached, brushed white flecks off her grandmother's shoulders.

Grandma jerked around, frowning. "What you doing?"
"Dandruff. You got dandruff, Grandma."

"No, I ain't." Grandma craned her neck, shook her collar. "More than likely it was lint."

Rilla waved to a greening willow tree. Mrs. Cranston at her mailbox waved back.

"Ma, Mrs. Cranston waved to you," Mama said.

"Law me and I wasn't looking," Grandma said. "She'll

just have to think I'm stuck up if she wants, but I can't help I didn't see her till we was past."

Mr. Ellis said he had to get some wire from the FCX. As long as he was making a trip to town, he might as well get some use from it himself.

A brown and white dog charged the car, barking. Mr. Ellis hit his horn, swerved to the other side.

Grandma said he should have gone ahead and hit the thing. It would have been one less to worry about. That if people had to have dogs, they ought to be made to keep them shut up.

"How much longer?" Rilla's head itched under the cap. She pushed it back until the ties were choking tight.

"Not much." Mama adjusted the cap. "You may have to wait in the lobby. I don't know if you can go see Daddy or not."

"She most certainly can," Grandma snorted. "I'd not leave a child of mine in a strange lobby. No telling who might come along and take her off."

Rilla squeezed her mother's arm. "Can't I see Daddy?"

"It would be a lesson for her"—Grandma looked straight ahead—"something she won't forget."

"That's what worries me," Mama said. "It might give her nightmares."

Rilla stood, held the back of the seat. "No, it won't. I promise." How could Daddy give her nightmares? Mares were horses. Horses to ride in the dark. Daddy used to ride her on his knee, sing, "Ride a cock horse to Banbury Cross to see a fine lady upon . . ." That was when she was little. Later she rode behind him on the motorcycle, flew through the wind, her hair floated like ribbons. Don't go so fast, she screamed. Slow down. Her words came back, hit her face—fast, too fast. Daddy went too fast and had a wreck. He was in the hospital. "What's a lobby?"

"A room with chairs in it." Mama sounded tired. "A

place people sit and wait."

They passed houses with fence-framed yards, curlicued front walks. We lived in a house with Daddy...before the baby died, when Mama still liked Daddy, before she cried so much. Grandma's house had a snaggle-tooth porch, nothing and nobody to play with. Only limp paper dolls cut from the Spiegel catalog.

Mr. Ellis stopped before the biggest building Rilla had ever seen. All glass and shiny posts, it seemed to have a thousand window eyes, a mouth that swallowed people. She tried to count the windows but tripped going up the walk, and Grandma said she better watch where she was going.

Inside, Rilla snatched off her ugly red cap, packed it in her pocket. Woodpecker cap Grandma knitted. When Rilla wore it she felt like going around pecking.

The lobby was filled with people, noise, and smelled funny. White like the doctor's office. Rilla pinched her nose together until it hurt.

They took stairs because Grandma said she didn't like elevators. "Don't want to be shut up in one of them things. If I'm going to be in a box, I want to be dead and not know it." The baby was dead, shut up in a box, and Grandma said it was all for the best.

Rilla liked to ride things. Did an elevator go up like the ponies on the merry-go-round at the fair? Daddy took her once, lifted her on a pony. It was fun. She waved to him every time she went past until his face wasn't there. When the pony stopped still and the music quit, a dirty man who smelled of liniment helped her down. Daddy was gone. She called to him, looked for his blue jacket with stars, the sign on the back. He was watching a lady dressed in pink feathers dance to a drum. Boom, boom. Rilla's feet went boom, boom on the stairs. Grandma's shoes clacked and Mama's high heels clicked.

Several times Rilla stopped, leaned over to look down.

Grandma grabbed her coattail. "You'll fall, bust your head wide open, if you don't watch out."

Rilla could see her head in two neat watermelon halves, her thoughts like seeds, arranged in rows. Red and juicy, some seeds would scatter, spill on the floor. She held the rail, walked carefully, not looking down.

"Shhh," Mama said in the hall. "Tiptoe. Sick people don't like noise. They'll make us leave."

Rilla tiptoed behind the nurse in her silky dress that whispered words she couldn't quite hear.

The nurse snapped on a light, said to a snow bank in the bed: "Mr. Lewis, you got company." Her voice was loud and Rilla wanted to turn her low. "Feel like waking up and talking to them?"

"Eugene!" Mama ran to the bed. A voice that didn't sound like Daddy said, "Merle, Merle, honey, I'm sorry. Sorry as I can be."

The nurse checked a chart, clipped her pen on a pocket. "He's a mighty lucky man and better take it easy for a few days."

Grandma stood behind the bed. "How you feeling, Gene?" Daddy didn't look at her.

"Stiff and sore, I reckon." She opened a dresser drawer, slid in the paper bag she carried. "You'll be needing another pair of pajamas or two. These were Merle's father's, but you're welcome to them."

"Thanks," Daddy mumbled.

Mama sat on the edge of the bed, talking. Daddy kept saying he would give anything in this world if all this had never happened.

Grandma adjusted the blinds, straightened the curtains, unpinned a card from some green plants. "That was quick," she said, reading the card. "Ebenezer Baptist. They was good to bother to send anything." She moved the plants to face the sun. "No more than Gene ever saw fit to go."

*Ruth Moose*

Mama and Daddy held hands, talked.

"Of course it was for my sake. Longtime-member-in-good standing." She poked the plants. "Haven't been watered in no telling when." She filled a glass in the bathroom, watered the plants, gave a vase of pink flowers a quick pour, as though they didn't deserve a drink since they would die anyway but she wanted to prove she was fair.

Sweet-smelling pink flowers in round rings stood on the grave when baby brother died. Grandma said his blood was bad and it was a wonder he lived two weeks. Gene's family had bad blood. Rilla had it too. Bad blood made her do mean things, hit the chicken with a hoe, break Grandma's tulips, lick spoons when nobody looked.

Grandma put the glass back. "You get well quick now, Gene."

Daddy closed his eyes, didn't move his swollen lips.

"Don't worry about a thing. Merle and Rilla are just fine with me."

Daddy opened one eye, looked at Mama. She was pale, her hair mussed.

"Jack Hunter said it was okay about those back bills."

Grandma wiped her wet hands on the sheet.

Mr. Hunter's store had a dozen different kinds of candy and Daddy let Rilla pick out as many of every kind as she wanted, fill a bag until its sides were fat.

"He's waited two years to get his money." Grandma looked out the window. "Guess he can wait a while longer."

Mama filled her cheeks with air, her face got red. "Ma"—she stood quickly—"I thought you were going to see Martha Allen while we were here."

Grandma tugged her dress front, patted her hat and left.

Rilla sat under the bed, wiped dust from the slats. Her foot hit the stool and it slid with a screech.

"Rilla, honey"—Mama reached down—"I forgot all about you. Come give Daddy a kiss." She lifted her to the bed.

*Ruth Moose*

The man was not Daddy. His head was bandaged white, his beard gone. "No." Rilla pushed back. "No!" She tried to wiggle away, but Mama held her.

Daddy reached up, stroked her hair. It wasn't Daddy's hand, the nails were clean and white. Daddy had black nails, his hands smelled of grease. "How's my girl?" His lips were thick, blue. Only his eyes, dark and deep, were Daddy's eyes. "Don't let them cut your hair, you hear?" He kissed a twirling rope.

"No." Rilla kicked the bed and hurt her toe.

"Put her down, Merle," he said. "She's afraid, that's all. It's okay, baby."

Rilla buried her face in Mama's scratchy skirt.

"I guess I do look pretty bad," Daddy said.

Mama's skirt smelled of Grandma's closet, the block that hung there to kill brown butterflies.

"I wasn't going fast," Daddy said. "The needle hit sixty, I saw gravel." His hand played with the sheet. "And that's the last thing I saw."

Rilla curled in a chair in the corner.

"Flying through the air," Daddy said, "I felt that. It was the craziest feeling."

When I jump from the peach tree, Rilla thought, it feels like flying.

"Funny"—Daddy shaded his eyes—"I don't remember ever hitting the ground."

"Hush." Mama bent over him. "Let's not talk about it."
"What went with my bike?"

"The highway patrol has it—what's left." Mama fluffed his pillow. "They said it was a total loss." She kissed his forehead. "You're here and that's all that matters."

Total loss. Lost. I'll never get to ride the bike behind Daddy anymore.

A nurse bobbed her white cap in the doorway. "Time for all visitors to leave."

*Ruth Moose*

Tiptoeing, Rilla saw Grandma in the hall. She talked to a nurse behind a desk.

"You don't know what my daughter's been through. Merle has never been one to turn tail and run, but there's just so much a person can stand. I said it wouldn't work when she married him, but you can't tell young people a thing." Grandma leaned closer. "He's always been wild. I told him about that motorsicle."

"He sure was lucky." The nurse shook her head. "The girl with him was killed instantly."

Rilla froze. *I'm not dead. I wasn't with Daddy. I wasn't killed instantly.* She toppled, caught herself against the cool wall. *Mama never rode behind Daddy on the bike, just me.*

Grandma stepped back when she saw Rilla, held her purse flat in front with both hands. "Where's your Mama? Is she coming?"

Rilla looked at her shoes.

Grandma turned to the nurse. "I walked clean to the seventh floor to see Martha Allen. She had gone for x-rays. I left a note I'd been. Don't want her going home, saying none of the neighbors come to see her."

Rilla spelled out the nurse's red badge: "M-R-S H-A-R-T." The nurse stopped writing, smiled at her. "You're a smart little thing. How old are you?"

"I'm six."

"Five," said Grandma, "six next month. She won't get to start school until she's seven. It won't matter though, as small for her age as she is."

"Smart as a whip." The nurse reached in a cabinet, drew out bottles. "Bet she takes it after her grandmother."

Grandma laughed, patted Rilla's head.

Mama walked toward them, head down, blowing her nose.

"Stairs are this way." Grandma pushed toward the corner. "Rilla and I will take the elevator." Mama watched the flashing numbers above the double doors.

"Stairs are quicker," Grandma said.

"I don't care." Mama blew her nose again.

"Suit yourself." Grandma snorted, banged shut the stair door.

"Five, four…here it comes." Rilla pranced.

Mama crumpled, recrumpled her tissues, tore them into small pieces.

In a concrete urn filled with sand and cigarette worms, Rilla buried her cap, covered it over like a cat. Nobody would ever find it and Grandma could not make her wear it now.

"Come on," Mama said as the elevator doors opened.

Rilla was pushed into a dark corner and the elevator started. It made her stomach hurt. She grabbed her mother's hand. "I want to get out. Let's go back."

Her mother laughed softly. "We can't go back."

Rilla couldn't breathe. Her chest hurt. "Let's go back."

"We're almost there," her mother whispered.

When the doors slid open, Rilla rushed into the lobby.

"We have to wait for Grandma," Mama said, looking up the stairs.

Rilla ran up, climbed a rail and locked herself around it.

"I'm going to slide," she called to Mama below. "Catch me."

She flew and Mama caught her in a tangle of arms and legs, laughed, and hugged her close. "Mama," said Rilla, "I'm Daddy's girl, aren't I?"

"Yes," her mother said, "of course you are."

*Ruth Moose*

# The Vinegar Jug

OVER COLD AND bitter coffee, Sharon said aloud thoughts she'd pushed around in her mind for a week. "You should have taken the job at the junior high."

"What?" Rob leaned around the sports section of the newspaper, stared at her. "Are you kidding? I couldn't handle it a month. That was no job, that was a sentence. Five days a week hard labor—breaking rocks. What makes you say I should've taken it?"

"Because"—she threw her spoon on the counter—"it would have been something."

"What?" He slapped the paper down. It slid off in a wide ruffle and drifted in a quiet flutter to the floor.

"A job." She gulped the last swallow of coffee, held the mug with both hands, tried to read the solemn stains on the bottom. "A job, that's what. J.-O-B." She spelled the letters loud, distinct, final, sharp as broken glass.

"Is that all you think about? Like there's some magic to it?" He snapped his fingers, pinched the crisp air. "The answer to everything," he sneered.

"No, not everything, but part of it. Something."

He took his plate to the sink, stood with his back to her. He'd gained weight lately, thick around the middle. And he wasn't even good in bed anymore. She hadn't said anything. Surely he knew.

"If that's what's worrying you," he said, "I'll get a job." When? She wanted to say, but didn't. There was so much she didn't say lately.

"I'll dig ditches, if that's what...I'll . . ."

"Do it," she said quietly.

"What?" He stopped in the middle of the kitchen. He stood centered under the light fixture.

She got up and flicked it off. "Do it," she said. "Dig ditches, do something. I'm so tired of all this."

He stalked from the room, his face milk-white, blue eyes icy.

She put her face against the refrigerator, leaned on her arms, but didn't cry. It was too hot, too dry, she was too empty for it. She and the weather burned, parched, had no moisture. Only the woods around them had warning signs, no burning, no campfires, no smoking, watch your matches. She ought to have a sign like that to wear, too. One spark and she was off and roaring. She was disgusted with herself for yelling, for sounding exactly like the thing she had promised herself she never would be. A fishwife, a regular bitch. All the things she'd told herself she wouldn't ever say, she'd said. And the ugly creature her words had made hopped around the empty room, made faces at her; green, purple, black Halloween witch faces.

In the beginning when Rob had been out of work two weeks, they joked about it. A vacation. It was great. What a life. Then a month, six months, now almost a year and they had stopped talking. Five days a week they had a pattern. There was a sort of tension, a hope. Businesses operated, schools were open, telephones rang; maybe theirs would. An answer to one of his ads, a letter, a contact he'd made would call. Saturdays were the end of hope. There was nothing to hide behind on Saturdays. No leads, as at first, little routes they traced zig, zag, zig on a map. Maps that went nowhere. He used to type résumés. She Xeroxed them at school. Impressive pages of credits, achievements, awards, publications.

*Ruth Moose*

"I'd hire you in a minute," she said once, hugged him as they looked over the pages he'd typed. Surely, somewhere there was a job for him, vacant, waiting and he would find it and fit in.

On the mornings she taught her class in Contemporary American Literature, he did the housework. Last year, they left together, going in opposite directions at the highway, honking and waving as they turned.

This year she went alone, left behind a mess in the bedroom, bath, kitchen. She never used to do that. She didn't like doing it now and she felt mean. It was a sort of rubbing it in. A reminder of who was important, who brought home the salary. Never mind how part-time it was, how small, never mind, only that it was she who brought it home. Home to the mess she left and he cleaned.

The first time she'd come home and found he'd cleaned the kitchen, she felt hurt and angry. She didn't know why. A puffy black anger that hung in the air like something burnt. And yet it was all she could do to keep from crying. Rob hated dishes! The kitchen work. He would do almost anything else in the house, vacuum, the bathrooms, scrub showers, floors, fixtures, wash, change beds—anything but dishes. Oh, he had done dishes several times, made a great show of washing and rinsing each piece, turning cup, bowl, plate carefully as a potter. Rinsing, wiping every tine of the forks, polishing pots, the stove. She tended to whisk through the kitchen, shove, stack, rattle, bang, but get the job done as quickly as possible, on to other things.

He followed her to the kitchen that first day like a child with a surprise on his face—a pleased look about his mouth. The kitchen sparkled, shone. Even the sink. He gestured like a salesman selling a house. "Look"—he pointed, rubbed his fingers across the hood of the stove—"no grease." He touched the top of the refrigerator. "No dust. It was thick as cloth up there. You never cleaned."

*Ruth Moose*

"I never looked up there," she said, and ducked into the hall. A laugh caught in her throat. She mumbled something about being in a hurry to go to the bathroom.

"You didn't say it was beautiful," he yelled.

"It's beautiful," she called behind her. "Marvelous, great, wonderful, terrific...how many adjectives do you need?"

After that, on her class morning, he cleaned and she never commented. Most of the time he had lunch out when she came home. Neat sandwiches, sliced tomatoes, soup, brownies on a plate. He was an adequate cook, but not good. She preferred hers, and cleaning the kitchen. What bothered her was knowing how much he hated doing dishes yet made himself do them, like a penance. Don't do this to yourself, she wanted to say, but didn't. There was so much she wanted to say and yet at times she felt she said too much. That she covered for him, protected him like an alcoholic's wife. Lying, but not quite, the times she told friends who asked, "Rob found a job?" She said he was working on his doctorate and had applied for a grant. That much was true. He had applied. And he had also been refused. To their friends she probably made it sound like he had the grant. The truth was that they were living on her salary from part-time teaching. Her meager two classes a week and promises for next year's full-time faculty. It was a small college, and they kept saying next year they would have a bigger budget, more funds; an endowment might come through. Rob had been the one with the secure job, a year to go to tenure. Her job was the iffy one, the fringe she was hanging onto reaching for the rope. Yet Rob's job had been the one canceled, his department discontinued, contract not renewed.

At first he'd had a few interviews, gone off whistling, excited. And he'd come back excited. "They seemed impressed with my qualifications." Then they never called back.

The last interview had been in the middle of the year, a

junior high two hundred miles away. They had called back, twice. "Biology," he said disgustedly. "They wanted me to teach biology and coach baseball."

She laughed. It was far from history, but there were books on the subject. And baseball. How much coaching was there to that?

"The pay," he said, "was ridiculous." He didn't have a certificate for public schools, only college.

They had talked about the job. Commuting was out of the question. She suggested he room over, come home weekends. Thoughts of being alone those nights frightened her. Could she manage? Make it on her own? If she had to.

Moving wasn't practical. The job was only for the rest of the school year and they could never find a place to live as cheaply as this. Their house was a cabin on the river and belonged to some friends of her parents who had chosen to travel for the winter. The Hoffmans also mentioned they might be interested in selling, since the cabin needed some repairs and was not in the most desirable section of the river lots anymore. What they had now, Sharon and Rob, was a sort of house-sitting arrangement. They paid utilities, and Rob was supposed to keep the heavy brush around the cabin trimmed, to make it look occupied, maybe prevent it from being burglarized. Last year, Sharon helped Rob clear brush, haul it to a ravine. All the while they watched for snakes. "Copperheads," Marvin Hoffman had told them. "They're around here. Color of leaves. You have to look for them." She and Rob had seen a few snakes, one on a rock by the river, a harmless water snake, another a black snake that she knew lived in the woodpile, also harmless.

Rob hated to clear brush, worried about snakes more than she did. "I wouldn't want to live out here with kids," he said once after they'd moved in.

Funny, and she had been the one holding back about having a child. Sharon wanted to wait until her teaching

*Ruth Moose*

job was secure, when she would have maternity leaves, could schedule between semesters and all. Maybe security mattered more to her than to Rob. There were so many ifs. If Rob's tenure had come through, if Marvin Hoffman had sold them the cabin, if her job were permanent, then would be the time to have a baby. First things first, her mother always said. Order. Sharon liked order and in the past Rob had been a big part of that order.

The cat, Smoky, a black Persian, rubbed against her leg and twined around her stool at the bar. Sharon sat back, let the cat leap into her lap, then stroked him until he settled down to a steady purr and kneading. She rubbed the cat's whiskers and noticed how gray he was getting.

"Thirteen's old for. a cat," the vet said a few months ago. "Even a well-cared-for cat like this one."

Smoky had burned with fever, weak, had been no weight at all in her arms. "He may not make it through," Dr. Frazier had said.

The cat blinked green eyes, poked out a paw, washed.

She and Rob had taken turns getting the capsules, food, warm milk, and liquids into Smoky. Rob had been the one who set the clock for night medications. Several times she woke to lights on, Rob in the kitchen mixing medicine, heating milk. He would be like this with a child, she thought, a baby. A gentle, caring father.

"But it takes more than that," she told the cat, who stopped washing and looked at her. "There's more to fathering than caring and 2:00 a.m. feedings, there's something called responsibility." The cat yawned wide and pink in her lap, its teeth shining thorns.

Their savings were almost gone. The savings they'd planned for a house, to travel, had melted like ice in August. Rob stopped writing résumés, reading ads. He worked off and on at a novel he had started the first year of their marriage. A book of dorm life, college pranks, panty raids, philosophical discussions. He hummed as he typed, distracted her as she corrected papers. He brought chapters for her to read, comment upon. She searched for things to say that wouldn't upset him, parts to praise. The truth was that academia had stilted his style, locked in his vocabulary. She tried to make suggestions for a clearer word, a description. He couldn't see them, argued, became loud.

The cat jumped off her lap, flicked his tail, and walked to the door. Sharon opened the door and heard a small, unusual noise. It took her a moment to decide the sound was Rob cutting brush. She saw his bare back in the woods, the flash of his axe. She hadn't heard him get his tools, hadn't heard the door of the workshop.

Sharon stacked plates, ran water, filled the sink with a great crest of suds. She watched Rob bend as he worked. Work. He was willing to switch jobs with her without hesitation. She'd helped him cut brush before. It wasn't the worst job in the world. Not the most pleasurable, but not the worst. No worse than scrubbing a burned black pot of greasy stew. Cutting brush was at least outdoors and had compensations. Number one, it was not an everyday thing. Number two, you had a sense of accomplishment when you finished. Number three, you never knew what you'd find. She'd found some unusual wildflowers...a carnivorous plant, she remembered; a blue-tailed skink; and once, the most beautiful blue beetle. The real thing, she told herself, was not jobs, nor roles, nor attitudes... maybe it was attitudes. What it boiled down to—she rinsed a spoon—was that she didn't want a wife for a husband. She didn't want someone who cleaned and cooked. Who kissed her goodbye at the door and drank coffee all day. (It could be worse, she told herself in a faraway her-mother's-kind-of-voice.) Sure it could, in all kinds of ways, but, Sharon told herself, what she really wanted was a husband, someone to share, take on half at least. She dried a glass, put it in a row with others on the shelf. Her feelings, spread out, looked to be of various sizes and though not as clear as the glasses, at least recognizable.

Rob's axe flashed in the sunlight as he swung. She wiped the counter, glanced out the window, and saw he had stopped and was standing, staring at the ground. Had he hurt himself? He was good with tools, careful, and though he didn't use them regularly, kept them oiled, dry, and in good repair.

"Rob," she called, "what is it?"

The McClintocks' dogs, a collie named Dan and a part shepherd, Lady, pawed the ground, whined, barked, their tails in the air like a workman swinging warning flags. "Get away," he yelled to the dogs. "Stay back."

Sharon almost tripped on the loose bottom step of the deck as she ran.

"Don't come up here," Rob called. "Stay back."

"What happened?" She still held the damp dish towel, walking closer.

"A copperhead." He leaned on his axe, almost smiling. "I think I killed him, but I want to be sure." His voice had more excitement in it than she'd heard in weeks.

"Where?" She was beside him now, looking into the brush, curled leaves.

"By the stump," he pointed.

She saw the twisted white underneath of the snake and shuddered, wrapping her arms tight about herself.

"I almost didn't see it." Rob poked leaves with a rake. "It moved when the dogs came up or I would have stepped on it."

He lifted the snake on the end of the rake, the metal fingers waving it like a string. ''About a foot long, wouldn't you say?"

The snake looked small to her...and large. Limp, dangling, dead, but with a large frightening danger about it.

Rob flung the dead snake into the woods, where it caught on the lower limb of a beech tree and swung. They watched it swing like a warning. He could have been bitten. God, it was close. And she was the one who screamed, Get a job, dig ditches, do something, anything, I don't care. And he had. He'd killed a snake. A thing he feared for the two years they had been here. She shivered. What if he had been killed? It would have been her fault. No, damn it, not her fault. She started crying, shaking from her shoulders down, her eyes burning.

She walked to him, slid her hand around his waist, dipped slightly inside his pants to the small of his back. His flesh was cool, hard there beneath the denim. "I'm sorry," she said.

He twisted away, threw the rake like a spear into the woods. "I hope you're satisfied now."

The rake hit a tree like a hand, clattered to the ground, its metal fingers frantic and ringing in the still woods.

"You said do something. 'Dig ditches.'" He mimicked her voice. "I could have been killed, thanks to you. Clear your own damn woods." He stalked to the deck, stopped once to wipe his forehead.

"It's not my fault," she started, then stopped. His axe lay beside the rotten stump where the snake had been. She picked it up, swung a blow to the stump which shattered into a brown powder that steamed in the air like a smoldering volcano. She kicked the stump, stepped on it hard, tamped it flat with the ground. What if there were more snakes? A teeming mass of them. She didn't care. Let them come. She'd destroy the copperhead castle.

Beside the stump had been a patch of the moss she used in terrariums. Gardens she made for friends, gifts she sent with a note when the occasion demanded—"A little bit of me under glass"—to cheer the sick, to celebrate the new baby, the promotion. She used to give books. She loved to give books and delighted in taking a long time in their choosing, the right one for the right person and special event. She took joy in their wrapping. Books made their own boxes, which was more than she could say for terrariums. She collected various containers, sizes, shapes and at one point, made them for the local florist. Rob had added up her costs, said she was only kidding herself that she was making any money, so she had stopped. Whatever it was she supposedly hadn't made had helped buy more at the grocery store, she remembered, and he hadn't complained about that.

Sharon cut and stacked brush. At one point she cut down a good-sized dogwood that hadn't bloomed this spring. It was hollow and black in the center around the pink heart. She sawed it into logs, pushing, pulling the curve-handled hand saw across the tree until it lay sectioned. Her wrists ached and there was a blister on her thumb.

She didn't think of snakes anymore. Or anyone. Or anything. Only the cutting, sawing, clearing of the area around her. Gnats buzzed around her at times, and she brushed them away along with the sweat from her face and neck. She was surprised once when some perspiration ran into her eyes and burned. It actually stung for a moment.

She picked up the logs and carried them to the stack beside the door.

The cat sat washing himself on the steps. He turned one wise eye toward her like a wink. She rolled the wood from her arms with a clatter, straightened it and noticed there was enough for several weeks of heating. If it ever turned cold. She couldn't remember what cold was like, only that it seemed clean to her and like something desirable.

She stopped to stroke the cat, who arched under her hand, rubbed against her leg. The hand that fed him and all that clichéd stuff, she thought. When he wasn't hungry, he was Rob's cat and wouldn't have anything to do with her. At times he hissed when she walked past his chair. Rob would laugh.

The stack of brush she had piled looked like a thatched hut from here, or an airy mountain. She'd like to light a match to it, finish the job. The air itself hung so hot, she felt it would spark, that one snap of her fingers and a blaze would flash, the green limbs crackle, burn orange coals, and become a mound of sifted gray ashes. She didn't know if the brush would ever get burnt. Rob tended to walk away from the things, not go back and finish. Actually the brush decayed and as it did, it made a protective thicket for birds and other wildlife.

The snake still hung on the limb, black, like a deep gash or wound against the tree trunk. She would have thrown that in the blaze, like a symbol, a gift, an offering to some god. She didn't know which one. The God of Eve? She snickered at the irony of her own thinking, her joke.

Sharon wiped her feet on the mat, noticing it was worn almost beyond the point of being effective. She heard the roar of a football game: "First down and twenty. The Black Hawks really want to win this one, folks." Rob's chair squeaked as she walked past and into the kitchen. He held a can of the coldest-looking beer. Frost driblets down the sides made her tongue wet.

She saw he'd left the bread open from his lunch, the small blue plastic twistem beside the sprawling loaf. There was a blob of wasted grape jelly on the knife and the lid was off the peanut butter.

She opened the refrigerator, rummaged behind the orange juice, milk, and container of tea, then checked the back of the bottom shelf, atop the meat-keeper, where they sometimes kept beer to get really cold. In the back corner, behind a jar of olives, she felt a can and pulled it out, tasting it already. Then she blinked when she saw the colors of the can. Refrigerator Deodorizer. She turned it around in her hand, half-laughing, half-crying. Then she read the expiration date—June...of last year. Last year.

In a haze she spun around, hit jars and bottles on the refrigerator shelf, knocked over a jar of dill pickles. It teetered,

*Ruth Moose*

turned over as she grabbed at it, and spilled a yellow brine down the shelf, which dripped into a puddle on the floor.

"The Vinegar Jug," she thought. "An old man and an old woman lived in a vinegar jug. . .." Two pickles leaned on the dry side of the jar.

In the bedroom, she got her car keys, purse, counted twelve dollars, plus the checkbook with almost a hundred in it, her overnight case with pajamas, robe, slippers, bra, and panties. Last, she folded in a shirtwaist dress and belt her mother had sent last year for her birthday and some dress sandals. She pushed the lid tight, grabbed the handle, and walked out. Rob didn't glance up from the game. An announcer blared, "And the Hawks are behind by seven—this may be the winning play."

All the way down the drive, she composed letters. Dear Dr. Omsby, Due to unforeseen circumstances.... Dear Marvin and Frances, Thank you for the use of the cabin....

When she thought of him finding the puddle of brine, she laughed. She hoped he'd think it was urine.

*Ruth Moose*

# The Summer Kitchen

MARIE IS MAKING jelly. Wild-grape jelly. The whole kitchen smells wonderfully ripe-purple. Even the steam above the stove is mauve and singing. Marie hums, alone and into the night, where the kitchen of this summer cabin is probably the only light for miles. She wears one of her husband's old shirts knotted at her waist, and panties. Her feet are bare. She likes to be barefoot on the cool kitchen floor late at night. And she likes a kitchen when nothing is expected of her, when no one will interrupt.

Earlier she pinned her blonde hair back, and then finally up and off her neck. That helped cool her in the steamy kitchen that slowly cools now in the fuzzy black night.

Three cats sit outside on the windowsill, watching her work. Marie likes to cook for an audience, even if the audience is only cats. The cats yawn one, three, two, as if she pointed a baton at them. Shame on you, she tells herself, keeping cats up past their bedtime. Through the screen, the cats stare; green eyes large as owls' follow Marie as she moves from sink to cabinet to stove, opening drawers, measuring sugar. She doesn't want to add sugar at all, the grape juice is so pure and strong. She wishes it were strong enough to stand, jell of its own strength. She feels she is cheating to add pectin to it, change it, charge it to become a product, bottled and practical, but that is all she knows to do at the moment. The only guide she has came with the pectin bottle.

*Ruth Moose*

The grape juice has dyed everything it touched. Dishtowels, wooden spoon halfway up its handle, cups, bowls, counter, sink, Marie's fingers, a spot on her shirt. Jon's old shirt. She thinks the spot won't come out quickly, maybe never, and will go through washings to remind her. She'll wear it like a badge. Perhaps add others it to like colors on an artist's smock, her uniform of the jelly-maker's trade. And Jon will find it funny, his old shirt gone soft next to her skin, hugging her breasts.

If Jon were home now, he'd be reading. She wonders how many tax accountants read Emerson. Thoreau. Emily Dickinson. He often reads aloud to her in the kitchen, sentences, paragraphs, prefacing them with an excited "Listen to this. . ." She misses his presence, his voice. At first, these summers, they telephoned each other a lot. Late at night. But he would be tired and she would be reading, or sleepy. What they said were not the things they wanted to say. Now they each save moments for the weekends. Lovely things they share like small, specially wrapped packages. Or collected coins, polished and dated, labeled.

If her sons were up, they would be playing checkers or a marble and dice game. They would not check to see what she cooked because it was not near a mealtime. If they saw the juice, they would not taste it as Marie did, tasting it in the morning by the lake, sun and dew and air heavy with wine. Marie is making jelly because she does not know how to make wine. Oh, what wonderful wine her father made in their damp and moldy dark cellar. She does not have kegs and crocks, white cloths to strain it through, thermometers. She remembers the more-than-grape smell, the heavy Burgundy air.

Marie has used a worn pillowcase for a jelly bag. She hung it above the blue-enamel cooking pot like an udder, warm and soft, squeezed it ever so gently, against the directions that cautioned not. She had listened to the drip of it all afternoon, through supper. They ate on the stone back steps and it comforted her to know the bag dripped without her there to order it, direct it. The jelly juice still dripped as she bathed the boys, let them run squealing and naked to thin pajamas and bunkbeds. It seems ages ago that she checked their curled and dream-wrapped sleep, before her pot of purple broth simmered and talked.

Marie stirs and wishes she knew words or chants to make her jelly magic, full of health and vitamins and summer. But she does not know chants or charms, so she hums and stirs, does small dance steps with her old woodstove partner. "Home Comfort." She loves the name, the ornate bowed legs, the little oven and warming cupboards above. She found the stove at an auction and Jon sanded, polished, and blacked until it gleamed like a genie's lamp.

She wishes Jon were here. That he could be a part of the kitchen late at night, enveloped, both of them, in the winy air. Breathing purple, watching everything through shades of lavender and pink. It seems Jon is never there when special things, little things, happen, and their magic is lost when she tells him. She can never quite capture that moment again in talk or telling.

He was in the city the night owls held a summer convention in their trees. Owls called and winged great, heroic speeches, nominations, orations across the lake. Marie and the boys, awake and sleepily subdued in the silver light of 3:00 a.m., watched from the porch. "I didn't know owls could be so big," Jess said when they told Jon about it that weekend.

"So loud." Martin made a face. "They scared me."

"Not my brave Indian." Jon ruffled Martin's thick red curls.

"Not really," Martin said. "Not next time."

"They were mating," Jon said later.

"Nine owls?" Marie asked. "It was the Southern Owl Association Big Meeting and Annual Convention. I know political speeches when I hear them. Nominations and seconds. Great horned hooting."

He rubbed the back of her neck. "How about pre-mating?"
"I accept that." She laughed. "Owl expert."

Actually he was the hawk watcher, keeping a tally each week of ones he saw beside the interstate. They seemed to like the clear vistas and high wires over the backwoods for hunting. He'd become quite a spotter, and one week reported he'd seen a hawk perched atop the steeple of a small white church on a hill above the highway. He had borrowed her worn leather bird book until she bought him one of his own. The last time she looked, he was still in the hawks section.

Marie was the only one to see the herd of deer move silently through their back yard. Does, thirty-five to fifty of them, and not an antler among the pack. They were the color of tree trunks as they weaved through the woods. She wasn't really sure she was seeing them until they were gone. But afterward their hoof prints patterned the creek banks, and she had those to show the boys and Jon. Heart-shaped prints embossed in the red clay. They were there for weeks. She wondered if the deer had even stopped for water or had simply, silently, continued their journey.

Jon was also away the afternoon shortly after she saw the does, when she heard a barrage of shots in the woods. The boys were on the porch, but she was apprehensive, thinking of the deer herd. Were they being chased by hunters? She called the game warden, who came in his brown car. Later he pulled into the drive and leaned out to tell her the hunters weren't hunters after game but were shooting swags of mistletoe from the tops of a stand of oaks. Nothing illegal.

When the road and creek and drive flooded, Jon missed it. For a week the creek roared like something gone wild. And she thought the rain would never stop. The boys, after exhausting every board game and puzzle in the place, resorted to building forts with the sofa cushions and pelting each other with jellybeans. On Friday, the first day of sun, the creek's waters pooled and spread like an ocean. They watched, fascinated, most of the day while water covered the drive, yard and bridge and swallowed a gap of road. They weren't afraid. The house was high above the creek, out of the way and dry. But all of them worried that Jon would get stranded on the other side. Would he park the car and walk? If he walked, where would he cross? Swim, with his clothes and briefcase? But the waters receded even faster than they came, left twigs and sticks in a dark ring where they had been. Jon examined the residue with them—wet logs and beaver "jam-up" (the boys called it) where the creek narrowed. For weeks afterward they talked of "When the creek flooded" and "Remember when the creek came way up here?"

Jess and Martin were the ones to find wild grapes. They'd come in with tongues and fingers stained.

"There's lots and lots," Martin said, pulling her to come see.

Lots and lots usually meant a handful. Summers before, Marie had left the few scattered grapes she saw for the birds and foxes. But she let the boys lead her to vines near the lake, near where the tree house stood. The lake where Jon taught Jess and Martin to swim last summer. Every Sunday morning, until the water was too, too cold, she watched them from her seat in the pines. Watched their bodies arch and dive, shiny as fish. Liking earth more than water, Marie brought along her bird book and binoculars, or her cross-stitch with its crayon-box colors of threads.

To her surprise, there were a lot of grapes. The air was ripe, alive with their wine smell. The vines hung heavy with sleek purple marbles. She ate one, then another, and more, let the wild juice linger as she chewed the tart, thick hulls. They were wonderful and she had to do something with them. To keep them. Make use of them.

*Ruth Moose*

All was quiet except for the plop as she piled grapes in her basket, the soft swish of leaves as she pulled them close, picked, let go, her fingers fuzzy. She felt steeped in grape smell and so heady she could have been drunk as she walked back to the cabin.

Drunk on the sweet, wild smell. A smell thick enough to spoon over ice cream or drink from the air. That world of grapes that must have been before people, before animals, before God? Maybe at one time there were only God and grapes and the air was wine.

Marie ladles foam off the simmering jelly into a saucer. Lavender whipped cream. A test as old as time. She remembers her grandmother, here in the kitchen, letting Marie taste the warm jelly, the lace around it.

She takes the jars from their boiling bath, sets them on a clean, spread dishtowel, pours jelly. Five full jars of jelly. She doesn't spill a drop as the dark-purple waterfall goes into glasses that have been waiting for this all their lives.

Her pot is empty except for a wedge of juice in the bottom. Not even half a glass. What to do? She pours it into a custard cup, where it sits like a small purple pudding.

Then she puts lids on hot jars, holds each one tight with a towel and twists, amazed at her own strength, sureness. She sets the jars aside in a row as orderly as a church pew. She sighs and stares around her. The kitchen is purple. Purple as the night outside. She looks and even the cats have gone to bed. Marie would like to leave right now, tiptoe out, flip off the light, and fall into bed. But she can't. She knows everything will be sticky in the morning. Pans, spoons, colander, counter. The floor is gritty, grained with sugar and sand.

She fills the sink with hot water and suds, begins. Not humming now, but working with speed and determination to rinse, dry, put away. Wiping stove and sink until at last everything is clean. The smell of grapes lingers and she takes the pulp, gray as eggplant, to the porch. Tomorrow she will spread it in the woods, return a share to the soil, the bees.

She gives the jars one more loving look, holds one up to the light. It is like looking through stained glass. She reverently sets the jar down. Its sister jar pings. Then another. Seals of approval. Comforting chimes of a distant clock.

Marie thinks of Jon, asleep in their house in the city. Three hours away. Alone. And she is alone. She wishes there were a way she could slip out of herself and into his bed until morning. Then back to motherhood, to self, to here. She sighs, takes one last look around the clean kitchen in the bare white light, sees the lonely custard cup of jelly. She takes a spoon from the drawer, holds the jelly high and spoons up the still-warm liquid, savoring each special drop. Then she turns out the light.

*Ruth Moose*

# The Swing

THE ROOM SMELLED of old hymn books, dust, and stale dry air. One window was curtained by two lengths of dark green plastic that once hung in someone's home.

When amid the opening, closing, and rustling of purses, the wooden collection plate of the Mary Magdelene Sunday School Class was passed to Margaret Rivers, she held it in her hands a moment, then passed it to Ellie Mason. Ellie Mason sniffed once, laid her dollar bill on the others, snapped her big black purse shut with a loud click, and passed the plate down the row.

Margaret could hear the low buzz of women's voices follow the collection plate around the room. Like hornets abuilding a nest, she thought. Let them talk, I don't care. She pulled a handkerchief from the loose bosom of her blue dotted-swiss dress, spread it across her knees, and began to smooth the folds. With the tip of her index finger she traced the bumps of the spray of forget-me-nots embroidered in one corner. These don't look like my hands, she thought suddenly. They look so rough and red, like I just them out of the washtubs. She turned the strange hands over in her lap. Papa always said I had such small hands. She sighed, quickly refolded the handkerchief, placed it in the middle of the black Bible in her lap, and glanced at the pink and purple map of the Holy Land that hung on the wall behind the teacher's desk.

*Ruth Moose*

"Mrs. Rivers." Letitia Hinson spoke from behind the desk. "I thought I'd call on our preacher's wife to lead us in our opening prayers this morning."

The sharp voice rapped out the command and Margaret was trapped by the dozen now silent and tight-lipped women. She shut her eyes, bowed her head, and began.

"Our Father"—yes, that was right, she was glad she remembered. "Our Father," she repeated. Father was Papa who never said a cross word to her in his life. "Thank you for every blessing we have received." Papa was so good to her. She was breathing more evenly now. "Bless us during the lesson this morning and be with us during the coming week. Amen." She finished, raised her head, and swallowed the lump that had grown to her throat.

Margaret did not hear the Sunday School lesson. It droned on and on like the constant irritation of a distant sawmill. She dutifully opened her Bible to the appropriate scriptures and sat watching the black letters run together like watery ink. When she heard the thud of Bibles being closed, she hastily shut hers too and stood in front of her chair while Letitia's long benediction rained like dust particles on her head.

When it was over, she reached up, felt for a wisp of hair and tucked it back into the tight, round onion of a bun on the back of her neck. I'm the only woman in the class not wearing a hat, she thought as she looked around the milling group. That should give their tongues something else to wag about next week, and she walked out.

Behind her, she could hear the chant. Nice lesson, Letitia; enjoyed the lesson, Letitia; a real blessing, Letitia. Bunch of hypocrites. She slammed the door. The hall was crowded and she weaved past groups of smiling, talking people who smelled faintly of fried pork, Rose hair oil and vanilla flavoring.

Just as she curled her fingers around the cold doorknob, he grasped her shoulder. She could feel the pressure of every finger.

His voice was a hoarse whisper, angry as wind. "Stay for the service, Margaret. It won't kill you."

She spun around. "What for? To hear you make a fool of yourself?"

He flushed dark and it spread to the inlets of his almost bald head, tinting his sparse white hair a pale pink. His mouth jerked open slightly as though he wanted to say more, but dared not.

Margaret yanked the doorknob, stepped outside and pulled the door shut with glass-rattling force, then leaned against the side of the building; rough edges of peeling paint picking through the thinness of her dress. A small breeze lifted her collar; she turned her face to catch the air and saw the cemetery, fenced with blackberry briars. High as my head, she thought, and nobody gives a hoot. Ellie Mason and them just laugh about all the pies they've had from cemetery vines. Her eyes followed the weed-tufted gravel path to the center of the cemetery and the largest stone. She knew the inscription by heart: "Lilly Reiley Rivers, Beloved Wife of Daniel Polkton Rivers, Her Price Is Far Above Rubies." Had to buy her the fanciest stone in the cemetery, lilies carved on it till there's not a place you can lay your finger. And my babies; my babies was lucky to get a marker.

The door behind Margaret opened, and children ran past like a herd of freed ponies; slick-haired boys yelled and whooped; little girls in bell-shaped dresses, their heads bent together in giggles, brushed past. Not one of them Laura. Margaret leaned back to wait. From the front of the church she could hear the squeak, squawk of the pump, the clang of the tin cup, and squeals at the rush of water.

The door opened scarcely larger than a crack and Laura squeezed out, head bent like an old lady.

Margaret laughed. "Cow's tail. You're always the last one out." As soon as the words were spoken she wanted them back. Laura's small face was pinched, her eyes large and wet under the severe line of dark bangs. She's tenderhearted like me, Margaret thought, not one to take teasing. "What's wrong, honey?" she asked gently.

Laura twisted a small handkerchief with both hands. "I couldn't get the knot loose, Maw Maw. I tried and tried and it wouldn't come undone."

Margaret took the crumpled handkerchief and began to pull at the knotted lump. "Honey, you got it wet, that's why. You worried with it so much you made it tighter." She tucked the Bible under her arm and began to pick at the knot. "Hold your hands under here and catch the pennies when I get 'em loose or they'll fly all over creation."

Laura cupped her hands under Margaret's large ones and when the pennies dropped, she caught them. "What'll I do with them now?" She pointed with her chin toward the doorway. "Take them in there?"

"Pshaw, I'd not bother." Margaret clasped her lips together in a tight line. "Just keep 'em yourself."

"I don't care what HE says." Margaret began to walk quickly around the church and through the yard. Laura ran to keep up. Behind them church doors closed with a loud scrape.

"Bringing in the sheaves, bringing in the sheaves." The voices rolled over their heads and Miss Bessie at the piano tinkled in the extra notes she was known for. "Weee shall come rejoicing, brin-ging in the sheaves."

Margaret muttered, "Picked out the songs too, didn't he?" "How do you know?" Laura asked, and stopped to grab a fallen oak limb.

They walked toward the old baptismal house, its paint gone, the weathered boards a greenish tint of moss growing between the cracks. Its tin roof was the color of red clay and two doors, side by side; faced steps that led down to the dirt-crusted concrete pool.

Laura ran down the steps and began to lift pieces of wet,

yellow paper and leaves with her stick. "Look, Maw Maw, somebody's old shoe's in here." She kicked it.

"Better get out of there before you get snakebit," Margaret said to Laura's dark head bobbing on the steps. She looks so much like Mary; little spindly legs, I worried they'd not make it up those steps. She was twelve and not much bigger than Laura. I tried to tell him that Sunday she was sick. He just felt her forehead, said it didn't feel hot, so get ready. I begged him to let her stay in bed. He said I was always putting my children before the Lord and I'd be punished for it. It was punishing that child to make her go.

"Margaret," Laura yelled from the third step, "was my daddy baptized here? Did they put him all the way under?"

"All of 'em were. All four of my children that lived were baptized here…and it like to have killed Mary. All week she hadn't been pert and I'd seen the stain on her britches. Knew it was coming on her. Dreaded it. Saturday night she was bent double with cramps. I filled the hot water bottle, wrapped it in an old sheet. Only thing I knew to ease it. The rest you got to live with, I told her. It ain't easy being a woman."

"Did she almost drown?" Laura was beside her now, skipping in the path across the broomstraw field.

"Who? Did who almost drown?"

"Aunt Mary?"

The saliva was bitter in Margaret's mouth. "No, it wasn't that at all. Something you wouldn't understand." The water in that pool was like ice, coming from the spring like it did, and Palm Sunday in March. I worried, was cold all over for her. He put her under and she came up dripping, face white as the dress she had on. When I heard a scream from the dressing-room after they had gone back, I tore in there. Scared me weak to my knees to see her laying on the floor, limp as a rag. I got somebody to take us home; left him standing in the water still preaching. He didn't speak to me that day, kept his jaws shut tighter than a bear trap. Mary took pneumonia after that and like to have died—he's made a fool of himself more than once in that church.

Laura stood at the edge of the woods under a large tree.

"Let's pick up hickory nuts, Maw Maw."

"It's too early." Margaret gave a short laugh. "They ain't fell yet. Wait till the leaves turn; you come back and stay with Maw Maw then and we'll pick up hickory nuts."

Laura hit the tree trunk with her stick. "I bet we get a bushel."

"Don't count on it." Margaret pointed to the top of the tree. "See those dead limbs? This tree's old. Your daddy and us picked many a bushel of hickory nuts, took 'em up town and sold 'em. Most we ever got was fifty cents a bushel. Course that was big money in those days."

"I'll get a dollar for mine." Laura jumped flat-footed over a big root.

"Whoa now, missy." Margaret's voice was tinged with amusement. "You're talking mighty big for such a little girl."

"Well," Laura said, her lips in a pout, "I'm getting that five-dollar gold piece, aren't I?"

"Don't count your chickens till they hatch, I've always said." Margaret walked ahead, leaned over and broke off a handful of pine needles, bent them across her hand and lifted them to her nose. Pine smelled so clean. He don't turn loose much for his family. Church now, that's different. It's in the name of the Lord.

They entered a thick grove of pines. Laura threw away her stick and walked sliding her feet under pine needles like two small plows.

"This is where your daddy wanted to build a house," Margaret said, and Laura didn't answer. There was only the soft shuffling in the dry needles. "He wouldn't have it though, said selling this lot would cut up the farm. Lot's already off from the rest of the land and it will never be any good unless the church wants it. Church don't need it."

*Ruth Moose*

Margaret snorted. "Just his excuse!"

Through the trees Margaret could see the black stretch of road, and across from that the rusted mailbox leaned on its rotten post. On top of the hill she could see the squat, reddish house, roof so bright it hurt her eyes. Painted it silver so folks'd think we had a new one. And that siding. Made to look like brick, but ain't. Any fool would know the difference. I wanted the house painted white if he was going to have anything done after all these years. My daddy always had our house painted white. Outbuildings too. Everybody always said we had the prettiest farm.

"Take holt my hand, Laura." Margaret shaded her eyes. "Guess we'd hear a car if one was coming." She checked both ways before they walked across.

Laura stood on tiptoes, pulled the mailbox lid, and peeped into the warm blackness. "It's empty."

Margaret stretched over her. "Let me see. Mail don't run on Sunday, but we might find something we missed yesterday." She patted the bottom of the box, ran her fingers around the corner, and thumped the back before shutting the lid with a dull clang. "One time a letter from Paul got stuck in the back and I didn't find it for over a week. I worried something terrible. I always get a letter from him on Mondays, 'less the mail don't run."

They started down the unpaved road, Margaret in one rut, Laura in the other, tall grass between.

Laura counted on her fingers, "You get a letter from Uncle Paul on Mondays, the Saturday Evening Post on Tuesdays, a letter from Aunt Mary on Wednesdays—what do you get the rest of the week, Maw Maw?"

Margaret laughed. "Not much! You got my mail all figured out, haven't you?"

Laura shook her head. The pigtails swung like twin whips. "Huh-uh. I can't figure out why you get the Saturday

Evening Post on Tuesdays. If they call it the Saturday Evening Post you ought to get it on Saturdays."

"Some folks get theirs on Saturday, I 'spect. I'm lucky to get mine on Tuesdays, whatever they want to call it. I don't complain."

They had begun to climb the hill now. On each side of the road, remains of the old orchard stood, trees gnarled like lepers' limbs.

"No siree." Margaret's breath was shallow and fast. I don't complain as long as I get it." And Paul said he'd see to it I got the Saturday Evening Post the rest of my life if I wanted it...and after his daddy wrote and told him not to send that trash. 'Course I wrote in the same mail and said don't do no such a thing. He keeps wondering when the subscription's out. Nothing fit to read but the Bible, HE's said time and time again. And every Sunday morning he starts the kitchen fire with my magazine. Rips it up page by page. I used to put my hands over my ears so I wouldn't have to hear it. Now I just go about my business and pay it no mind. I get a brand new copy on Tuesday and HE can't stand it. "Laura," she said suddenly, with more sharpness than she intended, "quit thinking about the Saturday Evening Post and let's work on your memorizing."

"I said my verses good yesterday, didn't I?"

"Yes, but that was yesterday and if you stumble one time he won't give you the five-dollar gold piece," Margaret said to the back of Laura's head. "He won't tell you the next word either."

"I know what," Laura looked back with a sideways grin, her eyes bright as a kitten's. "I'll study while you fix dinner. Listen to me say the first part now." Laura brushed her bangs to one side and began to sing-song, "The Lord is my shepherd, I shall not want. He maketh me to lie down in green pastures, he..."

*Ruth Moose*

Margaret paced each step with the words and when they reached the top of the hill said, "Slow down, honey, let me catch my breath." She took several deep breaths. "I was getting kinda swimmy-headed."

Across the front of the house on the open porch, wooden chairs leaned, their rockers upended like a row of menacing horns. At the far end a swing moved slightly in the breeze.

"Let's swing now, Maw, Maw. Laura's heels clicked like small horses hoofs across the porch.

"We better fix dinner," Margaret said. "Your daddy and mama might come and he'll be home shortly after twelve unless he gets wound up and forgets to stop." She chuckled.

"Just for a minute?" Laura patted the empty space behind her.

Margaret grasped the cedar post, pulled herself up on the porch and plopped down beside Laura. " It does feel good." She leaned back. "I always did like a swing. We had one at home."

"Just like this one?"

"No it was wicker, white wicker with green cushions in it and many a night Dora, Elsie or Pearl did their courting in it."

"Did you, Maw Maw?"

"No, I never did," Margaret's face was solemn. "I never courted atall. 'Thirty five years old and not married. Who'll look after you when I'm gone,' Papa said. 'You don't want to be a burden on your sisters and their families. Preacher Rivers is a good man, Margaret. He needs another wife. A good man.'" Margaret spit out a piece of grit that was cutting her tongue. "God himself that's who he thinks he is. Me and my children laboring on this farm, him off in a white shirt preaching. And when they wanted some little something he'd say it was sinful. I bought this swing," she said to Laura. "I bought and paid for it with my own money when your daddy wasn't any bigger than you are now. Paul and Mary saw this swing in Kistler's hardware store and commenced begging for it. Red, it was bright red then, bright as a Christmas bow. Sinful to spend money on foolishness, he said, work of the Devil. I'd not seen those kids want anything as bad as that swing in a long time. I went to the bank and drew out seven dollars of the money Papa left me and bought it. He was so mad he was about to pop, rared and pitched all the way home; kids huddled together in the back seat like they had been whipped. Me and the kids put it up that night while he was at prayer meeting. He's never sat in it to this day, acts like it's not even here. I've seen him bump into it many a time," Margaret smiled a thin halfmoon and ran her fingers along the wooden arm. "Hasn't been painted since David was home from service that summer, 'fore he was killed. He put in new boards, sanded it, and kept teasing about how pretty the blue swing was going to look. Had me worried for a while, till he called me to come see it when he finished. It was red, shiny as new." Margaret rubbed the dead paint into a powder between her fingers. "Needs painting again now."

Laura stood up and brushed off the back of her dress. "It sure does."

"Good heavens," Margaret said suddenly and stood. "I hear cars leaving from the church. Must be twelve and we got to get some dinner on the table. Let's make haste."

Laura held the door for her grandmother and they walked quickly down the narrow hall, past the front room with its black leather chairs and grass rug and the front bedroom where Laura and her grandmother had slept this week.

In the kitchen, Margaret grabbed her feed sack apron from its nail and slid it over her head, tying it deftly at the waist. She poked the fire and noticed a few shiny staples, some irregular bits of paper. She picked up a brown-edged triangle, turned it over, and said, "Tugboat Annie," then crumpled it and tossed it back in the stove.

*Ruth Moose*

Laura came into the kitchen as Margaret opened a mildew-covered jar of dark purple. "Damson," Margaret said. "Taste them." She gave Laura a spoon, then emptied the preserves onto the yellow circle of cake. "Not much, but it'll give plain cake a little flavor." Margaret licked the knife, then set the cake in the middle of the oilcloth-covered table. "Say your verses for me, honey, real quick."

Laura leaned over the back of the chair. "Make a joyful noise unto the Lord, all ye lands. Serve the Lord with gladness…"

Margaret looked at the page in the Bible on the table. "Come before his presence. . ." She took spoons and forks from a glass on the table and laid three places.

At the sound of a car, Laura lifted the corner of a muslin curtain. "Somebody in a blue car brought Granddaddy home."

Margaret poured water into a skillet, laid biscuits left from breakfast onto a plate, clanged the lid, and set it on the stove. "Brother Bassett, I 'spect." She stood in the doorway and watched as he put his notebook and the big zippered Bible on the small table by the window. "Dinner's ready, but I thought we'd wait and see if Dan and Julie come first."

He took off his black coat and hung it inside the closet on a nail. Slightly stooped, but lean and tall, he radiated strength. Don't look any more seventy than he did forty when we got married, Margaret thought.

He patted Laura on the head. "How's my girl?" Then turned to Margaret and said matter-of-factly, "I'm not eating cold."

Margaret checked the biscuits just starting to steam, stirred the pot of beans, and put chicken dumplings in a bowl. "Wonder what's keeping your daddy and mama?" she said to Laura and hugged her close. "Guess they ain't coming and I'll have to keep you." She cupped her hands on each side of Laura's face. "You could live with Maw Maw all the time then."

"And not go to school?" Laura's eyes were wide. She pulled away. "I've got to go to school."

"I know you have, honey." Margaret brushed one of Laura's pigtails back. "I was just teasing. Maw Maw wants you to go to school and learn everything you can so you'll grow up to be independent. Support yourself. Not have to depend on somebody else."

He stood at the table, white shirt open, exposing a neck wrinkled and scrawny as an old turkey's wattle. "What's holding up dinner?" He pulled out a chair. "I've got to be at a meeting at Shiloh at two." He poured a glass of buttermilk.

"I may preach their revival again this year." He folded his hands in his lap

Margaret put the hot biscuits on a plate, covered them with a cloth, set them on the table, and took her place. Laura sat with her palms together under her chin.

"Bless this food, Our Father," he said, and Margaret bowed her head. "To the use of our bodies. And bless. . ."

Margaret's stomach tightened, rolled, then murmured as he went on and on. "Bless the Worseley family," he was saying. "Thou has seen fit to take their youngest from them."

Yes, Margaret thought, and he's better off than in that squalor.".

"We knowest not why, Our Father, but we must trust in Thy divine plan. Bless. . ." His voice was like an old motor grinding, yet running forever.

Finally Margaret coughed, cracked an eyelid at Laura, who seemed to be asleep. Poor thing, his Sunday blessings are enough to last us a week.

"Amen," he said flatly, raised his head, took a sip of buttermilk and reached for a biscuit. "Cold." He laid it on his plate. "Biscuit's no good if it won't melt butter." He picked up his fork and raked chicken dumplings onto his plate.

*Ruth Moose*

Margaret pressed her lips together and reached for the salt shaker.

"Today's the day, Missy." He shoved a bite of chicken into his mouth. "You going to say your verses for me?"

"After lunch." Margaret took a swallow of coffee, "let her eat."

When he had cleaned his plate he reached for the cake, plunged a knife in its center, and pushed down until the plate rocked. "Wrap up what's left of this, Margaret." He lifted a piece of cake on his plate, dripping purple all the way. "I'll drop it by the Worseleys' on my way to Shiloh."

Margaret set her cup down with a clatter. "Dan, Julie and the kids is coming. I thought they'd be here for lunch. Besides, the Worseleys will have plenty without my little bit of sweetening."

"Yours. Yours?" He scraped the plate with the side of his fork. The noise set Margaret's teeth on edge. "Who paid for the butter and eggs that went into this cake? You?"

Margaret made herself get up from the table, take two saucers from the stack in the cupboard, cut two slices of cake, and still not look at him.

"Well," she said slowly. "It's my preserves on top. That damson tree came from my daddy's place. I brought it here and set it out myself. You can take the cake." She slid it back toward the center of the table. "But I'll scrape the preserves off first."

For a moment he looked like he had bitten down on something hard. Then he pushed his chair back, letting the legs scratch loudly, and left the room.

Margaret took a bite of cake, got strangled, and coughed until her face was flushed. Then she laughed. "Eat your cake, honey, he ain't taking it nowhere."

In the next room they could hear papers rattling, books slammed shut, and the hoarse voice of the zipper on his old Bible.

*Ruth Moose*

"Laura," he yelled. "Come say your verses. You'll be gone when I get back."

Margaret nodded and began to stack the dishes, prompting in a whisper, "Make a joyful noise. . ." She cupped clean plates over the bowls of leftover food, pushed them together, and spread a clean, white cloth over it all like some lumpy corpse.

As she poured water from the kettle into the dishpan she could hear Laura's small voice, "I shall not want. He maketh me..."

Margaret moved her lips with the words. When she finished the dishes she opened the back door and dashed out the dishwater in a stream that beaded on the dry ground. Used to have chickens scatter when I'd do that; squawk like a hawk was after 'em. And eggs. I had as many as five dozen a week to sell till the hens quit laying and he wouldn't bring me no biddies from town. Said they was too much trouble. Not to him—he never touched them. Just didn't want me to have that little bit of pleasure.

"Endureth forever." Margaret heard Laura finish. Then his voice and Laura's, talking, but she couldn't catch the words. She dried her hands and waited for Laura to run in, showing her prize.

Instead Laura rushed in, grabbed her grandmother, and wrapped her face in the apron, sobbing in jerks and gasps.

"What's wrong, Lauralee?" Margaret wiped Laura's chin with the apron. "Hush now, you didn't mess up, did you?"

"He says I didn't say it right." Laura's voice shook, she hiccuped. "But I did, Maw Maw, I didn't miss a word."

Margaret rocked her back and forth, cooing. "Hush now, hush." Laura's sobs stopped and the ache in Margaret's chest felt like an open hole. She settled Laura in a chair, pulled her dress over her knees and patted her leg. "What did you mess up on? Which one? We'll say it real quick and you can go try again."

*Ruth Moose*

Laura brushed her hand away from her face. "That's what I'm trying to tell you. I said every word right and he said it was still wrong. He said I left out the selahs."

Margaret hugged the child to her, "You just be still, I'll go talk to him."

He was bent over his writing table, the big pen scratching across the page.

"Daniel," she said and he didn't stop. "Daniel, why don't you give the child the gold piece like you promised? It's breaking her heart."

He laid the pen down slowly and began to fumble with the gold chain below his belt. The five-dollar gold piece dangled a small clinking sound. His voice was firm, distinct. "I told her, and you heard me, Margaret," he looked at his watch, snapped the lid shut and slid it into the small slot in his pants. "I told her she couldn't miss a word, not one—if she did, I'd not give her the gold piece."

"I know what you said"—Margaret's voice was controlled—"and she didn't miss a word. She said them perfectly before dinner."

He curled his lips slightly, "With the selahs?"

"Not with the selahs, no. They're not in my Bible and that's the one I taught her out of. They're not part of it anyway. You can't count that." Margaret's cheeks felt hot. "You're not going to disappoint that child. You hear me!"

She turned to go.

"What do you think you'll do about it?"

He was holding his position and Margaret shook. "I don't know." She was mad enough to cry. Papa always said I was tenderhearted and Daniel knows it. Treat his family like dogs and go around so mealy-mouthed. People saying what a good man Preacher Rivers is. "For all I care you can take that cake to those good-for-nothing Worseleys," she snapped.

"Fine," he said, as though the word tasted good in his mouth, "I'll do it. But that won't get you the gold piece."

*Ruth Moose*

"You don't care how you hurt people, do you?" She pushed her hair back, felt for a loose tendril, and jabbed it in place with a u-shaped pin.

"I'll give her the gold piece on one condition," he said quietly.

Margaret waited.

"I'll give Laura the gold piece if"—he paused, and still she did not turn to face him. "If you give five dollars to the church."

"Five dollars." She sputtered out the words. "From the money my daddy left me? I meant not one red cent of that was ever going to the church. It was for me and my children. What did that church ever do for me? Snicker behind my back, compare me to Lily. Nobody ever lived as perfect as they made her out to be. Keep your old gold piece. Let them bury you with it on." She said it and she was glad. She stalked out of the room, floors popping under wide, flat heels.

"Come on," she said to the frightened Laura, who jumped from the chair, her face white patches in red. "We'll find something better than his old gold piece if he wants to be that way."

"What?" Laura said as they went out the door, around the house to the porch and to the swing. "What, Maw Maw?"

Margaret leaned back, closed her eyes, and swung back and forth. Fast at first, then slower, the chains alternately crying and grunting.

"What can I have, Maw Maw?"

Margaret didn't answer and Laura snuggled close. "I meant for that money not to be touched till I was dead and gone. Papa left it to me and my children. They never had much all these years and I never touched that money but once and that was to buy this swing." She pulled Laura's dark head into her lap. She was warm and sleepy. Precious child. I never had time to hold Mary much when she was little. Always had work waiting on me, never finished.

*Ruth Moose*

Laura snored once, her eyelids twitched and Margaret rocked the swing back and forth gently. What will I give this child? She worked so hard, and it's my fault for not teaching her out of his old pulpit Bible. But he would have found something to keep from giving her that gold piece no matter what I did. Had her heart set on it and what can I give her in its place? Everything pretty I had wore out long ago, or got lost, or give away. The things the children send, she wouldn't want.

Margaret leaned back and stared at the rusty chain, followed it up as far as her fingers would reach toward the fly speckled ceiling. Got to take the swing down soon, put it away for the winter. Put the chains back in the oil cans to keep 'em from rusting. Can't leave it out in the weather, old as it is, wouldn't last no time. She sighed. Gettin' too old to be climbing in and out of that barn loft with this swing. Every year I'm scared I'll fall—break my leg.

"Laura." She shook the child gently. "Honey, I know what you can have." Laura didn't open her eyes, just wiggled closer to Margaret and slept on.

Margaret gave a push with her foot, it bumped a raised board in the floor and the swing jiggled, then was smooth. She drifted back and forth, lifted her feet and coasted. I want to remember how it feels for a long time. I've always liked a swing.

*Ruth Moose*

# The Wreath-Ribbon Quilt

WE SIT WAITING for Christmas, strangers whose lives are linked by blood, marriage, and memories. This is a rare calm. From the living room my daughters' voices float in a kind of music as they giggle and talk, shake packages and bells.

My brother Gary, tall in his blue V-neck sweater, flips channels on television, a montage of people, snow scenes, disasters, and commercials on digestion aids. The first year Gary went off to college it seemed he grew like a hollyhock. At his wedding I noticed for the first time he was taller than Daddy. Gary's wife, Anne, sits in the Boston rocker and feeds their six-month-old baby. Bubbles in her bottle float to the top, work like yeast.

Beside me on the sofa, Henry, my husband, leafs through an ancient issue of Reader's Digest. The comers are so curled he must press them flat to read, "I am Joe's Heart."

This lull is strange. Not peaceful, for there is a touch of tension present, but for the first time in days, I begin to relax. No cookies to roll, cut, and sugar-sprinkle, no gifts wrap, ribbons to fluff and tie; my hands, not in motion, lie like clay birds in a nest behind my knees.

My father's chair is empty. A blue plastic recliner, it looms large, casts a square shadow in the corner.

Mother bangs a spoon in the kitchen stirring oyster stew. We always have oyster stew on Christmas Eve, but before, Daddy in a red striped apron, arms at angles like airplane

*Ruth Moose*

wings, tasted and stirred. He heated it slowly, peppered, paprikaed twice, made us wait until he pronounced the thick broth creamy-perfect.

Gary, on the sofa now, moves an embroidered pillow, sits beside Henry. They discuss the Super Bowl, who's to win. Their talk turns to cars and Gary moans the loss of the sweet sports car he traded for Anne's station wagon.

"I could feel it," Anne says quickly. "He used to scare me half to death. Could have killed us both trying to see how much that car would do. I told him to either drive with sense or let me out. God, he tried to fly the thing."

My legs prickle under me and the sofa becomes a plush automobile seat. Daddy makes the speedometer needle move from 80 to 90 and past. My mother screams, "What are you trying to do? Kill us all? Make the car fly? Stop and let me out. You can kill yourself if you want to, but let me and the baby out." I watched the needle ease slowly back; the trees become trees out of the green fuzzy blur. The wind noise stops and my father, not laughing any longer, is angry, his face red as strawberry cake. Mother lets her breath out slowly and loud. My legs relax against the seat.

Mother comes from the kitchen, wipes her hands on her white apron, and pushes a footstool near Anne and the baby. She pats the baby's pink-knitted-bootie feet. "I'm surprised she can still wear these. She's growing so fast."

The baby smiles. Milk trickles from the corner of her mouth and down her hill of a chin. "If you don't want the rest of this—" Anne holds the bottle up. The baby reaches out a starfish hand, settles quickly back.

"I haven't made oyster stew in so long." Mother pushes back her hair. "I didn't know if I would remember how…and the only oysters I could find seemed small."

I used to fish oysters, large as shells, lift them from my bowl to Daddy's. He'd make some joke about lead in his pencil.

*Ruth Moose*

My daughters run in from the living room and swing onto Henry's lap. Jackie hugs his neck, whispers loudly toward his ear, "Can't we open just one present now?"

Henry glances at me. "No, let's wait. It won't be much longer." He tickles her stomach and she folds up laughing. Kate joins them in the horseplay.

I remember Daddy teasing me, making me wait, the suspense and surprise a mixture of aching delight. Now Christmas seems a whirlwind of duties, demands. Even the gifts we give and get are practical: pajamas and robes, toaster ovens and fry pans. Last year I gave Gary, as a joke, a book, "Making Wine at Home." Anne told me later the only thing they got was a jug of the darkest vinegar and a stain the size of a dinner plate on their kitchen ceiling.

Daddy used to make wine. I wonder if Gary remembers. Daddy made it before there were books on the subject, before wine-making was a fad kind of thing to do. He had wooden kegs in the basement and the air smelled purple, later a fuzzy gray. His wine, like Gary's, failed. He rolled kegs onto the grass, removed the plugs, let dark liquid, the color of blood, gush over the green lawn. Mother came out to ask if it would hurt the grass. Daddy didn't answer.

One of the girls, Jackie, whines at Henry's elbow, "I don't see why we can't open one present now."

Henry says after we eat they can open all the presents. Mother says if they don't stop fussing, Santa Claus will hear them and not bring the Teresa Tresses dolls they want.

They never saw my father as Santa Claus. The suit he rented sagged and bunched under the wide, black plastic belt. His curled beard could have covered two chins. After a drink or two at each of the first dozen homes Daddy visited, stomping snow from his boots and ho-hoing louder as the night moved on, he would have to hire someone to drive the car. Gary refused. He said if Daddy wanted to make a fool of himself at his age, he didn't want to be present to see it. When someone brought Daddy home, heavy after midnight, he was dressed in regular clothes. I never knew what happened to the Santa Claus suit.

Mother goes to the closet, rumbles in it. "You can't wait, can you, honey?" She gives the girls a box of toys. There is a rusty wind-up drummer boy Gary used to have. It lies broken on top. Hanging from one corner is a doll I never liked. She is wigless and her scalp a patch of sticky lint.

Kate carries the box to the living room. Mother winks at me. "That should keep them busy a little while. Their minds off opening presents, at least until the stew gets ready."

She pulls a plastic bag from a closet shelf, takes out a rainbow of ribbons. "Do you want these?" She strokes the ribbons, pulls a green one through her fingers.

"What?" I can't think why I would want the ribbons. They are too large for the girls to wear, if they ever wore such things, too limp for bows, too wide for gift wrapping. "Where did you get them?"

"Your father's funeral." She looks surprised that I had to ask. "The wreaths. I took them off the wreaths." She lays ribbons in a row down her arm. "They've been washed and pressed.'"

My head aches from the smell of carnations. A room filled and hot with carnations.

"You can make a coverlet," Mother says. "I've seen some beautiful ones. All ribbons of the same colors can be a border, others worked into a pattern."

I see Mother pluck bows from each wreath, gathering her arms full like .a garden bouquet. "No." I shake my head. "No."

She's disappointed. I think of the hours she's spent unwinding wires, washing ribbons, the work to iron satin without scorching. "There's enough purple ones," she holds several ribbons the color of awards. "They'd make a nice border."

"You keep them. You make a coverlet." I look to Henry for help. He's hiding in his reading. The Reader's Digest is desperation. I wish he'd notice what's happening, change the subject, say something, say anything.

Gary holds the baby, Lucinda. He pats her back until she burps loudly. "Atta girl," he says and kisses the top of her head wobbling on its stem of neck.

Anne restacks the diaper bag, folds in a terrycloth bib.

"I thought sure you'd want them." Mother closes the bag, stuffs it back into the closet. Her dress is a Christmas red. She never wore black or navy blue, not even to the funeral.

Ribbons the color of carnations. In my mind I see the wreaths still, my father's frozen face, the scar untouched; not even the undertakers would try to camouflage it. The scar that was a ditch of cuts and bruises, his face a mass of purple and red that night. "Go, you old tomcat, you," my mother screamed at him. He stood, head on his arms resting against the wall like someone being searched. "You got what you deserved," she yelled. "Some woman's husband came home too soon."

Gary, eyes bright with fever, dark hair limp, sat on her lap, hand over his ear. An infection woke him screaming in the night. Mother had been rocking him, I heard him cry, the even whump, whump of the rocker, was almost asleep again when Daddy came home and the argument began. Mostly an argument in Mother's voice. I stumbled sleepily into a room of people I knew but did not know. Mother pointed at Daddy, then the door. "Go on," she said. "Don't make me look at the mess you are."

He said something, pried my hands loose, and left. I didn't run after him and for the rest of the night, and several after, kept hearing his returning footsteps that weren't there.

In the weeks he was gone, Mother never used his name. I don't know what she told the neighbors, her friends, Mr. Edwards at the lumber company. If he was missed by anyone but me, if she was worried he wouldn't come back, I didn't know.

He did come back, one night. I came in for breakfast and he was in his place at the table buttering toast, his face healed except for the scar. He didn't look at me and I strangled on my orange juice. Mother came to lift my arm, help me stop coughing, but I ran to the bathroom. Daddy was gone when I got back.

"Where's Daddy?"

"Gone to work," she said, and started clearing the table.

Daily routines became routine again, no questions were asked, at least not in my presence, nor explanations given. The scar across Daddy's face stayed dark and ragged the rest of his life.

Mother startles me by slamming the closet door, saying, "I better check the stew. It may be boiling over. Goodness." Then she calls me to set the table.

I arrange crackers in a basket. She says it would be nice if we had some sprigs of artificial pine or holly to tuck in for color.

Jackie, my five-year-old, runs in, holds out a toy. "Look."

The toy is a plastic skull the size of a shrunken head. "Where did you get this?"

"The toy box."

Mother ladles stew. "That thing." She hands me a bowl to put on the table. "I found it in the yard raking leaves. Some child dropped it Halloween."

"It's horrible. Ugly.",

"Let's see if it still works." Mother presses a tear-shaped spot on the skull's forehead. Its eyes light red, blink; a harsh, grinding sound begins.

Jackie holds the skull to her ear like a shell. "It's laughing."

The tinnish laughter gets louder, grates on.

*Ruth Moose*

My father laughed at death when he watched the speedometer needle rise, when he talked of minefields, buddies blown up in his lap. Nobody dies until their time comes, he said. I worried for years he'd crash in a car, get a shotgun blast in the chest, or be found bloody in somebody else's bed. He died in his chair, newspaper spread across his knees. His reading glasses fell to the floor, dropped but did not crack.

I snatch the screaming skull and throw it like a grenade out the kitchen door.

"Don't let cold air in." Mother puts another bowl of stew on the table. "Let's eat while this is hot."

Lucinda starts to fuss when Anne puts her in the infant seat. She wiggles and waves her arms until I pick her up.

"Go ahead and eat," I tell everyone. "We'll go see the tree."

"Lights," I tell Lucinda. She finds my face more interesting. Eyes that blink and are wet. With a warm finger, she traces silver trickles down my cheeks, laughs. I am holding her tighter than I realize. She squirms to be free.

*Ruth Moose*

# The Eyes of Argus

AMY BASS HELD the black button on the red sweater with her thumb as she pulled the needle through. "Didn't know whether to use the black or red thread, but white's all you had, so I guess I didn't need to worry in the first place, did I?" She laughed through her nose and it tickled so she rubbed it.

At the ironing board, Mrs. Holly thumped the iron on its heel, jerked off the small brown gingham dress, shook it several times, then laid it back, spreading the collar like a doily. She attacked the collar with the tip of her iron, moving her fingers in the lace just a jump ahead of the iron. There was a small tearing sound like a weak cry and she lifted her iron quickly, frowning. "Snagged a place in that lace." She puckered her mouth as though holding pins. "Guess it's one you missed when you mended."

Amy looked up. "Law, I might have missed one, and more. I was lucky to catch as many as I did. Lace was nothing but hanging threads in some places."

Mrs. Holly worked slower now. "It still makes me mad—Lou Christen giving us these things the shape they was in."

Mrs. Holly was thin as a post with long stilt-like legs, dangling arms, and large hands. She had quick black eyes that didn't miss a trick and knew everything in the neighborhood before it happened. She often said, "I told you so," and nobody disputed her. Nobody disputed her when she said it was funny the fuel oil man kept stopping

*Ruth Moose*

at Granny Bakewell's and it hot weather. And a few months later Grovine was going around singing all day and looking like she swallowed a pumpkin seed. That was Eppie; and Eppie had hardly got into the world good when Mrs. Holly saw Peuse Ekins slipping around the neighborhood. She gave him a piece of her mind, but it was too late; Lucille was on her way. That's when Mrs. Holly sat down with Granny and had a long talk and nobody disputed that, either.

Amy fumbled in the tin box in her lap and the buttons made clicking noises as she shuffled. "They aren't going to match."

Mrs. Holly snorted. "Never understood why anybody would go so far as to cut buttons off good clothes." She banged the iron on the board. "Just do the best you can. What does it matter if the buttons don't match, long as it holds the sweater together. It'll be something to keep 'em warm...poor little things."

Amy finished the sweater, buttoned it, and held it out. It didn't really look too bad. She had put the black buttons at the bottom, where they wouldn't show so much. She tucked the sweater arms back, folded a neat red square, and laid it on the mound of clothes in four boxes lined against the wall like huge tins of bread dough rising. She and Mrs. Holly had collected all the clothes: dresses, coats, sweaters, pajamas, shoes, even three pairs of galoshes. Mildewed, but after they were wiped and wrapped in brown paper, they looked good. She did hope the rest of the clothes wouldn't pick up that awful, rubbery smell. She unfolded a pair of little girl's panties; fourteen pairs they had in all. Enough to do 'em for a while. Three boxes of things to go to Eppie and Lucille at the orphanage, and the last box was for Grovine. Most of the things in Grovine's box came from Mrs. Holly. Some dresses and a pair of brown oxfords she said "just killed her feet." Amy had put in a purple corduroy robe her children gave her Christmas, six years ago. She liked the robe, but every time she wore it, lint flocked to it like a magnet. "Grovine ought to like that purple robe," she said as she fingered it.

Mrs. Holly plumped a puff sleeve on the brown dress, picked up her iron, then set it back. "Here, Amy, you better do this. I don't know nothing about ironing little girls' things in the first place." She took Amy's chair, wiped long fingers across her forehead, and pushed back tassels of gray hair.

Amy spread the sleeve like a paper muffin cup and wiggled her iron across it. "It's been a while, but I guess you don't forget."

Mrs. Holly rocked. "Somebody has to see to them. If H.C. had been the kind of brother he ought to be to Grovine, we wouldn't have had to take so much on ourselves."

Amy switched to the other sleeve. "It's awful how people—and family at that—can have no more feeling for each other."

"'Course, it was to be expected. He didn't come around them when Granny was alive, and who'd think it now? Remember the funeral."

Amy touched a few places on the collar and nodded. "H.C. on one side of the church, Grovine on the other. If it hadn't been for you and me and John, and the rest of the neighbors, there wouldn't have been a soul setting with poor Grovine."

Mrs. Holly got up and pushed the boxes close together, sighing. "In a way you can't blame him. Grovine with her petticoat showing the whole time. And if I hadn't taken it on myself"—she tapped her finger on her chest—-"myself, to get those kids ready, no telling how they would have showed up at their own grandma's funeral. Naked as jaybirds, I reckon:'

Amy unplugged the iron, looked at the electric clock above the stove. "It's ten o'clock. I didn't know it was that late. John will be wanting his hot milk, says it helps him to sleep. You'd think the way he snores, he wouldn't need it."

*Ruth Moose*

She laid the iron's cord across the board and it dangled like a cat's tail. "I better be getting towards home."

Mrs. Holly took the brown dress, folded it carefully, and laid it on a box. "We done a good job, if I do say so. And everything's ready to go."

They decided to leave after nine the next morning. Mrs. Holly wanted to miss the mill traffic. Amy wrapped her shawl around her shoulders and darted out the back door, running across two back yards to her own. Her flashlight made zigzags of light as she ran.

John was already in bed when she got there and after rolling her hair in knots on yellow plastic curlers she ducked her head inside a flannel gown, yanking off her clothes as she pulled down the gown, then curled next to John's back. He did have the hairiest back.

She was asleep before she knew it and dreaming of cherubs in pink feathered pinafores who played flutes and danced. They danced so close their feathers tickled and she laughed. They begged her to dance too and she did, dancing on the lightest feet until the rain started. But it wasn't rain; it was hard drops like crystal candies that stung when they hit. And when the drops hit the street they melted in a hiss. The cherubs cried and started to run, but the street was hot and burned their bare feet. Their cries were still ringing in her ears when she awoke enough to realize the dog was whining to go out.

At breakfast she was tired and John grumped because his newspaper was late and the grits had lumps. She was relieved when he finally left for the store, flinging his jacket across his arm, his hat crooked on his head.

She dressed quickly in her navy blue crepe, her white Enna Jetticks, and got to the driveway just as Mrs. Holly finished loading the boxes in the trunk of her fat black Buick. The Buick had been her husband's before his death twelve years ago, and the paint had worn down to a mottled reddish-brown color.

Amy pulled on her gloves, holding her white purse flat against her stomach. When both gloves were on, she pressed her pancake of a straw hat flatter to her head and walked around the car. She got in, shut the door twice before she was satisfied. Didn't want to take any chances on falling out.

In the driver's seat, Mrs. Holly released the brake and let the car roll down the driveway and into the street before she started the motor. After she raced the motor several times the car jerked up the street, then bounced to a stop in front of a paintless two-story house with a leaning porte cochere. Under a bare chinaberry tree stood a straight chair, its seat torn and dragging the ground, making the new red-and-white "For Sale" sign sparkle in the yard.

"Just hurts me to see that," Mrs. Holly said, sucking in her lip. "But I guess none of us is going to live forever."

Amy folded her hands on her purse in her lap and crossed her ankles. It didn't seem possible. Six months ago Granny would have had the clothesline filled by this time of morning, and Grovine, Eppie, and Lucille out playing playhouse under the tree.

"Such a shock." Mrs. Holly stopped at the traffic light. "Her just to keel over like that. At least Grovine had enough sense to come get me. But you know, that girl wasn't any more excited or worried than if her mama had sent her over to borrow a cup of flour. I knew something was wrong when she said Granny was laying in the middle of the kitchen floor. Granny was one woman that didn't stop from sunup to sundown."

"No siree." Amy stared straight ahead. "Didn't stop till she dropped dead in her tracks. Like you and me, I reckon." She laughed and looked at Mrs. Holly in her gray wool suit and black felt hat.

"Well, I hope not." Mrs. Holly stiffened her shoulders. "One of these days I want to sit back and let my younguns wait on me."

"That's right." Amy nodded quickly. "At least our younguns have minds and won't be a burden on us like Grovine was. I said a long time ago she was going to be the death of Granny." She took a handkerchief from her purse and blew her nose loudly, then lowered her voice. "If Grovine had been sent away someplace when she was little. . ."

"I know, I know." Mrs. Holly held the steering wheel tightly, and sighed. "I hated to be the one to call the County on Grovine, but somebody had to. Pitiful the way those girls was running around barefooted and it frost on the ground." She slowed the car, pointed to a neat white house framed by a mat of green lawn. "Look at that. Ethel Shaw's got buttercups blooming already. Mine ain't even come up yet." She twisted her neck and moved her lips as if she were counting the blooms.

"I declare, they sure are pretty." Amy stretched to get a better look. "Ethel always been so smart. Give me two bags of dresses her Sybil had outgrowed, said they ought to fit Eppie, if they didn't she could grow into them. There was a red polka-dotted one, and a—"

"There's Ethel out in her yard now." Mrs. Holly nosed the car across the road and parked facing traffic. A blue truck tooted loudly as it swerved around them. "Yoo-hoo, Ethel," Mrs. Holly yelled as she lowered the window. "Your yard sure does look pretty."

Ethel, in men's striped coveralls, laid her trowel in a tulip bed, dusted dirt from her hands and walked toward the car.

"We're going to the orphanage to take Eppie and Lucille them things we rounded up. You want to go?"

"I'd love to"—Ethel had a dirt streak like a dark scar across her cheek—"but I'm fixing to feed my boxwoods and I need to get it done before they start putting out. You all go on without me this time." She stepped back from the car.

"Sure do thank you for all them dresses," Amy leaned toward the window and hollered.

Ethel nodded. "You're sure welcome. Glad to get shed of them."

Mrs. Holly said, "Amy told me how you did every one of them up, too. Not everybody was that nice." Her tone was cold. "I was up till ten o'clock last night. Lou Christen give me a box of things and I had to wash and iron every one of them myself. Some of 'em was nothing but rags—and she'd cut the buttons off—"

"Lou Christen?" Ethel's face stretched. "I never wouldn've thought it of her. All the money she and Ham's got and her cutting buttons off. They could buy a whole storeload of buttons."

"Now, Ethel, don't let on I said that." Mrs. Holly shifted gears. "I wouldn't want to spread anything. It's what's in a person's heart that counts, I've always said."

Amy wiggled a gloved finger at Ethel as they drove away. When they crossed the center line, a blonde in a red convertible had to screech her tires to avoid hitting them.

"Did you see that hussy?" Mrs. Holly asked. "Bet she keeps the drugstores in business buying peroxide. Nobody's hair's that color naturally."

Amy put her handkerchief in her purse and snapped it shut. "I think we did real well rounding up as many things as we did. And Mr. Andrews at the store giving five dollars for Grovine—"

Mrs. Holly speeded up. "He said give it to her and tell her to buy what she needed, but I'm not handing her money. She wouldn't know what to do with it if she had it. I bought her a slip and three pair of step-ins. They had 'em three pair for a dollar in Belk's basement—seconds, but she won't know the difference."

As they passed the old Pickens place Amy fussed about

how it had run down since old man Pickens died and his children fighting to keep one from getting a cent more than another. When they passed the Weatherfords' new house, Mrs. Holly said she had heard there was a bathroom for every bedroom and could remember when John Weatherford was knee-high to a grasshopper and didn't have a rag to wipe his nose on.

"You never hear of him going out of his way to do nothing for nobody," Mrs. Holly said angrily.

"Must be kin to H.C.," Amy shot back, and they both laughed.

They rode in silence when the road became familiar. Finally Amy said, "One good thing about it, the county sure didn't waste any time getting those kids taken into the home, and Grovine settled too."

"She won't last." Mrs. Holly shook her head. "Somebody'll have to tell her every step to make."

"I know it." Amy swallowed loudly. "And then what'll happen to her? And what do you reckon will be done with the money from the sale of Granny's house? You think H.C. will stick it in his pocket and Grovine not get a thing from her own mama's estate?"

"Lord, it's no telling what's going on. If Grovine can just hold out to work I'll feel better. And knowing Eppie and Lucille is being taken care of is a load off my mind. That orphanage may not be the fanciest place in this world, but they'll be raised right. There's a church there, I heard, and the kids march in every day for chapel and twice on Sunday."

"Is it an orphanage for girls, or girls and boys both?"

"Both, I heard, but I think the boys' home is on the other side of the road and somebody said they even have separate dining halls." Mrs. Holly squinted. "What's that sign say? Tillman's Home?"

"Tillman's Home for Orphan Children," Amy said proudly. "This is it."

*Ruth Moose*

Mrs. Holly steered the car toward the center of the brickpillared entrance with a series of short pulls, tugs, and audible grunts. "Which one of those buildings do you think they'll be in?"

They parked on the grass in front of the first brick building, under a large oak tree. Mrs. Holly got out, looked at the gray sky, held her hand palm up and said, "Sure looks like rain" to a large dark cloud.

Amy waited at the car trunk until Mrs. Holly took her elbow, leaned close, and said, "We'll leave the clothes and things in the car and surprise them later. Poor little things, aren't they going to be tickled?"

Amy patted her purse. "I had John bring them some penny candy from the store…little younguns need a bit of sweetening once in a while. You don't think they'll take it away from them, do you?"

"Naw." Mrs. Holly breathed hard and grabbed the wrought iron rail beside the brick steps.

Amy pushed the wooden door and waited as Mrs. Holly sailed mightily through. "Well." She stood inside and looked around. "You can say one thing. This place sure is clean." She smiled and whispered to Mrs. Holly, "Just like a living room. They got reading lamps, a rug, and even a television set."

Mrs. Holly marched to the desk, holding her purse to her chest like a shield. "We'd like to see Eppie and Lucille Bakewell, please."

The lady in the pink blouse smiled, handed her a card and pencil. "Just complete this form while I call them. Are you expected?"

Mrs. Holly turned to Amy and said, "Don't see why I have to fill out any card—I'm just visiting—not wanting to adopt them."

"It's routine," the girl said, still smiling. "For our records."

"Very well." Mrs. Holly wrote her name large, the H straight and stiff. She was still writing when the lady behind the desk sang out, "Here's our Eppie and Lucy. You girls have company, isn't that nice?"

Like a color snapshot, Eppie and Lucy stood in the doorway, side by side, holding hands. Eppie, the seven-year-old, had her hair in a neat brown pageboy with bangs, and her red plaid pinafore was crisp and new-looking. Lucille, her blonde ringlets topped by a bow, pulled at the lace collar on her blue dress and stood with one toe of her black patent shoes against the floor. There was lace on her blue socks.

"My goodness." Mrs. Holly went to them. "You girls must have known we was coming and got all dressed up."

"No, ma'am." Eppie didn't smile.

Lucille dropped Eppie's hand and grinned.

"They must be feeding you girls good up here." Amy pinched Lucille's pink cheek. It was warm, smooth as cream.

"Oh, yes," Lucille said. "We had strawberry shortcakes last night and today we're having—"

Mrs. Holly frowned tight bands across her forehead.

"Eppie," the lady behind the desk said, "why don't you girls take the ladies to see your room? Then show them around the grounds."

"Yes, ma'am." Eppie turned and started down the hall. Lucille took Amy's hand and Mrs. Holly followed.

"It's room twelve," Lucille said, skipping beside Amy, her head bobbing like a buoy. "We can see the lake from my window, and Joanne, she's my best friend, says in the summer we get to go swimming and have hot dog roasts and—"

"That's fine...just fine," Amy panted.

Eppie went inside a door at the end of the hall and Lucille led in Amy.

When Mrs. Holly got to the room she stuck in her head like an old turtle and muttered, "This sure is nice... nice."

*Ruth Moose*

Amy sat on one of the hobnail bedspreads on a maple twin bed and Eppie sat at one of the desks on each side of the window.

"We can't stay." Mrs. Holly stood rooted, like a large. potted plant, in the hall.

"Just for a minute," Amy said, and patted Lucille's leg.

"We wanted to see how you girls was getting along." She picked at a tuft on the spread. She'd been saving stamps to get one just like it and only needed three-fourths of a book more. "Do you like it here?" She untied Lucille's bow and retied it, crookedly.

Lucille bounced on the bed beside her. "Oh, yes, Mrs. Adams, my teacher is so sweet and I go to kindergarten. I drew these." She pointed to the pictures on the wall.

"You ever see your mother?" Mrs. Holly inched inside the room.

"Yes, ma'am. Mr. Ervin brings her every Sunday."

"Mr. Ervin?" Mrs. Holly's eyebrows shot up as though someone had pressed a spring.

"Yes, ma'am." Eppie turned the pages of a book on her desk.

"He brings us candy," Lucille chirped, "a whole box and we can give some to our friends."

Amy pulled the two little brown paper bags from her purse. "I was about to forget to give you girls this. My memory's no longer than a minute. I'd forget my head if it wasn't fastened to me."

Eppie peeped inside her bag, squeezed it shut, and set it at the back of her desk.

Lucille ran her hand into her bag, pulled out a pinkish square, and said, "Is it peppermint? I don't like peppermint." She shut her bag and handed it to Eppie.

"Well, my goodness." Mrs. Holly's face was flushed. "You can certainly give it to someone and not let it go to waste." She stared hard at the closet door. "Do you all have plenty to wear—or is what you got on all you have?"

"Oh, no." Lucille ran to the closet. "We got lots of dresses. The first day we went to Wardrobe and they let us pick out what we wanted." She flung the closet door wide, revealing two neat rainbows of dresses.

Mrs. Holly turned, one foot in the hallway as if she were getting set on her mark. "I guess we better be going."

"But we haven't—" Amy stood, stretched her arm after Mrs. Holly. "Wait, we got all those things in the car yet—" She turned to Lucille. All the work she and Mrs. Holly had done, surely…"Honey, does everybody up here have as many dresses as you do?"

"Oh, no," Lucille said, "they got more 'cause they been here longer."

Eppie gave them a cold look and went back to her book. "We'll see you girls again," Amy said from the hall. Lucille dashed after them. "We didn't show you the cafeteria or the library, or—"

"We'll go next time, honey." Amy patted Lucille's shining hair.

The girls sure did look good. She hurried after Mrs. Holly. She'd never thought Eppie was pretty. Her forehead was too broad, but with bangs. . .

As she passed the desk, the lady in the pink blouse sang out, "You ladies come again. We'd love to have you any time."

Mrs. Holly drew in her breath as she marched past, but Amy smiled and waved.

Mrs. Holly went down the steps faster than she'd come up them and left Amy to close the door. In the car she started the motor and was backing before Amy got settled.

"Wait," Amy said, "I got my dress-tail caught. I was in such a hurry—wait." She opened the door, pulled her dress in and held a corner of it in her lap, brushing it. "Hope I didn't get any grease on it." She banged her door shut. "Grease is so hard to get out."

"My doors don't have grease on them," Mrs. Holly said flatly.

Amy leaned back, her dress spread across her knees."What are we going to do with all those—"

Mrs. Holly didn't answer, just looked in her rearview mirror, her lips clamped together.

"This isn't the way we came, is it?" Amy said as they turned onto a dirt road.

"No," Mrs. Holly slowed down. "Look at that dust boil up…whew. At the county they said this is the quickest way to the place where Grovine's staying…They could've told me it wasn't paved."

"Six months." Amy played with the handles of her purse. "It's just been six months since Eppie and Lucille was taken to the home. I never thought I'd see such a difference in those younguns. Looka yonder"—she pointed to a large windmill near a barn. "You reckon them things really work or are they just for looks?"

Mrs. Holly glanced at the windmill quickly, then went back to reading names on mailboxes. "White Oak Farm, Hope Crest Farms, Four Pines, Treetops is the one we want…"

"Treetops," Amy said excitedly. "Right there. On that big mailbox."

Mrs. Holly saw nothing but another dusty road and trees. "Can't see the house for the trees," she muttered. They crossed a creek, the car jouncing on a wooden bridge, then up a hill. "Hope we don't meet anything. This road isn't wide enough to pass a cat. Don't see why anybody ever—"

They rounded the curve and saw the house for the first time, a gleaming white house with four large columns across the front. "Law, it looks like something out of a picture, don't it?" Amy craned her neck and pressed her nose against the cool windshield. Beyond the house she could see rows of gleaming metal chickenhouses like huge bars of silver in the sun. "Wonder if Grovine works in the house or with the chickens? She ought to do real good at gathering eggs."

Mrs. Holly stopped the car and turned off the motor. "I'll see if anybody's home," she said, her hand on the door handle. "They might not want us visiting Grovine during the week. Some places is funny about their help."

Amy watched as Mrs. Holly wiped her feet and walked across the neat flagstone porch. In a moment, the big front door opened and she turned, beckoned Amy to come on. She swung her arm wide as if she were gathering a bundle of air.

Amy left her purse and gloves on the seat, then took her purse, leaving the gloves. You never know who might walk by and decide to help themselves.

Grovine and Mrs. Holly waited as Amy crossed the porch. "You sure do look good, Grovine, honey, real good." She hurried toward them. "Why, you used to be nothing but skin and bones…A big gust of wind could've blowed you away."

Grovine laughed and put her hand over her mouth. "You all come to see me way out here?" She twisted her terrycloth apron, wringing it like wet wash, then let it go. It twirled against her like a drill and Grovine caught it with both hands, then started flapping it. "You all come to see me!"

"Of course we did, Grovine." Mrs. Holly's voice was soft, sweet, as she patted Grovine's arm, and walked to the white brocade sofa.

"This is the nicest house, Grovine." Amy took a seat beside Mrs. Holly. "Everything's so fancy." She ran her hand over the shiny coffee table.

Grovine smiled, making a church steeple with her fingers.

"It sure is," Mrs. Holly echoed.

The sun poured through stiff organdy curtains and made a rainbow on the cut glass vase on the marble mantel. "You keep everything this clean?" Mrs. Holly glanced around. "Must be a big job."

"Yes'um." Grovine lifted her chin. "I dust in here and Matildabelle runs the sweeper and waxes and—"

"Matildabelle? Is that Mrs. Ervin?"

"Oh, no," Grovine giggled, cupping her hands over her mouth. "Matildabelle's the maid. Mrs. Ervin's been in bed three years. Don't have no use at all for her legs."

"You have to lift and do for her?"

"Oh, no, ma'am," Grovine pulled her hair and held it behind her neck.

"Lifting a sick person—if they're any count at all—will just kill you. Grovine, you can't hold out to do that kind of work and they shouldn't expect you to. Should they, Amy?"

"Oh, no." Amy stopped admiring the ornate gold-rimmed mirror above the mantel. She'd seen pictures in magazines of rooms like this. "It's just too hard on your back."

"I don't do things like that." Grovine stuck out her chin. "Mr. Ervin does. I mainly straighten up her room, and pick some flowers for her, and comb her hair. . ." She looked at her hands in her lap. "I do some of the cooking, but Mr. Ervin helps me with that too."

"Well." Mrs. Holly let out her breath. "I'm glad about that. And he pays you too, does he? Along with your room and board?"

"Oh, yes." Grovine's cheeks looked pinker than ever. And he's so good to me."

"You're fixing your hair different," Amy said excitedly. "I knew there was something new about you."

"And you've gained weight," Mrs. Holly smiled.

"Yes, ma'am." Grovine blushed.

"Guess you have plenty of milk and eggs, fresh things from the garden, living on a farm." Mrs. Holly picked up a magazine from the table. There was a woman with a low-cut dress on the cover, and big red letters said, "My Husband Is

Not My Lover." Mrs. Holly began to fan with it.

"All you can eat, I guess," Amy laughed.

"Well, Eppie and Lucille are doing just fine." Mrs. Holly fanned harder. "We went there first."

Grovine crossed her legs and swung her foot in its trim black shoe with the big gold buckle on the toe. Amy thought of the lace-up brown oxfords in the box. "Eppie and Lucille look so pretty," she breathed.

"Is H.C. doing anything to help you out?" Mrs. Holly's black eyes pinpointed Grovine.

"He got me this job," Grovine said quickly, jumping up. "And that's the best thing ever happened to me. H.C. just leaves me alone, and that's the way I like it." She glared at them, her nostrils enlarged slightly.

"I guess we better be on our way." Amy poked Mrs. Hollywith her elbow. "Grovine's probably got things to do."

Grovine held the door for them, wiggling it back and forth, her feet doing little dance steps. "Bye," she said, "bye."

Mrs. Holly fumbled her keys in the ignition, started the motor, then rolled the window down and leaned out. "You make Mr. Ervin bring you to see us now. You hear?"

Grovine had already shut the door.

"Well," Mrs. Holly said, "I guess she didn't hear me." She watched the rearview mirror as she backed. "Keep an eye on that big tree over there, will you? Let me know if I get too close."

"You're okay," Amy said just before they heard the scrape of metal.

Mrs. Holly jammed on the brakes and turned to Amy, her lips in a hard line, eyes snapping. Then she got out with a rush.

Amy held her purse and looked at the house. "Imagine Grovine living in a place like that. Just imagine."

*Ruth Moose*

Mrs. Holly got in the car and shifted gears. "It tapped the bumper, but didn't dent it—sure was lucky. Could have been worse. I thought you was watching," she fussed. "I told you to."

Amy didn't say anything and they drove in silence for a while until Mrs. Holly leaned back in her seat and said, "Grovine looked the best I've seen her, didn't you think so?"

"Right fleshy." Amy took off her hat and laid it in her lap.

A car zoomed around them and Mrs. Holly blew her horn. "Smart-aleck. They ought to keep people like that off the roads. Let them go to the racetracks if they want to race."

"I don't think all that weight was Grovine." Amy slapped her gloves back and forth on her purse.

"What was it then?" Mrs. Holly turned to her.

"You know."

"I know what?"

"You know…like before. She always did start to show early."

"You don't reckon?" Mrs. Holly's lower lip dropped and her mouth stayed open for a good two minutes. Amy was about to say if she didn't soon close it, the bugs was going to fly in, but she didn't.

"Who?—How would anything like that happen? Out there on a farm she don't see nobody but Mr. Ervin . . ." The car veered off the road and Mrs. Holly jerked it back. "Mr. Ervin!" she swallowed loudly. "And his wife right there in the same house?" Mrs. Holly clung to the steering wheel. "Oh my…oh."

Amy nodded. "I'd bet my life on it." For once she had beat Mrs. Holly to it and it felt good.

"Well." Mrs. Holly stared straight ahead. "It's H.C.'s fault and he can just see to this. He got her the job and got her into the mess. I'm going to write him and dump the whole thing in his lap."

Mrs. Holly spluttered and Amy half-listened all the way home. When they turned the corner, she heard the boxes slide in the trunk and couldn't help smiling.

Ethel Shaw, pruning her Crimson Glory rosebushes along the fence, waved as they passed, but Mrs. Holly acted like she didn't even see her, just sped up.

# Knotty

THROUGH THE SAVE Mart plate glass window, Beryl saw a shadow dart between a row of parked cars. "Fay," she said to the girl at the next register, "he's still out there."

Neon lightning flashed. Red, green, blue…would he try to get in her car? It was locked, wasn't it? Lately she locked everything. Would he try to kill her? Yellow, red…maybe now he was aiming a rifle over her fender. Glass would shatter, people scream and she would be shot…killed. Dead. Oh God. She ducked, squatted, pretending to straighten her paper bag file. He couldn't see her now. Knotty, she wanted to scream. Knotty.

Her fingers stuck to the bags. She crushed, wrinkled, rather than straightened them. Their irregular edges looked barbed, menacing.

"You're crazy," she said to herself. "Downright nutty." Of course Knotty would not shoot. No, never anything so noisy. He hated noise. That was one of the things they shared. Hours in bed listening to everything around them. Silence in their own warm world. The fish mouths they made kissing…Beryl clamped her hand over her mouth, felt her cold, dry lips.

Fay's register rang, the drawer jangled open, and she clinked change into the customer's hand—a bald man with a buglike mole on his cheek. He counted with Fay, moving his lips, "Ninety-nine, one dollar."

Beryl whispered loudly to Fay's green smocked back, "What am I going to do?"

*Ruth Moose*

"Thank you for shopping Save Mart," Fay said to the customer. She shrugged her shoulders and turned to Beryl, "What can you do?"

Fay had a long face, hair rippling to her waist and fanning across broad hips. The original Plain Jane, Knotty called her. He used to pull his chin down, mock her. Beryl had laughed, spilled beer on her robe.

"I don't know." Beryl watched the parking lot. Cars left, winking their tails like fireflies. Was Knotty curled in her car? Back seat? He would hide, spring on her, wrap a scarf around her neck, and pull, pull, pull. A scarf was quiet. Her throat felt dry and tight. She needed a drink of water. Never leave the register unattended, Rule Number One in the book of Save Mart. Sometimes Beryl felt chained to that damn register like an organ grinder's monkey.

"Are you going to ring me up, or not?" a fat lady in black stretch pants snapped. Riding her hip like some deformity, a moon-faced child kicked the counter with dirty, bare feet.

"I'm sorry." Beryl cleared her register, picked a pink girdle from the pile of goods and read, "Six eighty-eight, lingerie." The price tag pin jabbed Beryl's finger and a drop of blood burbled. "Ouch." Beryl put her finger in her mouth, sucked. Blood tasted rusty.

"Don't bleed on my girdle." The woman snatched it up, laid it carefully out of the way. "Don't want it messed up. I ain't even got it home from the store yet."

Beryl punched seventy-nine cents for a can of motor oil. Her finger stopped bleeding, but it looked pale and. drained on the tip. "Socks, ladies socks." She hunted for the department fifty-seven key. Slow tonight, her fingers would not work. "White cotton socks." Knotty wore white cotton socks. She washed them. Maybe he was out there now wearing socks she had washed. No, it had been two weeks since...

Beryl picked up a package of training pants. "Eighty-eight cents," she said. The pants in assorted colors, tight under their plastic wrap, looked like rolls of pastel mints.

The woman shifted the child on her hip. "Two years old," she said, "and he ain't broke from wetting his pants."

Beryl rang up a red-handled spatula. "Forty-nine cents." Then a hairbrush. She couldn't find the price sticker, turned it over, looked on the back. The bristles bit her hand and a chill crawled down her back.

"They're a dollar eighty-six," the woman said, "on special. I thought they was a real good buy."

"Yes." Beryl's hand shook as she fingered the keys. "I need a brush. Mine's broken." Knotty broke the handle after he held and scrubbed her with it. Laughing, at first she laughed. Then he wouldn't stop. Her skin burned for days, there were scabs. He was gone for a week after that and she had gotten used to being alone when came back.

"I thought that was a good buy." The woman smiled. There was a large gap between her two front teeth, her eyes were large, rimmed with brown like a raccoon.

Knotty had small darting eyes. Kin to a squirrel, he used to laugh. Fast on my feet.

Beryl picked up a sticky package of marshmallow peanuts. Several rolled onto the counter. She put them back, twisted the bag shut, and gave it to the boy. "Thirty-three," she rang on the register.

"Now you got your candy." The woman jiggled the child. "See, I told you, you'd get it back after the lady rang it up. You happy now?"

The child stuffed both chipmunk cheeks. Orange drool dripped down his bare belly.

"That's a total of twelve seventy-two, including tax," Beryl said. She slipped the items into a paper sack, glanced toward the parking lot. Dark, it was too dark to see anyone out there now.

"Thank-you-for-shopping-Save-Mart." She shut her register, leaned upon it. The register was warm, like

*Ruth Moose*

something alive.

Beryl watched the double doors swing open, the woman hitch the child higher on her hip, clutch her package tight to her chest and sway out, the child dangling like a doll.

"Fay?" Beryl whispered. "You think he's gone?"

"Could be." Fay peeled a stick of gum, folded it into her mouth. "He's your problem, not mine."

At first Fay had liked Knotty, kidded with him. After he moved in with Beryl, she acted different. Jealous, Knotty said. You got a boyfriend and she hasn't. Never will have unless she learns to loosen up a lot.

"Attention all shoppers," the sound system boomed.

Fay gave her mock salute. Beryl usually laughed, but tonight she stood on tiptoes, surveyed the store. Not much of a crowd.

"Save Mart will close in ten minutes. Please make your purchases now."

The lights dimmed, brightened.

I could stay here all night, Beryl thought. Not go to the car, not go home. I'd sleep in the linen department. "Ha," she wanted to say. That fluffy-looking display bed was plywood and hollow underneath. Knotty hid under it the day the police came. The last time she had seen him.

"How can they expect a body to get her shopping done?" A thin lady in a faded floral dress pushed her cart beside the register. "If they turn the lights off and you can't see the price of nothing."

Beryl rang up a flyswatter, some knitting yarn, and a box of chocolate-covered raisins. The woman saw the total and put back the flyswatter, and Beryl had to void the ticket, ring everything again.

Fay locked her register, threw her smock across the bath oil display.

Beryl penciled figures on a sheet.

Ruth Moose

"Hurry," Fay said, stamping her red-sneakered feet, "these dogs are killing me."

Beryl erased, wrote in another figure. Knotty is going to kill me. He thinks I called the police, that I put them on to him, but I didn't. I didn't.

Knotty bought things at Save Mart. Beryl rang them cheaper. When he returned them for a refund, he got the marked price. At night they giggled, made up stories. Reasons For Refund, they called them. Nothing as simple as "too large," or "too small," but things like, "The dog barked at me when I wore it." Or, "This color clashed with my favorite nail polish." Silly, silly things.

"Come on!" Fay lifted one leg like a flamingo.

"Do you see him?" Beryl counted change. Knotty never needed money from "the game." They had her pay and his macrame sales. But he got bored with all those strings and knots and loops that became belts and bags. It was more string and belts and bags, wall hangings—he got bored with it all. Had he been bored with her too?

Fay cupped her hands, pressed her face to the glass. "Not a creature was stirring," she laughed, "not even a mouse."

Beryl shut her drawer, handed the brown drawstring bag and sales sheet to Lorita Willis. "Machines," said Lorita, glancing over her shoulder for Mr. Phelps. "He thinks we're machines that don't have aches or pains or feelings."

Mr. Phelps pranced by. Lorita jerked the bag shut and swished off. He held the door, jangled his keys like a jailer. "Good night, girls," he called. "See you tomorrow."

Humpty Dumpty, Fay called him behind his back. Round, he bounced when he walked.

Two checkout girls filed past him numbly. "Tomorrow's another day," he sang, wiping his shiny forehead with a monogrammed handkerchief. The ring on his little finger caught the light and flashed meanly.

"Another day," Fay said outside, "another dollar—for him."

The lights in the parking lot went off almost immediately. Only neon lit the area. Red. Blue. Green. S …A …V …E.

Beryl looked at her VW alone in the back row, listened and heard nothing. Knotty never made noise.

Fay waited for Beryl to unlock her door. "Every customer I had today was a pure, capital B, Bitch." Fay rubbed her feet together. "Do you know what one customer had me do?"

Beryl looked behind the front seat. Only an empty Cheerwine bottle and some popcorn puffs from the last drive-in movie she and Knotty had seen. What was it? Who starred in it? If someone held a gun to her head and said remember, she couldn't. Numb, my head is numb, she thought.

"This one customer"—Fay popped Spearmint—"had the nerve to ask me to open a bag of cookies so she could count to be sure it was 'the exact figure stated on the label.'"

Beryl locked the car door, leaned back, and took a deep breath.

"Say," said Fay, "you are in a state, huh?"

Beryl nodded, started the car, and headed down the boulevard.

"I'm so tired." Fay stretched. "I feel like digging a hole somewhere and crawling in it."

Is that what Knotty would do? Dig a hole and bury her?

"Fay?"

"Yeah," said Fay, chewing rapidly. "You want to stay with us?"

Beryl braked for a light. "No. . ." That stuffy house that smelled of mildew and death—those old people. "No, I don't think so." I'll be okay after I get home. Fine.

"You don't seem so shook anymore." Fay drummed on the dash, hummed. "I mean, that might not have been him in the parking lot. Right? It could have been anybody."

"I guess," Beryl said quietly. "Knotty could be a hundred miles away." She let out a little laugh. Maybe it wasn't him. Maybe.

"A thousand miles," said Fay. "You're not still in love—"

"Love? Knotty?" Beryl's throat hurt. "No. Not anymore." Once she loved him, loved him a lot. At first he had been gentle, tender. She had not known…waking with him beside her, not being alone anymore. . .

"That's it." Fay swung her purse strap over her shoulder." Home again. Thanks for the lift."

Beryl parked, let the motor idle. "Night."

Fay blew a tan bubble, pulled it flat with even teeth. "Bye," she said. "See you."

There were lights in Fay's house; people. For a moment Beryl wanted to call, to turn off the car and run up the walk. Fay's mother blocked the light in the doorway. She waved.

Beryl pulled away from the curb. Eight blocks to her apartment. Apartment. That was a joke. Knotty said the house must have been built in 1722 when Mrs. MacCauley was brought there as a bride. Mrs. Mac rented rooms with adjoining closets. Kitchen closet, bathroom closet, bedroom closet.

Beryl parked beside the crepe myrtle hedge. Its wicker limbs wove a fence of shadows along the walk. Mrs. Mac said it was pretty when it bloomed. She wanted a yard full of it.

Beryl locked her car, dropped keys in her purse, and looked up. There was a light in her apartment. A light! One of the small round windows in the eaves glowed. Knotty. Knotty was in her apartment.

She grabbed the car door handle hard and pulled, reached for her keys, then stopped. Where would she go? Fay's? No.

In the empty hallway, Beryl checked her mail. Nothing. Not even an "Occupant" today. How could she expect mail when no one knew where she was?

You left the lamp on, she said to herself, climbing the stairs. Reading the newspaper, you forgot. This morning she was looking for something about Knotty. Two weeks ago she had read on page 11B, "James Null Crowell, released, pending further investigation." She read it a dozen times. There had been nothing since.

On the second floor Beryl paused. Someone in Apartment C was watching TV. They drowned the canned laughter in all the right places. Across the hall, a baby cried and a voice yelled, "Make that kid shut up."

Before she reached the top of the second stairs she saw the light from her apartment and stopped. Oh God, what if Knotty was waiting?

No, she decided. He wouldn't have the light on. Would he? Her key made a small, sharp click when the lock released.

She shoved open the door, stepped back and hugged the hall wall, broken plaster tearing her pantyhose. If you are in there Knotty, come out…now.

Nothing.

Beryl peeped around the facing. Her apartment looked as she had left it this morning. Fuzzy slippers on the floor, newspapers sprawled across the sofa, dirty slacks and blouse draped like a corpse across a chair.

She walked in, closed the door and went to the bedroom. "Knotty," she whispered. Under the bed she found a rumpled magazine, an empty tube of lipstick, and some dirty panties. In the shower, the faucet dripped. In one closet she banged hangers and said, "Knotty?"

Finally she sank on the sofa. Knotty was not here. Had not been here in two weeks. She stared at the fly-speckled ceiling, the stain made when the roof leaked. She would relax. Relax until tomorrow when she would have to go through the whole thing again. If he were here, she could deal with him. Yell and scream and throw things. He'd run.

*Ruth Moose*

But out there—she didn't know. Didn't know how mad he was, if he hated her. Mr. Phelps called the police. Not her. Sometimes she wished she had and told them everything she knew.

She closed her eyes, exhausted, too weak even to cry. In the next apartment a dog whined to go out. Someone opened the door, jingled a leash. "Come on, boy," they called, "come on."

If Knotty came back; Beryl thought, it would be like before. They'd sleep late on Sundays, make love on the Times and take turns afterward reading their backsides. They would pour salt on slugs and watch them curl black. They would send Mrs. Mac a plastic funeral wreath for Mother's Day and laugh until they cried. Laugh until she cried.

*Ruth Moose*

# Sisters under the Skin

THE LIVER-COLORED PONY, four legs spread, lay in the pasture stiff as a carnival horse.

"Lord." Leona nosed the faded blue Plymouth down the road. "If that pony don't look for all the world like he's dead."

Her sister Betta'lain sat between two bags of groceries on the backseat. Celery stood from one bag, a loaf of bread hung from the other, and in her lap Betta'lain held a bag of oranges.

"The way he's laying ain't natural.'"

"He was standing when we left." Betta'lain pointed. Her finger, pale as the celery, shook under the sleeve of her brown poodle cloth coat. She wore a purple beanie with an aluminum propeller on top. "Right there"—she said—" he was leaning over the fence like he wanted to say something. 'Bye, pony,' I said. 'Bye now."

Betta'lain pulled her beanie tighter. She wore it every waking minute, her short silver hair curling around it like moss.

"Right there." She made a smudge on the window with her finger. She made another smudge beside it, laughed, made a whole row, then another, until it looked like a school of minnows. "Hey, pony," she called, "bye, pony."

"If he's dead"—Leona stopped the car, reached inside the rusty mailbox twisted on its post as though somebody had tried to wring it off—"I'm not having it. Pearly Postom can pay what he owes just the same. Just the same."

*Ruth Moose*

She read her electric bill of $6.37 and crumpled a folder that said that "Little George," the famous midget singing cowboy minister, would lead a revival next week at the Big Oak Baptist in Luthersville. "Only four-feet-six and every ounce the gospel," the circular said.

"Anybody with a head as big as that"—Leona threw the folder into a kudzu-covered ditch—"can't be all there."

The pony still had not moved as she turned into the road and headed for the garage. He had belonged to the last family to live in the "old Tew Homeplace." It made Leona mad when anybody called it old. That place, she'd snort, is warm and tight and more than good enough for anybody who's ever rented it the last twenty-five years. Grandpa Tew built things to last and all the lumber was cut off this property and dried for two years before the house was built.

She pumped her brakes. Betta'lain bounced in the back seat, her mouth opening, closing like a puppet. "Stop."

"Stop," Leona told the car, and it did, two inches from the garage door.

Oranges spilled into Betta'lain's lap. She held one to the light, turned it around until she found the navel, and laughed. "There's nothing you can do about it," she said to the orange. "Nothing in this world. A dead pony can't be made alive."

"I most certainly can do something about it," Leona huffed. "If my foot didn't hurt, I'd had the sheriff after Postom long ago. Even if that pony is better off where he is now, dead, or in my pasture. He's got privileges here he wouldn't have in town. No big boys to ride him down…grass to eat."

Betta'lain peeled an orange, dropped each bit of skin out the window.

Leona tied a green scarf over her head. It had irregular polka dots on it and as many wrinkles as a paper hat. "Somebody in this family has got to see to that pony, even if it's somebody who's not able in the least."

"Nine, ten." Betta'lain dropped peels.

*Ruth Moose*

"Doctors don't operate on ingrown toenails every day of the week and say, 'Stay off your feet, Leona, take it easy, Leona.'" She looked at the bandaged swollen foot in the pink terrycloth slipper. "If I go getting this foot wet. . ." She buttoned her coat. "There's still dew in that tall grass. . ."

"It's after three." Betta'lain spit a seed, poked in another orange slice, and chewed. "I heard it on the drugstore news."

"Anybody who stands in a public place and watches demonstration television sets looks stupid. You ought to know better." Leona unlocked the car door. "Most people go about their business. The world doesn't always wait, you know."

The pony had not moved. "I can't believe he'd lay that way if something wasn't bad wrong."

"He was all right this morning." Betta'lain wiped sticky juice from her chin, licked her fingers. "I said, 'Bye, pony,' and he—"

"Don't you carry a handkerchief?" Leona snapped. "Mama always told me never to leave the house without one somewhere on me."

"She never told me," Leona said. "When she died, she didn't have as many lines as I got now." She handed Betta'lain a blue handkerchief with a tatted edge. "But then she didn't have you to look after all these years."

"What?" Betta'lain munched another orange slice.

"Don't eat so many you won't eat supper. You may have to be the one to cook it." Leona stepped from the car, held her foot carefully up. "Pony, honey," she called.

The animal didn't move. She couldn't tell if he was breathing or not; his rear and flanks looked bloated, swollen.

"If I take cold in this toe," she said to a dark cloud directly overhead, "I could die and then what would happen?"

Betta'lain pulled white membrane from the orange skin with her teeth; they protruded like a horse's. No manners, Leona thought, and no help. None whatsoever. Eat, eat, eat, and that pony out there dead or dying.

*Ruth Moose*

She hobbled to the gate and unlatched it. The gate was made from the iron frame of an old bed headboard some renter had left. Most of the time it was hire somebody to haul junk to the dump, but this time she got use from it. She'd showed Pearly Postom the picture of such a gate in the "Handy Helps" section of "Today's Farmer" and he'd made it.

She swung the gate shut. There was a lot you could do with things, if you took time. She didn't know about the pony. All he'd done so far was eat hay and run up her winter feed bill.

"I heard ponies are the worst thing there is on a pasture fence," she told Postom once.

"Naw," he said, rolling his wad of tobacco around stumpy yellow teeth. "Ain't no worse than nothing else."

"I heard if ponies aren't watched, they'll tear a fence down in no time."

"Little pony like he is"—Postom propped on his hoe handle in the cornfield—"why, a good puff of wind could push him over. He can't do a fence no damage."

Leona was not satisfied and watched her fence for signs. A month after Postom took his job working third shift at the mill, she made him move. How long he'd been working there before she found out, the Lord only knew, but Len Ralston let it slip one day in town. "That renter of yours is turning into a pretty good hand," he said. "Looks like it would kill him to move, but he gets his work done."

"What?" she said, and almost dropped her cup of Caroline's best Russian tea.

No wonder she hadn't been getting any work out of him. He was worn out from his mill job, sneaking off when she wasn't watching and coming home before she knew he'd been gone.

"You're doing more work for that mill than me," she told Postom, "so go live in one of their houses. See if they let you get behind in your rent."

The morning Postom and his boys packed stuff in some pickup truck they borrowed (it looked held together by baling wire), she stood on the porch and watched.

"We ain't got no place for the pony," he said. "Is it all right to leave him till we do?"

"You can leave that pony till you pay for what he ate of last winter's feed bill," she said.

Postom turned on his heel like a gear, got in the truck, and gunned it thundering and roaring down the hill. "He's doing that on purpose," she told Betta'lain. "Never had a lick of sense."

Betta'lain sat on the steps holding one of the multicolored cats that kept multiplying like mushrooms. Everywhere she looked, there was a new one. "I'd rather have somebody working this place that had some common sense than a person with all the degrees they give away at State College."

"Shoot," said Betta'lain, holding the cat's face to hers, "you never get neither."

Sometimes Leona was surprised at the clearness of Betta'lain's mind. She could be almost like a normal person, the things she came out with at times. Most days she trotted room-to-room wearing her beanie, carrying her wicker Easter egg basket. In the basket she had broken strings of beads, every Christmas card she or Mama ever received, valentines they'd made and never sent, some crochet hooks, half a box of raisins, and some nibbled cookies.

Leona didn't know how she'd manage—Betta'lain, the pony, her toe. She walked the path, dodged two greenish-black stacks of manure. "I wouldn't mind having a goat or two on the place, if it wasn't for the stink of them. At least they do their business neat and it don't pile up a pasture."

She held her bandaged foot away from the grass as much as possible, hobbled slowly. If the pony was to get up, she'd turn around and go back to the car this minute. Not waste her energies.

*Ruth Moose*

As she got closer, she saw gnats and bright green flies circling the pony in a haze.

The pony flicked an ear; or did she imagine it? The sun glared so. She cupped a hand over her eyes, plodded on.

She knew Betta'lain would have all the oranges peeled before she got back. I'll make ambrosia, she thought, I'll have to. Her feet hurt now, both of them.

The pony's eyes looked leaden. She heard a whinny of a rumble from his stomach, like he'd swallowed something alive. How long did stomachs live after an animal died?

"Lordy." Leona squatted over him. "You're not a bit dead. Fooling me all the time.'" She reached out to him and he flounced his head, neighed nasty teeth. His breath smelled like an old man's…'

"Oh, oh…"

She stepped back too fast and felt moisture seep through her slipper and stain the bandage.

"Betta' lain," she hollered, hopping toward the car.

The pony rolled a few times, beat the ground with his limp mop of a tail and got to his feet. He hobbled a few steps like his feet hurt, all four of them.

"Pony"—as he came around beside her—"what happened to you?"

He pulled past her, limped toward the gate.

Betta'lain had the drive littered with peel. They can lay there till they rot for all I care, Leona decided. I don't have the strength to pick them up. Her toe ached like a decayed tooth and the smell of the slipper and bandage was making her head hurt. . .

"Lain," she called at the gate, "somebody's hurt the pony."

Betta'lain had all the peeled oranges back in the sack. She carried them dripping from the car. "I saw him," she said. "Who? Saw who?"

"Him that had the pony before us."

*Ruth Moose*

"Postom?" Leona followed Betta'lain toward the house. "What are you talking about?"

"He was behind the barn all the time. Didn't you see?" Betta'lain waited for Leona to open the door. "Him and the biggest boy. They had a rope."

"He was trying to take him without paying me," Leona screamed at the barn, shook her fist. "The only pay I get from his bills, three months' back bills, and here he comes stealing it away. Tried to ride the pony off and it couldn't hold their weight, that's what."

"He left," Betta'lain said.

Leona looked toward the bent pony by the gate. "Any man with common sense would have known to lead him off, not try to ride a little thing like that."

She sat on the steps, watched the sun that lay like a spent gold piece. Her toe hurt, throbbed like a pump that drained everything in her out.

She could hear Betta'lain singing in the kitchen. "I'm a little teapot, short and stout, tip me over, pour me out."

"I'm poured out," Leona said. "That Postom—there's not a drop of me left."

The pony whickered at her, turned and stumbled toward the pond.

Leona blinked in the kitchen light. Betta'lain had set the table, two spoons on each of the four "Our State Bird" plastic placemats. The bald oranges were stacked in a pryamid in a bowl.

Leona took her seat and Betta'lain tied a chain of tea bags around her neck. She wore an identical one. "Sing." Betta'lain waved a wooden spoon. "I'm a little. . ."

"If I had a gun"—Leona stirred her tea—"I'd shoot him."

*Ruth Moose*

# Pieces of Crow

THE SCRAPS OF yellow taffeta lay on the floor like shattered sunshine. I held Joey, warm from his nap, clean in a freshly ironed sunsuit. Keeping him quiet while Daddy slept and Mama sewed was my job. It wasn't always this easy.

Mama knelt at the stool where Nina Baldridge stood turning like the ballerina on my music box. I hummed "Sweetheart Waltz" for Joey. He laughed, reached for the sun spangles in the air.

"Am I pinning this too short?" Mama stood, brushed back her hair. The pincushion on her waist looked like a nest of spiders, all with silver legs.

Mrs. Baldridge, feet fat in black lace-up shoes, sat with her ankles crossed. She wore a veiled hat and under the net her face was damp as though a mist rained on her.

"We can make the dress longer if you like. I have plenty of material for the hem." Mama stood back from the fidgeting Nina.

Mrs. Baldridge walked around, ducking, unducking her head like a chicken. I could almost hear her cluck.

"It's about an eighth-inch shorter over here." Mrs. Baldridge pinched the air as if she were making a bird's beak.

Joey clapped his hands for her to do it again.

"Cute." She patted him on the head. A minister's wife had to go around doing things like that.

*Ruth Moose*

"I check it all the way around before I hem," Mama said. "Right now we're more interested in the right length." She helped Nina step from the stool, the long yellow gown swishing like a curtain. Nina was fourteen, two years older than I was, secretary of the student council, a cheerleader, and one of the most popular girls in school. "We don't want the dress so long you trip over it," Mama said.

"I'd die if I tripped." Nina made a face under her thick makeup mask. Pimples made her cheeks rough as an orange. She also had pimples on her back. "If I fell"—Nina slid into high-heeled pumps—"Susie would say I did it on purpose to ruin her wedding."

"Your sister would not say anything of the sort," Mrs. Baldridge said. "Nina, what makes you say such things?"

Nina stuck her tongue out. I giggled. Mrs. Baldridge was behind her adjusting the back of her dress. "I still think it's cut too low, neck and back."

Mama had shaped darts so Nina could wear a padded bra. She looked nice.

"I don't see why Nina thinks she's supposed to have as much up there as Susie's friends," Mrs. Baldridge said. "They're all college girls."

I rocked Joey. Nina, as she paraded by, said, "He's cute." I wondered if she planned to marry a minister when she grew up and was practicing. Since Mama had been sewing this bridesmaid's dress, Nina said "hi" to me in the hall at school. I always said "hi" back.

This was the first dress Mama made for anyone for pay. She made my clothes, hers, some for Joey, and several things for women in the neighborhood, but she never charged them—they were neighbors. They were the ones who told her to start sewing for the public. That's. when Mama ran the ad in the paper and Mrs. Baldridge answered.

"Taffeta has to be one of the hardest things in the world to sew," Mama said after they left. ''And a bridesmaid's dress—I've never made one before. I'll be glad when it's finished and I get paid. I'll have earned every cent of it."

Mama was trying to earn some extra money. School would open in three weeks and all my dresses were too short. Joey needed winter things, Daddy a jacket—so many things, Mama said.

"You must think you're going to get rich," Daddy said at the table. He worked at the all-night gas station, his first job in four months. It was late afternoon and he looked sleepy, tired. "It's not that easy, nothing is." When he lost his job at Coleman's after ten years, Mama said it hurt him more than anyone knew.

"Every little bit helps," she said, putting beans on to cook. "It costs so much these days to live."

Daddy drank coffee. His eyes seemed as deep as cups.

Mama's second customer was a Mrs. Lanning who had a crippled daughter my age. "She's been in a wheelchair all her life," Mama said when she hung up the phone. "Poor thing." She looked at me for a moment, then hugged hard. "Sometimes I forget how lucky we really are."

The afternoon the Lannings came, I waited by the window. Mama told me to meet them at the car and help Cloene, the crippled girl, be nice to her, play dolls or games if she could from her wheelchair.

A Buick, big, black as a whale, stopped in the drive. It crunched gravels like they were being swallowed. I ran to the car and saw myself in the shiny hubcabs, all moon-faced and fish-eyed, as I waited for them to get out.

Cloene lay against the seat, eyes closed as if asleep. Her mouth jerked open once and I saw teeth too large and crowded for one person.

Mrs. Lanning came around the car, yanked off leather gloves like she was mad at them. She opened the door so fast I was pushed into a prickle bush. "I been doing this so long, nobody but me knows how!' She handed me her purse and gloves to hold. A scalloped handkerchief was caught in her purse and flowered out like a purple blossom.

"When Cloene falls," Mrs. Lanning said, "she goes sprawling and there's nothing you can do but get out of her way." I saw rubber-tipped crutches step to the ground, then one leg in a heavy brown shoe, then another. Both were held in cages of silver braces.

"Look out," Mrs. Lanning called, helping the huddle of shiny bones toward the house. "Look now!"

Cloene thrashed and flailed metal. Deep cries choked in her throat.

"No." Mrs. Lanning pulled at her. "No, we're not going back in the car. No." She turned to me. "Cloene would ride twenty-four hours a day. Sometimes when I can't do anything with her, we get in the car and ride. But with the price of gas these days..."

Mrs. Lanning pushed Cloene into a porch chair, took her purse and gloves, pulled out the handkerchief, and wiped and fanned herself. "I don't know why I pick the hottest day of the year to do things."

Cloene lay to one side of the chair as though she'd been tossed there. Black curls that looked carved clung to her head and the dress she wore was a faded green thing, zippered like a sack. One sleeve had a tear. She kept kicking her feet, made clanking noises on the porch.

"No"—Mrs. Lanning slapped her leg—"we are not going. You calm yourself down and sit still."

Mama came then. "Bethann, get one of your dolls or something for Cloene to play with."

I ran for Rosalie on my bed. Grandma had mailed me Rosalie for Christmas. She was my favorite and best. She had pigtails, her own straw hat, patent shoes with buttons no bigger than a bug's eye. Mama had made her polka-dot dress with tucks, scraps of lace, and a ruffle.

*Ruth Moose*

"Cloene looks about the same size as Bethann," Mama said.

"We can measure and find out. If she is, I'll be glad to use some of Bethann's patterns and save you buying some."

Cloene stared straight ahead, one foot tapped the floor. Her hands lay like dead fish in her lap. I gently gave her Rosalie.

She screamed and swept my doll to the floor in a clatter.

I grabbed poor Rosalie. Her hand was broken off. I held it, almost crying. "Mama, look."

"We'll glue it back, honey," she said. "Go put Rosalie away. One of your old cloth dolls might have been better."

I kissed Rosalie, held her hollow stump like I wanted to hide it.

"I'm sure Cloene didn't mean it," Mama said.

"Yes, she did." Mrs. Lanning spanked Cloene's arm. "Bad girl. Bad."

When I came back from bandaging Rosalie's arm, Mama and Mrs. Lanning had black material spread across their laps, the chairs, and spilling onto the floor. If you looked at the cloth closely enough you could see tiny blue dots, but the rest of it was black as thunder. "Ugh," I said.

Mama gave me a look that said don't say anything else. Her eyes added, please. "Don't you think a brighter color would be better for Cloene? Little girls like—"

"I know what little girls like," Mrs. Lanning said. "But Cloene isn't any little girl. If she weren't my sister's child, I wouldn't be doing all I do for her."

"She isn't your daughter?" Mama smoothed the fabric. A large wrinkle had been folded in the center.

"Not for a minute," Mrs. Lanning said, "even if we have had the responsibility for her since she was a month old. Elsie died and we were the only ones to take the baby. That's before we knew she was so …damaged."

*Ruth Moose*

Poor Cloene. No mother and having to wear black dresses. "I think there's enough material here to make her five dresses." Mrs. Lanning folded the fabric.

"Five?" Mama said. "Alike? Don't you think she'll get tired of—"

"It doesn't matter." Mrs. Lanning waved her hand. "Cloene never notices what she wears and what she doesn't."

I couldn't watch Mama and Mrs. Lanning as they tried to take Cloene's measurements. I heard from inside the house. Mama tried to soothe her, show her the tape measure wouldn't hurt. Mrs. Lanning shouted and pulled her around. The chair scraped.

"Now do you see why I can't take her into a store and buy a dress? She fights me every step of the way."

Mama helped Cloene to the car and Mrs. Lanning said she appreciated what Mama was going to do. She said she had tried to order things for Cloene by mail and never got what she wanted. "They send you the worst stuff they have just to see if you'll keep it," Mrs. Lanning said.

The car sped off in a loud blast. Mama folded the awful material and took it in the house.

When she cut out the dresses the next day, the black material fell to the floor like dead birds. Pieces of crow. Mama told me to get out her remnant box and look for any scraps of blue. She would use them for pockets or collars or trim, any way she could to dress up that deathly black. "Did you notice what beautiful blue eyes Cloene had?" Mama asked.

At the fabric shop Mama bought lace. "It won't take much for a collar," she said, "and all little girls should wear some lace once in a while." Before we left the store we looked again at the material we wanted for my school dresses. I held the red and yellow plaid out from the bolt, rubbed the green cotton with its red apple design. "Mrs. Lanning should buy material like these for Cloene," Mama said. "A pity. She bought good material, paid a lot for it, but what a color."

*Ruth Moose*

At night Mama hemmed near the lamp. The yellow taffeta talked as it slid through her fingers. Poured like a waterfall off her lap as she worked. She couldn't sew on Cloene's dresses at night.

On Friday when the Baldridges picked up Nina's dress, Mama had it pressed and floating on a hanger. They examined the seams and sleeves, said she had done a fine job, and paid her nine dollars. She put the money in the top drawer of the sewing machine.

I built blocks with Joey on the cool linoleum floor. All the colors were gone. Mama had mopped and scrubbed and swept them away.

At the sewing machine she finished Cloene's dresses. She had used scraps to make sashes and pockets on some, round as muffins. Another had buttons in a row on the yoke. Each dress was different and Mama was pleased. She pressed and hung them around the room.

Mrs. Lanning hurried in, left the motor running in the car. When she saw the dresses she drew up her face, took a breath big enough to blow the house down. "You mean you made all five dresses like this?" She snatched at the first one.

"I tried to make them as different as possible from the same material," Mama said.

"They're not what I had in mind at all." Mrs. Lanning threw a dress on the bed. "They're not practical. She'll only get a collar dirty, tear off a pocket. Lace is a waste of time. She doesn't know the difference." Mrs. Lanning threw three other dresses down. "They simply won't do."

"I'm sorry," Mama said. "I didn't think you'd mind if I tried to make them as attractive as possible. The material was so drab, depressing. It needed—"

"You've ruined my material." Mrs. Lanning's face was red.

"I'll have to start over."

*Ruth Moose*

"I don't understand," Mama said. She put the dresses back on hangers. "You don't want the dresses. I don't know what to do."

"I don't care what you do with them." Mrs. Lanning spun around. "That's your problem. But I do expect reimbursement for my material. It's ruined as far as I am concerned."

"I didn't ruin it," Mama said. "I've never had anyone who didn't like my work. I double-stitch seams, sew buttons by hand—people say they're better than ready-made."

"I expect replacement for my material," Mrs. Lannin said. She patted her purse. "Five dollars at least."

"What about—"

"The fabric cost more than that, of course," Mrs. Lanning said. "But five would be fair."

I thought of the money in the sewing machine drawer.

"Don't," I said under my breath. "Don't."

"My time is worth something," Mama said.

"I'm in a hurry." Mrs. Lanning stood at the door. "This did not turn out like I had hoped. A matter of communication. I should have known." She gazed around the room.

Mama took the money from the drawer, counted out five ones.

I felt sick. In the other bedroom, Joey started to fuss. He would wake Daddy.

Mrs. Lanning shoved the money in her purse, snapped it shut, and walked out.

For a minute Mama didn't move. Then she put the rest of the money back, got up, and closed the machine.

"It's not fair." I ran to her. "You worked hard and the dresses were nice."

"I know." She touched one.

I took a dress and held it before me. "Will I have to wear them now?"

"They would fit, wouldn't they?" Mama said.

Joey yelled from his crib. He wanted up.

*Ruth Moose*

I thought of the plaid I wanted, the pretty dresses Mama and I planned. .

"No." Mama took the dress. "You won't have to wear them. I'll give them to the Clothing Closet or somebody, but you don't have to wear them." She put her arm around me. "We're not that poor. Not now, not ever."

# Green Lightning and the Tablecloth Bride

TALK ABOUT FAST weddings. I think my mother and Aunt Harriet once set some kind of record. In less than three hours they had the wedding dress, bride's bouquet, cake (complete with wedded couple, a borrowed piano, and Uncle Elmo in his stocking feet, playing "The Yellow Rose of Texas."

It happened the summer I was twelve. The longest, hottest, driest summer anyone had ever seen. Green skies boiled daily, cooked with lightning, burned black, and ended up spitting a few hot drops that plopped hard as marbles in the dust.

Neighbors sat on porches and fanned with cardboard fans labeled, "We Are Your Friend in Time of Need," compliments of Herman's Funeral Home. Aunt Harriet had a painted, folded Japanese fan with a pink tassel. The tassel flicked around her wrist like a fly as she fanned. She kept the fan in a tall crystal vase on the piano in her dark and mothball-smelling living room. "Go get me my fan, May Kay," Aunt Harriet sat on our porch and sang. Mama added, "Run, honey." And gave me a look. I ran across the street, got the fan but not before I tried it out a few times posing in the long mirror above the piano. I fanned, tried to make my eyes look slanted. They never did. Nothing I did worked out right that summer. I was too big and awkward to take turns with the kids playing with the hose or jumping through yard sprinklers. The pool in the backyard was for little kids like

*Ruth Moose*

my brother Lester. "Baby Squirt," I called him when Mama couldn't hear. Everybody I knew had gone to the beach or mountains for the summer. It was awful. I read a lot, walked downtown to the library and carried home armloads of books. When I wasn't reading, I pretended to be. Held a book in front of my face and listened for all I was worth. Everybody forgot I was there.

Twelve was bad, but being the only girl in the neighborhood was worse. Except I wasn't really the only girl. There was Frances Anne Gurley on the corner, but she was twenty-one and treated me the way I treated the rest of the kids. Like I was the lowest kind of brat. Frankie dated Shorty Privette every Sunday, Tuesday, and Thursday night. For their thirteenth month going-together anniversary, Shorty gave her a fuzzy black ball of a dog named Mop and took her to the Riverview Fish Camp where you get all you can eat for two dollars.

One of the differences between this summer and last, was that on Monday, Wednesday, and Friday nights Frankie's new boyfriend, Leon Futty, came to see her. Saturday nights she stayed home.

"What for?" my father once asked.

"A girl has to catch her breath once in a while," Mama said, "and wash her hair."

"Oh." Daddy went back to his VFW magazine with the jumping deer and bow and arrow on the cover.

Mother gave him a look to freeze any deer in midleap.

Saturday nights Frankie did wash her hair and do her nails.

She held her fingers wide apart, waved them in the air like a handful of matches. She sat in her green and white gingham robe with cherries embroidered on the pockets, her feet tucked under and hidden in a fat, red velvet chair. Mop curled on her lap and we watched the Texaco Hour with Milton Berle, Beat the Clock with Bud Collier, and Your Hit

Parade with Snooky Lanson and Dorothy Collins.

"Don't Bud Collier look just like Shorty?" she said once. "With that high forehead and all?" .

I didn't know. We watched everything that moved on the television, even the test pattern, which didn't move and which Frankie said looked like the Indian on the nickel, only bigger.

Frankie's mother, Sudie Gurley, knitted while we watched. Her needles clicked and scraped like grasshoppers, a dry sound like the one Frankie made scraping off three coats of nail polish in chips and peels.

"Why don't you use remover?" Sudie asked. "It wouldn't be half the mess."

"Because I can't stand the smell." Frankie stuck out her tongue. I giggled.

"Anybody who can stand doggy breath. . ." Sudie's needles snapped faster. "It can't be good for you to sleep with that dog every night."

"It's my room"—Frankie wrinkled her nose—"and I'll sleep with whoever I want to."

The way she talked to her mother made me feel tough inside, and I kept a file of things to say when I got her age. I doubted I'd ever get around to it, though.

Frankie's room had been added onto the duplex where the Gurleys lived, five years ago. One time her father came home from wherever he stayed, started the room, got it framed in, roofed, and floored, then was suddenly called away on business, or so Sudie told Mama.

"Poker game," Aunt Harriet said. "Monkey business." She also told Mama that Ed Baynes, who owned the duplex, told her one day he drove up to collect the rent and there was a man on the roof tacking shingles. He never said a word, just lifted his hat and kept tacking. Sudie counted out the rent and didn't mention it. Ed said Sudie always paid her rent on time and she had for the last twenty years and he didn't want to ask questions that might embarrass her or cause hard feelings. So Ed paid for the rest of the room to be finished and felt it was a good investment, even if he hadn't thought of it himself.

Grover Gurley was in and out, mostly out, most of the year. He came home for Christmas, the Fourth of July, a few times in between. He sent money every month though. "At least they aren't living off the county," Aunt Harriet said whenever anyone snipped or gossiped about Sudie or Frankie.

All Sudie Gurley ever said was, "May Kay, don't you marry a gambling man. He'll write you fancy letters, then walk off and you'll never know when, or if, you'll ever see him again!' She showed me a packet of dusty-looking letters tied together with a bluish-green ribbon. "Isn't that the most beautiful handwriting you've ever seen for a man?" She traced the curls of her name in the crinkle of brown ink.

Mama and Aunt Harriet wondered what her choice was in Frankie's boyfriends. She told them Shorty was as steady a boy as you'd ever want. Not a minute late, never a second too early, and he always had Frances Anne home on the very tick of twelve. And Shorty's gifts to her, other than Mop, which she was sure was Frances Anne's idea, also pleased her. A Blue Waltz perfume set—the big one with bath powder, spray, and twelve-ounce perfume. For her birthday a watch, and at Christmas a toaster. On Valentine's Day he had given her a diamond. You had to squint to see it, but if Frankie held her hand out and at an angle to the light, and you looked really hard, you could see a tiny glint. Sudie said his car was paid for and he had eight hundred dollars in the bank. When he dated Frankie, he wore green pants with a sharp crease and his hair was wet combed, so wavy it made you dizzy to look long. He was smart, Sudie told Mama and Aunt Harriet. He drove a Pepsi truck and had taught himself to play the guitar in twelve easy lessons.

*Ruth Moose*

Leon, Frankie's new boyfriend, or Number Two as Daddy called him, was a preacher's son. He brought his daddy's old pulpit Bible once to show Sudie and Frankie, led them in a devotion. "That boy"—Sudie wiped her glasses—"can pray the prettiest prayer. It will tear your heart right out." She said she wouldn't be a bit surprised if Leon didn't get the Call any day to go preach.

Daddy laughed, hooted out loud and slapped his knees when he heard that. "Anybody who calls that boy deserves him," he said. "Ha…haw. That's a good one."

Leon's last job had been in the poultry plant and he said he'd die if he ever so much as had to look at another chicken in any shape or form.

"That ought to be proof right there," Daddy laughed. "If he don't eat chicken, he'll never be a preacher."

After the chicken job folded, Leon didn't seem in a hurry to find anything else. Daddy worked him one day at the hardware. "He couldn't count nails," I heard him tell Mama. "Lester can do that and he's just a kid. Nails," Daddy groaned. Mama and Aunt Harriet didn't say anything after that. Daddy had tried. He had given the boy a chance and if he didn't choose to take it, whose fault was it? They looked to Uncle Elmo, who ran a plumbing business. "Not for a minute," he said. "You gotta know what you're doing when you mess around people's pipes. I'm not taking a chance."

Leon didn't own a car and walked nine miles to eat supper with Sudie and Frankie on his date nights. Then he and Frankie sat on Gurley's stoop and batted bugs that sizzled and hit the light. Or they'd walk around the block, go downtown to a movie or the drugstore. Several neighbors said Leon sure didn't look like any preacher's son they'd ever seen and he walked like he didn't have enough sense to put one foot in front of the other.

Mama said it was wonderful Frances Anne had two calling on her and she could make a choice.

*Ruth Moose*

"Some choice," Aunt Harriet sighed behind her fan. Everyone waited for the day Shorty and Leon would meet, either by accident or plan. "After all," Mama said, "she is engaged to one of them." I wondered if it would be pistols or swords for Frankie's flame-nail-polished and fat-fingered white hand. Fists or duel at dawn? Mama said I'd been reading too many old romance books and she didn't know where I got that kind of thing. Maybe I was in the section I wasn't supposed to go in the library. "Children's is on the right, May Kay," she told me, "the right side." I had been slipping through for years and Miss Laura Kelsey just stamped out my books and didn't bother to read titles and authors anymore.

I wanted them to duel. That would be exciting.

"Those two—" Daddy said, one night after Leon walked past, "when he and Shorty do meet—they'll probably take one look at each other and run."

I frowned at him. What an awful thing to say.

"Hush," Mama said. "Somebody might hear you."

If Sudie worried about her daughter's decision, she didn't show it. France Anne dated during the week, watched TV on Saturdays, and kept saying Shorty sure did look a lot like Bud Collier. Same handsome high forehead.

"A sure sign of intelligence." Sudie counted stitches in the sweater she knitted. "My daddy had a high forehead and he served as Court Solicitor for Harnet County four terms in a row."

"Leon's got the prettiest eyes." Frankie reached between her legs, lifted up Mop, held him high in the air, and blew fluff off her face. Mop swam in the air, snapped small, pointed teeth.

I told Mama about the business of high foreheads meaning a lot of intelligence. She canned peaches, pushing them in jars with the back of the spoon. "Don't bet on it," she said.

*Ruth Moose*

"Is that so?" Daddy walked into the kitchen, took half a peeled peach and bit into it. "All the time I thought Frankie loved Shorty for his musical abilities."

When Shorty drove his Pepsi truck down Woodward Street twice a day, he played "Shave and a Haircut" on the horn.

"Thank God for Saturdays and Sundays," Mama said. "Sometimes I hear that tune in my sleep."

Shorty also played the guitar, picked and pulled it more than singing with it. Sometimes he sat on the stoop with Frankie for hours. Frankie in a blue dotted-swiss dress that took Sudie four hours of hard ironing, fanned out like a lake around her. Frankie, blue satin bow in her curls round as radishes, crossed her ankles in their white socks, patted her sandaled feet and listened, her face upturned as a bird.

Leon didn't look like he could lift a guitar without getting a hernia. But he could hold more lightning bugs in his hands at one time than anyone I'd ever seen.

We counted 206 once until Frankie started goosing him under his arms and he got so tickled he let go. That was when Mama called me in.

"It's not late," I fussed, "and you can't say tomorrow is a school day because it's not." School wouldn't start for two weeks yet and I both wanted it and yet dreaded for the summer to end.

"I know when it's time for you to come home," Mama said and shut her mouth before anything else came out.

A week before school started, the last of the hottest August on record in forty years of weather-keeping, Frankie made her choice. She gave Shorty back his diamond, the toaster, what was left of the Blue Waltz perfume set, and kept Mop. Sudie walked the street telling first one neighbor, then another, how "that boy actually broke down and cried." She twisted an embroidered handkerchief when she said it. "Frances Anne broke his heart plain and simple. I told her,"

Sudie went on, "that whatever became of him now would always be on her head. That boy came up and hugged me, said he'd always love me and a real mother couldn't have treated him any better. I cried, he cried some more. We had us a crying good time."

When Sudie was telling Mama, I wondered what Frankie was doing while all this crying was going on. She was probably watching ''As the World Turns" and not hearing a thing being said.

"When are Frances Anne and Leon planning to get married?" Mama asked.

"Why, right now," Sudie said. "The sooner the better, that's what she said. When Frances Anne wants to do a thing, she won't wait. Once she makes up her mind, you have to—"

"Now?" Mama's jaw dropped low enough to spring a hinge. (That's what Daddy always said she did.) "Now?" Mama said again.

"Well, today." Sudie looked at the little gold biscuit of a watch she wore on a neck chain. Her grandmother's watch. One of the few things she ever got from her family. "They never accepted my marriage," she said once, "never forgave me."

"But it's Wednesday," Mama said. "Nobody gets married on Wednesday. Besides, the stores are closed this afternoon."

"That's what I said." Sudie snapped her watch shut. "But you know Frances Anne when she makes her mind up."

"Can't she wait until Saturday?"

"Leon's gone home to tell his daddy, change clothes, and get his things now," Sudie said.

As soon as Sudie left, Mama stopped peeling apples for supper and dashed for the phone. She came back to the kitchen a minute later, sat down and sighed. "There's not a preacher in this town. I don't know what we'd do if somebody decided to die."

*Ruth Moose*

Aunt Harriet slipped in the back door. "I know it and as I walked across the street, I remembered old Mr. Ledbetter—over on Hathaway. He's retired, but that won't make any difference"

"He's deaf." Mama peeled and quartered an apple.

"If he can say the words and sign his name, it ought to do the trick," Aunt Harriet said, and picked up an apple.

Mama went to the phone in the hall, came back in a few minutes waving her arms. "Victory," she said. "He'll do it, but not until after three o'clock. That's his rug-hooking time and his nap."

"May Kay." Mama looked at me. I'd just taken an apple, was open to bite. "Go tell Sudie it's three o'clock and we'll do the best we can with what we got."

"What about her dress?" Aunt Harriet spun a red peeling around in her hands, the apple balding with each stroke.

"Sudie says they've got her white organdy graduation dress and Frankie was freshening it up with some spray starch."

"And I've got a new lace cloth for that little round table in the front bedroom." Aunt Harriet took another apple. "She could wear that for a veil, even if it is heavy. It's never been used."

I ducked out the door and across the street so fast the hot tar didn't burn my bare feet. Frankie was not ironing her dress after all. She was deep in the dark corners of her room behind towering columns of magazines, True Heart and Intimate Romances. "Don't you ever let your Mama know I give you those," she said as I left with my arms loaded. "She might think the wrong thing."

Aunt Harriet had sent all the kids in the neighborhood out to pick Queen Anne's lace and "anything white that's blooming." "All I got is red geraniums," she said, "and orange gladiolas—and we sure don't want those."

I couldn't see why not. Red was a pretty color. So was

orange. White was no color at all.

Lester and I were sent uptown to the Martin Sisters' Sweet Shoppe. "Hurry," Mama said, and pushed twenty dollars in my hand. "Take any kind of white cake they got—round or square or sheet—and decorated—as long as it doesn't say Happy Birthday or Bon Voyage—just plain cake."

We had to wait for the train to pass. It had seventy-seven cars and I won because I'd guessed seventy-two. Lester punched me in the arm and I ran after him as he whizzed around the corner. The Sweet Shoppe was closed and there was nothing in the window but a few scattered cupcakes with clowns on them and a sign saying, "Fishing." A station wagon disappeared down the street with two white heads bobbing and a bunch of fishing poles waving their corks like a game at the county fair.

"Fools," Aunt Harriet said. "Don't they know it's too hot for fish to bite on a day like this? Fish got more sense than some people."

Mama said that was what she was afraid might happen and she'd whipped up a mix cake. "We'll put white icing on it and call it cake," she said, dumping powdered sugar in a bowl. It swirled up a sweet-smelling cloud. Lester went across the street to get the little bride and groom dolls that were from the fiftieth wedding anniversary cake Aunt Harriet and Uncle Elmo had in June. Aunt Harriet cut the gold foil "50" from behind them and said, "Now...that's the same thing, isn't it?"

I planned to loan my bride and groom paper dolls from last year when I played junk like that, but I was glad I didn't have to. They'd get icing on them and I might play with them again when nobody would know.

"Girls don't get married but once—or shouldn't," Aunt Harriet said. "And at least the first time ought to be a little special." Aunt Harriet stood back from the cake. She had made marshmallow flowers and put white borders with a tube Mama used for our birthday cakes. On a lace doily and milkglass stand, the cake looked pretty after all. You never know what you can do until you try." Aunt Harriet wiped sugar from her fingers.

"It does look better than I thought." Mama gave me and Lester the bowls to lick.

"It will have to do," Harriet sighed. "In the time we've had, I think we've done well."

My father came home at one. Mama met him at the door and backed him out. "Don't take your hat off," she said.

"Frances Anne is getting married and we have to move the piano."

"Whoa," Daddy said. He held his hat, had it ready to sail across to rest on the radio. "Not me," he said. "You all can just get Frances Anne married all you want to, but leave me out." All he wanted was a hot lunch and a cool nap in the swing under the fan.

"It can't take more than five minutes," Mama said, "and it's all downhill." She had a hand on his back, pushed. "We can't have a wedding without music."

"It's a hell of a lot of work to move a piano," Daddy said.

"I'll sing."

"Lord." Mama raised both hands in the air. "That would be all we'd need."

"It's the mountain to Mohammed." Daddy rubbed his hands together. "I hope Elmo's hernia's in shape for this." He hitched up his pants, followed Mama out the door, humming "Home on the Range."

After they pulled the piano from the wall, Aunt Harriet made everyone wait while she cleaned behind it. Christmas cards, church bulletins, her crocheted pineapple doily. "I wondered where that thing went." She shook lint tags off.

"I thought the cat ate it," Elmo chuckled.

"You accused Amy Rothwell of taking it after you had

the circle meeting here last Easter." Mama cupped her hands over her mouth.

"Well, she always said she wanted it." Aunt Harriet bent to pick up marbles, pieces of chalk, crayons, bobbie pins, and an old key. Lester took the key, put it in his pocket, and grinned. "It's a skeleton key. I can get in every house on this street any time I want."

"I'm as good a housekeeper as the next, and better than some, but pianos don't get moved every day of the week." Aunt Harriet swept.

"Thank God." Daddy wiped his forehead.

The vacuum cleaner salesman who appeared at the door was invited in. His eyes lit up at Aunt Harriet with the broom sweeping the corner. "I got a tool that gets to places like that."

Lester and I carried the piano bench. It was full of sheet music that kept slipping and fluttering into the ditch. We finally had to park it on the lawn and take some out. We left it under the magnolia tree with a rock on top to keep it from blowing.

The men had the piano tilted on the steps like a sailboat about to be launched. "Hold her steady there, Revco," the vacuum cleaner saleman said.

"Elmo," my father said.

"If he does make a sale afte this," Mama said, "you can't say he didn't earn every cent of it."

The piano rolled on the walk smoothly, old wheels squealing like cats fighting over a fence. As they turned the piano into the street, Sarah, Aunt Harriet's black and white tabby cat, strolled by and was nearly hit. Uncle Elmo said something I couldn't quite hear. Aunt Harriet frowned, said, "Hush." Mama, who followed along behind with a dustcloth and furniture polish, said, "Wouldn't that look good in the News and Enqirer? Cat Killed By Piano on Woodhaven Street."

*Ruth Moose*

"Wouldn't be half as dumb as most of the stuff they print," Uncle Elmo grunted.

"Pictures." Mama's hand flew to her cheek. "We haven't called someone to take pictures."

"Lester's got a camera," I said.

"I'll take the pictures," Daddy said. "I want to be standing behind something while all this is going on, even if it's nothing but a camera."

The piano moaned and leaned as the three men carried it across the yard to the empty apartment next to where Sudie and Frances Anne lived. It was Mama and Aunt Harriet's idea again. "Why not?" they said. The apartment had been freshly painted, floors refinished, windows scraped and washed. "It's clean as a church," they said. Ed Baynes said sure, it was fine by him :to use it, just save him a piece of cake and cup of punch. He'd try to get by.

"I tell you," Daddy said after they rolled the piano to the corner of the living room, all the squeaks chasing around the empty room like ghosts. "Never again. Not for any man's money will I ever move that piano."

Uncle Elmo sat down and began "Chopsticks" and a rollicking version of "The Yellow Rose of Texas." "How's that for bridal music?" he asked.

"Not much," Aunt Harriet said. "I know you. You'll scandalize us."

She and Mama set up folding tables, covered them with sheets. "Blue candles were all I had—and the stores closed. What does Frances Anne think you can do on Wednesdays with the stores closing at noon and no notice?"

"It looks just lovely," Mama stood back, hands on her hips. She had arranged Queen Anne's lace in a white basket and sent Lester back out to see if he couldn't find some kind of blue flowers growing somewhere, "to add some color."

Grandmother's carnival glass punch bowl was in the table's center. "Thank goodness Mama had the good taste to have the blue kind and not that horrible red-orange stuff." Aunt Harriet slid the bowl an inch to the right.

Sudie came flying in, waving her hands as if she were erasing something. "Her dress won't button. It's too tight. There's a gap at the top this big." She measured air with her fingers.

"I'll fix it." Aunt Harriet left. Mama always said Harriet was so good with a thread and needle she could outwit a spider if it came to it.

"What if you're going to all this trouble for nothing?" Uncle Elmo said. He took a handful of mints from the bag Mama opened. Aunt Harriet found them in back of the freezer, left over from her anniversary party. "What if Frances Anne backs out? What if Leon decides not to show up? What if—"

"The sky fell?" Daddy said as he went out the door. "My wife and your wife would pitch in, start sweeping up the pieces and never look to see what happened or where it came from until after they finished."

Daddy dressed and fussed. He refused to wear a suit on his one afternoon a week off. "A sports shirt will do," Mama said, "if you'll wear a tie." Daddy sighed wetly.

She made me wear my yellow Easter dress, even though it was so tight I could hardly breathe and too short by three inches. "We're going to do our best for Frances Anne." She tugged on my skirt. "Nobody can say we didn't."

I wore white sandals and socks, my ankle bracelet with the one blank heart. I was waiting for the right initial to scratch on the other. I carried my gloves and the white Bible I got when I passed the Catechism at church.

Preacher Ledbetter was there in polka-dotted stockings. A bee stung his ankle as he walked across the grass. His foot swelled so, Mrs. Ledbetter had to go home for his carpet slippers.

*Ruth Moose*

Uncle Elmo was on the second round of "Here Comes the Bride" when Frances Anne came in the front door. Leon came in the back. He said there was such a crowd at the front, he couldn't get in. He wore a shiny blue suit with red striped tie and white shirt. His hair looked dark and wet combed back from his face. His forehead was pale as the underside of a melon.

Preacher Ledbetter cleared his throat and began, "We are gathered here today. . ." His voice ground like the motor on Lester's rock polisher.

At the end, Leon took a small jewelry box from his pocket, picked something from the blue velvet lips, and slid it on Frances Anne's finger. Then he kissed her so hard the veil slid off. Aunt Harriet dashed to catch it before it hit the floor, then shook and brushed it as though it had. I'd never be able to look at the tablecloth again without somehow seeing Frances Anne's face under it.

Uncle Elmo let roll with "The Beer Barrel Polka" and then Sudie danced with Preacher Ledbetter until her face was the color of Daddy's tie and she was making little gasps with her breath, laughing and hiccupping in between. Daddy swung me around a few times and Lester danced with Aunt Harriet who said thank goodness all this was taking place during the day or we'd be arrested for disturbing the peace.

"Who's to complain?" Daddy wiped his face. "We're all here." He had bubbled a quart of Uncle Elmo's homemade wild cherry wine in the punch bowl when Aunt Harriet wasn't looking. Aunt Harriet, cup in hand, said to Emmie Lou Ledbetter, the preacher's wife, that somebody, she wasn't saying who, sure didn't know how to brew tea for a punch so that you had a tea taste, yet wasn't too strong and bitter. She looked at Mama when she said it and I almost let the secret out by giggling. Then Aunt Harriet and Emmie Lou talked of ways you can brew tea to keep it from clouding.

The wedding cake was chocolate inside. Mama said that

was the only mix she had in the house. Frances Anne said it was her favorite and how did Mama know? She cut the first piece and fed it so fast to Leon his cheeks bulged like a chipmunk and he had to put his hand up for her to stop. That was when Daddy snapped his picture. The flash froze everybody either bug-eyed or chewing.

Outside, kids came from six blocks away and stood in line for cake and punch.

"I never thought we'd have this many," Mama said and glanced at Lester. "It wasn't up to you to invite everybody you knew." She cut smaller pieces of cake. Aunt Harriet ladled out half-glasses of punch until the bowl was empty. They sent me home for Kool Aid and frozen lemonade. Daddy and Uncle Elmo said that was the worst-tasting stuff that ever got caught in a cup and traded glasses with the kids that got punch before the punch ran out.

Frances Anne left to change clothes to "go away" and Mama sent Leon to pick up all the plastic cups scattered around.

"Go away?" Daddy said. He folded up the table after Mama took off the cloth. "How far can they go when he doesn't have a car?"

"He's got Elmo's." Mama packed the tablecloth in the box with the punch bowl and clean cake plate.

"Does Elmo know?" Daddy looked at Uncle Elmo's back on the piano bench. He and Lester were doing a "Chopsticks" duet now.

"Well...no," Mama said, "but that will still leave him with the truck."

"Why couldn't the happy couple take the truck?"

"Harriet and I discussed this"—Mama pinched in her mouth—"but we decided nobody should have to start their married life going on a honeymoon in a Futty's Plumbing truck."

"Why not?" Daddy said. "When it's free."

"It rattles so," Mama said.

"So does a tin can." Daddy grinned.

"Now, what is that supposed to mean?" she asked. But he had turned away and was going out to get a picture of the honeymooners as they "went away."

Emnie Lou Ledbetter held my Bible while I helped chase kids away from the kitchen door after we ran out of Kool Aid. She thought I was Frances Anne when I came back and handed me the Bible. "Now honey," she said, "you just read every word and you'll never have any troubles you can't handle." She patted my hand. "Commit to memory all the verses you can. Why, there are sometimes I don't know what I'd do if I couldn't say a little Bible verse or two when things go wrong. And honey, they will. They will. Life is like that."

The preacher hooked his arm through hers and pulled her away. I let them out the back door. All the kids were in the front yard now, waiting for Frances Anne and Leon to leave.

Frances Anne stood in the doorway and everybody clapped. She did look pretty. Her hair was long and combed and curled. She wore a green linen suit the color of a January pine and a yellow print blouse with a bow tied at her neck. She took off her white corsage—Aunt Harriet's silk orchid from Easter—and threw it. Aunt Harriet's shoulder jerked a little. I knew she planned to wear that corsage next Easter and the next and the next.

"She's not supposed to do that," Mama frowned. "Only her bouquet. What happened to it?"

"Sudie put it in water," Aunt Harriet whispered. "I told her there were more flowers where those came from, but she did it anyway."

Aunt Harriet had made Frances Anne's bouquet from Queen Anne's lace and some paper doilies she had in the drawer with white gift wrap ribbon streamers.

*Ruth Moose*

The corsage landed in the shrubbery hedge and yellowjackets flew out like sparks. Everyone jumped back. The kids ran.

Uncle Elmo stood beside his blue Plymouth. "I told Lester and his friends that the first one I saw with a bottle of white shoe polish or shaving cream would see more than the back of my hand." He said he'd washed his car yesterday and be durn if he was going to wash it again when they brought it back. "I don't have much finish left on that car," he said, "and shoe polish won't help."

He had let them tie balloons and crepe paper streamers on the door handles, radio antenna. While he wasn't looking somebody painted a big heart with initials and an arrow through it on the driver's side. The paint looked like the same rust-red Uncle Elmo had used on his porch last year.

Shorty came by in his Pepsi truck, stopped to wish Frances Anne and Leon "the best." He passed out Pepsi to show he wasn't a sore loser. Mama made us take ours to the refrigerator, but some of the kids started shaking theirs, held their fingers on the top, then let them spew out a Pepsi fight. That's when Aunt Harriet sent everybody home and asked Mama whatever in the world Frances Anne and Leon kept standing around for when they had a honeymoon to go on and reservations at the Heart of Cottonville Motor Inn. She sent Uncle Elmo a hint by narrowing her eyes, saying, "I got supper to cook and a thousand things to do."

"Me too," Mama said. "I think we've done enough for one day. Sudie seemed to really appreciate it."

"She really seemed to enjoy it. She's got a good heart, even if she does try your patience at times. And, after all, what are neighbors for if not to help when there's a need?"

Uncle Elmo came back looking tired. "Leon says he can't drive. Never learned how."

"What?" Mama asked. "And of course Frances Anne can't drive either."

"We'll have to—" Aunt Harriet started.

"Don't look at me," Daddy said. He took the camera strap from around his neck, began to wind film. "Not me."

"I guess I'm elected," Elmo said. "I feel better about driving my car myself."

They left in a roar with a puff of exhaust. Everyone waved. Sudie stood beside Aunt Harriet, wiped her eyes. "My little girl is gone. I can't believe it. Why it seems like last week I plaited her hair in pigtails, waved her off to school."

"They grow up," Aunt Harriet said, "and we have to let go—get on with the rest of our lives. I've said that every time."

Sudie hugged them, thanked everyone over and over. "Nobody could ask for better neighbors. I just want you to know I appreciate it. Everything you did."

"We do what we can," Mama sighed. "I only wish we'd had more time…but everything turned out okay."

"Just fine," Daddy said. "You got the knot tied."

We walked home together. I changed clothes and went back to Nancy Drew, Mystery of the Old Clock. Getting married, I decided, was a lot of fuss with everybody all the way around and meant having to wear stiff clothes and tablecloths on your head.

Supper was late, but Mama had made an apple cobbler. "I was too tired to make crusts," she said. I helped with the dishes and didn't have to be asked.

"I made a cake and cobbler today," Mama said, "and there's not a crumb of either one left." She scrubbed the pan. "The rest of those apples go in the deep freeze as soon as I can get them there."

The whole family had to help peel and core, though Lester ate more than he peeled. We sat on the porch and joked, peeled apples until it was too dark to see. Daddy said if he turned on the lights it would attract bugs, so we finally stopped peeling and looked at stars. I wondered what Frances Anne and Leon were doing? If they saw the same stars? Probably they watched television. Frances Anne had certain shows she wouldn't miss for Mr. Anybody. Life or death.

We were almost ready to go inside when Sudie Gurley crept around the corner of the house. "Sudie!" Mama jumped. "You almost scared me to death. What's wrong?"

"I feel just lost.," Sudie held her hand over her heart. "That house is so quiet I can hear myself think. It's awful."

I heard Daddy give a little chuckle. "If you all are going to be out here awhile," he said at the door, "I'll turn on the lights, but I'm turning in. Tomorrow's another day."

"Good night," Mama said, then turned to Sudie. "I'm so tired, thunder couldn't keep me awake."

"What?" Aunt Harriet came across the street. "What's going on?"

Sudie told her. "Of course you are," Aunt Harriet said, "and having that empty apartment next door is enough to bring out the ghosts."

"A whole empty house." Sudie almost burst into tears. "I can't bear it."

"Surely there's somebody who can put you up for the night." Mama waved away a moth who had bumped the porch light, gotten stunned.

"You got sisters," Aunt Harriet told Sudie.

"You can't depend on them," Sudie said. "They wouldn't give me air if I was in a jug. Why, I couldn't call them about Frances Anne getting married. They wouldn't come or bring her any wedding gifts. My family never forgave me for marrying Grover Gurley. They all married above. I was the only one who married beneath. It hasn't been an easy life." Sudie twisted a handkerchief. It looked wet and limp. Like she'd been crying.

"Get your pajamas, May Kay," Mama said. "You can spend the night with Mrs. Gurley."

"But—" I started.

"Just once," Mama said tiredly, "for tonight."

I got my things, packed them in the plaid zippered bag my grandmother had given me for Christmas, and started to tuck in Nancy Drew when I remembered Frances Anne's bedroom and her stacks of romance magazines. I wouldn't need anything to read. I could close the door and leave the light on, read all night without anybody telling me to turn it out and go to sleep.

I helped Sudie change the sheets. By the time I got in bed and all settled down with True Love and Secrets of Love, it was nearly eleven o'clock. I read until after twelve. All the stories were alike. She loves him, he doesn't love her, they finally love each other. Or he loved her and so does his best friend. I turned out the light.

The next thing I knew I heard a noise that sounded like a scratch across a screen. Then whispering. Heads bobbed and shadows brushed across the window. I crept from bed, my heart leaping like a yoyo in my chest. Somebody was trying to break in Sudie Gurley's house! Robbers? A rapist? The floor creaked once under me and I froze. The voices stopped, then started again.

I ran across the living room, thankful the carpet muffled my feet. "Wake up." I shook Sudie Gurley. She lay curled in an oval like the old woman in the moon, her gray hair in a rope on top of the sheet. "There's somebody breaking in."

"Huh?" she said. "What?"

"They're breaking in Frances Anne's window." I shook her harder.

"Call the police." She had her eyes open now and rummaged under her pillow for a flashlight. She nearly knocked the telephone off the table reaching for the receiver, but she dialed the number in the dark, told them the address and hurry, there were two women alone in the house. (This was the first time I'd been called a woman and it made me two inches taller, my arms stronger.)

*Ruth Moose*

Sudie got a broom from the kitchen. I took an oval framed portrait off the wall. I'd cream somebody with it if they came through the door. Wring them around the neck.

We heard more noises, the screen being pulled, scraped against the house. Then somebody said "ouch" and "dammit." I wanted to call my daddy, to run home and get him, but my legs wouldn't work.

We waited behind the living room door. The thumps got louder. "They're in the house," I whispered.

"Lord," Sudie said, "I wish I had a gun. I wish I had a gun."

I shook. Where was Mop? Why hadn't he barked? The dog had gone to sleep on his rug in the living room when I went to bed, but why didn't it bark? I knew. They had killed it. Poor little dog. The robbers had snatched Mop and choked it to death without a sound. Two of them against the two of us and I was only twelve. I'd spent my whole life growing up and just when I got ready to live it, somebody tried to kill me. No, I said inside. No. I saw shadows come closer. They would be through the door any minute. I held the picture higher. One, two, three...ready! I whanged it hard over the first burglar. "Oh," he hollered. "What the hell was that?"

Sudie flammed away with her broom and her robber finally held his hands up. "Don't. Stop. What's going on?" Then finally someone cried, "Mama." It sounded like Frances Anne being beaten there on the floor with the broom. "Mama! What's wrong with you? Don't you know who we are? Are you crazy?"

I turned on the lights and Sudie hugged Frances Anne and Leon, said she was sorry but we were scared half out of our minds. How had they gotten home?

"We took a taxi, Mama, what else?" Frances Anne said.

Then we heard the police car stop, saw lights flash blue and white in every window. They knocked. "Open up. It's the police."

Sudie flung open the door and two blue policemen burst into the room. "All right, fella." The taller one walked toward Leon. "Let's not have any trouble." He held handcuffs. Leon backed away.

"He's my son-in-law," Sudie said. "Wait."

"The police," Frankie said. "Mama, you called the police on your own daughter."

"I'm sorry, officers," Sudie said. "It's been a mistake. They were on their honeymoon and—"

"It's okay, lady," the pear-shaped policeman said, "as long as you know what you're doing."

"He's my son-in-law," Sudie said.

"He can be part of your family all you want," the policeman said, "but you need to get some things worked out." He let Leon go, looked at his partner, said, "I'm going to the car for a minute. Long as you got things under control here."

Frankie and Leon sat on the porch. She held Mop, half the time kissing him, half hugging him on her lap. You'd think she'd been gone from that dog a dozen years the way she acted. Leon just looked at the wall.

"Mama," Frankie said, "you embarrass me to death."

The remaining policeman took out a pencil and tried to scribble in his notebook, reached in his pocket for a penknife, and sharpened his pencil.

Sudie watched pencil shavings dust down to her floor. "You people need the name of a counselor?" the policeman asked.

"We only got married yesterday," Frankie said, kissing the dog. "We've never had a fight. Except this one. And that's just Mama. She gets scared of anything that moves in the night."

The second policeman came to the door, called his partner out. "Excuse me for a minute," he said. "I'll be right back. In the meantime see if you can't work things out among yourselves."

*Ruth Moose*

"I feel faint," said Sudie, laying her hand like a white feather across her forehead.

I went to the kitchen for a glass of water, hurried, sloshing a trail behind me as I ran back. All this was too good to miss.

"Mama," Frankie said, "you have embarrassed me all my life."

Leon looked at his toes like he was seeing them for the first time. Hangdog, was what Mama and Aunt Harriet would call it. He had a hangdog look. I don't know that he ever had anything else, but at that moment, I thought he'd just disappear, get as invisible as a ghost, if he had the power, which he didn't, so he just stared at his scuffed old tennis shoes like they had writing on them.

Frankie tucked the dog under her arm, flounced into her bedroom, and slammed the door so hard the house rocked. We heard the lock click like a final word.

Then a knock on the front door. A knock from someone who knew how to do it. One of the policemen. "Ma'am," he said, "we got a problem."

Sudie handed him her glass of water, but he refused it. "My partner—he's got this memory for faces and he thinks this Leon fellow here looks like somebody he's seen before. We'd like to take him in—nothing official—just a friendly little visit downtown to see if there's anything we need to talk about. If that's okay with you."

"No." Frankie lunged from the door. She'd been listening all the time, and she made a bear hug for Leon. "I won't let you go."

Leon gave a half smile, shrugged. He'd never been in such demand, had so much attention in his life. He eased toward the door the policeman held.

"I won't let them keep you," Frankie yelled, grabbed his arm, tried to pull him back. "I mean it. I'll break that jail down."

*Ruth Moose*

"Nobody said anything about jail, lady," said the policeman. "We're just going to have a cup of coffee and talk about some things. Real nice like."

Frankie grabbed the policeman's hat from the TV where he'd laid it earlier, flung it at him. "You want to ruin my honeymoon. The only one I'll ever have."

"It takes all kinds," the policeman said. "If there's one thing I've learned in this business…it take all kinds." Mop crawled from under the piano and barked like he'd been stepped on.

Frankie picked up the dog, buried her face in its fur, wiped her nose, and sniffled. "I'll never forgive you for this, Mama," she said, "as long as I live. "She slammed her door again.

I wondered where I was going to sleep the rest of the night. Maybe I could sit on the steps, still warm from the tracks of Leon and the policeman, and wait until day walked in.

Sudie gulped the last of her water. "May Kay." She fastened me tight to one spot with her command. I'd never heard her speak so directly before. "You are not going to say one word about this night to your mama or daddy or Harriet or Elmo or anybody for the rest of your life. Hear me?"

I said I heard her. I didn't say what I would tell and what I wouldn't.

She made a bed on the couch for me. I tried to read the rest of Nancy Drew, but fell asleep sometime before dawn looked in the glass on the door. The minute I woke and realized where I was, I couldn't wait to get home. First, I had to tell Mrs. Gurley that I enjoyed spending the night. Which was a lie. I hadn't enjoyed it. I surely never wanted another like it in my life. Did it all happen?

Sudie Gurley thumped in the kitchen. "Sit down," she said.

I sat.

*Ruth Moose*

She rolled piecrust, lifted it like a paper plate into the pie dish, then fluted it like a sculptor, turning and pinching, turning and pinching. Mama always said her pies were works of art if they did take all day to make them. I waited.

She poured in cherry filling, laid on the top crust. It had a design of stems and leaves and cherries.

"I've always thought fresh pie made the nicest breakfast in the world," she said. She wore an apron so white it hurt, with ruffles crisp as the crust. Her hair, in twisted braids, rode her head like a crown.

I knew I had to stay for breakfast or hurt her feelings. The clock ticked.

I watched the pie bubble and brown in the oven.

Sudie Gurley made a regular path to Frankie's door and back. She begged a dozen times to please come out. She tried to bribe her with pie. She said she'd forget everything that happened.

There was only silence.

I couldn't believe all I'd seen. The Police! The Police had been over at the Gurleys' in the middle of the night and hauled Leon off.

"Good Lord," Mama said. "The police? I was tired enough to sleep through thunder, but looks like I'd have heard some of all that going on."

I think she was upset because she missed the excitement or maybe she felt the neighborhood was no longer safe if she didn't have an eye and ear alert to anything out of the ordinary.

Aunt Harriet said she never for a minute had seen what Frances Anne saw in that Leon and if Sudie had thought twice she would have stopped the whole thing before it got started good.

"That's that," said Mama as though she dusted her hands and her mind of the whole affair and was ready to be on to the next thing.

*Ruth Moose*

Three months later I heard Mama and Aunt Harriet in the kitchen and something in their tone made me ease closer. When I stumped my toe on the Queen Anne leg of the huntboard and only made a small bump, they immediately stopped talking. Then Aunt Harriet started in about the Christmas bazaar and how she was the only one crocheting a thing for it. Everybody else would wait until the last minute, end up with felt and glue things that never had sold and never would and why did they vote to have a bazaar if they didn't intend to make something for it?

They had been talking about Frankie. I'd heard that much.

And how she was showing already. Maybe that's why they'd been in such an all-fired hurry to get the wedding going in the first place.

"If I'd known that," Aunt Harriet said, "I wouldn't have had any part of it. Not the first part."

"Yes, you would," Mama said, "and you know it. At times like this you have to think of the future and those innocent. We can't let them suffer the rest of their lives for something they couldn't help. Something beyond their control that happened before they were born."

Next thing I knew Aunt Harriet was crocheting baby booties and matching cap and carriage robe. "Not that it will ever have such a thing as a carriage," she said, "not with a daddy in jail, a mama that don't know the first thing about babies and where they come from and what they need when they get here." The booties weren't for the bazaar. She crocheted Christmas ornament bells for that and white snowflakes that she starched and spread on her kitchen table to dry. Or had in years past. This year everything she crocheted was blue.

"You act like you're going to be its grandmother instead of Sudie Gurley," Mama said.

*Ruth Moose*

They talked about it in front of me now as though I'd known it all along. I knew more than they thought but not as much as I wanted to.

Aunt Harriet looped blue wool around her little finger and said, "I know my Christian duty doesn't lie in some foreign country with strangers I'll never see, when someone right here on this street needs help."

In February they gave Frances Anne a baby shower, again baking cakes and making her a corsage by stuffing little socks with cotton, tying them with ribbons. They invited everybody they knew whether Frances Anne or Sudie knew them or not.

"You reckon any of Sudie's sisters will come?" Mama asked, wrapping the receiving blankets she'd bought.

"I'd faint in the front door if they did," Aunt Harriet said.

She wiped her icing spatula with two fingers, then licked them. "I know white looks better, but everybody likes chocolate. And you've got to admit"—she took the batter bowl from me—"this is not your ordinary baby shower."

"Not with the daddy in prison and the mama refusing to say the baby's even due." Mama set her lips in a straight line.

"Sudie said Frankie felt it might be bad luck."

"Bad luck! I've heard every superstition to do with any thing all my life and I've never heard that one," Mama said. "That's one of the first things anybody always asks—when's the baby due."

"Well, Frances Anne has always been funny about things."

"She gets it honest," Mama said, trying to fluff up her curly tie bow. "I bet she made up that bad luck business just to keep from having to lie."

"Lie?" I said. "What about?"

Mama cut her eyes at me, said sharply, "Premature babies that come into this world weighing ten pounds that's what." I knew the subject was closed.

March came and went, so did April. Mama and Aunt Harriet kept counting on their fingers. "I don't think she's ever going to have it," Aunt Harriet said.

"I've heard of ten-month babies," Mama said. "This could be one of those."

I hadn't seen Frankie in months. "What does she do with herself?" Mama asked Aunt Harriet once.

"Reads, watches TV."

"Anybody watches TV that much, looks like they'd go blind or crazy one," Mama said, "which ever came first."

We had Easter and I got my first shoes with one-inch heels. I was on my way to being grown-up.

"I hate to see it," Aunt Harriet said when I tried them on for her. "Next thing we know she'll be like Frances Anne Gurley."

"Over my dead body," Mama said. I figured she really meant my dead body first.

The second day of May in the middle of the morning Frances Anne had the baby before the taxi could get her to the hospital. "In the car," Mama whispered. "Curt Cleveland says he'll have to have the whole seat reupholstered."

"Just think," Aunt Harriet said, "if I'd been home instead of at the circle meeting, I would have taken her and my car would have gotten it instead."

"You read about things like this in the newspaper or see them on television, but you never think of them happening right in your own neighborhood," Mama said.

Frankie had a girl she named Diana Lee. Lee was her daddy's middle name... –

Aunt Harriet and Mama both counted on their fingers and the baby had been born nine months to the day after the wedding. "It could have been late," Mama said, trying to swallow all their months of speculation. "First babies usually are by two weeks."

But Aunt Harriet said no, this time she thought the calendar and the marriage ceremony were in direct line. And that was something. If it had to be, it had to be and we must not hold it against the baby even if she did have those same criminal little eyes just like her daddy.

"If she's raised right," Mama said, "maybe it can be got out of her."

"We'll have to do all we can," Aunt Harriet said. "And if Sudie and Frances Anne won't take that baby to church, I will. I mean it," she said, "as soon as it's old enough."

Mama opened her mouth to say something, then stopped and quietly closed it.

Neither of them ever got a chance to raise Frankie's baby "right." When it was six weeks old, Grover Gurley came driving up one day in a ten-year-old Lincoln the color of a canary and packed everything they could into it. A van he'd hired followed behind. They moved to Tryon, North Carolina, where he'd bought a farm. "Plantation." Sudie giggled, put her hand over her mouth when she said it. She almost clapped her hands when she told Mama and Aunt Harriet. "There's almost fifty acres and it has barns and horses and—"

Daddy said Grover must have won it off somebody or got in with the mob. He probably wouldn't have it long.

But he did. All of them came back to visit—Sudie, Frankie, and the baby. She had dark hair, and blue eyes round as chicory blooms. She laughed, played pattycake. I held her warm and soft against me, pushed the porch swing back and forth.

"She seems a bright little thing," Aunt Harriet said after they left.

"She doesn't take after the daddy then," Mama said, snapping the first beans from the garden. "I never trusted that man's eyes."

*Ruth Moose*

Daddy put his paper down. "Grover Gurley told me he quit gambling the minute he got that farm."

Uncle Elmo laughed. "He's really gambling now. Whether he knows it or not."

Since then there have been two families in and out both sides of the duplex where the Gurleys had lived. Aunt Harriet's piano stayed. She used to mention moving it back and Daddy and Uncle Elmo would both groan. "You want it done, you hire it," they said. "Once was enough for us."

So she hushed. "Nobody played it anyway."

"I just hope whoever lives there appreciates it," Mama said. "It was such a lovely wedding."

"Even if it didn't last," Aunt Harriet said.

*Ruth Moose*

# Peanut Dreams
# and the Blue-Eyed Jesus

WHEN SHELBY JEAN FOSTER first hears about the photograph of Jesus, she is twelve. She has long dark hair, thick bangs, and wide eyes. She has never known anyone like Ellis Nickerson in her life and she doesn't know what to think. She doesn't believe Ellis. Shelby hasn't believed a lot of what Ellis has told her, but this photograph stuff is the most unbelievable thing Ellis has said yet. Ellis says she has not only seen the photograph, but knows the girl who took the picture. Two weeks after the girl first took the picture, she died. Just like that. Ellis snaps her finger in the air.

Shelby Jean has been going to Sunday school all her life and she knows, if she doesn't know anything else, that Jesus died a long time before the camera was invented.

When Ellis sees that Shelby Jean doesn't believe her, she gets red, puffs out her cheeks, and acts huffy. That's the only word for it—huffy. Ellis says she can get the photograph and show Shelby. Then Shelby will have to believe her.

"If the girl who took the photograph is dead," Shelby Jean says, "how are you going to get it?"

"She lives in Locust Lick." Ellis lights a cigarette, tilts her head, and blows smoke in a blue cloud toward the ceiling.

Shelby Jean really doubts the whole thing then. She never heard of Locust Lick until Ellis started talking about it. And when she tried to pin Ellis down about where Locust Lick was, Ellis would say quickly, "Down in the eastern part

*Ruth Moose*

of the state."

"What's it close to?" Shelby would ask. "I mean what's the largest city?"

"Nothing," Ellis would say. "It's between nothing and close to nothing." Then she would laugh big, as if she'd made a joke. Shelby thought. that was rude, but then that was Ellis.

Shelby tried to find Locust Lick on the North Carolina map, spreading counties and roads, rivers and cities across her desk, trailing some over onto her bed. Nothing. Locust Lick wasn't even a chigger-sized dot on the map in the eastern part of the state or anywhere else. It wasn't even in the index of cities.

When she told Ellis, Ellis snorted, "I'm not surprised. Half the county don't even know where Locust Lick is. Much less the state. They never heard of Raleigh down there. For your information"—she paused, looked Shelby Jean directly in the eyes—"Locust Lick is a little slow-down place in the middle of the road between Elizabethton and Warrenington. It's got five houses, a service station, and a post office. I should know. My daddy runs both."

Shelby didn't know whether to believe Ellis or not. Locust Lick, her daddy, and all. Ellis said every seven years people remembered Locust Lick because that was where they had the festival. The Locust Festival, she added when Shelby acted like she hadn't heard.

"That's when they have the locust races," Ellis said, "and eat fried locusts to see who can eat the most. Last festival a man ate six hundred. Fried! They have chocolate-covered locusts for dessert and locust beer," Ellis went on. "Then at midnight there's a street dance and fireworks. Don't tell me you never heard of it."

Shelby hadn't. She asked her mother who said Lord knows what people would do these days. And she had heard of a locust beer. It was made from pods off a locust tree she thought grew in North Carolina but she'd never seen one that she knew.

Shelby still doesn't know whether to believe the Locust Festival, Locust Lick, and all. She doesn't know how much of Ellis to believe. It seems Ellis appeared out of nowhere. One day late in August, she and Truett Deal moved into the Hyatts' garage apartment. "It didn't look like they had six sticks of furniture," Mrs. Hyatt told Shelby's mother. "Kids. Both of them. I got my rent in advance though so I won't be out. If they move tomorrow, I won't be out anything."

The next day Ellis Nickerson, she never called herself Ellis Deal, which made Shelby's mother and Mrs. Hyatt glance at each other, knocked on the Fosters' front door. She asked if she could use their phone, then started using it twice, three and sometimes five times a day. Shelby's mother didn't mind the first few times. They were new in the neighborhood, a young couple and all. After a while she said she didn't see why Ellis came to their house, it was Hyatts she rented from. If anybody should bend over backwards to be nice to Ellis and True, it should be the Hyatts. But she never says this to Ellis, who most of the time doesn't even call back a thank-you when she finishes with the phone, just leaves and slams the door.

When Ellis comes to use the phone she is usually calling Truett, True as she always calls him, to bring her a popsicle or sack of potato chips or mostly just to ask how much longer it will be before he comes home. He never gets home before dark. It is as if Ellis thinks by calling him she can get him to hurry or change things. But he doesn't.

Shelby's mother says that if she keeps it up, she will make Truett lose his job. That George Arnold doesn't pay people to stand around his service station and talk on the phone.

In the weeks before school starts, sometimes Ellis and Shelby Jean walk to town. The town has a few old-fashioned stores that have not yet moved to the shiny new mall out on the bypass. Shelby likes to get her school supplies early. She can spend an hour choosing a notebook, clicking the rings, testing the backs of the binders. She likes to see her school supplies laid out neatly and newly bright on her desk in her bedroom. Ellis says, "You aren't going to find out what life's all about in a book, sitting in some dumb room copying words off a blackboard." She says she spent more time riding school buses than she ever did in a classroom. That's where you learn things. Who is going with who. Who did what after the last football game. Who is going after who with a shotgun. "You don't need to know anything to be married," she tells Shelby Jean with a wide smile, "except the most important thing."

"What's that?" Shelby asks.

But Ellis only licks her lips and says, "If you have to ask, you don't need to know."

Shelby knows. Her mother gave her a book with diagrams and little drawings and pictures. She has seen the film at school. The whole thing doesn't seem like such a big deal. She thinks of married people as old. Like her parents. Like the Hyatts. Like everybody in the neighborhood, except Ellis who is too smart for her own good, Shelby's mother says. In every way but where she needs to be. It'l will catch up with her," Mrs. Foster says. "Wait and see."

Every Sunday Ellis and Truett sleep late. Sometimes they never leave their apartment at all. The door stays closed, shades pulled all day, even though Mrs. Foster, Mrs. Hyatt, and others in the neighborhood have invited them again and again to the red brick Methodist church on the corner.

Shelby has gone to the church forever, it seems. Sometimes she stands under the lighted picture of Jesus in the basement hall that smells of cement and paint. She studies the picture. The kind blue eyes, thick brown hair, very dark beard. She thinks of Jesus as very good-looking. Her father, most of the men she knows and sees every day, are very

*Ruth Moose*

plain, or bald, wear glasses. Jesus looks healthy, like he has a year-round tan. She thinks it is from being outside with all those sheep. The picture is cardboard, loose from its frame. When some of the older boys go by, they take a swipe at the picture, send it askew. Shelby always waits for lightning to strike them immediately or at least a hailstorm outside when they get there. Ice balls pelting their head and them crying help, help. But nothing happens. She straightens the picture and wants to feel some good blessing fall around her shoulders.

When Shelby describes the picture to Ellis, Ellis says it sounds like the ones you can buy everywhere and a church as rich and fancy as the one on the corner ought to have something better. She's seen those Jesus pictures at the dimestore. Ellis spends a lot of time in the dimestore in town. She goes maybe two or three times a week. She walks to town just to look. Most of the time she doesn't buy anything but a cherry Coke and some Nabs, sits in the drugstore booth and sucks ice. "They got the prettiest towels in Rose's," she tells Shelby. "Yellow leaves. They'd look so good when we get our house." She slides a plastic ring from the bubble-gum machine back and forth on her finger. Truett was going to buy her a wedding band, she says, but she didn't want one of those plain old things like her mother had. She wants a real diamond. A big one. And until then she doesn't want one at all. .

In the few days before school opens, Shelby Jean walks with Ellis to town. Ellis wears cut-off jeans, a tank top Tshirt, and flat, floppy sandals. Beside her Shelby's wearing pink shorts and a frilly white blouse and bounces when she walks. She feels like an ice cream cone. Strawberry. Shelby's hair is pulled back and tied with a pink ribbon so it flips and sways. Truck drivers hoot their horns, whistle and wave. Ellis waves and whistles back, acts like she is going to run after them. When one slows and opens his door, Ellis grabs

Shelby's arm and acts like she wants to run and hide behind the nearest bush.

Ellis is pregnant now. Even though she keeps saying it, Shelby Jean doesn't know whether to believe her or not. Her stomach doesn't seem to be getting any bigger. Not in one spot. She's gaining weight all over; face, arms, hands, feet, especially her breasts. Ellis says she has grown two cup sizes in two months. Shelby Jean is still in a training bra. Ellis shows Shelby some of her black lace bras, pink satin ones, flesh-colored ones. When Shelby's mother sees them on her clothesline she says they are the tackiest things and she hopes for goodness sakes no one thinks they belong to anyone in her family. She looks at Shelby when she says this, as though Shelby is tainted being around Ellis. Mrs. Foster knows Shelby owns no underwear that is not the whitest of white. It is Mrs. Foster who lets Ellis use their clothesline after she goes to the coin washerette on the corner. Ellis pushes their laundry in a shopping cart that squeaks in all four wheels. Mrs. Foster thinks it was probably stolen, but Ellis swears True says someone left it at the station. Most of the time Shelby's mother has her own wash dried and folded and put away before Ellis gets around to hanging hers out. Then at eleven o'clock at night, Shelby sees Truett like a ghost in their back yard gathering in laundry. He always whistles some Willie Nelson tune that Shelby can hear long after he leaves.

Ellis sleeps late, then watches her "programs"—soap operas that make Shelby's mother shake her head and say, "All that will change once the baby gets here." And, "Then she'll see what she got herself into." She sighs, but Shelby hears the warning aimed at her. It has hit its mark. Shelby does not plan to let her life go in the same direction Ellis has taken, but something about Ellis interests her. Ellis seems so much much older than anyone she knows, but not old in the same way as her mother or Mrs. Hyatt.

*Ruth Moose*

Now that Shelby is in junior high she rarely sees Ellis. Shelby is caught up in school. She is trying out for cheerleader and stays after school to practice. She can do the yells and the motions that go with them, but she never kicks quite high enough. And she absolutely cannot do the split. Her mother doesn't like to see Shelby trying to do the split in the back yard. She says girls can damage themselves. They spend the rest of their lives paying for it. Shelby doesn't care if she can only be selected cheerleader. The white wool skirts are so short and cute. The red vests with the big letter A on them. And the red pom-poms. Shelby can see one hanging in her room above the mirror on her dresser with her dance card from the Spring Fling. She was one of the few fourteen-year-olds invited, but she is not chosen cheerleader and cries herself to sleep for several nights. Her mother buys her a new plaid skirt and yellow sweater, leather loafers, button bag.

On Shelby's night stand is a plastic cross that glows in the dark Mrs. Frome, her Sunday school teacher, gave every girl a cross last year for Christmas. Sometimes Shelby wakes in the night and her cross is not glowing. She wants to ask the other girls if theirs work all night, but she is afraid Mrs. Frome will overhear and be hurt. Once in a while, the thing Ellis said about the photograph of Jesus crosses Shelby's mind. She knows it is something Ellis made up because Ellis has not mentioned it since. Nor Locust Lick. Ellis was trying to impress Shelby and now that she has seen she doesn't have to, she has stopped, settled down.

One day after school, Ellis is sitting on the bottom step of their garage apartment. She invites Shelby in for a Coke and to see her new maternity clothes. Ellis has jeans with a hole cut in the stomach, a dotted blouse with little tucks and smocked yoke. She shows Shelby her baby bottle filled with pink and blue capsules she takes every day. Each time she gets her prescription filled, she gets another bottle. By the time the baby comes, she will have enough. The way she says it, by the time the baby comes or when the baby comes, Shelby feels like glancing at the door, as though the baby is expected like any guest to step through it.

It is Christmas vacation before Shelby sees Ellis again. She taps at the door and Ellis, in the same quilted robe full of burn spots, pulled threads, and dangling buttons, answers it. There are greasy dishes in the sink and the whole apartment has a sour smell. Shelby doesn't stay, but when Ellis says she has a doctor's appointment the next afternoon and Shelby has to go to the library to research a paper on the American Revolution, they decide to go together.

Shelby feels as if she ought to get Ellis a Christmas present, but she doesn't know what. The little green bush of a tree Ellis has in the middle of her table is so sad. Ellis tried to decorate it with a dozen red and blue balls, a few strands of icicles. There is one present under it.

"I know," Shelby tells Ellis. "Why don't you get your ears pierced? That will be my present to you for Christmas. And you get a set of earrings when they pierce them."

Ellis looks excited. She likes the idea. They stand in line at Belk's, and Ellis signs the release form. They select earrings. Ellis doesn't like the tiny gold button ones, but wants earrings that dangle. Shelby tells her you have to start out with the plain ones. Shelby and Ellis lean over the glass counter looking at all the earrings while they wait. The smell of alcohol is strong. When the nurse punches holes in the ears of the little girl in front of them, she lets out a scream you can hear all over the store. Tears roll down her face and wet her dress. "That didn't hurt," her mother says.

"Yes, it did," the little girl screams. "It still hurts." She holds her ears. The mother pulls her from the store, still screaming. Only one ear pierced.

Ellis steps from the line. Shelby Jean follows. "Aren't you going—?"

*Ruth Moose*

"I've changed my mind," Ellis says. "I didn't like any of those earrings anyway."

They buy popcorn from Rose's and share the bag all the way home. The popcorn is warm and fresh. Even the butter flavoring doesn't taste stale. "I bet I've gained ten pounds," Ellis giggles. "True says he doesn't care if I get big as a house. He loves me just the same."

In January, Shelby is at the drugstore. This is where all the kids from school stop first thing. There is no music, but no one could hear it if there was. Everyone screams. You can't hear yourself think. Shelby and some of the seniors she knows get a booth together. They like the tables better because the booths are old and have splinters and sometimes pick their pantyhose. She sees Ellis at the prescription counter. Ellis is wearing a bulky green coat and looks big as a truck. Her hair is oily and limp, her face blotched. The dotted top is hiked in front and wrinkled. Shelby hopes Ellis won't see her, but she does. She stops at Shelby's booth, stands With her packages and purse against her protruding stomach. She says hello, looks at Shelby with a weak little smile.

Shelby thinks Ellis looks as old as her mother or Mrs. Hyatt, yet she knows she is the same age as Leigh beside her. Or Ann across the table. Not yet seventeen. Shelby sips her Coke, stirs her ice with the straw, stares at the tabletop. The room is a field of books, letter jackets, cheerleading costumes, so noisy. She doesn't know what to say, so she mumbles something about the crowd. Her friends stare at her, their eyes amused, asking how do you know this person? Who is she? Ellis smiles and waits. She brushes her hair back and Shelby sees her nails are chipped. Ellis used to spend hours on her nails until they looked like pictures in magazines. She isn't wearing any lipstick. Ellis shifts her packages. She stands on one foot, then shifts her weight and bulk to the other.

Shelby feels hot. Her mouth is dry and all her friends are waiting for her to say something. Ellis drops her smile into a look that hits the floor like something Shelby can hear. Her eyes get dull and hurt. She turns and waddles through the crowd.

Shelby watches her back until it is out the door and down the street. Out of sight. She can still feel the pain in Ellis's face, the asking. Almost the please in her voice and eyes. Why didn't Shelby invite her to sit down? She should have asked. She should have introduced Ellis to everyone. She could have done that. It wouldn't have hurt...but what would her friends have thought? And Ellis was probably too big to get in the booth anyway. Still Shelby knows if she doesn't do something, she will feel that hurt. So she grabs her books, the rest of her Coke, and hurries out.

When she catches up with Ellis, neither of them says anything. They walk two blocks in the wind and silence. After a while Ellis rummages in her packages and opens a clear plastic purse full of chocolate candies. Peanut Dreams. From the drugstore? Shelby's favorite. Ellis eats one, crunching the peanuts loudly. Then she eats two more. Three. Finally she hands one to Shelby, who tries to refuse. Ellis forces it into Shelby's hand. The candy is sticky, lumpy with nuts, whitish on top. It looks stale and possibly wormy. It smells like mothballs and the oil Rose's uses to sweep their floors. And cardboard boxes. Shelby never eats anything from the Rose's counter. Those open glass bins. You don't know who has had their hands in there, her mother says. Or where their hands have been. Shelby doesn't want to hurt Ellis's feelings. "Eat it," Ellis says.

But Shelby cannot.

Ellis eats the rest of the way home, pushing crumpled red papers from each piece back into the plastic purse as she empties them. "Probably make my face worse," she says, her voice flat and tired. "I'm already retaining fluid."

Shelby's candy has melted in her hand, stuck her fingers together. If it were forced down her throat she would immediately throw it up. That would hurt Ellis more. She slides it into the deepest corner of her coat pocket where she hopes it won't stain through. At least not until she gets home.

Ellis doesn't talk about the baby today. Nor True. She used to tell Shelby being married was the sweetest thing in the world. Today she doesn't talk much at all.

In March when Ellis has her baby, Shelby hears her mother and Mrs. Hyatt talking. A little boy. Not little really. It weighs almost ten pounds. And Ellis didn't have the easy time of it she thought she was going to have. "You never do," Shelby's mother says and Mrs. Hyatt quickly adds, "Amen to that." They have bought receiving blankets for the baby. They take their gifts to Ellis along with a meatloaf and casserole of scalloped potatoes. When they come back they talk about what a mess the apartment is. Newspapers and dirty clothes everywhere. Everywhere. Mrs. Hyatt says she is glad she didn't see the bathroom. The sight of that kitchen was enough. They talk about calling Ellis's parents—or the county health department.

Shelby doesn't know who they call and she doesn't know what she can do. She wants to see the baby. She has even bought a pair of white felt beaded moccasins for it. They have been in a clear plastic case on her dresser for several weeks now.

When she gets home from school the next day, there is a rusty red pickup truck parked in front of Ellis's garage apartment. It has wooden rails on the sides and something about "Farm and Home Supply" painted on the doors. Then below it, "Locust Lick, N.C." So there really is such a place, Shelby thinks as she changes from jeans to a wool jumper she wore a lot last year. It is so tight she can hardly get it zipped, but it looks dressier than jeans. She wraps the moccasins in white tissue and puts a blue bow on top. At Ellis's door, she knocks so timidly she has to knock again. A large woman in a sweatshirt and black polyester slacks opens it. She is wearing an apron and wipes her hands as she invites Shelby in. Shelby sees a man in a hat in the brown chair Ellis usually sits in to watch her soaps. The man is watching a game show on television or asleep. He doesn't turn around or speak. The woman says she is Ellis's mother and takes Shelby to the bedroom.

Ellis is in a gown in bed. There is a wicker basinette beside her and she gets up when she sees Shelby, smiles and takes the present. "Look at my big boy," she says, "while I open this."

Ellis holds the little shoes up and laughs, then unwraps the baby's foot from the blanket and compares them. The shoes that looked little on Shelby's dresser now look huge. They laugh and Ellis covers the baby back up. It is red and wrinkled. Shelby doesn't know what to say. "Isn't he beautiful?" Ellis says. "My big old boy."

She gets back in bed, arranges her pillows. "Don't ever have a baby," she says. "They do awful things to you. It wasn't having the baby that was so bad. It was the stuff they did to you first."

Ellis has a new robe, but Shelby sees one burn spot on the front already and her hair looks tangled and wild. Her eyes dart back and forth like minnows in a jar.

Shelby doesn't know what to do. She doesn't want to be in this room alone with Ellis. She has never seen Ellis like this, and when Ellis's mother comes in to ask if she would like a cup of coffee, Shelby is relieved. She says she really has to go and Ellis's mother says she understands. That Ellis doesn't need to wear herself out, but she is glad she has met some of Ellis's friends.

Some? Shelby thinks on the way home. There was nobody else. And she didn't really think of herself as a friend to Ellis. She was just someone who lived in the neighborhood closer to her age than her mother or Mrs. Hyatt. She and Ellis never did any fun things friends do. Not movies and football games, pajama parties, the drugstore—not any of those things.

After church on Sunday, Shelby has helped her mother with the dishes and started a report on the French and Indian War when her brother tells her someone is at the door to see her. She can't imagine who.

It is blustery cold, but Ellis and her mother are on the porch with the baby wrapped in a thick blue blanket. You can't even see his eyes nor face but the blanket wiggles so Shelby knows the baby is in there somewhere.

"I told Mama when she came to bring the photograph," Ellis says, "and she did."

For a minute Shelby thinks Ellis means a photograph of the baby. When Ellis hands the photograph to her, she can't understand it. The photograph is old. One of the corners is bent, another missing. All Shelby sees is black and white shapes, like a puzzle or shadow. "The photograph of Jesus. I told you about it," Ellis says, "the one the girl who lived in Locust Lick took."

"Oh." Shelby remembers, but she still can't see anything in the photograph.

"Right there." Ellie points. "See the beard. And hair. And his robe." All Shelby can see are two dots someone has made with a ballpoint pen.

"Eyes," Ellis says.

Shelby squints. For a moment she thinks she can see a figure in white with arms outstretched and a beard. But she isn't sure. It's just shapes. She hands it back to Ellis.

"I told you Mama would bring it," Ellis says, then adds that she is going home for a while.

"Till she gets straightened out," her mother says.

In the red truck someone honks the horn and they yell they are coming. To keep his shirt on. Ellis grinds out a cigarette on the Fosters' freshly painted porch. Shelby knows it will

*Ruth Moose*

leave a scorch mark and her mother will say good riddance to bad rubbish.

Shelby tells Ellis goodbye. Then calls after Ellis, "I'll see you when you get back. Maybe it won't be so cold. Brrr."

She wraps her arms around herself and shivers, runs back into the house.

For the next few weeks there are lights in the bedroom of the apartment, then none at all. True has moved out. Left. Gone. Just like that.

"Where did he go?" Shelby's mother asks Mrs. Hyatt.

"Who knows?" Mrs. Hyatt shrugs. "All I know is, he didn't leave owing me rent. If there's one thing I've learned all these years, it's get your money in advance."

One night as Shelby is almost asleep she remembers the photograph. That the girl who took it died two weeks later. She wonders if because she looked at it, she will die. Every night, she puts on a fresh nightgown and sleeps on her back so her hair will not be mussed. She gets a crick in her neck and makes a failing grade on a math test. Jimmy Reese invites her to his party. Nothing else happens.

*Ruth Moose*

# The Women's Club

THEY WANT TO do away with October...it's convention month and nobody is at the meeting anyway. And January. Do away with it too. January comes so soon after Christmas. Everybody agrees. Their voices seem to say the nerve of that January coming so soon after Christmas whether it's wanted or not. January will be done away with unless someone speaks up. Anyone opposed?

No one is really opposed, but one member in a navy suit with white blouse of long frilly lace at neck and wrists waves her thin many-diamonded old hand. "January is Lee and Jackson month, Madam President, and I don't think we can do away with them."

Madam President says no one said anything about doing away with Jackson and Lee, just moving them to another month.

"State won't like it," another member mumbles.

"I don't care what State likes and doesn't like," says Madam President, her nose slightly wrinkled, pencil poised.

She seems about to strike the papers on the table beneath. "State isn't the one who has to do everything. Everything! Is there more discussion?" Her pencil checks out the room.

"What about June?" Another member leans forward on her cane. "That's always been Jefferson Davis month and I don't think we can change that without State saying something."

*Ruth Moose*

"Nobody," says Madam President Lucille Eppworth, "nobody said a word about doing away with June. If you'd just listen...just listen before you speak, you'd know which months are being done away with." As president of the chapter, Lucille wears a red, white, and blue ribbon pinned to her left breast. It dangles to her waist, gleaming with ten gold stars that dance in the candlelight. Candles for the Installation service.

"Anyone opposed?" Lucille says again. "Now's the time to speak up if you are. Not next week. Not next year. Not when it's your turn to hostess and you've got the month we tried to do away with. Speak up now so you won't grumble later."

No one opposes and the motion carries. Savannah Beauknight, the youngest member in both club years and age, sits in the last seat in the last row. Lucille bangs the gavel when she announces with vigor and a little smile that the motion carried. Savannah expects to see Lucille gather something in her arms (the motion?) and set it properly down. But she doesn't. Lucille goes on to the awarding of scholarships. The first one goes to her own "dear niece and namesake, a darling girl talented in every way and smart to boot." Lucille beams as she calls the girl forward.

"Just like her aunt." Lucille's vice-president, Jolene Husucker, smiles at the table. Jolene is cool in green linen and pearls.

The niece, Drucilla, goes forward. She's seventeen and fresh as a rose. Pert and pink and yes, even bright-looking, Savannah thinks. Drucilla wears a hat that matches her dress, the only hat in the room. Odd, Savannah thinks, because most of these women have worn hats on most occasions most of their lives. She mentally puts hats on them, feathered red ones, white sailor straws, wide brims with fruit and flowers and ribbon trims. She can't think why she is at this meeting. Yes, she can. Because she still reacts to Lucille Eppworth as she did when she was in the sixth grade and bit her nails. Miss Eppworth was school principal, who did things like nail examinations and behind-the-ear checks. You never knew when she'd come to your classroom. Savannah remembers wanting to sit on her pink and stubby fingers to hide them from Miss Eppworth's eyes.

When Savannah and Charles moved back to Elliston, Lucille called. "We need you, dear," she said. "So many of our members have passed." Passed? Savannah thought of grades first, then realized with a little shock that wasn't what Lucille meant at all.

"We don't seem to be getting any new members," Lucille went on. "Young women today stay too busy for their own good and don't feel their obligations and responsibilities to their communities like they should."

Guilt. Lucille ladled it out. "Your grandmother was one of our dearest members and though your mother never joined us, we so hope you will."

Savannah joined, was installed, pinned, hugged until she felt she reeked of Estee Lauder in all twenty-eight flavors.

"Energy," Lucille said. "We need some of that energy to help us out."

So far Savannah hadn't seen they needed anything but her dues. She'd been in line at the A&P when Lucille approached her from Produce, a honeydew like a newborn in her arms. "Sweetie, I know you've forgotten…it's so easy to let time slip right past…your dues come up this month. If you'll give me yours right now, I'll see Irene gets them on time and you won't be a minute late."

Savannah planned to drop out. She'd been to one meeting all year. The meeting where they showed slides of the Grand Canyon one of the members had taken from a mule. Everything tilted and blurred. But Lucille blocked the aisle at the A&P with her hand out, purse open. Savannah wrote her check for dues.

They made her Chaplain when she missed the next meeting. "Your grandmother could pray the sweetest prayers ever heard," Lucille said, "and I know you learned at her knee."

Lord, thought Savannah, get me out of this. "I'm really not very good . . ."

"Of course you are, darling," Lucille said. "And we'll all help you. It's a wonderful way to start. We need you so much.".

At the next meeting (the time was ungodly—Friday afternoons at three o'clock—Savannah led the Collect. It was printed on little cards with Chaplain in italics, then Response in bold. They all pledged three times. The United States flag, the state flag, and finally the Confederate flag, "in remembrance." And because they didn't know if Savannah would be present, Randleman Sipes had written a prayer just in case. Savannah was relieved. Off the hook for another month.

Then she honestly forgot the next meeting. She bumped into Zillah Mayfield at the post office, who clasped her forearm and said steelily, "We missed you at the meeting."

"Meeting?" Savannah couldn't think what meeting.

"The chapter, of course, darling," Mrs. Mayfield said.

"You're our Chaplain, you know. And when you don't come, someone else has to take charge."

Six people pushed around Savannah, still held in the iron grip of Mrs. Mayfield. "I forgot," she said.

"Forgot?" Mrs. Mayfield said. "Forgot!" Blue tears gathered in the corner of each pale eye. Oh, my dear, we mustn't ever do that."

She let go as Savannah pulled toward the door. "Promise to try to do better next month, dear." Mrs. Mayfield's silver curls ringed her head, each sculpted and individual. Light shone through them in a halo effect.

Savannah would have forgotten again, had a member not called to remind her. "May we expect you tomorrow?"

*Ruth Moose*

Savannah gulped, "I don't know if . . ."

"It's our covered dish and last meeting of the year. We install new officers and I want our attendance to be good."

She'd said the two magic words. Last meeting. Savannah said yes and forgot again until noon. No time to make anything, she really had a good excuse this time, but she kept thinking last meeting, last meeting, so she quickly put together a Three Ps Casserole, dropped on some grated cheese, ran it under the broiler and shoved it into a silver dish, then dashed out the door. Somehow she had a feeling the food didn't count as much as the container.

There were a dozen cars in the parking lot. Last meeting, Savannah remembered. One car's motor idled with the doors locked and no one in the driver's seat. Savannah tried to turn the ignition off, but couldn't get in. She asked in the kitchen, but no one seemed to know whose car it was until Lucille bustled toward the meeting room. "That's Lauraellen's car. She does that all the time. It's a wonder that car hasn't run off and left her, or tried to. Give me the keys." She went to a woman in red silk. "Let me go see to it."

They formed a serving line, pushed Savannah in front. "You go first. You come so seldom, you're like a guest," Lucille chirped.

Savannah took a corner table and placemat of a white columned azalea-blooming plantation. She was joined by her high school music teacher, who hadn't seemed to age as much as grow smaller and speak slower, more precisely. "You know I wrecked my car," Mrs. Priester says.

"No." Lauraellen Mayfield leans across the table. "I bet you went to sleep at the wheel."

"How did you know?" Mrs. Priester bends her head, ashamed.

"Because that's what I always do," Lauraellen says with a jerk of her chin. "Last time I just steered right off the road and even in my sleep I turned that curve as pretty as you please."

"In your sleep?" Mrs. Priester raises an eyebrow. "Really?"

"If I hadn't, I would have gone right into a tree. I was sound asleep, but I knew to turn that wheel." Lauraellen turns an imaginary wheel in the air. "And there was Harold sitting right beside me all the time reading the map. He didn't know we'd gone off the road until we stopped."

"What did you do then?" Savannah asks. She has taken a mound of chicken salad onto her plate. It looks like wallpaper paste. It tastes like wallpaper paste. She can't possibly eat it.

Lauraellen stops her fork and stares at Savannah. "Why honey, this was in Florida. I just drove right back up on that road like I'd never been off and nobody knew the difference."

"Oh." Savannah can't think what else to say. She has swallowed the mouthful of chicken salad.

"I had three people with me," Mrs. Priester says.

"And nobody said a word," Mrs. Priester repeats. "Until we all got out and looked at what I'd done."

"Oh," Savannah says again, drinking tea to wash down the wallpaper paste that is stuck in her throat. Tea so thick with sugar it coats her tongue. She waves away offers of dessert. Pound cake. Miss Ann made it. Her mama's recipe. "We can always depend on our Miss Ann for dessert," Lucille says loudly and everyone laughs. Miss Ann is also a music teacher. She loves to emphasize that she teaches privately and has her own studio downtown. "I could never use my home," she said once to Savannah. "That wouldn't do at all. You simply have no privacy, and privacy is one of the basic needs."

Miss Ann is nearly seventy, lives alone in a house that looks down over the town and can't be seen except in winter for the high unpruned magnolia trees around it. Trees and a tall wrought-iron fence. Miss Ann wears white cotton socks with sandals and a blue bow in her hair. She blushes as pink as her scalp when Lucille says she has never tasted a pound cake as good as Miss Ann makes.

When the dishes are returned to the kitchen (they never use paper plates; never have, never will) Savannah puts chairs back in rows, folds up a table, the only one left standing—hers. Somehow everything has been whisked back into place in the blink of an eye. Savannah slides the table toward the hall closet where others are stored behind louvered doors. "Darling, you are so sweet to help." Lucille flies past, taking off her organdy apron as she goes. "But that's the table we always leave out for the guest registry. Leave it there for now, that's all right…for now."

Savannah puts the table up again and by the double front doors underneath the shiny photograph of Miss Agnes Overmyer. Miss Agnes passed last year at ninety-eight. She had been the one to donate land for building the woman's club. "We needed a little place to ourselves," she said, "for little meetings, parties and bridge."

"But we paid for the building," Lucille has always been quick to point out. "Every cent, every dollar, and it wasn't easy."

"How?" Savannah asks.

"Why, honey, don't you know? Every way we could. That's how you do things. You have bridge benefits and bake sales and more bake sales until before you know it, the thing's paid for." Lucille's eyes don't stop moving the whole time she talks. Nor her hands. She's like a hummingbird.

The officers of the woman's club are installed by Mrs. Priester, whose musical voice Savannah remembers rolling along in folksongs over and over, silver pitchpipe sounding the first twangy note. As each officer is called, Lucille serving as Madam President again, the green linen lady vicepresident,

Lauraellen Mayfield secretary—again. And Irene Hautman, treasurer—again. They go through program chairman and corresponding secretary until every member is standing at the front of the room being installed. Only Savannah sits in the audience. She is the audience. She wants to laugh, but it is like the chicken salad, stuck in her throat. Instead she coughs. The ladies blink. It is as if she has taken their photograph. This is the moment later. They move from the ranks and back to their lives. Savannah takes the photograph home and for a long time finds it hard to flip past the images lodged like a slide caught crosswise. in a projector, light cutting off the corners and edges until the whole thing rounds like an eye. The projector fan hums in her head and the dust motes of all time dance, dance like things alive in the air.

*Ruth Moose*

# The Girl Who Looked Like Irma Budd's Little Sister

THE WOMAN IN the red coat with fur collar, wind whipping her waxy cheeks, walked through the three o'clock throngs of children knotted in front of Fairview Elementary. At the corner, she turned on her heels like a sentry, walked back again. Ted Hartman, the bus driver, Ronnie Apple, the cop at the crossing, the kids, some with books balanced on their heads, others playing keep-away with a purple toboggan, acted as if they didn't see her. The woman walked as invisibly through them as a spirit, untouched by their scuffling, yelling, and screaming. At the opposite corner she wheeled, walked through the crowd again.

Across the street, Mary Emmett Spratt stood on a stool by her bay window. "That wind won't do Rosalie Ritchie—"

"—any good," said Loveda, Mary Em's sister. Lov sat at the table cracking pecans. A gray wool plaid skirt covered her legs in folds to the floor where toes of her embroidered black slippers peeked out like kittens.

"Especially not in—" Mary Em glanced out the window.

"—her condition." Lov squeezed the silver jaws of the nutcracker until the pecan exploded, popped hulls that landed like insects on Mary Em's red braided rug.

"I wish you wouldn't do that." Mary Em studied the part in Lov's gray hair, the woven figure-eight braids across the back of her neck.

Lov wrinkled her forehead like a paper fan. "It's the only way I know to get the meat out."

*Ruth Moose*

Mary Em meant she wished Loveda wouldn't always finish her sentences for her. It got tiresome. A person had a right to finish something she started, her own thoughts even. It's still my house, she wanted to say a dozen times a day. Lov had retired from her Civil Service job in Washington six months before and moved in with Mary Em. There was no reason she shouldn't—with Hilbert dead and Mary Em rattling around in that big old house. No reason at all.

"Every day"—Mary Em taped another Christmas card to the red streamer attached to the cornice—"rain, shine, snow—Rosalie's out there, back and forth in front of that school." Lov's cards covered the left half of the streamer. Cards from people Mary Em didn't know. Cards with strange names that made Lov coo and give her silly laugh. "People cut down their mailing this year," Mary Em said. Her end of the streamer was a few cards scattered as patchwork. It looked skimpy even after she put up some cards from last year. If Lov had so many friends, why didn't she go live with them?

"I feel so sorry for her." Lov shifted the basket in her lap. Pecans piled high, like little brown eggs a wooden bird might have laid. "Rosalie Ritchie is young to have been through so much. Losing first that boy and now this one."

"What do you mean, this one?" Mary Em watched the tiny treadmill figure of the red-coated Rosalie. "She ain't had it yet."

"But it's dead." Lov threw a shriveled nutmeat into the trash. "The doctors say there's no chance it's still alive. And she won't give it up. Won't let her baby be taken."

"When did you find this out?" Mary Em pressed her nose to the cold glass that frosted so quickly she couldn't see anything but a blur of colored dots where the children stood, a smear of cars, black fumes of bus exhaust, and the wavering figure of Rosalie, walking, walking. "She looks like—"

"—Irma Budd's little sister," Lov said. "I've thought so too for a long time. There's something about her—the way she holds her head, that dark hair . . ."

Irma Budd had been Mary Em's best friend in high school, killed in a car accident the night of the spring cotillion. Her little sister had a nervous breakdown afterward, was "sent off."

"Whatever happened to—?" Lov lifted out the perfect pecan half, held it with long, tong-like fingers.

"Darlene Budd? I don't remember." Lov had such long fingers and Papa spent a fortune on piano lessons for her. What did she do with them? Once in a while Mary Em heard her out in the cold, dark old music room picking out onefinger tunes. Recital pieces children played. It helped her typing, Mama used to say, and that got her that good job. Manual dexterity. "If you're going to do that"—Mary Em wiped the frosted window with her sleeve—"be careful of your nails. I read in the paper you could sell them for so much a quarter-inch."

"I got a fortune then." Lov held her hands to the light, spread her fingers, white nails shining like candle flames.

"When did you hear about Rosalie Ritchie's baby being dead?" Mary Em shuddered. She couldn't imagine carrying a dead thing around inside you. How awful.

"Somebody who lives next door to the Ritchies told it at Circle last week."

"I didn't hear it and I—"

"—keep up," Lov said. "Yes, I know you do."

"I must have been out of the room." Mary Em put away the stool she'd stood on. "I sure didn't hear anything said about Rosalie Ritchie." Several cars clogged the crosswalk and a cluster of kids chased each other around a stop sign, swatted each other with books. A boy walked by carrying a trumpet case. Rosalie passed again.

"As cold as it is," Mary Em said, "nobody should be out who doesn't have to be out. The radio said ice this morning. She could—"

*Ruth Moose*

A camellia bush rubbed against the house, shook in the wind. If there was a hard freeze tonight, the blossoms would be killed, turn brown and rot on the stems.

"There won't be any blooms." Lov shook the bowl of pecan halves.

"If you're planning to make fruitcakes, they should have been done weeks ago."

"I know." Lov held a large nutmeat shaped like a skinny heart. "I'm planning to make fudge and leave the nuts whole. That makes it twice as luxurious."

"Fudge." Mary Em wiped dust off the table with the side of her hand. "Don't leave any lying around here." Rich chocolate stuff. She could taste it thinking about it, so good, the sweetness melting down her throat. Inches added to her like another layer of clothes. "Give it away," Mary Em snapped. "And remember whose money paid for the sugar and stuff that went into it."

Lov's faded blue eyes darkened. "Why, Tigee—"

Mary Em hadn't been called her baby name in years. She kept sweeping dust with her hand.

"You know I'd put both our names on the gift enclosure."

Lov emptied hulls from her lap into the wastebasket.

She's never gained a pound, Mary Em thought, taking the wastebasket to the back porch. And those long skirts she wears, the fringed things—all my friends talk. Why can't she wear pantsuits like the rest of us? Why does she have to be so fancy?

"That woman needs help." Lov stood by the window now.

"Sent off." Mary Em washed her hands.

"No, they don't do that any more. People aren't institutionalized so much these days. Why add strange surroundings, uproot them when there's no need? She's suffering pain as real as any disease."

*Ruth Moose*

"She didn't show her grief." Mary Em wiped an already clean counter. "That's what some said who went in when the boy died." Jimmy Ritchie was killed last spring, only a few months after the family moved here. He was pushed, they said fell, down a stairwell, hit his head and died. Weak blood vessel. The doctors said it would have happened anytime. Mary Emmett. had seen the stretcher carried out the glass doors of the school, slid into the quiet ambulance. She knew somebody was dead when Charlie Swanner didn't burn his red light, blow the siren. He'd do it for the least reason, especially after he first got the job driving the ambulance. Maybe it got old for him.

"It's like she's pacing," Lov said. "That's so frightening." People said Rosalie Ritchie never shed a tear, at least not where anybody could see her, but went on with that funeral like it was all somebody else's child. Then when school. started back this fall, here she came every day with a look on her face like she didn't know what world she was in.

Lov dropped the drapery. "Let's invite her in. She needs something hot—tea."

Mary Em was a coffee person herself. Before Lov came she kept a pot always hot on the back of the stove. Now it was a fat teakettle for hot water. Lov drank odd teas, ones she ordered in tins from companies that kept sending her brochures, catalogs showing all kinds of expensive things. Things people could get along perfectly well without. Mary Emmett always had and she didn't think she'd missed much.

Lov tapped the window. "Maybe I can get her attention now that everyone's gone. If she'll just look this way. . ."

Mary Em put the kettle on, clicked the button to HI.

Lov lifted her skirt, started toward the enclosed porch.

"I'll just—"

"I'll go." Mary Em pushed past her sister, slammed the kitchen door so hard the glass rattled and the wreath kept banging against it like a muffled clock striking.

"Mrs. Ritchie," Mary Em called. "Dear—" She waved across the street to the woman walking.

Finally the woman glanced in Mary Em's direction. "Can you come—?" Mary Em yelled.

The woman stepped off the curb, started stiffly toward her, and slipped into the path of a blue Page's Delivery truck cruising the wrong way down the one-way street.

"Watch…out," Mary Em: called. "Do be…careful."

The truck screamed to a stop, past the crushed rag doll of a woman, who lay in her red coat with her arms and legs at odd angles, anxious eyes frozen in her face.

"It's—" Mary Em put her hands over her face.

"—not your fault." Lov came up behind her, laid her arm across Mary Em's shoulders, drew her close.

They were standing there when the first faint scream of the teakettle started and got shrill, hurting louder.

Ruth Moose

# The Pink Bed

THILDALEE TOLD RONNIE she had to have her bed. Just had to have it. She sat cross-legged on the edge of the tub, smoking. She'd gone three nights without sleeping, two weeks before that of light and fitful sleep. It was beginning to show. Bags under her eyes were dark as pansy petals. And she felt wrung out, limp, like an old T-shirt used to mop with, flung across the clothesline, sour and dry.

"Over my dead body," Ronnie said. "You know that's what it will be. No way I'm going into another man's house when he's not home and steal his furniture." Ronnie shaved without looking in the mirror. With his cheeks and neck soaped he looked like an old man with a white beard. Is that the way he'd look when he got old? Thildalee didn't want to think about that now. That night when she had met Ronnie in the diner and gone back to his motel, she'd thought he had more muscles than anyone she'd ever seen. "Driving a Cat every day for fifteen years will make you or break you," he said.

"What makes you say it's his furniture?" She reached for a Q-tip, poked her ear. "I'll have you know that's my bed. Always has been, always will be. I can't sleep right in anything else."

"Seems to me anybody who's up and down as much as you are every night don't need a bed anyway."

"That's what I'm trying to tell you." She threw her cigarette butt in the commode. "I can't sleep without my bed."

*Ruth Moose*

"Aw come on, Sugar Foot." He reached around, tweaked her toe. "You know it's not the bed anyway—it's who's in it."

"Ouch," she said.

"That didn't hurt one bit. You're the touchiest thing I've ever seen in the mornings. A regular old cactus puss."

"You'd be touchy too, if you didn't sleep."

"Get your mind on something else," Ronnie said twenty minutes later when he left for work, coffee mug in one hand, lunchbox in the other. "It ain't going to happen. Not by me anyway."

She leaned out the door for his kiss. He smelled like some spice she remembered as being Christmasy …that and orange. He smelled like her father. That made her throat ache, her chest tighten.

He raced the motor, plowed the dust-colored pickup in a cloud down the road.

"Get your mind on something else," she mimicked, pulled on jeans and a black Coors sweatshirt, hung her nightgown on a hook in the bathroom. That red plastic hook was one of the things she'd added to the doublewide since they bought it. There wasn't much you could add. Everything came as a package, furniture, curtains, shades; Ronnie made them throw in the pictures on the wall, silk flowers on the coffee table, mugs and ceramic canister set in the kitchen. He bought the display model and by durn he wanted it delivered just like he saw it or he'd take his money somewhere it was good.

"Oh, it's good here," the sweating salesman had said. "Right here." Three days later everything was delivered. That was two weeks ago and every night Thildalee slept less. All Ronnie could talk about was that king-size bed and the bathroom with two tubs and all those mirrors. All she thought about was her bed—her pink upholstered heart-shaped headboard she'd had since she was twelve. Her daddy made it for his little girl. He'd cut out the wood and had it upholstered in the brightest pink marbled plastic she could find. "Don't you think it's bright?" Mama asked. "Yes, ma'am," Thildalee answered. "And that's what I want. Exactly what I want." It was a prettier bed than any movie star had, Marilyn Monroe or Elizabeth Taylor or anybody. When she added white eyelet spread and pillows the whole thing looked like a valentine.

Deane never minded her bed. "You sleep with me," she said the first night they came back from Myrtle Beach. "You sleep in my bed." He smiled, reached to turn back the spread. Never said a word. Deane was as easy-going as anything—at first. So how come in three years a man could change so much? Day and night, there was that much difference to him. One day she was all he ever wanted, the next he came in and cried all over her nightgown. But not until after she'd called every cop in town. They knew. Had a running list. Kept it quiet and took their Christmas bonus every year like they'd earned it.

Ronnie wasn't going to help, Thildalee could see that as she cranked the Mustang. First car she'd ever owned, only car she wanted to own. Her daddy had rebuilt it, repainted it new blue, the works. Let her pick out the seats.

At least there was Mama, Thildalee thought as the Mustang's muffler popped and roared. She'd have to tell Ronnie again how her muffler was acting. Trouble was he wouldn't hear her. "I might as well tell the table," she thought.

Mama was putting out tomato plants in the garden. She straightened up, dusted her hands on her hips. "You would come when I finished," she said. "Ten minutes earlier and I'd let you set out the last half-dozen. Make sure you haven't forgotten how."

Thildalee and Deane never had a garden. Mama gave her a tomato plant to put in a whiskey barrel once. Thildalee planted petunias and the tomato plant got crowded out. Plus it got the wilt, blossom-end rot, droops, white mites, black spot, everything a plant could get. "You spray things," Mama said. "Any fool can grow one tomato plant."

"Not this one," Thildalee said.

In the kitchen Mama handed her a glass of iced tea, took a long drink from her own, tilted back her head, said, "Ahhhh, I needed that."

"I need a favor," Thildalee said. She wanted lemon, but she wasn't going to ask for it. "My bed's still at Deane's."

"So?" Mama said. "What else is new? Any woman who takes off in the middle of the night wearing nothing but her nightgown and not taking a stitch with her, left more than her bed behind."

"I don't care about all the other stuff," Thildalee said. "Besides, Deane put everything that had my name on it in a mini-warehouse. I can go get it any time I want. He told me so."

"Maybe the bed's in that."

"I checked," Thildalee said. "You think I'd come asking if I hadn't?"

"I think you'd better leave well enough alone. What do you want the old thing for? It's never been pretty. Your daddy didn't get the sides even. Left side was always higher."

"It's mine," Thildalee said, "and I just want it." She ended up leaving her glass on the table. Any other time she'd put it in the dishwasher, but today she wasn't doing one thing for people who refused to do a single thing to help her. Wouldn't lift a finger. If her daddy was alive, he'd help and they'd have that bed out of Deane's house, loaded on somebody's truck, and be down the highway before now. Two months ago, one morning at the mill, they said her daddy took a coffee break, went to sit on the stoop in the sun, and just kept sitting there. When somebody thought to call him, he was dead. Heart attack. "Went in a wink," the doctor said. "He never knew a thing."

*Ruth Moose*

Thildalee drove around awhile, through the square, past all the empty-eyed stores downtown, past the new shopping center with a big J.C. Penney's and Rose's just completed. Maybe she'd get a job selling lingerie at Penney's. That might be something she'd like. She imagined herself unpacking all lacy and silky things, easing and patting them onto hangers.

She cruised by her old high school where everybody seemed to be in class or out doing gym on the athletic field. She bet old Miss Wilkins was still teaching Home Management, making those girls bake cakes from scratch when the minute they got out of her lab, they'd buy all the mixes they could get their hands on.

She and Deane met in Home Management. He was the one who baked the best coconut cakes in the whole world. That and the fact he could iron must have had something to do with her marrying him. His shirt collars always looked so smooth she wanted to press her cheek against them. And he smelled clean, like soap and starch and sheets when her mama dried them on the line in summer.

Thildalee parked across the street from the drugstore, went in and ordered a fountain Coke, sat in a back booth carved with the names of everybody from Eatonsville. There was probably Adam Loves Eve, that booth was so old. She traced carved hearts and arrows, initials, nicknames...Who was Pep? And Duck Frommer? Crazy Legs? Why did girls never have nicknames? Maybe it was all jock and locker room jokes anyway. Girls in locker rooms spent all their time taking showers, shampooing hair, blow-drying and hot-combing. Maybe hair made the difference.

She finished her Coke, bought a bottle of some new shampoo called "Sure Enough"—which sounded more like a deodorant—and left.

She cruised by her old neighborhood...just in case. She didn't know in case what, but just in case. The Bakers still hadn't fixed their smashed mailbox. The dead pines in Miller's yard weren't down, just looked browner, more dead. Tony Braswell's bike lay flung next to the street where anybody could steal it in a second. If they wanted the rusty old thing. Maybe nobody did.

And Deane's car was in the drive. What was he doing home in the middle of the morning? Was he sick? She started to pull in behind it, go in. She still had her key. Instead she decided to drive around the block. Maybe he took a day off to do errands, take the dog in to be clipped, do the laundry, shampoo the rug, go to an afternoon movie. Sometimes he took a sick day to do those things. Not that the company ever found out. They'd have a fit. Him out hosing off his car when he was supposed to be in bed with the "bug." But usually those were half-days he took, not mornings. Not unless he really was sick.

She rounded the corner when she saw the two of them come out, smiling and walking all hugged up. It was sickening. Two adults acting so icky. That's all you could call it, sickening…icky. Lucky Thildalee was going slow so she could pull in the Braswells' empty carport, get the Mustang out of the way before Deane spotted it. Not that he was looking at anything but that guy, whoever he was, all long legged in short shorts cut up at the thigh. Not the kind of thing a decent person wore out the door. Shorts like that might be right for some workout club or the YMCA, but you didn't go around in public for everybody to see everything you had—unless you were advertising.

Deane didn't even open his car for his "friend." Both of them got in on the driver's side and stayed stuck together as he backed out.

That's when Thildalee made her move. She was out of Braswells' and parked across her own drive, blocked Deane's car before he got it in reverse good.

What's all this about?" He got out and came around her indow after he stopped honking and saw who she was. "It's about my bed," she said.

"What about your bed?"

"I want it," she said.

"Is that all?" He ran his hand through his uncombed hair.

She noticed he looked grayer than two months ago. Or maybe he was then and she didn't see it. "Thildalee, you just take anything you want in that house—except my exercise bike. That's new and I want it for the condo."

"Condo?" she said weakly.

"At Jim's place. They got a pool, tennis courts." He bent to tie his shoe. New Reeboks, she noticed. "I was going to call you. The yard sale's Saturday."

"Oh," Thildalee said, and moved her car to let him leave. The blond boy waved, friendly as anything. Bleached, Thildalee thought, and too skinny. He looked like a stalk; a sunflower.

She watched in her rearview mirror until there wasn't a trace of a taillight. That was all there was to it, she thought as she let herself in the kitchen. His dishes were still in the sink. Their dishes were still in the sink. Jim must have spent the night. "Well," Thildalee said to the walls. "He didn't even let my side of the bed get cold before he's got somebody hopping in it."

That was all right, she told herself, and a little catch of her breath echoed in the still house. That was perfectly fine. All she wanted was her bed.

The house smelled like cigarettes. She opened the den window on her way to the bedroom. There was half a bottle of vodka on the coffee table, two glasses, some sort of sticky green dip and taco chips. She looked away.

She dreaded seeing the bed. Unmade beds always bothered her. She'd never left one unmade behind in her life. Not even on their honeymoon. Deane kept saying that's what they had maids for and why did she have to be so prissy. And

*Ruth Moose*

she said she wasn't prissy at all. It was just one of the things her mother taught her. Always make your bed. He finally thought it was cute. He just didn't think it was cute the way she never wiped the shower after she finished, never turned the hot water completely off, and wouldn't drink a Coke from anything but a bottle or glass. "They taste like the can," she said. But that wasn't why she left. Not that Mama nor Patsy or anybody else would ever understand. "You got the perfect husband," they all said. "I could stay married forever to someone who does all the cooking, food shopping and cleans the house the way Deane does. You just don't know how good you got it." She knew. But cooking and cleaning wasn't what marriage was all about. She'd like to tell Miss Wilkins a thing or two now.

The first thing Thildalee noticed when she got to the bedroom was the perfectly made bed. Her white eyelet spread and pillows, ruffles all in place. That was when she began to cry. And cry and cry. She cried until she hiccupped. Her face was hot and she looked for something to wipe it. She saw something under the bed and reached for it. One of her old terrycloth scuffs. On her knees, she looked for the other and saw only dust bunnies, a curling paperback book, and a pencil with a broken point.

She wiped her face with her hands, straightened up, tucked the bedroom shoe in the back pocket of her jeans, and walked out, closing the door with a small click that sounded like the echo of one last hiccup.

*Ruth Moose*

# Daisy Wars

I HAVE ARGUED with that woman and argued with that woman. But when she gets Shasta Daisies planted in her brain, there's no uprooting them.

"They fall over, I told her. Little spindly things. Nothing to them but a stem and blotch of fuzz. She won't hear it.

"Therma Ann," I said, "you're going to split the garden club right down the middle. You're going to turn friend against friend, neighbor against neighbor, and preacher against preacher." She won't hear it. Goes traipsing around to the Lions Club, the Wednesday Night Men's Fish Fry, and who knows what-all with her little rolled-up drawings. Loves for them to say what a wonderful job the ladies in this town are doing to make it a better place to live. Acts like she thought of it all by herself and is doing it single-handed. That garden club has been selling Chocolate Nut Crumbles and Pecan Pralines-in-a-Can for the last six months. Fronnie Laidlom is so mad now she's not speaking to half the members. Said they knew when they voted she'd never been able to resist chocolate in any shape nor form. They made her drop Weight Watchers. Said they saw she was losing and couldn't stand it. I said the rest of them could have sold candy; she didn't have to. Nobody held her arms and made her. I tried to get them to order stationery. It's harder to sell but not impossible, I said. They said it wasn't something people had to have and there wouldn't be repeat orders. And besides, nobody in this town wrote letters anyway. I said

*Ruth Moose*

well, why don't we just close down the post office too, but nobody heard me..

This town is dead enough as it is. We don't need any more empty buildings to sit and watch run down. If it wasn't for the bank, drugstore, hardware, and Baptist church, we could just close up shop. Strike Eddysville off the map—if it's on any. I'm the only business still open on my side of the street and it's awful. Those empty stores attract mice and who knows what all slips in from the back alley?

I remember when this town had four hardwares, an FCX, and six churches. There was a dress store in every block, three dimestores and more shoe stores than you could get into on a Saturday, if you tried on a pair each place. I have known Saturdays when you had to park a mile from the square. When you saw everybody—neighbors, cousins, preachers, people you hadn't seen since the last funeral.

One shopping center will ruin a county, I've always heard. They put in a chain department store, drugstore, and hamburger drive-in, run the local businesses out. Joe's Grill had been on the lot behind the jail for twenty-five years. Wasn't big enough to stump your toe in, but Joe could cook with his eyes closed. He made the best fried sandwiches in town. I ate one every day of my life as long as he was in business, except Sundays, and then when I had a funeral. Ten o'clock sharp, Joe would send whoever happened to be passing around with my order. Half the time he'd throw in a fried pie. I don't know how that man stayed in business. Sometimes I don't know how any of us does, with the way people in this town like to take their business elsewhere. Not to the one who is your neighbor and best friend and does the job at half the price, but for no reason. Whim. Fickle. I have had to face the truth that people will listen to somebody talk a fast streak and smile a lot even if she is wearing a five-year-old hundred-percent polyester dress most of us threw out years ago. Mine was made from the same pattern, Simplicity

#6066, but I pushed it to the back of my closet and forgot it. Some people don't keep up, won't keep up, whether it's clothes or other things. I say if they don't see fashion, how can they see something as complicated as landscape design? That's what this boils down to—simple landscape design.

Not many towns this size have two entrances and one exit. You have to keep that in mind. Marigolds, I said. You can depend on marigolds. Nothing touches them. Not dry weather, not rot, not mildew, not mealybugs. I've worked in flowers all my life and I know my Abelia, my Pittosporum, my hollies, and my Buxus from a name on the page. Why can't people trust a trained eye? I know daisies and design. I see them. And trouble at the same time.

Every year I take two days off, close my shop and go the Convention. No telling how much business I lose. Don't anybody die the second week in July, I tell people. Because Lallah Carpenter won't be here to help you out. I gas my station wagon, run up motel bills you wouldn't believe, and come back with it loaded to the rims.

I see to it personally that people in this town hold their heads up with the best of them when it comes to weddings and funerals. I was the first to go with artificial flowers—nobody called them that but us in the floral industry—and they almost took over. Silk flowers? When they started, I filled my shelves with every color rose and carnation made; blue, black, and orange if they wanted them. I was the first to make bridal bouquets in silk flowers for "keeping" and I've looked the other way when some have been used twice.

I know how to put on a wedding. People give me credit for that. Women who wouldn't speak to you if you ran over them in the streets will come calling when their Tanie or Mona Rae or Louine starts thinking wedding. Asking what dates I have open. I got lace cloths and secret wedding punch recipes nobody can touch. And I have sugar flowers put on my wedding cakes. Those little bride-and-grooms are overdone, I tell my people. Flowers are my middle name. Sometimes I dream them all night long. Arrange them in my sleep, take orders and deliver. It's not a business you can let go at the end of a day.

Especially the funeral part. After the preacher, I'm the next to know. And I do a good job. Nobody has ever said they didn't get their money's worth on a neighborhood wreath. There are families in this town who won't let a permanent arrangement in their door. And those who welcome them for every holiday in the year. People appreciate your knowing things like that.

My sweet daddy-in-law had a yard full of flowers. Plus every houseplant you could name.

"You could start a business," Daddy Bell said one morning, making his way to the breakfast table. We always drank coffee together. That was the one thing he taught me. I'd never touched a drop in my life until I married Tom Bell and he brought his daddy to live with us. Now I can't do without it. Can't find one hand with the other until I have my first cup. So Daddy Bell was the one who started me off. And this business has been running nights, days, and weekends ever since.

Everybody in the garden club said I was the one with the natural green thumb. For a while I thought of calling myself that, but it sounded too much plants and shrubs and nursery. So I ended up with ''Budding Beauty'' because I could see the B's with two big loops.

I can see things. That's what I tried to tell the garden club after their civic beautification committee came calling—after they'd asked Therma Ann to draw up their plans. If they'd come to me first I could have saved a lot of heartache and heartbreak. But no, they go to Therma Ann. Let her make some little chicken scratches on paper, put color over them and get everybody excited.

For somebody who never had a single art lesson in her life, she does draw a straight line. With a ruler. And the brick entrance-way with "Welcome to Eddysville" looked good when you thought how bare that place was now.

Highway #701 is not your heavily traveled road. Thank goodness, I say. But it is two-lane and paved and we have a stoplight.

There wasn't an evergreen in the plan, but did I point that out? I did not. I was the soul of sweetness. They said bricks had been donated and Therma's husband offered to lay them free. I said be sure he works on a day when he's...ah...feeling well. I did not mention his drinking habits which everyone knows. And if you don't watch him every minute—stand right out there—then you'll get a wall crooked as that bend in the road to the river.

And little gas lamps? Donated too. Weren't they tickled? I asked if anyone had considered electricity? Something not quite so eternal, but which could be turned on and off. They have lights burning all the time and while it may look friendly and "welcome to our town-ish," somebody will complain. They will cry taxpayers' money, even when it's not.

Too late to change their minds, I could see that. All them acting like hens on a nest of Easter eggs. Jelly beans, I started to say, but didn't. Wasn't going to shoot off my mouth to anybody who would listen. Those things come home to sit on your mantel and roost. Therma Ann ought to know.

She was the one calling the baby premature when it came two months too soon. Nine pounds? All along I said it didn't matter if things were hurried up. Of course I wanted Tommy Lee to finish school before marriage, maybe take a course or two in auto mechanics if he wanted, but I have learned with children what you want and what you get aren't always the same things. I said boys will be boys, especially if girls let them. Make the best of it, I said when they told me. You weren't the first and you won't be the last. It's nothing to be ashamed of, nothing new since Adam and Eve.

*Ruth Moose*

I was the one who insisted on a church wedding though. Every girl needs a memory like that in the back of her life, I told Rita.

It will mean more to you as time passes. And Tommy Lee agreed when I mentioned the showers for Rita and bachelor party for him. He didn't mind waiting a few weeks until we could get things in the works. I think he'd still be waiting if it was up to him. But he's like me. We make the best of things and more.

I mean how many mothers of the groom do you know, who plan, direct, and pay for the whole wedding? While Therma Ann is in the background the whole time pushing them to go across the state line to Cheraw so she can fudge the date a little if she has to. And she did. She was scared to death Rita would show walking down the aisle. She wouldn't have been the first. I expect to see bridal gowns in the maternity shops any day now. It wasn't anything the town didn't already know. Out in the open, I've always said. That's the way I've been. The only way to be.

When my first husband up and left and little Tommy not but two, I told it. Good riddance I said. Then when Charlie Flaggle was dying with his trouble I told it. We didn't keep it to ourselves even if trade did fall off at the barber shop. Picked up some afterwards and stayed steady until he couldn't hold the trimmers and got to nicking too many ears. Nobody cut hair like him. Three generations in the same barber shop. I even thought Tommy Lee might take it up, but it's too much indoors all the time for him. Gilda made the best beauty shop there though…those mirrors down one wall and that old pole out front. She cuts men and women. Only store open in that whole block. "We are in the same boat," I tell her, "and no beautification project is going to change a thing."

Try telling that to Therma Ann. I would if it wouldn't mean breaking my word not to speak to her again. Six weeks next Sunday. I said it and slammed the door. Billy is her

*Ruth Moose*

grandson same as mine. Or more. If you go back and look at some things. I never let my son go swinging his hips up and down the streets of this town in cut-off jeans so short they showed what they were supposed to cover. Little terry tops no bigger than a washcloth and everything spilled out. Advertising. I never claimed my son was any stronger nor weaker than a regular man. Make the most, I said, but it was a marriage he was caught into. Trapped. At least he hasn't gone running home every time somebody turned their face upside down at him.

"Make your bed," I said. "You sleep in it." And he has. If Rita's mama had been home showing and telling her a thing or two, not running around from club to club, she might be holding her end of a marriage up.

Park benches. That's what Therma wants now. For the vacant lot where Miller's Drugstore stood for fifty years. She'd got them drawn into her plan. That's one thing I agree with her about. If she's bound and determined to plant the lot, then I'll help her with them. If people are sitting, they can't be parading around, showing all they've got. I give Therma Ann credit where credit is due. But I will fight her until the Fourth of July on Shasta Daisies. I know my flowers.

As my sweet daddy-in-law used to say, "Lallah, you got more wheels in the road than anybody I know." And I don't intend to let somebody in a five-year-old polyester dress with Shasta Daisies on the brain run the show.

*Ruth Moose*

## Wooden Apples

THE OLD CEDAR made a dark triangle of shade. Patsy had spread her quilt in the widest part so close to the tree she smelled its spiced clean scent. When she closed her eyes she smelled it stronger, but she hadn't made a pallet in the yard to sleep, just read.

In August no place was cool, but the cedar shade was cooler than the house and there was an occasional breeze.

She heard her brothers' voices from the kitchen. "Rat. You stinko. You're not playing fair and I'm going to tell." They played Monopoly, fought over Boardwalk and Park Place, who got the railroads and utilities. They were mad at first when she wouldn't play, wanted to take a quilt and go outside. Then they forgot about her.

She was almost asleep when someone said, "Wish I had nothing to do all day but take a nap in the shade." Ladella Honeycutt leaned over her.

Ladella lived across the street. She was tall and blonde, tanned in white short shorts and some fluffy pink halter top.

She had pink hoops in her ears and smelled like warm strawberries. Her nails were much too long and perfect for anyone who did much in the house, Mama said, yet when she strolled her baby in the evenings both of them looked fresh and clean. "She just does it to show her legs," Mama said once. Patsy helped her snap beans. They sat on the back porch. It was late on a Saturday afternoon and Mama wanted to get the canner on before she started supper. It would be

*Ruth Moose*

the third canning of beans she'd done this week. When she made the remark about Ladella, Patsy looked up. It didn't sound like Mama saying that. There was an edge to her voice. "Some people wouldn't know a fresh vegetable if it ran up and jumped in their face." Mama tossed a handful of snapped beans in the flat metal pan between them.

Patsy thought Ladella ever so beautiful. "That hair's not real," Mama said. "It's bleached-proxided-whatever they do."

Patsy didn't care. She wanted to be tall and blonde even if it wasn't real and have a sweet baby like David to play pat-acake with, push up and down the street in his stroller.

"If there was anything much to her," Mama said, "her husband would live with her—if there is one."

That was the mystery. If Ladella had a husband she never mentioned it, and when Patsy babysat David at night, Ladella always left and came back by herself. "Maybe she's divorced," Patsy said. "Maybe her husband's dead."

"Maybe there never was one," Mama said.

Patsy couldn't imagine anyone who wouldn't want to marry Ladella, have a baby like David who hugged everyone, laughed, and went to sleep quietly sucking his thumb. She'd never heard him cry.

"Can you babysit Saturday night?" Ladella asked.

"Where's David?" Patsy looked around.

"Asleep," Ladella said. "He's teething and didn't get his nap out this morning. I've got the fan on him and he's sleeping like a baby." She laughed. "But then he always does, doesn't he? I mean what else could he sleep like?" She turned over the book Patsy had on the blanket. "I've read this. Want me to tell you how it ends?"

"Don't you dare." Patsy snatched back her book. She knew how it ended. Happily ever after. All the books did, but somehow she didn't quite know until she got there.

"Hey, gorgeous." Patsy's father came down the back

porch steps. "I'd been home early if I knew I had two beautiful girls waiting for me in my back yard."

Ladella laughed, pushed back her hair. She spread her legs on the blanket, wiggled her toes in their white patent sandals. "How do you like my new nail polish?" she asked. "It's called Cherry Smash."

"I like it," Patsy's father said. "Looks good enough to eat." He reached for one of Ladella's feet.

"I meant Patsy," she said. "I was asking Patsy how she liked it."

Patsy didn't know her father knew Ladella well enough to tease and talk like that. He'd only seen her a few times when she came in to borrow a stick of butter or something. She'd lived on Harper Street a few months. Moved in the last of May, a week or so before school was out. David was three months old, a really little baby, and she didn't leave him then. Patsy had sat with him a few times or so and mostly when he was already in bed. She only had to check him, be there to change him if he woke, heat a bottle if he cried. He never had. And Ladella always paid her ten dollars a time, plus a tip when she washed the dishes soaking in the sink. About a week's worth of dishes, Patsy thought. She couldn't stand to be in the house with that many sticky dishes. That's the real reason she washed them and the baby was asleep. There was no TV and she was bored. Ladella gave her five dollars for washing the dishes. "It was worth every cent," she said the first time, and lit a cigarette, slipped off her shoes, and slid down on the couch. She wore the same nail polish then, Patsy remembered. It wasn't new. So why had she said so?

Her father teased Ladella some more about her tan, how he bet she had it all over and she acted like she didn't know what he was talking about. Said she didn't have any tan at all compared to how dark she used to get going to the beach and she hadn't been to the beach forever. "A couple of lifetimes ago," she said.

*Ruth Moose*

Patsy wanted her father to be in a good mood. She had been asked to go to the movies with Linda. Linda's mother would pick her up, bring her back a little after nine. Patsy had money to pay for her ticket. All her father had to do was say it was okay and stay home with her brothers until she got back. She didn't know if he'd do it. Her mother worked nights in the sock mill, going in at three and coming home after eleven. She said those machines turned out millions of socks; enough socks for every man, woman, and child and dog in the world to never have to go barefooted again. She said they spit socks out faster than you could catch them and cut the threads.

Patsy had to make supper for her father and two brothers.

Usually she heated things left from lunch—garden vegetables, cornbread and biscuits—peeled tomatoes and cucumbers, put vinegar over them.

In the summer her father grew enough vegetables to give half the county. Her mother said she didn't care if those people he gave it to would come help hoe and pick it when it got ready. Those were the hard parts. Corn her father planted was now so tall she couldn't see across where Ladella lived unless she stood...

Patsy smoothed a wrinkle from the blanket and asked her father about the movies.

"You hear that?" He cocked his head at Ladella. "My little girl's going on a date."

"Not a date, Daddy," she said. "It's with Linda. You know Linda. Her mother's going to take us."

"Skinny kid with the braces and big ears?" he said. "Looks like somebody left her out in the rain."

"Daddy," Patsy said, "she's my friend. She's nice and her mother's nice and—"

"I guess you can go," he said, "if you put on a skirt."

"Bring a brush and I'll comb your hair for you," Ladella said.

Patsy ran, pulled a dress from the hanger and over her head. The dress felt still warm from her mother's iron, though she knew it couldn't be, and smelled like soap and sunshine. She grabbed a brush and comb, flew down the hall and back steps. She was afraid Ladella hadn't meant to comb her hair at all and would be gone to check on David.

Ladella was still there, talking to Patsy's father, who laughed, showed all his teeth. He didn't laugh like that much. Mostly he frowned or yelled they made too much noise or the TV got on his nerves. Then he'd slam down his newspaper and say he was going where he could get some peace.

The service station. That's where Patsy's mother said he went. Once when Patsy knew they needed milk for breakfast she called, asked to speak to him, and he wasn't there. Then someone corrected in the background. "Yeah," the man said, "Roland Lentz was here—till a few minutes ago. He just left. You want to call back? I can give him a message."

She left the message about bringing home milk but the next morning there wasn't any and her father acted mad, said he forgot.

Sometimes he wasn't home when she went to bed. Her brothers had to be in bed at ten, no later, but she could stay up until ten-thirty, take a long bath, have the rest of the hot water all to herself. She'd be almost asleep when her father came quietly in, went straight to bed, not even turning on the lights. Minutes later her mother came from work. Even her footsteps on the porch sounded tired.

Patsy wondered if Ladella ever got tired. She never looked nor acted it. She took the brush and began on Patsy's hair, giggling about something. Her hands were smooth and Patsy closed her eyes as Ladella brushed. It had been a long time since her mother had time to brush, comb, do pretty things to Patsy's hair, but that was okay. Patsy liked doing things for herself. She'd just forgotten how nice it felt to have someone do things for her. Soothing things.

*Ruth Moose*

"Now," Ladella said, "you'll knock 'em dead. You'll be the prettiest girl there." She pulled Patsy's collar from inside the neckband, buttoned the top button. "I've got a cute pin that would look just perfect on that collar," she said. "Let me go check on David and I'll get it."

"I'll go along and look at that water heater for you," Daddy said. He winked at Ladell, who said, "Oh…sure. That will be fine."

Patsy watched them walk across the street. Ladella was almost as tall as her father and she walked with a little jiggle, almost a bounce, her hair lifting and falling, her legs almost gliding over asphalt, grass.

Patsy folded the blanket, was starting toward the house when Ladella called from her door. "I found it. Come let me pin it on."

"I'll bring it back in the morning," Patsy said as Ladella patted the red wooden apple pin in place on her collar.

"Oh, no need for that. You keep it. I want you to have it."

"Thank you," Patsy said, and took the blanket in, set places for supper, and listened for Linda's mother to toot the car horn.

When she came in from the movie, her father wasn't home, and his plate was still clean on the table.

The next morning when her mother woke her she picked up Patsy's dress, started to hang it up, and saw the wooden apple pin. "Where'd this come from?" she asked.

"Ladella," Patsy yawned. "She gave it to me."

"When?" Mama closed the closet door.

"Yesterday…on the blanket…when she came over."

"Over here?" her mother said. "Where was the baby?"

"Oh, he was asleep," Patsy said. "And Daddy went to fix her hot water heater. He said I could go to the movies with Linda. Her mother picked us up."

Mama took the pin off the dress. "I don't think you better keep this. She's not a very nice person."

*Ruth Moose*

"But I like her," Patsy said. "She's nice to me."

"She's nice to a lot of people," Mama said. "A little nicer than she's supposed to be. I think Miss Ladella's middle name is trouble."

The pin left a rusty mark on the collar of Patsy's dress. It didn't even wash out. Mama and Daddy talked a long time the next Sunday afternoon. Sometimes her mother cried. Sometimes her father yelled. Then he finally left. Patsy and her mother and brothers had supper alone, but that was nothing new. Her mother red-eyed, not saying much. Not making jokes over toasted cheese and milk, nothing.

Sometime during the night, her father came home. It was late, but Patsy was awake, thinking. She thought it was funny how you could live in the same house with four other people and not know much about them. Not know them at all. How you found out little things you didn't really want to know, things that hurt and made you worry if the world was all right. And how her brothers could sleep and play and sometimes argue and fight and not know anything at all.

*Ruth Moose*

# Across the Bridge

LYNNE HAD READ to him all night. "And the wicked old troll called, 'Who goes trip-tropping across my bridge?'" She read with her eyes closed; the print felt raised on her eyelids as she sing-songed the words. "'It is I, the littlest Billy Goat Gruff, who goes trip-tropping across the bridge.'"

At times when she thought Danny asleep, Lynne stopped reading. He'd cry, "Read, Mama, read!" in such a shrill, feeble voice it hurt to hear him.

So she read, every book they had brought to the hospital, every book she could remember reading Danny; sang songs in a voice she tried to make steady; and said rhymes, "One, two, buckle my shoe." She stopped, then went stumbling on. Danny's scuffed shoes were in the metal locker at the foot of the bed. The day they brought Danny to the hospital, he asked a dozen times for his clothes, to see his shoes. She took them from his locker, held his shoes, jeans, and brown jacket so he could see them. Later, when his eyes swelled shut, he stopped asking for his clothes and begged for a blanket; he was cold, so cold. But she couldn't give him a blanket. Not even a sterile sheet was allowed to touch his raw body. Fmally he curled into a fetal position and withdrew inside his cocoon of pain-killing drugs. Her voice was the only link between that world and the hospital room. Her voice and the bottle of blood draining slowly into his veins from an umbilical cord to a machine. The machine throbbed its desperate rhythm. Lynne wanted to cry faster, faster.

*Ruth Moose*

Toward morning Danny dozed and Lynne stopped reading but didn't move from her chair beside his bed. Sometimes she sipped warm water to ease her dry throat. Fluids. The doctors said Danny was losing all his body fluids and there was nothing they could do. When the pairs of doctors came and went, mumbling behind masks, she read bewilderment in their eyes. "When these wonder drugs backfire. . ." they murmured. Danny had had measles, then a strep throat. Dr. Barger gave him penicillin as he had before. Only this time it reacted. It was like nothing anyone had ever seen before. "We don't know what to do," the doctors said. "What to do."

When Jim came, Lynne was sitting in the rocking chair, her arms wrapped tight around herself to keep them from swinging empty as the chair thumped back and forth on the cold tile floor. He touched her shoulder, walked to the crib, and stood quietly like someone paying respects. Lynne closed her eyes, leaned back. From behind, Jim stroked her hair. Danny used to do that sometimes. She squeezed herself tighter. Jim's voice was low. "No change?"

Lynne shook her head. "None." She stood, hands on the chair back, and Jim pulled her close. His raincoat was damp, smelled of the outdoors. How much older Jim looked, as though this hospital week had been years that wore his face long and sad.

He drew tight lines on his forehead. "Honey, you have got to get some rest. Go home for a little while."

"I can't. I can't leave Danny."

"You've got to. You're going to make yourself sick." He took her coat from the locker. "Put this on. It's raining out." He slid her arms into the coat, buttoned it all the way down, as she used to do for Danny. Then Jim took a scarf, tied it under her chin, tried to laugh at his big, slow fingers, and in the dresser found her purse, closed her fingers around its leather edge. "Now, go." He opened the door, gave her a small shove. "The car is in the A parking lot."

*Ruth Moose*

Lynne gripped the door facing. "When Danny wakes...if he asks for me, tell him I'll be right back."

"I will," Jim whispered, closed the door.

In the hall, Lynne waited for an elevator until she realized she hadn't pushed the button. Running, she took the stairs and her shoes made loud, hollow echoes as though someone followed. One more turn, she rounded the corner, to the glass doors, then parking lot.

Lynne felt for her car keys. A lock of hair tickled her cheek as she started the car. She pushed her hair back and across a wet cheek. It was rain. She wouldn't cry, she wouldn't break down.

She eased the car into an almost deserted street, reminded herself to turn on the wipers and drive slowly. Red traffic lights blinked their scared doe eyes as she drove. Main Street, Greenway, past the A&P, then home.

In the driveway, she stopped the car and sat, just sat. Cold, she hadn't turned the heater on, stiff and numb. She jumped as rain pelted from the oak tree onto the car. The lowest limb on that tree was Danny's. He bounced on it, played "horse," cowboy hat sideways on his head.

Quickly Lynne slammed the door and ran up the walk. There was a light in the kitchen and Mother Grogan, Jim's mother, sat at the bar. Jim had driven to Bolton for his mother to come care for the baby the day they took Danny to the hospital. The day the blisters—huge water balloons—formed all over Danny. And broke, leaving him raw. Never saw anything like it, the doctors said. The nurses' eyes grew soft and misty as they looked at him.

Lynne blinked, tugged off her scarf, coat.

Mother Grogan stopped turning the newspaper. "You scared me for a minute. I didn't hear the car. Where's Jim?"

"At the hospital with Danny." Lynne laid her things across the empty highchair. This room didn't seem like her kitchen anymore. Different, things moved; her planter of

Sansevieria on the counter instead of the window, a bowl of fruit atop the refrigerator, a rug she used on the porch spread before the sink.

Mother Grogan stacked a section of the paper. "I didn't hear Jim up or I would've fixed him breakfast. A man shouldn't go around on an empty stomach."

"That's okay," Lynne sat in Jim's chair. "He can eat Danny's breakfast. Danny hasn't been . . "

"How's Danny? Any change?"

"No." Lynne thumbed comers of the newspapers. "The doctors don't say much. They don't know. If the transfusions can be completed before the vein gives out…if his skin would start to heal. . ."

Mother Grogan rattled pans under the stove, found Lynne's coffeepot, filled it. She wore a blue chenille robe Lynne gave her one Christmas. It was almost white now.

And Jim's bedroom slippers. They flapped as she walked.

"It took me a while at first to find where you keep things." Mother Grogan held the coffee canister. "I'm used to it now."

She could have borrowed my slippers, Lynne thought. They might be more comfortable. "We appreciate your coming like this, Mother Grogan, taking care of the baby and all. I don't know what we would have done."

"That Eddie." She jammed on the coffeepot lid. "He's the sweetest thing. So good. Don't cry or fuss. Just plays with his granny. It's the most I've ever been around him and I didn't know how he'd take to me, not all the time that is." She clicked the stove button, went to the refrigerator. "He wakes up at the crack of dawn, cooing and carrying on in his bed. Soon as I get up and give him his bottle, he goes right back to sleep." She took the chair across from Lynne, smoothed her crinkled short hair. "Usually I stay up, but this morning was so bad, rainy, I crawled back in, and was asleep before I knew it."

"Is Edward awake now?" Lynne listened. She heard the crib rattle and ran down the hall to him. "Precious." She hugged the sleeper-clad baby. He smelled of milk and the strong ammonia of his diapers stung her nose. "Soaked," she said, changing him.

The baby gurgled and pulled at her as she dressed him. Red overalls, striped T-shirt. Danny always said Edward looked like a jack-in-the-box in that outfit. Danny. The drawers where she kept Danny's clothes were tightly shut. Danny.

"Boo." Lynne tickled the baby, tugging on his shoes and socks. She felt guilty. This week all she had thought about was Danny. She'd forgotten Edward. Danny needed her so desperately.

She carried him to the kitchen, hurrying past Danny's too neat room, toys in a line on his shelves.

At the stove, Mother Grogan waved a spatula. "You sit down. I got some sausage fried and these eggs will be ready in a jiffy."

"Coffee will be fine." Lynne popped the baby in his high chair. "I'm not hungry."

Mother Grogan shoved a plate with two large yellow eyes before Lynne. "Now you eat all that."

The egg eyes glared at her. She never liked eggs and didn't think she could get them down this morning. "I'll feed Edward." She got up. "You eat your breakfast."

"No, I already mixed Eddie's cereal with applesauce. He eats it better that way." Mother Grogan poked the gray matter into Edward's open mouth.

Lynne cut brown rims from her eggs. She wanted to feed the baby. Do that much for her week's neglect.

"Fred's coming today." Mother Grogan scraped a blob from Edward's chin, pushed it back in his mouth. "He said when I left if he didn't hear anything he'd be over Saturday. He must have had a time this week. Doing for himself."

Lynne thought of Jim's father, wide-shouldered, gangling outdoorsman of a fellow in the kitchen, dropping, spilling things.

"Course he could eat over at Estelle's," Mother Grogan went on. "If she ever cooked and he knew when she'd have a meal."

Estelle. Jim's sister. Jim said his sister might have learned to do a few things for herself if his mother hadn't always been right there to do everything for her. Including raise those children.

"I got a letter from Estelle this week. Said she and the kids might come over with Fred." Mother Grogan wiped Edward's face, then laughed. "I bet those kids have sure missed me this week. There's not a day goes by that one of them, Billy, Tina, or the baby ain't over there. Spending the day, the night, half the time. I feel like I've raised those kids myself."

Mother Grogan and her old-fashioned way of child-raising. That survival-of-the-fittest business made Lynne's skin crawl. When any neighbor child had measles, mumps, chicken pox, Mother Grogan took Estelle's children over to be exposed. Might as well have it and get it over with, she said. Lynne disagreed and Mother Grogan said she was too particular with her children. Always carrying them to the doctor's for things and shots when they weren't sick. Tina had the measles after Mother Grogan's exposing her to a neighborhood child. Danny caught the measles from Tina. Mother Grogan said it wouldn't hurt him and he'd be glad to have them done and over with before he started school. Measles, then strep throat, penicillin, now this…God, now this. Oh God.

"I thought since Estelle and the kids was coming"—

Mother Grogan put Edward's dish on the counter—"I'd see if Tina didn't want to stay over here. I've never been away from those kids this long a time. I know it's about to kill them not seeing me everyday."

"Sure." Lynne stirred sugar in her coffee. "She would be a lot of company to you and maybe help with the baby." Lynn could see Tina swinging on Danny's swings, her hair blowing in the wind.

Mother Grogan stabbed her eggs, dipped toast in the yellow blood. "Only thing is"—she broke off more toast, chewed loudly—"Estelle won't be planning on Tina staying and she won't have her any extra clothes."

Lynne watched the baby rub his sticky cereal hands in his hair.

"I thought"—Mother Grogan went on eating—"since Tina and Danny are about the same age and she's not much bigger than she is, Tina could wear Danny's clothes. It won't hurt her none to wear boy's clothes for a week."

"What?" Lynne's cup crashed on the saucer, sloshed an ugly stain on the mat. Tina in Danny's shirts and jeans, asleep under his warm blanket. "No," Lynne said quietly, "no." Her shoulders shook in hard jerks and she couldn't stop them. Danny was so cold and he couldn't even have a sheet. And his clothes...

"No, you don't understand." Lynne gripped the table.

"I understand all right. You don't want Tina wearing Danny's clothes. That's okay. I wouldn't let her touch a thing of Danny's if that's the way you want it."

"No, don't you see?" Lynne reached for Mother Grogan's arm, but she pulled away. "Danny can't..." Her eyes blurred. "He can't wear his clothes...He's dying." It was the first time she had said the word, allowed it. Now the tears tore loose. The tears she'd held in a week came out in great heaving gasps in the bedroom until she lay there empty. Drained and weak, her head was heavy but she slept a fitful sleep, exhausted. The telephone awoke her and Jim's voice.

"Lynne, honey, are you there?"

*Ruth Moose*

"Yes," she said. The spread had left waffle marks on her arms. She felt them on her face. It was dry now.

"Danny has started to heal. The doctors were by and found a place on his back. They think he's going to be okay now."

Healing. The sign they had waited for, watched for. She had begun to think it would never happen.

Danny was going to get well. He would make it.

"They say he's not out of the woods yet, but they're optimistic."

"I'll be there as soon as I can. Tell Danny I'm coming." She hung up the phone.

Mother Grogan stood in the doorway, Edward sagging on her hip. She put him on the floor. "Was it Danny?"

"Jim says the doctors think he's going to make it." Lynne picked up the crawling baby and hugged him. "Your brother is going to be okay." The baby laughed and reached up to pull her hair.

"Did you hear?" She swung the baby and embraced Mother Grogan. "Danny's not going to die."

Mother Grogan began to smooth the bed. Lynn put the baby down and helped her.

"I'm sorry about before," she said. "It's okay for Tina to wear Danny's clothes. I don't care if she wears everything he has."

"No." Mother Grogan's hand was on the door knob. "I wouldn't think of it." She turned and left the room.

Lynne started after her, then stopped. She felt the baby's diaper. He needed to be changed before she left again for the hospital.

*Ruth Moose*

# Happy Birthday, Billy Boy

MAMA SETTLES HERSELF in the back seat, twisting her navy pleated skirt like she's smoothing a nest. "If I'd known you were going to be this late," she says, "I could still be fixing my face. I told your daddy to get the camera and come on."

Evanelle doesn't answer. The baby, Billy Buttons, threw up twice and she had to change him skin out, every stitch. Then she had to pick up the cake and flowers. Mama insisted she get silk. "Anything fresh won't last five minutes in that place. They keep it hot as an oven. I took your grandmother an African violet and it didn't live three weeks. Three weeks!"

There are roses on the cake. Thirty-six. Evanelle had to wait while they put on every last one of them. And she'd called in her order Friday—decorated. Done everything but spell it. And all the time she ordered, Darren Ravel rubbed her thigh. He kept saying he just loved the feel of Arnel. Arnel, her ass. When she told anyone she worked at WKIS, they'd get so excited, their eyes would bulge out and they'd say, "You know D.R. the D.J.?" And she'd say Lord yes, she ought to as long as she worked at KIS. What she didn't say was she knew D.R. more than she wanted to. More than anybody ought to, but that was water over the dam or spilled milk or whatever you wanted to call it.

Billy Buttons sleeps in her arms and Evanelle thinks he is the most beautiful baby in the world. His dark lashes curl

*Ruth Moose*

up from round cheeks and he sucks air with a pink pucker. He looks stuffed, fat as a frog in his blue terry jumpsuit with anchor buttons and little red sailboats embroidered on the collar. He's growing so fast, no matter what Mama says about bottle babies. It worries Evanelle though when he spits up and that's why she can't say the reason they are late.

Earl pushes in the cigarette lighter, pulls it out again when he remembers he isn't smoking anymore. This is not his idea of a good time. He couldn't have been any slower getting dressed if he tried. Which is another reason they are late. He put on too much musk cologne and Evanelle thinks she may be sick. She feels dizzy, nauseated.

"Let me hold that sweet thing." Mama leans over the front seat, brushes Evanelle's forehead with her stiff hair. Evanelle thinks she feels a red, ugly scratch there. "I never get to hold him," Mama says. "People say I bet you spoil that grandbaby to death, now you finally got one, and I say I don't even have a chance. He's in that awful nursery all the time."

Evanelle would love for Mama to hold the baby. That way if he spit up again Mama would go around the rest of the day smelling soured. "He's asleep," Evanelle says. It almost comes out a sigh.

Mama dangles an earring close to Evanelle's eye and she pulls away from the sharp edges. Mama always said earrings were her weakness. She's got two hundred pair in every color and shape. Drawers of earrings, little trees and cats and birds that hold earrings. When Mama went to get her ears pierced, Evanelle had to hold her hand and it made her feel strange in the middle. There was Billy Buttons kicking her inside...only she didn't know it was him then. Earl kept calling him girl names—Tammy Lynn and Loretta Rae and Crystal Sue—all names of his old girlfriends. And Mama kept pulling her on the outside. It gave her a funny feeling she still thinks about sometimes. A feeling that comes back and grabs her from behind like somebody sneaking up when she was little, playing Hide and Go Seek. Sometimes Evanelle feels her life has been turned upside-down like that game they used to play on rainy days in the sixth grade, Fruitbasket Turnover.

Mama folds her rain bonnet. She rattles it like paper and says, "I don't know what on earth can be keeping your daddy." She says this even though she knows Lester Pedy is not Evanelle's daddy; never was, never will be. She just says that to Evanelle to try to make up to her for remarrying and to make her feel more family. "All he had to do was get the camera and close the door. He was right behind me." Mama fans with her folded bonnet. "How long can it take somebody to close a durn door? If he'd been any closer behind, he'd been on my heels and we're late enough as it is." She keeps fanning, making little steam sounds with her breath. "And this rain. I'm proud of Earl for driving."

Earl grunts. Evanelle is proud he's even going. That's all. For over two weeks now, Mama has planned this four-generation thing and Evanelle has worried. Worried about taking Billy in that place. Worried he'll catch something. She doesn't know what, just something. Worried that Earl will act up. He said he didn't see any sense in this business. That it didn't amount to a hill of beans. Evanelle said her family wasn't a hill of beans and she didn't appreciate him talking like that. Then he said that was kinda cute, the way she got mad like she used to and he called her "Pepper Pot" and "Red." He used to say she didn't have red hair for nothing. Actually Evanelle could have hair any color she wanted, but this was one she'd gotten used to and so had everybody else.

Now it covered the gray that was creeping in a hair at a time. At forty-two she saw it coming and she didn't want to be solid white like Mama and going all Easter egg colors; pink, blue, and lavender. Mama had been going to Eunice Platt all her life. Every Friday. And everybody knew Eunice never measured when she mixed. Evanelle had nightmares that she'd be gray-haired in the hospital and the nurses would say things like, "Why honey, this can't be your first!" or ask wasn't she the baby's grandmother? Or giggle behind her back that at her age she should have known better. Well, she couldn't help it. The baby wasn't something she went out and decided. He just happened. Earl acted more surprised than she did. After twenty-two years you just forget, don't expect. She'd never been in love with the idea of kids in the first place and here she was in the middle of this fourth generation thing, just so Mama could show up her sister Faith Anne who never liked Evanelle from day one. Faith Anne's three daughters had married and divorced and moved twenty states away so they could stay away as much as they liked. So here goes Evanelle, baby and all, to some party in the nursing home. Grandma wouldn't know any of them and Mama would probably hold the baby right up to her face so both of them would have to fight for breath. She accused Evanelle of being peculiar, then taking him to that day nursery where he was exposed to every kind of germ there was. He was in that place so much, Mama said, he wouldn't know anyplace else. Not his real home, nor who his real mama was. It made Evanelle feel like two cents. She didn't work for the fun of it. Lord, she didn't know what they'd live on every week if it wasn't for her paycheck. Earl's didn't seem to go anywhere. She tried to save, but something always came along.

"Where is that man?" Mama rolled down her window. "How long can it take somebody to pull a door shut?" She was ready to yell when Lester backed onto the porch, settled his hat sideways on his head. He had a wide rear like two brown pillows pushed together, a bald doorknob of a head. In some ways Evanelle felt sorry for him; that he lived with Mama seven days a week, twenty-four hours a day. How does he stand it? How do I? How do any of us stand each other? And somehow we'll go on putting up with each other until

*Ruth Moose*

they put us off in a bed with sides and chairs with wheels to push like Billy Buttons in his stroller.

"Faith Anne has called me fifty times about that cake," Mama says as Lester gets in. "You got it?"

"Right here." Lester pushes the camera in her face.

"I can see that," Mama says, "I'm talking about the cake."

"In the trunk," Evanelle says quietly. What she doesn't say is the cake has only thirty-six roses instead of the eighty-six Mama wanted. Even after Evanelle telephoned the order. She was going to be mad, but it was too late to do anything. Let her be mad, thought Evanelle. I've got this baby and a job and husband to look after. I can't do everything. The baby snored wetly, wiggled like a puppy and snuggled closer. He was sweet even if he did cry a lot and spit up. When he wasn't crying, his face didn't look so puckered and red.

Earl turned at the light and Lester kept clicking the camera, twirled in a roll of film. It snapped like a beetle or something.

"Is that camera what took you so long?" Mama asks.

"I had to find the film," Lester grunts.

"Well, that didn't have to take you all day."

"It wouldn't if you kept things in the place they ought to be." Earl puts the camera to his eye. "I like to never found the film."

"It was in the linen closet the whole time."

Earl hunts a country/western station on the radio to try to drown out the back seat. All he gets is the Radio Gospel Hour and Ministry of the Air. "I've seen the blind learn to see," some preacher yells, "and the lame throw down their crutches and walk. I've seen drunkards lay their bottles down and never reach for them again." Earl turns the radio off...

Evanelle shifts the heavy baby in her arms. It's a wonder all that door-slamming and fuss hasn't waked him up. He makes a snuffling noise and sucks his fist. She hopes that means he's not going to spit up again.

Lester has rolled down his window and Evanelle hears Mama make a noise like she is going to say something about her hair being blown to shreds and changes her mind.

"I sure like this car," Lester says.

"I'll sell her to you." Earl peels off a breath mint, chews. "Nothing down and a hundred when I catch you."

"Har," laughs Lester, "har. I heard tell of deals like that." Mama pats the back of the front seat. "This is a nice car, Earl. Yours or the company's?"

Mama loves to rub it in that the only car Evanelle has ever owned is the blue one she bought herself when she still lived at home. And Earl has a different one every week, all belonging to the dealer he works for. It's a wonder he hasn't traded or sold Evanelle's, but that's only because she won't let him.

Sometimes Evanelle thinks she's been married a hundred years. Fifty at least. Her life seems to be running away from her and she can't slow it down. It wasn't good having a baby at her age. Not when she'd shut off her mind to the idea a long time ago. Billy Buttons would grow up with a bald daddy and the oldest mama in the first grade while her own mother was going around saying, "1 never thought I'd have a grandbaby in the first place and here you go off leaving it with some stranger every day. Nobody could pay me to be away from the only baby I'd ever have when he was at his sweetest and most precious stage."

When Mama says that, Lester always says, "Hush. Now that Nelle's got started, who says she's going to stop? She and Earl may end up with a baseball team yet."

Earl always blushes and grins, says, "I'm all for it." Then he pokes Evanelle in the ribs like he wants her to laugh.

She doesn't see anything to laugh about. Earl slept right through the midnight feedings and on past 5:00 a.m. when

Billy Buttons woke up the day. There wasn't one thing slow about him, even if that's one of the things her doctors worried about at first. Her age. They did the test and everything came back normal. Evanelle knew it would be. Billy Buttons kicked and turned and twisted too much to be the least bit slow.

"If you go slow by here"—Lester leans over the front seat and points for Earl—"right up there. That service station. That's where I found a man with my name once. I tell you that was a crazy feeling."

"I don't know what's crazy about it," Mama snorts. "It's a common name."

"I was selling soap for the car washes and when I walked in that station and saw my name, I like to have backed out. Scared me so." Lester points. "Right there."

The only thing that sits in the spot now is a fruit stand and adult book store. The sign reads "JOY" in big, orange letters. "Tapes, books, records and films."

"It's got so nobody can stay in business anymore," Lester says as they drive past. "Used to be a Gulf station. And the fellow that ran it was honest as they come."

"How you know?" Mama asks. "He buy you out?"

"He didn't buy a thing," Lester says. "But anybody with my same name has got to be an all right fellow."

"Shoot," Mama says. "You're lucky he wasn't a crook. One of the ten most wanted. Picture in the post office. How would you like that?"

"My liking wouldn't have anything to do with it," Lester says. "His face, my name. Now my face in the post office would be a different story. It might just pretty up the place."

"I found my name once." Earl brakes for a light. "In an obituary. Like to have scared me to death."

Then Mama has to tell about the time H.A. (who is Evanelle's real daddy) stopped in a cemetery somewhere in Kansas. "Never been there before nor since—and there was his name big as anything on a tombstone. I tell you if that don't set your mind to thinking, nothing will."

Evanelle has heard the story ten hundred times. She could tell about the time she was scared to death, right recently. When Billy Buttons was born and nobody, nobody was there. Not Earl—he'd gone to Nashville. Not Mama—she'd gone across the river to some outlet store with Gladine Williams and they stopped to look at bedding plants and got to talking and forgot her only daughter in her time of need. Evanelle had called a dozen places from the grocery store to the beauty shop to church and couldn't find one trace of her. Here she was two weeks late and Mama had called every single day for the last month, driving her crazy, asking, "You gone yet?" Then the one day Mamma didn't call, Evanelle's water breaks and she has to call a taxi to get to the hospital. She's never been madder nor more embarrassed in her life. Then the driver didn't have change for a twenty and she'd had to stand in front of the hospital and wait—in her condition. Sometimes she didn't know how she got through half the things she did.

They were nearing The Home now. Seven Oaks, but it was only some bent little pines and seven smooth, gray stumps. The oaks had been cut down to add on to The Home and it was too much trouble to change the name. The Home was long and low like a pink motel without a marquee. It had a porte cochere with an ambulance parked under it.

"I called here yesterday," Mama says, "and they're supposed to have her up and dressed. Faith Anne is bringing her an orchid. That's what they told me at the florist. She didn't. Yellow. I said orchids aren't orchids unless they're purple, but it's not me buying. It's her money."

"Florist?" Evanelle shifts the sleeping baby. There is a damp spot on her dress and his hair is plastered down. She tries to fluff it. "I got silk," she says. "That's what you told me."

*Ruth Moose*

"I know. I know," Mama says. "But I was by the florist and just dropped in. You know how Harmon is. If you're within ten miles and don't stop, he gets his feelings hurt."

There are three flags flying in front of Seven Oaks. The state flag, the regular red, white, and blue one, and the other Evanelle can't figure out. It is purple with some sort of yellow trim and design. She can't think what it stands for. Council on Aging? Presidential Seal of Approval? Duncan Hines rating?

Earl eases into a parking place that looks too small. It is an end one and marked off for a small car. "Foreign," says Earl. "I wish they'd outlaw the things. Not let them in the gates of this country."

"I hate to wake him," Evanelle says to nobody in particular.

"Well, if you want to sit in the parking lot all day," Earl says, "we'll let you." He slicks back his hair with both hands, looks in the mirror. When Evanelle was in the eighth grade and Earl was a senior, she fell all over herself trying to make him notice her. He wore duck tails and white loafers and when he did the twist, it was "locomotion." Everybody said they had never seen anybody who could move so much standing in one place. And she'd been a little bitty thing with a ponytail, but he'd noticed. He even said then that she had more up there than most women would have in a lifetime of wishing. Then he went off to the Navy, never wrote once. When he came back, Evanelle was still there, living in the same house, doing the same things, seeing the same people. She worked after school for the radio station, answering the phone, typing spots.

"I hope I never live long enough. to have to go to one of these places," Mama says. Earl hands her the flowers, Lester takes the cake, and they leave Evanelle with the baby, diaper bag, and her handbag. She can't figure out how she's going to carry it all, but they have gone up the walk, past an old man in a sea captain's hat sitting in a wheelchair on the porch.

*Ruth Moose*

The baby wakes with a wail and Evanelle shifts him to her shoulder, the diaper bag to the other, and somehow grabs her purse. She doesn't have a free hand to shut the car door, so she gives it a boot with her foot and leaves a print on Earl's fresh wash job. She doesn't care. Serves him right.

She's glad it stopped raining or she'd be getting soaked to her toes and the baby too. He turns his eyes to the sky like he sees something, stares.

The old man in the wheelchair holds the door for her with his cane. There is a beach towel spread across his lap that has pictures of punk rockers and the words, "It's a Wild and Crazy World." Evanelle thinks it sure is. Earl and Mama aren't in sight.

"They brought me here and dumped me and haven't been back since," the old man says. He has stubble on his chin like cactus.

"Who?" Evanelle thinks of Earl and Mama.

"My daughter," he says, "and that good-for-nothing she married. That's who."

Evanelle adjusts the baby on her shoulder. Something has fallen from the diaper bag and she drags it behind her like a tail.

"You're losing something," the old man says, pokes at it with his cane.

"I got too much." Evanelle thrusts the baby onto his lap, where the baby begins threshing his legs and cranking up to cry. The old man pokes a stubby brown finger in Billy Buttons's face. "Dooba, booba doo," he says. "This boy won't turn his old daddy out in the world not caring if he lives or dies. Not this boy. No siree."

Evanelle repacks the diapers. Under the wheelchair she notices a lint-ball big and gray as a mouse. Faith Anne has been saying all the time this place wasn't kept clean.

"Yar," the old man says to the baby, who is sucking in air to let out a sharp, red-faced howl. She takes the baby, gives the old man the diaper bag, and he rolls after her. "Some around here," he says, "got chairs that go by themselves. I like to roll my own, thank you."

When they round the corner, Mama and Earl are nowhere to be seen, but Lester is leaning against the wall next to the Coke machine. "Don't tell your mama," he says, draining the last drop. Air in this place makes my mouth dry."

Evanelle wonders what Coke does to his diabetes. I must look like a parade, she thinks, with the old man in his wheelchair following her, then Lester in the rear. She feels like a drum majorette with her skirt hiked up in front and her thighs showing. Lord, Faith Anne was right, she thinks. This place almost knocks you out with ammonia. It reeks like a giant diaper pail.

There is a crowd of nurses at the nurses' station, pulling at some flowers brought over from a church service. Evanelle thinks the gladiolas look rusty and the mums limp and brown-edged. She feels something bump the back of her knees and the old man says, "I didn't go to do it, honey. It's hard to stop when somebody slows down and you got all geared up to go ahead."

The door to her grandmother's room is open and she hears Mama and Faith Anne rattling paper, moving things around. The bed is completely covered with a display of gifts and the cake they've placed at her grandmother's feet. Her grandmother looks small, plastic as a doll in a box, her silver hair screwed in tight wads like French knots. Mama loves to tell everyone The Home has its own beauty shop and everyone gets their hair done once a week whether they want it or not.

Faith Anne and Mama are taking turns posing with Grandma. "Smile, Mama," Faith Anne says. "It won't hurt you."

Grandma flickers her eyes, but keeps the same stony expression.

*Ruth Moose*

"Grandma," Evanelle starts.

"Not now, honey," Mama says, cradling Grandma at the same time she elbows Faith Anne back and smiles for Uncle Frank, who holds the camera. "Hold the thing straight," Mama says. "I don't want you cutting me off. Get both of us in there. Me and Mama."

The baby jumps when the flash goes off, squeezes shut his eyes. He'll probably do that on the picture, Evanelle thinks, but she doesn't care. Lights probably aren't all that good for his eyes anyway. Not so much at one time.

Faith Anne tries to move closer to her mother and sister, but Mama steps in front. "I don't know how many flashes he's got left"—she motions to Frank—"and we want to get the four generations in. That's what we come for."

Faith Anne makes a face and Evanelle thinks if she'd been any younger she would have stuck her tongue out at Mama. Faith Anne looks that peeved.

"I thought it was birthday," Faith Anne says. "That's what it was supposed to be about. I've had four generations three times and nobody made a fuss."

"Well," Mama says, "this is my four-generation." She takes the baby from Evanelle, jostles him upright so that he reaches out both arms like someone has a gun in his back. "Look what I brought," Mama shouts to Grandma. "You ever seen anything so cute?" She props him beside the prone woman. "Now Evanelle, honey, you come get on this side and Frank, you get us all in the picture and see if you can not make me look as big as you did the last time."

Mama jerks Evanelle around close to the bed.

Frank shoots three pictures and each time Evanelle blinks when the flash goes off. She is sure the baby does too. That ought to be next week's winner in the Horsepoint Herald. Sometimes they put generation pictures on the front page if nobody robbed a branch bank, there wasn't a flash flood or fire, and nobody shot a deer or killed a big rattlesnake.

*Ruth Moose*

"I've waited long enough for my turn." Faith Anne squeezes close between Mama and Evanelle. "I got Mama something she's never had before. A happy birthday card from Ronald Reagan—the President. Look, it's got her name right here." She pushes the card under Mama's nose.

"I can read," Mama says. "It's one like they send to everybody who asks for them."

"You got to be over eighty," Faith Anne says, "and you got to write in months ahead of time. Not everybody in this world gets one."

Evanelle looks at the gold-trimmed card. It does have some signature on it that looks real and it says Ronald Reagan.

"What's she going to do with it?" Mama asks. "I've seen prettier cards before. It's got no design, no color, no flowers, no nothing."

"Nothing but the President's signature," Faith Anne says, and waves the card. "She can put it on her bedside table for all the nurses to see"—she props it behind a water pitcher—"or hang it on the wall." Faith Anne holds the card against the wall, then presses it to her chest. "I just might have it framed for her. Myself."

"You do that, "Mama says. "Now move over. We got pictures to take here."

The baby lies like he's been stunned and Grandma reaches one old yellow hand toward him, tries to stroke his hair. She makes a deep noise in her throat that comes out like a bird squeak. Evanelle pushes the baby closer and sits on the edge of the bed.

"We've got to have at least one more picture." Mama motions to Frank. "Let's finish out the roll. Where's Earl?" She goes to the door. "We need Earl. Earl," she calls.

"That's okay," Evanelle says, and takes off her shoe, rubs her foot. "He didn't have anything to do with it." But Mama goes down the hall and comes back pulling Earl, who poses at the head of the bed just like he belongs there, which almost makes Evanelle smile. She knows a secret she'll never tell. Not if she lives to be a hundred. Not if Earl behaves himself like he has lately. Not if D.R. the D.J. goes his merry way and keeps going.

When the pictures come back, Evanelle's eyes aren't closed but she's making a funny mouth and her nose looks like she's been crying. Everybody who sees it in the Horsepoint Herald says it's a good picture. After a while Evanelle thinks, "Well, it could've been worse." But she knows different."

*Ruth Moose*

# The Green Car

IN MY DREAM someone is stealing the car, my old station wagon; its concave side, rusty rear, and temperamental starter. The dogs bark. I stand by the window, watch headlights tarnish clean white moonlight into something tawdry. Two loud men yell to each other like carnival barkers. I can't hear what they say as they slam doors, race the motor; and my car glides down the road smooth as liquid seeking a level.

I watch the scene like something on television. A moment later I get angry. How dare that car start so easily for strangers, when I, its owner, its caretaker and oil-giving friend, have to baby and coax and wheedle it into action, to get it to take me to market and classes, on errands, the girls to school. Where does its loyalty lie?

After anger, there's fright. Why would anyone steal my old car? Are they taking it first and will come back later for more and better things? I see them hauling out my grandmother's silver service, wedding china, the stereo, our TV, Kate's coin collection. I see them tying my hands, gagging my mouth, so I can't scream rape or whatever I'd scream if there was anyone to hear me.

Most of the time there's no one on this mountain but me. When everyone is home, there are six. Dave and me, the girls, Kate and Chris, and our neighbors, Thad Reeves and his wife, Betts. They live a mile away. Between us we have an assortment of cats, dogs, uncounted wildlife.

*Ruth Moose*

The Reeveses have two dogs who visit daily, frolic with our beagles. I know the dogs better than their owners.

We met Thad and Betts once before we moved and I've called her a few times. Mostly at night when she's home from work. She sounded either unfriendly, distant, or bored. I did learn the dogs' names are Red, the setter, and Plasha, the collie.

The dogs' barking wakes me and I'm shaking, but not cold. Dave is snoring steadily when I slide from the bed and stand by the window. Moonlight, pure, unbroken except for the trees, close as pickets, covers everything in a soft snow. It was only a dream. There is no one out there, and my car, worn and wearing the autograph of my city days, stands beside Dave's pickup truck. The dogs bark at deer who touch small feet to trails they knew before we came, built this house, invaded their world.

I know what triggered the dream, what mixture made it. The chilling leftover of yesterday. Another thread knitted into a garment of a shape I refuse to wear. Fear. It fits me like a shadow. I've cleaned and shaken, brushed and put away this garment, mothballed in a closet. But it does belong to me and it hangs there waiting.

I stand by the stove, wait for the fat lady of a teakettle to sound the first note of her scream. Despite the snores, Dave sleeps lightly. He has an eight o'clock lecture class. He was making lesson plans at eleven last night.

After eleven years in the business world, he returned to the university to teach. We left the city and moved to a tiny mountain near a national forest, seventeen miles from the town where the girls go to school, Dave teaches, and I shop. Three days a week, I take a class. "The Progressive Era in America, 1890-1920: Years of Protest and Reform." Someday I'll have my degree.

"You live in paradise," our city friends say. "All this clean air, trees, your own creek, and not a soul for miles,

miles." They envy the quiet, the peace of the place, our ferns, wildflowers.

I got a book, tried to identify them, teach the girls. Bloodroot, bleeding-heart, rattlesnake plantain. Our woods are full of birds. I try to learn their names and calls. Of ones I can't identify, Dave says, "Name them yourself. Call them anything you want. Red bird, blue bird, brown bird."

I hear birds now; a cardinal flies to the feeder as I make coffee.

With my steaming cup I wind through the house, in and out of rooms, touch things. The girls in blanket cocoons, polished tabletops, moist soil around plants.

The prayer plant in the living room has its leaves closed tight for the night. I never see it closing, or opening, but only fully awake and asleep. I sleep only to dream the bad dreams, the dark residue of yesterday.

Yet I like the soft hours before dawn, the silence of the sleeping house, the even breathing of the furnace, the way early light slants through the trees.

I feel in command, mistress of the manor with my family in tow. It's only after Dave leaves, the girls are gone, that I am afraid. Can I make it alone?

At the market in town, when I cash checks and clerks read my address they ask, "Aren't you afraid out there?"

Before yesterday I had given a negative answer. Said, what was there to fear? The quiet was so nice, the woods and creek beautiful; the feeling of owning all the mountain, acres, acres of it.

Someday there will be other houses here. The town will grow, grow, land sell, other people build.

"It will never be a gossip-over-the-back-fence-type place," Dave said. "No houses close enough to smell back yard grills."

People who choose to live out here have an independence about them, Dave said. Like us, I thought, like the Reeveses.

*Ruth Moose*

I hadn't recognized Betts's voice last night when she phoned, only that she was someone upset. She wanted to know if I had seen anything unusual, any strange cars? Strange men?

Nothing. I had been to class, the library, picked up the girls at school, then home.

The Reeveses' house was broken into, Betts said. A few things taken. Nothing valuable, a rifle, some money and food, but she was upset.

My first thought was that it could have been our house.

That I could have been home when the thieves came. Alone.

"What could I do?" I asked Dave.

"Simply say, 'I have a gun and if you take one more step, I'll blow your head off.'"

"But I don't have a gun," I said. Dave has talked for weeks about buying a gun. I refuse. Feel it is more dangerous to have a gun around the house. Home accidents, the girls. I would worry so much with a gun in the house.

"That person out there"—Dave pointed toward the door—"won't know whether you have a gun or not. Living out like this, he might well assume you do."

But instead I am the pioneer wife, at home alone, protecting the homestead…with empty arms. I think of all the women on Gunsmoke and inside my head I practice my line. Take one more step, Mister, and I'll blow your head off. I can't convince even myself. My voice sounds thin, silly, and anything but fierce. Even the dogs don't listen to me.

These city dogs. They go partway with me to the mailbox, sniff, take small side trips, hit a fresh deer track, and are off for half the day. None of my calls brings them back or keeps them home. At those times I feel deserted. The dogs are not really protectors. They would melt under a stranger's touch. But I bank on the fact that most strangers wouldn't know that. They do bark convincingly at times, growl to protect

*Ruth Moose*

the bones of dead deer they bring up. Our woods are posted against hunters, but they come anyway. I often hear shots, sometimes very close, and I worry the dogs, or I might be mistaken for deer.

I check the dogs' bed outside. It's empty. They are off even now, chasing the deer they saw earlier. The barks that woke me.

The mist through the trees is lovely and I like the smell of early morning, dew-damp woods. I take several deep breaths and go wake the girls.

"Your face is cold." They snuggle deeper into their blankets.

Dave's electric razor is going and by the time he is showered and dressed I have bacon on plates, an omelet in the oven.

"What's the occasion?" He pours coffee.

"Two more days until Saturday." I take the tongues of toast from the toaster.

Kate fusses, "Isn't there any jam but grape?"

Dave tells her to eat grape or plain, or not at all, but they do have to hurry. An early class means he takes the girls and I am spared the struggle with the car. I won't have to hear the usual gripes from the back seat as I jiggle and coax the old car to life.

"Why don't we get a new car?" Kate said last week.

"Because this is a good car," I said.

"If it's a good car, why won't it start?" Chris sat, fat in her overcoat, hair streaming down her back like ribbons.

"Because it needs something fixed." Dave has said one of the guys in Vocational at school can fix it. Why take it to a garage and spend forty or fifty bucks when Frank says he'll do it for free?

"When?" I asked.

"When he gets around to it," Dave said. "One of these days."

I get so tired of waiting for one of these days.

"You're hurting the economy," Chris said one morning. "When people like us don't buy new cars, it puts other people out of work"

"If people like us buy new cars when they can't afford them, then we hurt our economy."

"We have the truck," Kate said quietly, books on her lap.

Kate, the practical. "Yes, we do, don't we?" I laugh. "And the truck starts." It roars at a touch, leaps like a huge wild horse. Scares me. I need a mounting block to get into it.

Dave loves to drive the truck, gets teased at school. I drive it reluctantly. It isn't me. I'm not the size or temperament, not the self-sufficient farmer's wife. When I shop, the groceries sit beside me on the seat like brown bagged people.

"Is everyone ready?" Dave grabs his briefcase, gives me a gritty toothpaste kiss.

"Take the car today. Leave me the truck"

"I didn't think you liked the truck" Dave looks puzzled.

"I don't. It's just that. . ."

"What?"

"If the truck is here…I mean, if there's a truck parked in the drive, they might think a man is home."

"Who might think a man is home?"

"Whoever broke into the Reeveses' house yesterday."

"Why do you think they'll come back?" He tries to read my eyes, looks long enough to see down to my toes. "Don't you?"

"No, I really don't. What did they take? Food, some loose change, a gun. They weren't pros. I think it was kids hitchhiking, taking a trail through the woods."

I think they could still be here, hiding. Waiting. "Betts was quite upset."

"And her hysteria rubbed off on you, right?"

I swallow a lump of cold coffee. "Not really, but what if—?"

"They won't." He sounds positive. "Most break-ins happen during the day when no one is home." He checks the door locks, gives me a kiss. "Make sure the doors are locked."

Last week I had come home from class to find the door open, living room full of leaves, and a dog asleep in each chair. I was frightened and went through the house checking closets, under beds, behind shower doors, and even then could not relax until Dave and the girls got home.

The door had simply blown open. It had not been shut tightly. But I asked myself, what would I have done had I found someone? I don't know.

I scrape dishes, load the dishwasher, look up to see a shadow flick past my window. My imagination. The first week we lived here, I saw someone outside my kitchen window and was near a scream, when he lifted his cap, said, "I'm from the electric company, ma'am. Here to check the meter." There had not been a single bark from the dogs. They had been off for a swim in the lake, hunting a delicious scent, leaping after a deer. No loyalty—like the car.

"Sandy," Pete calls from the drive, "I can't get the car started. And if I keep working on it, I'll be late. Sorry."

I wave from the deck until the truck disappears—stand there until I no longer hear the motor, only birds and trees and my own breathing. I go back to the dishes, routine things.

While the vacuum runs, I try to organize my term paper. Number my notes, footnotes.

When I glance up and out the window I see a green car slowly going past our road. It almost stops, then goes on.

At first I'm frightened; then I relax. A lot of times people take a wrong turn off the highway and often there are inquiries about buying property, since most of it is still unsold.

The car comes back, turns in our drive, stops. Two men get out. One is a boy in jeans. His boots crunch across the gravel as he walks to my car and gets in. He gets in my car.

*Ruth Moose*

This is last night's dream, but real. It's happening and I don't know what to do. The other man comes toward the house.

The car starts and goes halfway down the drive before it stops, idles.

I run to the phone, find the number I typed on a card taped to the base. 983-111 ...large black type. My fingers are wet and slip as I dial. Hurry, hurry, hurry. The sheriff will know where to come. He was at the Reeveses' yesterday.

Someone knocks on my door. Do thieves knock? Is it a guise? Should I say nothing, wait for them to break in?

"Mrs. Paxton," he calls.

I still don't answer. He could have read our name off the mailbox. The phone is ringing at the sheriff's office. Once, twice, three times. Where are they? Why don't they answer?

"Pete sent us to get the car."

I hang up the phone.

"It's Frank Willis from Vocational, over at school," he says. "Pete told me a few weeks ago he wanted me to take a look at the car. He reminded me a while ago."

I remember Frank from the faculty picnic—thin, dark haired, glasses, very unlike my idea of a mechanic.

"Pete gave me his keys and I brought one of the students to drive it in." Frank stands on the deck, smiles. "I thought I better tell you, so you wouldn't think we were stealing it."

He laughs.

"Thank you." I can't laugh, or even attempt any sort of a smile. ''You did scare me."

"Gosh." He waves his arms. "This is a great place to live. Don't you love it?" He reaches down to scratch the ears of one of the dogs who have come from the woods, sit thumping, smiling at his feet.

I glare at the dog. Where were you when I needed you? Frank waves, goes back to the green car. "See you later." The dogs run, circle around me, jump for attention. "Why don't you stay home?" I ask them. They only thump and smile, fenced city dogs relishing in their new freedom. They want to explore coves, creeks, follow every trail.

I go into the house for my red jacket, slip it on, tucking my hair into the knitted red hood. Keys in my pocket, I carefully lock the doors and head toward the mailbox. The dogs rush past, look back as if to say, come on, let's run. Sometimes I do run and laugh and look at my shadow like a child. I whoop and call hello to hear my voice, to know that I am not afraid.

I walk between trees, over the bridge. The creek rushes around the rocks, charges and roars like a tan beast. At places it rises up full of challenge and spunk.

I take a deep cool breath, then hum as I walk up the road, hands deep in my pockets. I've never learned to whistle. This is a good time to try.

*Ruth Moose*

# Rules and Secrets

MISS MELODY MCLEAN was from Virginia. No one knew how she came to teach that one year in a small town in the North Carolina mountains, but there she was the first day of school, sitting on her desk, rollbook in hand, checking us off as if we were a shipment of rare goods she had waited a long time for. Her red-orange hair waved and curled with a mind of its own and her green eyes always saw something to smile about. She wore a plaid skirt, white organdy blouse, green vest, and swung her long freckled legs. She had more freckles than anyone I'd ever seen. Arms, legs, face—more freckles even than Vaden Stringer, who had a million. One time Miss Mclean hugged Vaden and said, "If there was a freckle-counting contest, Vaden and I would tie for first place." He smiled wider than anyone had ever seen him. Maybe because nobody had hugged him before. Most of the teachers tried to stay as far away from him as possible and nobody wanted to be the one in front of or directly behind him in line. He usually smelled. Like car motors or oil or grease. His father ran the local garage, the family lived above it, and Vaden must have played in and around the grease pits. Teachers gave up long ago when they inspected nails. Vaden was always passed over. Except by Miss Mclean. Vaden began to come to school with cleaner shirts, sometimes ironed and free of grease spots, and he started combing his hair. He worked on his hands and they were cleaner. Not as clean as anybody else's hands, but wonderfully clean for Vaden.

*Ruth Moose*

Miss McLean always noticed when anyone wore anything new—scarf, blouse, shirt, jeans, sweater, socks—and commented. "That's a pretty new dress, Lucy," she'd say. Lucy Estridge looked down to see what dress she was wearing and said, "It's just one my mother made."

"How wonderful to have such a talented mother." Miss Mclean touched the collar. "Not everyone can sew and it means you can have so many more clothes."

Lucy looked like she'd never thought about it like that before. And began to say when she had something new, before anyone could comment," My mother made me this dress." Or blouse, or skirt. Her mother even made Lucy a coat and jumper of soft green wool. We envied Lucy now and wished our mothers could sew.

Lucy was pretty that year. Maybe she always was and we'd never really looked at her before. The way no one had ever listened to Carolyn sing. We didn't know she could sing until Miss Mclean picked her for the part of Dinah Shore for the Friday assembly. And Kenny Stone. "Crooner," we called him for weeks afterward, and he looked. it. All the fifth-grade girls got his autograph and used to follow him on the playground. Skinny Kenny Stone with the thick glasses and pointed nose. Miss Mclean took the glasses off, combed his hair back like Bing Crosby, and put him behind the broomstick microphone. He had a wonderful, deep voice. There was swooning in assembly that Friday. Carolyn wore her older sister's pink satin evening gown with the sweetheart neckline and borrowed her grandmother's fox fur piece. She was glamorous, she was Hollywood, after Miss McLean made her up, swept back her hair on one side, and pinned in a silk carnation. Bing—er—Kenny was clear and strong. The rest of the year Carolyn and I sang as we walked home from school.

But Miss Mclean wasn't all play and music. She said a lot, "Work when you work, play when you play." We worked when we worked. But it was fun. Arithmetic problems became real when she substituted our names for the ones in the book, or the names of businesses in town. History was acted out—if you read your assignment and knew what to do. Spelling was always two teams chosen for six weeks at a time, with the winners receiving certificates Miss McLean made. She had two shelves of her own books, brought from home, for us to read, check out, and take home. We'd read all the good ones in the library and I loved books with her name in them in that fancy, curling handwriting.

"I don't know what that teacher's doing," Mama said one night, "but your math grades are improving. She's got you really interested and working like you should for the first time."

Miss McLean had us working in partners. We switched every week, graded each other's papers and studied together. It was fun every week but the one I had with Sylvia Hurley. She cried when you marked one of her answers wrong, begged you not to. How was she going to learn if you didn't mark wrong answers? And she missed a lot of them. She copied over every paper and put in the right answers. I had to mark 100 on it so she could show her mother.

Sylvia was the only one unhappy that year. She'd always come to school looking like she'd been crying. Sometimes there were bruise marks on her arms or legs. She was last in line to everything and nobody wanted her on their team for softball. Most of the time she wouldn't play anyway, but sat on the bank by herself and didn't even watch. If the ground was damp, Miss McLean spread her jacket or sweater for Sylvia to sit on. That was one of the few times Sylvia smiled, looked even a little happy.

We were on the playground the day Sylvia's mother came to school and argued at Miss McLean. We couldn't hear everything she said, but she kept jerking Sylvia by the collar of her dress, pulling her arms, and Sylvia cried. "My child wouldn't steal your handkerchief," Mrs. Hurley yelled. "She's not a thief."

"Of course not," Miss McLean said. "Nobody ever thought she was."

Mrs. Hurley yelled some more things that didn't make sense and Miss McLean kept saying, "I gave Sylvia my handkerchief. She had a cold and didn't have one."

That seemed to make Mrs. Hurley even more angry and she started yelling a lot of things about taking care of her own child's needs and Miss McLean kept saying she knew she did and Sylvia was such a well-behaved student, tried so very hard in every subject and so on. Miss McLean's voice was sweet and nice. Once she reached to put her arm around Sylvia but Mrs. Hurley jerked her away. Finally, more upset than ever, yelling and screaming things, she grabbed Sylvia's elbow and pulled her away. We watched them walk off the playground. When we grouped around Miss McLean to return to class, tears had dried on her cheeks and she excused herself to stop by the teacher's lounge.

Nobody could understand what the fuss had been about. Of course Miss McLean had given Sylvia the handkerchief. She was always doing things like that, loaning her books, pencils…to all of us. Whatever we needed. And when we finished, we returned them. Sylvia must have kept the handkerchief, wanted it, because Miss McLean was so special, and everything that belonged to her was special. Her handkerchiefs had monograms in the corners and were trimmed with lace. Miss McLean wouldn't have cared if Sylvia had stolen the handkerchief. She would have let her keep it, if she'd ask. What was one handkerchief? Who would steal one? Who would accuse anyone of stealing something so silly? Something at all. Not Miss Mclean. But why did she cry?

We were all in our seats and strangely quiet when Miss Mclean, face washed and lipstick freshened, came in. She still looked pale, moved some books and papers to sit on the corner of her desk. "I wish that you had not had to witness the incident on the playground a few minutes ago. And I hope you won't feel or act any differently toward Sylvia because of it. Except to be more understanding with her and toward her. She can't change the way things are in her life, not yet—maybe not ever—and we can help by being more patient, less critical. We won't mention this again." She picked up the geography book, turned to the chapter on "African States," pulled down the pink and green map, got down to business.

On the way home Carolyn and I talked. Last year, other years, Sylvia had been called "Bird Legs" or "Bird Brain" or "Feather Face"—ugly names—and she'd shrugged them off, even smiled. I was glad we'd never called her things, but I remembered times I'd giggled when somebody else did, and felt terrible. Times when I got to choose teams and waited until last to pick her, hoping the other captain would, then yelled at her when she dropped a fly ball on the third out and we lost.

Carolyn and I invited Sylvia to the church Halloween party, offered to give her a ride. At five-thirty she called, said her mother was going out and she had to go with her. Sylvia sounded like she'd been crying.

"I'd cry too," Carolyn said, "if my mother made me miss the Halloween party."

Lights were on at Sylvia's house, the car in the drive, when we drove past at nine, taking Benny Cushman home. "I bet she didn't go out at all," Carolyn said. We didn't mention it to Sylvia—the party or anything. Some things are better left unsaid, Miss Mclean had said a long time before about anger and retaliation. We liked the sound of that word, new words, but she didn't write it on the board as she usually did any new word we heard or asked about.

Anger was like a shade pulled over her face the day

*Ruth Moose*

she read aloud—according to instructions—the new school policy toward Christmas, against gifts and "any said and possibly planned parties" at school. This was the word sent down from the superintendent's office. The law of the red brick land. "No student shall give any teacher a Christmas present. Due to the differences in circumstances, since all students are not able to give gifts of equal value, none shall be given. And consequently, no teacher shall give students gifts of any kind. There will be no Christmas parties allowed in any classroom in the system. To facilitate janitorial and maintenance services, holiday decorations should be kept to a minimum." Miss McLean's face got darker and darker as she read the notice. We didn't understand it. In the past, I'd given teachers gifts, small gift-wrapped boxes with the bow the biggest thing about them. Usually earrings, lotion or perfumed soap, a scarf. Carolyn and I spent hours in the dime store picking out the perfect gift for our teachers. The day we left school for our holidays was always party day. With cupcakes and punch, games (how many words can you make out of the words "Merry Christmas"?) and carols, listening to the Nutcracker Suite or a teacher reading Dickens's "Christmas Carol." We could have none of that this year? It wouldn't be Christmas. Who was the superintendent of schools? Scrooge? There were cries of protest around the room, Oh no's and How could anyone be so mean? At Christmastime? It was awful.

Miss McLean thought so too, but she didn't say much. "In Virginia, I gave my class a party. I was planning—"

She was going to give us a party? No teacher had ever done that before. Room mothers came in and gave parties with cupcakes and candy canes, Santa napkins, but a teacher giving her class a party was something else. "Please, Miss Mclean," we begged, "isn't there any way we can still have the party? We won't invite the superintendent. We won't tell the principal. We'll be so quiet no one will know."

*Ruth Moose*

She grinned with a small shake of her head. "I wish I could."

Why can't you?" Kenny Stone stood at his desk. "No one would have to know. We can keep it a secret."

Miss Mclean laughed, looked at us in a warm, sad way. "Oh my little dears…it would never work."

"And if she went against the rules, she'd be fired," said Bruce Stern. His daddy was a deputy for the sheriff's department, wore a uniform with a badge, carried a gun. Sometimes he picked Bruce up at school in the county car. "Using taxpayers' gas," Daddy said. "I don't think it's right." But he did it anyway and nobody said anything.

Miss Mclean's giving the class a party herself was not using taxpayers' money, nor school funds. Why couldn't she do it? Carolyn and I discussed it walking home. Life was unfair, school was unfair, and whoever was superintendent wanted to make Christmas miserable for us.

The next day, Miss Mclean asked everyone to stay for a few minutes after final bell. We would have stayed forever for her.

"This class is going to have a Christmas party," she announced, her eyes sparkling.

We looked at each other, mouthed oh boy, oh boy. Then remembered. "How?" asked Carolyn. "The rule made by the superintendent. You'll—"

"Maybe not," Miss Mclean smiled. "I'll have the party at my apartment, on my own time, and that shouldn't get anybody in trouble." She wrote the time on the board. An open house, six until eight o'clock, and her address.

She never told us not to tell. Somehow we knew. We were breaking a rule and keeping a secret about it. That made the party even more special, exciting. But what to tell our parents?

I solved that by spending the night with Carolyn. We did that on Friday nights often. And we simply told Carolyn's

*Ruth Moose*

mother we were going to an open house at Miss Mclean's.

Carolyn wore her blue velvet dress with lace collar and cuffs, her new coat with the white rabbit collar, and both of us wore our Sunday slippers, white ankle socks and matching charm bracelets we exchanged for Christmas, opening them early to wear to the party.

The streets had been scraped dry of snow that frosted yards, shrubbery, and rooftops and made the world look like a Christmas card. Chimneys ballooned out plumes of smoke and we stopped every block or so to admire our bracelets or try to puff out a perfect ring of breath.

Miss McLean had a wreath of fresh balsam on her door with holly, pine cones, and a soft red bow. Christmas music and the smell of something hot, orange, and spicy met us at the door, opened by Kenny Stone, in sport coat and tie. Sylvia took our coats, hung them in the closet.

Miss McLean, with a moss-green bow in her hair, matching long skirt and red gingham blouse, poured punch, gave us small sandwiches and decorated cookies.

We stood around like strangers. Everyone looked so dressed up and so pretty—even Sylvia. I wondered what she'd told her mother, and if she came alone? Probably Miss McLean would take her home, though none of us lived more than six blocks or so from school.

I'd walked by this apartment building every school day for six years and had never seen inside. Four teachers lived in four apartments. Sometimes we saw wash on the line and guessed what belonged to who. Sometimes we giggled when we recognized a blouse or shirtwaist dress of the second-grade teacher or Miss Beal, the librarian.

The living room had bookshelves on each side of the fireplace that reached the ceiling, all painted white, as were the walls; green wool carpet, matching drapes, and an armchair of the same color. There was a small desk by the window, a yellow lamp with a shade of different kinds of birds. I decided Miss McLean graded homework papers there. Unless she used the kitchen table, my favorite place at home rather than the kneehole desk in my bedroom. There was a mirror above the fireplace and I looked at all of us framed there, the lights, laughter, and Miss Mclean lifting red punch from a crystal bowl, candles reflecting in her cheeks, her eyes. Sylvia, by the door, important, collecting coats, placing them carefully on hangers. And Kenny Stone by the fireplace, Bruce Stern putting on another log.

Later we sang carols around the piano, Miss McLean playing softly, as she sometimes did on rainy days when we could get the music room off the auditorium. Carolyn sang "Silent Night" as a solo, then "O Little Town of Bethlehem" as a duet with Bruce. Everyone sang "We Three Kings" last and as we left Miss Mclean gave us gifts—two new red pencils apiece, saying, "I don't want to hear anyone say they don't have a pencil next time I announce a spelling test."

We laughed, gave mock groans. Then she gave us each an envelope with our names written in red ink, said, "Merry Christmas."

Carolyn and I didn't open the envelopes until we were outside. Under the streetlights we dug from the envelope three movie passes, "Admit One" to the Center Theater. We hugged each other, dancing in the cold. Movies! Three free passes. Nothing could have been as wonderful. She was giving us the world for three Saturday afternoons: Tom Mix, Superman, Wonder Woman, Roy Rogers and Dale Evans, Lash LaRue...the Pan-a-View News, popcorn and Cokes. Each other. No teacher had ever given us a party before, certainly not at her home, with gifts. Pencils, because she was serious about school and leaning and wanted us to be too. Movie passes because she believed life should have some fun in it.

Fun was movies on Saturdays, but it was also school five days a week. I denied colds, sore throats, and low fevers that year, to keep my mother from keeping me home. Missing a day would have meant missing everything, seeing everybody, Miss McLean. Almost nobody was absent, even Sylvia, who last year had been on the absent list several days a week, looked bluish, pale, and thin shivering in her chair when she was there. She moved that spring, an oddity for the town and our lives. Each year we had the same people, from first grade on. You knew who you wanted to sit beside, be on your relay, dodge ball, softball team. Sylvia didn't say goodbye. No one knew until the Monday morning Miss McLean, with a firm mouth, made the announcement and started the day's work. We wondered where she moved? Why would anyone move before school was out? And especially since we were planning a May Day. Lucy's mother was making costumes, Carolyn's blue and mine yellow. A long dress with the skirt a complete circle. We couldn't wait.

My father grumbled behind his newspaper that he was "paying good money for a dress that will only be worn once. Somebody in this town has big ideas."

A seventh-grade girl, Sarah Grambling, was May Queen. She was beautiful, blond with round blue eyes, the longest dark lashes in the world, and a different angora sweater for each day of the week.

Three of us were chosen for the May Court. We were to wear lacy picture hats, carry bouquets of real daisies. Daddy said it was too much for a little elementary school in a small town.

Mother said it was going to be beautiful and she hoped he could get off work to come.

He didn't answer.

Mother kept rolling my hair on leather curlers, twisting them tight to my head. "I try," she sighed, "even if it doesn't stay in."

I thought of Miss McLean who never had to roll her hair at all, how it waved, curled, and did things by itself. Like she did. All energy and sparkle and fun. She suggested the May Day, planned and directed it. And it was beautiful, more beautiful than even my mother thought.

The whole town turned out to see the king and queen crowned, the throne Miss Mclean borrowed from one of the churches set atop a platform covered with red felt. There was a red runner on the front lawn and a processional for the presentation of the court. I bobbed and bowed, didn't spill flowers from my basket. Court jesters did card tricks and juggled. Toby Simpson rode his unicycle and Kenny Stone's black and white dog did tricks. ,

Fathers took pictures, some movies of it all. The Maypoles were braided to music, unbraided, then woven again. Everyone said it was beautiful, and parents kept repeating this to the principal, superintendent, who stood stiff and out of place in dark suits, narrow ties. They didn't smile much, complained about the heat "so early in the year," and brushed playground dust from their polished shoes.

Summer vacation and the end of the school year came too fast. The last day nobody wanted to leave. We stayed to stack books, rewash boards, put chairs on tables, take down decorations, divide up the plants, discard dead science projects, and clean out closets. Anything to linger. Miss McLean shushed us when we said there would never be another teacher we'd love as much as her, another year that would be more fun. "Go on with all of you." She headed us toward the door. "Get on with the business of growing up." She hugged everybody, tousled Bruce Stern's hair and told Carolyn to keep on singing.

What was she going to do this summer? "Going back to Virginia," she said.

"See you next year," we called, feeling lightheaded to leave the classroom without an armload of books, homework assignments.

*Ruth Moose*

The next week Carolyn and I went to her apartment to visit. We promised ourselves we wouldn't go in--or maybe only for a glass of iced tea—if she invited us. For an excuse we carried potholders we'd woven on a lap loom Carolyn got for her birthday.

There was no answer at the door. We heard it ring when we rang again. It was working. Surely she hadn't packed and left so soon. Not for the whole summer. We weren't tall enough to peer in the door glass, so we had to find a low window, one that looked in the living room. The empty, empty living room. And kitchen and bedroom.

We couldn't believe it. "Maybe she found a better apartment," Carolyn said.

"In this town?" It wasn't possible.

Or moved to a house? My daddy would have said something. He sold real estate—but not lately. I heard him tell people, "I used to sell real estate."

She had moved. Disappeared, left our lives. We would never see her again. Carolyn and I said it must have been Sylvia who told. Or Sylvia's mother.

Bruce Stern said once at the swimming pool he had gotten a letter from Miss McLean. But he never showed it to anyone and he liked to tell lies.

*Ruth Moose*

# Who Cooks for You?

WHEN BONNIE ROSE set out with her basket and tester, she always felt a little like Red Riding Hood. She went over highways and past woods, to country homes and city apartments. She was your handy-dandy microwave demonstrator "by appointment only." It wasn't a bad job for part-time. She made her own schedule juggling appointments between other people's hours and her classes and family. It wasn't easy, but she liked most of the people she had met, and she usually outran the wolves. Since her husband, Pete, lost his job eighteen months before, the wolves always seemed to be after her: the food market wolf, the mortgage wolf, the utility company wolf, the charge account wolf. They snapped at her heels, threatened, nipped and snarled. She felt their hot breath on her neck, heard them groan in her sleep, but she kept them away tossing tidbits.

Today's wolf was real. He had glittering eyes, a neat little beard, two steaks and a chilled bottle of wine. She walked right into his parlor with her basket and job. How could she not have known?

21C Brakston Court was a brick duplex with peeling trim and torn black shutters. Bonnie Rose checked her notebook as she rang the bell. Yunger, Fredrick. The space beside Wife's name was empty, but sometimes the company salesperson simply failed to fill it in. The shrubbery beside the porch was shaggy and behind it were beer cans, an upended pizza box.

*Ruth Moose*

She's been in this demonstration business for a year now and in all kinds of houses, met all kinds of people. The ones who apologized for their "mess" were usually the ones with a spotless house, a kitchen that looked like a floor covering ad in magazines. They waxed and polished even drawer pulls. She loved those kitchens. In others she smiled and started with how to keep their microwave ovens clean: glass tray, interior walls, the door.

"Mr. Yunger?" Bonnie Rose saw a maroon terry jogging suit unzipped to his waist, dark curly chest hair, and lizard-skin cowboy boots. "Is Mrs. Yunger home?"

"I'm it," he laughed. "Come in. The oven's in the kitchen like a good little oven should be. Or do you want it some other place? I can move it for a lady's convenience." He smiled, held the door.

"Wine?" he asked, and poured a glass.

"No, thank you—I'm really on a very tight schedule. I need an ice cube, though."

"In your wine? You like it iced? It's more bodied at room temperature. If you've never tried it—"

"An ice cube for the demonstration," she said firmly between her teeth, and reached inside the freezer, past a decal on the refrigerator door of a huge pink panther holding a glass of champagne.

"Here, let me." He brushed against her. "Oops, sorry."

She didn't know if he was making a pass, extremely clumsy, slightly drunk, or all three. All she knew was she wanted to get her demonstration done and get out of there fast.

"This is your program for defrosting," she said, but he didn't seem to be listening. He poked in a drawer. "You smoke?" he said.

"No," she said. Her head felt wooden. She could go through her talk in her sleep, like a nursery rhyme…And this is how we thaw our food so quickly in the evening. Her feet ached. Her throat felt scratchy.

*Ruth Moose*

"For temperature-controlled cooking," she continued, "use your probe."

"So that's what the little devil is." He twirled the probe in his fingers. "Well, I'll be probed and prodded and—"

"In this mode"—she inserted the probe—"you can program the temperature and it will hold indefinitely."

"That's me," he said. "On hold indefinitely unless you can do something about it." He moved around the counter, reached toward her. "Look, honey—"

She stepped back. Her elbow hit the wine glass, knocked it over. She grabbed her basket and ran. She probably left the door open, churned and spun gravel in his driveway getting away so fast. She didn't care. All she knew was to get out as fast as she could. She remembered his open mouth as she ran. She should have shoved the oven in it.

Still shaking, she screeched to a stop at a traffic light. The nerve of the Hairy Little Bastard. She'd heard other demonstrators talk of HLBs at their monthly meetings. Several had bachelors or newly divorced guys make suggestive remarks about flanks and being well-done. "Everybody gets at least one," her supervisor had said. But Bonnie Rose had never had one until today. Well, they can have it, she thought, and this job too. She wanted to pound her dash, sit on her horn, kick and scream and yell. Something. She looked in her mirror. What if he followed her? But a blue sedan was behind, a man who looked tired, distracted. Beside her, a station wagon with two blond toddlers batting balloons. She glanced down and saw she was still wearing her red "Deluxe Foods" apron. She laughed and kept laughing. Anyone seeing her would have thought she was some runaway housewife. People in the cars around her probably thought she was some madwoman. She was mad—angry, angry, angry. Bonnie Rose pressed the accelerator; the car surged forward.

There was an ache between her shoulders. When she pulled in at home she noticed Pete's truck parked at an odd angle, the tailgate down.

She heard hammering as she put her books on the hall table. What was Pete doing? She followed the hammering to Marty's bedroom, where everything from the closet lay heaped on the bed—toys, clothes, shoes. Pete was putting shelves in Marty's closet. The organizing shelves she'd mentioned months, maybe two years before. Pete poked his head out, grinned. "Hi, babe."

"It's going to be neat, huh, Mom?" Marty said.

"Great, but what about Scouts?" Bonnie Rose looked at the shavings, sawdust, scattered tools. "And what about dinner?"

"Do I have to go?" Marty said. He picked up a baseball mitt, kneaded it. "I'd rather help Dad."

"It's okay by me," Bonnie Rose said, "but what about your derby entry and money for the campout? It's due tonight."

"I guess I'd better go." Marty laid the glove down.

"Hey," Pete said somewhere from the closet, "I guess I forgot."

He also forgot dinner. She'd left instructions on the refrigerator door to thaw the ground beef and make the Chili Casserole.

She didn't say it was okay, because it wasn't."

Breakfast was still on the table. Cereal, sugar, coffee cups. God, she hated a dirty kitchen, and she wasn't going to cook in one when she wasn't being paid to do it.

She checked the schedule. Lucy's turn. So where was Lucy? In the library. Lucy had scribbled a note on the telephone pad. Thanks a lot, Bonnie Rose thought. Other people around here have to study too.

I won't touch it, she thought. I won't touch a thing if it's midnight when she gets home. Someone around here has to teach responsibility.

Bonnie Rose picked up her textbook, went to the porch. She was glad she made good notes. Now all she had to do was carve out time to really go over them, to concentrate. She couldn't do it! She was tired, hungry, upset, harried, and at the bottom of the well. Pete had been out of work a year and a half now. His company had relocated and was consumed by a merger, and the parent company had someone on staff for his job. Cost Accounting. He was good at it, but there wasn't a vacancy within two hundred miles. They could move, but not for another six months. She had one more semester to get her teacher's certificate. "Wherever we are there will always be schools, and schools have to have teachers. Teaching is a job and that way at least one of us will have a job." She'd been back in school almost a semester and she both loved and hated it. She loved the fact that the classroom and her assignments took her mind off money worries. She liked her classes. She liked looking at learning and how it worked, why certain methods were appropriate to certain types of learners, but she hated the way her life was scheduled down to minutes. Even sleep was a luxury.

Beside Pete's chair was his coffee cup, an overflowing ash tray. He could at least pick up around here. Mail lay on the floor. Most of the time the people Pete contacted through the classified ads never bothered to reply. She flipped through circulars, envelopes addressed "Occupant," a dentist's bill, utility statement—$89.75, and that was not even using the dryer. It was broken. The last letter had the Deluxe Foods logo. Bonnie Rose's hand shook. More demos. She couldn't. She just wouldn't—not after today. She was still so angry she wanted to bite something very hard and scream very loudly. Damn, damn, damn.

"Hon." Someone touched her shoulder and Bonnie Rose jumped. "Don't. Don't." She started crying, shaking.

"What's wrong?" Pete said. "What's wrong?"

"Don't touch me."

"I only wanted to say Scouts meet in twenty minutes and I can stop by for burgers on the way back."

*Ruth Moose*

She didn't answer, but rushed past him to the bathroom, where she cried into a towel until her cheeks felt raw. Pete rubbed her back, hugged her. "Whatever it is, it isn't worth it." He rocked her. "You do too much. You don't have to make Dean's List. You don't have to be the best Deluxe Foods demonstrator. You push yourself too hard."

"And you're not pushing at all," she screamed. "You charged more lumber and the account is past due now and—and."

"I'm taking Marty to Scouts." His mouth was a hard, dark line. "Then we'll talk."

When he came back she had washed her face, put on fresh lipstick, and made a cup of lemon tea. She told him about the latest wolf.

Pete's face flamed. "Who the hell does he think he is? Who do you report this to?"

"No one, really." She shook her head. "And nothing happened except he tried. I don't have to go back there."

"But what about the next one?"

"I can handle it."

"Why don't you quit? Tell Deluxe they can have this great job."

"I'd love to, but it's three hundred dollars a month that's paying some bills and it's something I can schedule in with my classes. We have to think about that."

"It doesn't pay enough for that kind of harassment. You don't have to do it."

"I don't want to do it. I don't want to ever go through my song-and-dance this-is-how-to-cook-your-food-so-fast—"

"There's got to be other things." He let go her hands, walked to the window. "I'd like to do small jobs for people… home contracting, repairs …little things the big companies don't have time to fool with. Things like building decks, like the shelves I'm doing for Marty's closet—that kind of thing.

I think we could make a living. Not a great one, but enough to hold us together for a while."

She didn't know. She didn't doubt he could do the work. He loved building, remodeling, adding things to the house. He'd completely built an entertainment wall in the den; cabinets he made for the kitchen cost half the original ones. But as a business…she didn't know.

"What say we try?"

He said "we," which was a start.

Bonnie Rose didn't really believe he'd do it, and certainly not make a living at it, but she smiled. It was one thing to know the HLBs existed. It was another to know she could handle them.

# King of the Comics

MAMA MAKES ICED tea in her white-curtained closet of a kitchenette. She, who used to think small kitchens were a curse and closed her in, loves this one. She has any extra inch filled with plants. An asparagus fern brushes my head, tickles my neck. Begonias, spider plants, geraniums, others crowd out the light. Daddy used to say Mother not only had a green thumb, she had green fingers to match it. Plants are a part of my childhood; this apartment is not. Mother moved here after Daddy died, kept few things from the house, a chair, her small drop-leaf table, mirror and chest. Mostly everything is new and it is strange to me to see her here.

"I don't remember any Beasleys living on Harmon Street." She hands me a wedge of lemon, thick and large the way I have always liked it. "Lemonade," Mother used to say, "that's what you drink—not tea. Leave the tea out and be honest with it."

"The Beasleys lived in the white two-story house at the top of the hill." I drink my tart-sweet tea. An ice cube bumps my nose, chills the tip.

"You mean Clara's house," she says. "Clara sold it to—"

"No, I mean the one across from Clara's house. Beasleys. They had a maid."

"Nobody on Harmon Street ever had a maid." Mama lays her spoon on a napkin, holds up one finger. "Wait. Old Mrs. Toliver. She had a maid once. No, that was a nurse and just before she died. Poor old dear, I haven't thought about

*Ruth Moose*

her in years."

"No, I'm sure the Beasleys had a full-time maid. She used to walk down the street early in the mornings." I remember her carrying an umbrella and shopping bag. The shopping bag bumped her legs and she used the umbrella to keep the sun off her head when she waited for the bus.

Every dog on Harmon Street yapped at her every morning. It was quiet when I walked toward the Beasleys' in the soft black tar later in the day. A broken strap on one of my sandals made me clop like a crippled horse, but the street was hot and I didn't dare take them off. I couldn't go barefooted beside the street because there were clumps of nettles, sharp, spiny things with evil-smelling yellow berries my brothers loved to shoot in their slingshots. I did better with gravel and liked the sound it made hitting something. Roger and Rich also shot chinaberries, and wild cherries.

Anything to make a stink or stain, Mama said, and send one of the neighborhood kids running to her or home screaming. But that was mosty last summer. This year we were older, read a lot, played games. A single Monopoly game continued a week if the fights settled peacefully and nobody moved the board. Mostly it was comic books. "Thank the Lord for whoever invented them," Mama said. "I haven't had so much peace and quiet in the house at one time since they were all sick with the mumps."

I carefully carried a stack of comic books under my arm. "Superman" was on top, "Masked Marvel" next, "Tales of Horror." "Wild West Adventures" and "Archie," "Baby Huey" and "Casper" on the bottom.

"Don't trade for any mush stuff," Roger said as I left. "No 'True Romance' or that junk."

"He doesn't have those," I said, and decided if he did, I'd trade for them.

"Be sure the beat-up comics are on the bottom," Rick said.

*Ruth Moose*

"He won't notice."

"The heck he won't," Roger said, jumped and tried to touch the door frame. "He'd make you trade two of ours for one of his if you didn't watch."

I was to trade with "Bug" Beasley, since the last time Roger and Rick went they came home cheated. A rotten deal. He wouldn't take one of ours if a cover was loose, page torn or anything.

"Bug has his comics written down," Rick said. "A list on his wall. He checks off when you borrow one, knows when you bring it back. Won't trade for one he's had."

"He's crazy." Roger rolled his eyes.

"Crazy smart." Rick flexed his muscle. "His room's neat. All those planes and stuff."

The Beasleys had only lived on Harmon Street a few months. Bill was a year older than me, three years older than Roger and Rick. He played with us evenings. Games in the dark. Hide and Seek, Run Sheep Run, Snake in the Gully, Sling the Biscuit…games where somebody always gets hurt, Mama said. "Why do you kids think it is fun to run and scream like something crazy in the dark?"

I shifted the comic books under my arm, yanked up my elastic halter and felt my breast rub against me. Mama had been trying to put me in a bra all summer. I had held out so far and only wore one to church. Dressed up it wasn't so bad. "Boys don't wear those things," I told Mama.

"They don't have to," she said.

I made a face as she left the room.

A bra was all straps that held me down, reined me in like a horse.

On the Beasley porch, I took off my sandals, left them beside the brick steps and made dusty shadow prints as I walked the slick, gray paint to the door.

The doorbell sounded harsh over the kitchen radio tuned to "Our Gal Sunday…Can a young girl from. a small mining town in the West find happiness as a wife of a wealthy and titled Englishman?"

"Yes," Mrs. Beasley called. Her tiny heels tapped the waxed floor toward me. Always dressed to the teeth, makeup, perfume, and dangling earrings…Mama said she was "artificial as a doll." Mrs. Hendon across the street said, "The rest of us could go around dressed up all day if we had someone doing our work too."

"It's Frances," I called, "Frances Bolt."

"Come in, dear." She held the door, her orange hair in curls like carrot peels covering her head.

"I came to trade comics with Bill." I shifted the books. In the kitchen, the ironing board groaned as the maid ironed.

"Bil-lie," Mrs. Beasley called up the stairs, hand on the rail. A ring with a green stone big as a grasshopper sat on her finger.

Bill came to the top of the stairs, rubbed his head as if he'd been asleep. "Okay"—he saw the books—"if you got anything I want."

The lenses of his glasses were so thick it was hard to tell what he was thinking.

"Let me see what you got." He took my books, sat on the floor of his room, spread them around. "I've seen this one." He slid "Superman" across to me.

I studied his stamp collection framed on the walls.

He flipped "Masked Marvel" at me. "This is old. Where do you get such junk? The trash can?" He flipped another. "'Archies'…I don't read."

That made three strike-outs. Eight left. I wondered if he'd like any of them. Spread on his desk like a fossil were the ribs of a model airplane.

"Don't touch that," he snapped. "Glue's not dry."

I put my hands behind me.

"There's comics under the bed," Bill said. He lifted the spread, pulled several out.

Ruth Moose

I saw a "Spider Man" Roger and Rick would like, a new "Horror Tales" halfway back. I slid under to reach it. There were dust bunnies and I had to rub my nose to keep from sneezing. Mama would laugh to know that prissy Mrs. Beasley had dust balls as big as cotton bolls under her bed.

I slid out three comic books. One was "Love Secrets" but it was marked up in red ink, a mustache drawn on the guy holding the girl making kissy lips. "Five Exciting Romances in One Big Issue." If I traded for that one, Bill would have to give me two, it was so scribbled up.

Bill fell against me. I rolled over and away. ''Watch...out...what are you trying to do?"

He grabbed my halter and pulled it down. His hands were hot, sticky and smelled like glue. There was brown on his nails. "Stop," I said. "Don't do that."

He kissed me hard. "Stop." I tried to twist away. His breath smelled of peanut butter and his teeth hurt. He was squeezing my breast. "That hu ...Let me go." I squirmed under him, kicked the floor, pounded on it with my hands. The zipper on his pants bit my leg.

He grabbed my wrist and as he loosened the grip on my mouth, I bit his finger so hard I felt the bone crunch between my teeth.

"You bitch," he screamed, "you little bitch."

I scrambled up, pulled my clothes on, and flung comic books right and left, pages ripping.

Bill sat beside the bed, looked at his finger. "Look what you did. You made it bleed."

I dived out the door, half fell down the stairs, almost bumped into the maid on the landing.

"What's the trouble?" she puffed. "What's going on up there? You kids—"

I swung past her and out. Halfway home I noticed my feet burning and remembered my sandals. I wouldn't have gone back for them if they'd been gold.

*Ruth Moose*

In the kitchen, I flung down the comic books, ran to my room.

Roger and Rick spilled sugar, stirred Kool-Aid. "Hey, these look like ours—You didn't—"

I locked my door, hit my bed, and cried hard into the pillow. I didn't care if it soaked through and I had to sleep on it wet. Bug Beasley was the worst boy in the world. I hated him. I didn't want breasts if boys pulled and hurt them. Roger and Rick pounded my door, yelled, "Open up." They finally went away.

Mother knocked then. "Are you sick? What's wrong?"

I didn't answer.

She got a skeleton key and came in. What good was a lock if anybody could get a key and come in any time they wanted? I cried harder.

"Does your stomach hurt?" Mama whispered.

"It's not that," I said.

My periods had started three months before and I was afraid. At first I thought I was dying. That I would bleed to death. "Hush," Mama said, "it's part of growing up." She showed me how to wear a belt like another harness and pad of a saddle between my legs. It was awful. I couldn't walk. Felt bowlegged. "All part of being a girl," Mama said. "You get used to it."

"I don't want it," I whined. "I don't want to be a girl."

"I'm afraid you don't have any choice." She had a sad, odd smile.

I lay on my side, studied my postcard collection on the wall. The one of the Empire State Building, as high as I could go, then France, as far as I could go…and away from Bill Beasley.

Mama ran water in the bathroom, came back with a cool cloth. She folded it across my forehead. "What happened?"

I told her Bill Beasley tried to pull my clothes off.

"You didn't let him," she said with a gasp.

*Ruth Moose*

"No," I said, "I pushed him away."

"Where was this? Where did it happen?"

"In his room."

"What were you doing in his room?"

"Trading comic books."

"You shouldn't have gone to his room," she said.

"That's where the comic books were."

"You should have made him bring them downstairs then." She acted mad at me.

"It's not my—"

"Where was his mother?"

"Downstairs," I said, "in the living room."

"The whole time?" Mama said.

"Yes—and the maid was—"

"If you had been wearing a bra," Mama said, "this would not have happened."  .

"Get out," I told Mama. "Go away and leave me alone."

I cried some more and slept. Daddy brought me supper on a tray. Macaroni-n-Cheese and a Jell-O salad. Mama had made gingerbread with lemon icing for dessert. She knew I liked it. I didn't touch it.

Daddy talked while I ate, promised me we'd go riding this weekend, that he thought I was big enough to handle one of the other horses and old Ted was too slow. He never mentioned it, but I knew he knew. Mama told him everything. Always.

I heard her later on the phone. "No, I don't think Frances has an active imagination. I'm sure she wouldn't make up a story like this. She has no. reason . . ."

"Frances is not that kind … Well, what kind of boy are you raising to do a thing like this? Oh, I'm sure your precious Bill always tells you the truth …that he would never touch…"

Ask the maid, I wanted to say through the door, she'll tell you. She saw my clothes. . .

"If that's the way you want it," Mama snapped. I heard her slam the receiver in its cradle with a jolt. "Forget it, forget the whole thing."

"Like mother, like son," she said to Daddy later. "I might have known."

"You are not to go near that house," Mama told me the next day. "And if you see Bill Beasley, you come home fast."

Roger and Rick giggled. They had no idea what happened, I am sure. Probably thought it was because of the comic books.

"And another thing," Mama said after the boys went out. "You are not to leave this house again without a bra."

"Never," I said. "Never."

I put on the bra and an old blouse with roll-up sleeves. Stayed in my room a lot, reading. At night Roger and Rick, the other kids would yell for me to come play Hide and Seek.

"Leave her alone," Mama said. "She's getting too big to be out running around in the dark. Somebody is going to get hurt yet."

I knew what she thought. That if Bill Beasley was out there he'd grab me again. I hated him, hated, hated.

From my room, I could see his room, a light on at night. Sometimes he undressed and didn't pull the shade.

When I saw the moving van backed up to the Beasleys' a week or so later, Mama said, "Good riddance," and I echoed her in my head.

I never knew what happened to the maid. Surely she had no trouble finding another job. Good maids were hard to find then as now. No one else in the neighborhood hired her or ever had a maid. Even in time of sickness, they helped each other.

"Everyone but Mrs. Hendon has moved from the old neighborhood," Mama says now as she sits across from me in this greenhouse of a kitchen. "The day they bulldozed down our house, Lou Hendon called me to come watch. I asked her what for? It's not part of me anymore. What do I care if they tear it down, build apartments?"

I care, I started to say. A part of me is being flattened out, erased, rumbled over, covered. My childhood and more. Some parts I want to erase, yet they sprout like rubble.

"Have you driven down Harmon Street since you've been home?" Mama asks.

"Yesterday, as I was going to the shopping center." Only the willow tree stood where our house had been. The rest of the lot was flat, waiting. The Beasley house was the same, shiny wedding-cake white. Porch floor polished now as then and there were fluffy ferns in white wicker stands.

"The maid's name was Radie," Mama says. The word pops from her mouth like a fruit pit. "That was her name."

I know then that Mama remembers. Remembers the Beasleys, Bill, the whole business.

She doesn't look at me, instead reaches up and crumbles off a brown leaf from one of the begonias. She pokes the soil to see if it needs watering. "When you go, take some of these plants with you. I'm crowded out of this apartment—there's not room for them all."

I feel that way now about bad memories. I don't have room for them all. They crowd my life and cause blight. And as I leave, two begonias and a rose geranium in my arms, I lean back to kiss Mother's cheek, something I haven't done in a long time. It's all right, I want to say. I love you. She waves as I start down the stairs. She knows.

*Ruth Moose*

## The Silver Crescent

IF MY GRANDMOTHER were alive today and I gave her a pair of pantyhose, she'd unwrap them, examine the package front and back, thank me graciously, and hand them back. And if I protested, she'd say, "Honey, I never wear them."

"But Grandma," I'd say.

"I wouldn't know how to put the things on in the first place," she'd say, "and you know I don't like any stockings but silk."

And I'd remember. Yes, I ought to know. To know very well. That was all I heard the summer I was thirteen. She and Aunt Rennie.

Every fifteen minutes they came in. "Are you asleep yet?" And when I said "No," they'd say, "Well, you better be, because it's going to be a long night."

I felt like it had been a long night already. I hummed songs, told myself stories, leaned out the window, listened to dogs bark and cats howl. Just after I closed my eyes, Aunt Rennie woke me saying, "Hurry, hurry, trains don't wait."

If the Silver Crescent had been a horse it would have snorted, stamped its legs, and whisked its tail to be off. Instead the doors stood open and my grandmother clutched her black leather-strapped suitcase like a life preserver..

"Give it to the porter," Aunt Rennie said gently.

"No." Grandma tightened her grip and her mouth.

The porter in his navy blue uniform and red cap bowed at the waist, touched his cap. "Ma'am."

*Ruth Moose*

"No." Grandmother stepped back.

"But why, Mama?" Rennie moved closer. "It's his job. You don't want that thing in your way the whole trip."

"He can't have it." Grandmother rearranged her sweater across her shoulders, tightened her grip on the suitcase handle. "I might not get it back." She eyed the waiting porter, who crossed his ankles, tugged the tip of his small, curled black mustache.

"Of course you will." Rennie was exasperated now. "I've never heard of such a thing, have you, Patsy?"

I shrugged. It was my first train trip too. Aunt Rennie had gone to New York twice a year since she started working for Foto's Department Store in Fairmont. Buying Trips, she called them in capital letters. She ran the millinery department at Foto's and all year long she'd hold up some hat like a freshly decorated cake on a plate and tell Mrs. Foto and her friends she thought of them the minute she laid eyes on this hat in New York City. That it was perfect for them and she couldn't imagine anyone else in town wearing it. Then she'd whisper that of course it was an original, a one-of-a-kind, and whoever bought it would never have to worry. about meeting herself coming or going in Fairmont, or anywhere else for that matter.

The ladies would buy the hats, leave in a swirl of gold-striped and corded boxes. Mr. Foto would take out his half cigar and with the handkerchief from his pocket would wipe his oily, brown, and balding head. Aunt Rennie was tall, gray, and fifty, but she knew women and hats and everyone in Fairmont, so Dick Foto staked her to the New York trips.

I imagined Aunt Rennie in New York. She'd be like she was anywhere, hatted, of course, usually a large one with flowers or a trailing feather and always her pink umbrella folded tight as a fresh petunia and ruffling at the handle. With the sharp tip she got attention, sometimes by poking people in the chest. I'd seen her poke Louis Mehew. "Young man," she said, "if that's gum you're chewing, I'd advise you to stop the nasty habit right now if you know what's good for you." And Louis gulped down his gum.

Now Aunt Rennie aimed that same arrow of an umbrella off the side of Grandma, whispered loudly, "For Lord's sake, Mama, you're holding up the whole train, making a spectacle …let the man have your suitcase."

Grandma loosened her grip, finger by finger. The porter eased it from her and, almost tripping, ran to the baggage car.

"That's the last I'll ever see of my suitcase," Grandma said in a little-girl voice. "I know bad blood when I see it."

"Ohhhhh. . ." Rennie blew out her breath like steam. "He's in a hurry because you held up the train. Of all the— He's putting it on the baggage car beside my suitcase, with Patsy's. With everybody else's who's already on this train. And if we don't get on soon. . ." She pushed Grandma up the narrow metal stairs. "We've been laughed at enough. See if you can find a seat without another commotion."

I looked around. There was no one on the train platform. At 2:00 a.m. the whole town was as deserted as any small town in the South. Nobody had laughed at us. I giggled. Aunt Rennie reached a hand back, grabbed me, and yanked just as the train shuffled, blew a stinging skirt of sand, and started off.

We stumbled into the car as the train lurched, released brakes in a scratch of metal. Grandma toppled into the first seat atop a sleeping fat man who snorted, "What? What is this?"

"Not there." Rennie pulled. "You don't want a seat back here. Let's get one where you and Patsy can be together. Don't sit with strangers."

We wove toward the front, past people with pillows, seats tilted, heads back and mouths open like fish. Some slept curled in their seat, others sprawled, dangled arms in the aisles.

*Ruth Moose*

The dark was heavy as a cape and sparks shot from under the wheels like firecrackers.

I sat bolt upright beside Grandma stiff in her best navy blue crepe with the lace collar. Not even red silk roses on her hat wiggled. She could have been one of Foto's Department Store mannequins, still as she sat.

The train moaned through an occasional town, rocked easy as any toy horse. New York was a world away.

Across the aisle, Aunt Rennie promptly went to sleep. She snored like a grinding motor. I hoped nobody knew she was with us.

Grandma and I made a mirror picture in the train window. I saw the part in my hair, touched my birthday string of pearls from Belk's, and posed with my neck arched, chest out in my white dotted Swiss dress and ballerina skirt ruffling around me. I wore white socks and black patent-leather shoes, my first with heels. On my ankle, a bracelet of two hearts initialed PM and BH, Buddy Harkey. He'd given it to me for my birthday. Mama said not to wear the bracelet next to my skin or it would leave a green ring.

Riding the train at night was like going into a tunnel only you never came out. I kept looking, waiting for the light at the end, but it never came. I pretended it was at the movies and I waited for the picture to start, but there was nothing but people breathing and the everlasting black flannel.

My seat prickled under me and the linen napkin behind my head was stiff as paper. The whole train was a rolling box of snores. Finally Grandma said, "I coulda kept it at my feet."

"What?" I looked at her.

"My suitcase," she said. "No reason to let him have it." Lights outside the window winked at me and once I saw the silhouette of a horse on a hill. I drifted to sleep and woke to find Grandma hadn't moved a breath. She still stared at the gray wall in front of the car, held her purse hard in her lap, the clasp with both hands.

*Ruth Moose*

The conductor came through, punched our tickets, tipped his cap to Grandma. "Have a good trip, ma'am."

She smiled a little, nodded her roses.

Outside, the sky greened in streaks, became orange and pink silk. A few people in the car lifted green shades at their windows, yawned, stretched. One man opened his briefcase, took out a razor, and shaved. I felt embarrassed, as though I had seen someone in a private act. Several people took trips to the bathroom, came back tugging ties, patting down freshly combed hair, headed for the dining car. I'd wanted to eat in the dining car but Aunt Rennie said, "Who can afford it? Not me. We got more sense than pay six prices for things just because it's a train we're on."

I would have settled for a Coke, but Rennie and Grandma had packed a lunch the night before in a hatbox with cellophane see-through on top. .

Aunt Rennie woke, rustled in her box, passed across chicken, ham biscuits, deviled eggs, chocolate cake.

Grandma held the chicken toward me. I shook my head.

"You got to eat." She took a dark bite off a drumstick, nicked the bone. "You don't know when you'll get another chance."

Grandma chewed loud. The whole train echoed and the sulphur smell of eggs made me turn away. I hoped nobody knew where the smell came from.

Aunt Rennie kept passing across food. I kept refusing. Grandma ate.

Finally I took a plum, a handful of green grapes, cool and wet in my hand. "You'll get that juice on your dress," Grandma warned, "and it won't come out."

I cupped my hand under the plum, bit deep and sucked the red sour juice that tasted good down to my toes.

A group of people got off the train at a small yellow station in Virginia. I tried to read the name of the town but couldn't. They reached overhead for briefcases, boxes, paper bags with handles as they left.

"I coulda kept mine," Grandma said. "They're back there going through it."

"Why would anyone go through your suitcase?" I asked.

"Money." Grandma rounded the word. "What else?" She patted her breast and paper rattled. "I fooled them. I got mine pinned to me."

I saw two shining stitches of safety pins small in her dress. In my suitcase, I'd packed six Bit'-O-Honey bars and some Juicy Fruit gum. If they were missing, I'd know Grandma was right.

Aunt Rennie passed us a damp paper towel to wipe our hands and pass back. She folded everything back in the cake box, tied it with gold cord, and got into a long conversation with her seatmate, a widow from Pleasant Grove. I heard Aunt Rennie tell about Foto's and what a perfectly lovely little town Fairmont was and how she'd have to come visit when the dogwoods bloomed. That she'd only be in New York three days, but Grandma and I would be with her sister, my Aunt Lucille, and Uncle Taylor in Trenton for two weeks. They lived in New Jersey. The way she said New Jersey I knew it wasn't as good or as important as New York, but Aunt Lucille had written if I'd come with Grandma they'd take me sightseeing. Since Uncle Taylor was a Ford dealer, I figured we'd go a lot and Trenton was farther from North Carolina than I'd ever been.

We changed trains in Washington and that worried Aunt Rennie. The Crescent didn't go any further north, she said.

I didn't see what Rennie was so worried about since the conductor took us right to the other train, helped Grandma get settled. She hissed, "Is my suitcase still on that train?"

"No, no," Rennie said. "They switch everything. Now hush."

*Ruth Moose*

She told me to wait until we got out of town to use the bathroom and cross my legs and hold it if I had to. I edged past her and walked the aisle like a plank until I reached the bathroom with its pink sink the size of Ruthie's playhouse one. Grandma would say this room wasn't big enough to cuss a cat in. I giggled. When I flushed I saw the track riding gray and steel under me and grass, shiny bits of metal.

Aunt Rennie helped Grandma, her hand under her elbow guiding and Grandma saying, "I'm fine," and pulling away.

They came back with their hats on straight, hair freshly combed, and gloves smooth.

As the train eased toward the station and between other trains, I held my breath it seemed so close. Like we were sliding into a slot. Aunt Rennie was ready. "I'll help you out," she told Grandma.

"My suitcase. . ." Grandma said.

"It's with the others, for goodness sakes." Rennie waved to Lucille.

Aunt Lucille hugged us, got lipstick on my collar. She smelled of narcissus and cherry blossoms. "Be good," she called to Rennie, and Rennie yelled back, "And if I can't be good, I'll be careful." They both laughed loud. I wanted to stand behind a post but there wasn't one.

"I want mine." Grandma walked toward the suitcases on the platform.

In the rack of suitcases, I saw my plaid zippered one and pulled it out.

"It isn't here." Grandma said and bent, read tags. "I know it isn't."

Lucille picked up a black one. "This looks like yours."

"Well, it's not." Grandma reached for the tag, turned it over. "See, I know my own suitcase."

Lucille put it down, called a porter, had him check the luggage.

*Ruth Moose*

Grandma fidgeted, fussed. "I knew all the time something was going to happen. Never should have let it from my sight."

Lucille checked inside the station, came back frowning. "They said some luggage was left on the other train by mistake and your suitcase must have been one of those."

"Oh," Grandma moaned. "Now he's got it and he'll just keep it. Everything in the world I had to wear."

"It's supposed to be on the next train," Lucille said.

"Lord knows when that will be." Grandma rolled her eyes toward the ceiling.

"Three o'clock," Lucille said. "We might as well have some lunch, kill some time until then."

Grandma wouldn't eat the club sandwich Lucille ordered for her. She complained the mayonnaise was old. I had a toasted cheese and licked the melted threads between bites. Lucille only had black coffee and worried about her office. "I told them I might be a little late getting back"—she rubbed out her cigarette—"but not the whole blessed afternoon."

"I knew all along this would happen," Grandma said to anyone in the room.

We waited on a bench in the station until four a' clock and every parcel of luggage had been unloaded and checked. I knew all the cracks in the wall, ceiling. There was a map of Italy in the corner, overhead the Mississippi River.

When we left with only my suitcase, Grandma sank into Lucille's car, fanned herself with her hand. "Here I am in this Godforsaken place without a stitch to my name but what I got on."

"They said they'd find it and have it delivered tomorrow." Lucille started the hot car, backed from the parking place.

Grandma and I had twin beds in the pink wallpapered guest room. Grandma paced while I unpacked, gave her the top drawers in the bureau. "I don't know what for," she mumbled.

*Ruth Moose*

After dinner she said she guessed she'd have to just sleep in her dress.

Lucille, loading the dishwasher, said, "Mama, I'll get you some of my gowns, a robe, slippers and things. Just give me time."

"I'll rinse out my step-ins," she said, "and hang them in the upstairs bath. They ought to dry overnight—as hot as it is up there."

"If worse comes to worse"—Lucille scraped a plate—"you can always buy a few things. It won't hurt you to have a new dress or two."

"I had a new dress," Grandma said from the stairs. "Rennie got it for me at Foto's. Green with blue and white stripes. Not worn yet. Price tag still on it. No telling who's wearing it now."

"It's for sure that porter isn't," I said.

She gave me a dark look. "Probably got a wife that is. I don't trust anybody whose eyes are too far apart. One look and I knew."

The next day, Lucille took us shopping in a big, bright, flower garden-smelling department store. I rode the escalator about a dozen times. Grandma wouldn't get on and Lucille went in the elevator with her. She didn't want to buy anything, and none of the things she looked at were as wellmade or as pretty as what she had in her suitcase. She did buy one dress and some underwear, a nightgown. "A change," she said, rolling down the top of the silver-colored bag.

"Something you could use, anyway," Lucille said. "Don't begrudge it."

Grandma fussed. "No use spending money on things I already had. If I'd just let my common sense rule . . ."

Uncle Taylor took us to Radio City Music Hall. "I've never seen a Rockette I didn't like." He winked at Aunt Lucille.

At the top of the Empire State Building, Grandma wouldn't get near enough to the rail to look over and held the tail of my dress, yelled the whole time for me to stay back. "She couldn't fall if she tried," Uncle Taylor laughed. "The rail's eight feet high and glass-enclosed."

I bought postcards, wrote all my friends and Buddy Harkey every day the first week. Aunt Lucille introduced me to Lisa Ponte, who lived three houses down and was fourteen. Lisa introduced me to the rest of the kids in the neighborhood, including Ronnie Martinez, who had the blackest hair and eyes I had ever seen. When he smiled, I almost lost my balance. "I don't know much about those kids," Lucille said. "They seem awfully fresh to me."

They loved my southern accent and begged me to talk and talk. They thought "you all" was supposed to be in every sentence and I had to start saying it all the time. When we went out for pizza, they made me order and the girl couldn't understand a word I said, we laughed so much.

In Atlantic City, I rode the ferris wheel out the roof and looked hard and deep toward North Carolina, couldn't see a speck. Lisa helped me buy short shorts and an elastic halter like hers. Grandma said, "If your daddy knew you were running around parading everything you got, he'd jerk you home fast."

I wasn't planning to ever go home.

Grandma spent her time washing out underwear and moaning. She wrote all her friends back home about thieving Yankees who wanted to rob an old woman of every stitch she owned. Next she worried about me going wild. She said New Jersey people looked strange, talked funny, too fast. She couldn't understand but every other word they said and I was getting to sound just like them. She said I ought to hear myself talk.

I stuck out my tongue when she turned her back.

Aunt Lucille had called the railroad every day since we'd been there and they had done everything they could to trace Grandma's suitcase.

*Ruth Moose*

"Trace," Grandma shouted. "Find is more the word." Ten days after the suitcase was lost the railroad called to say it had been found—in Florida.

"It couldn't have gone any farther," Grandma sneered, "or it would've been in the ocean."

"I told you the whole time," Lucille said, "things don't just disappear and people don't go around stealing suitcases."

"Humph," Grandma said, adjusting her glasses on her nose. "You just wait and see. It could be stark empty. He could have taken everything he wanted and sent back the rest."

The suitcase was delivered by special messenger and the first thing Grandma did was check the lock. "It's been opened," she said triumphantly. She examined her dresses, still folded flat and careful, counted her "step-ins," slips, nightgowns, her "good" robe and sweater. Then she patted the elastic pouch on the suitcase divider. "Not one," she said, "not the first one."

"What?" Lucille and I peered around her and into the suitcase.

"Stockings," she said. "I had a dozen new pair—never been out of their wrappers and there's not a one left—not a sign of them." Her face was long, mournful, ready to melt.

"What in the world is a few pair of stockings after all this time?" Lucille snapped. "You got your suitcase back, the rest of your things in perfect condition. I don't want to hear any more about any of it."

Grandma sighed, set her suitcase on the luggage rack that had been waiting empty almost two weeks. She put things in it to take home. "No use to unpack now, when I'd just have to pack again."

When she wasn't worrying about what to do with her suitcase on the trip home, Grandma perked up a little, tried to have a good time, let Uncle Taylor take us out to eat, said she'd had a fine visit in spite of everything.

*Ruth Moose*

Lucille winced at that, but didn't say anything.

Uncle Taylor ordered another glass of beer for everybody and a Coke refill for me.

"Beer?" Grandma said. "Was that what I had?" Her mouth hung open like a pocket. "I thought somebody up here sure didn't know how to make iced tea so it didn't cloud and bitter."

We all laughed and Grandma laughed so hard she hiccupped.

On the way to the train station, Grandma pulled her handkerchief between her fingers. I saw it becoming a string by the time we got there. "I'm going to keep it with me," she said, "if I have to sit on it the whole trip."

"Okay, okay," Lucille said. She rolled down her window and took a ticket from the parking attendant.

"And if I see that porter again, I'm going to go right up and demand to know what he meant by stealing my stockings?"

"For goodness sakes, Mama," Lucille said, "you don't know for sure. Anything could have happened."

"I bet he sold them."

"Porters are well paid." Lucille held the door, carried the suitcase. "They don't need your stockings. Black markets went out with the war."

We sat with the suitcases while Grandma went to the ladies' room. She told me I'd be sorry if I didn't go now and I said, "But I don't have to."

"I don't have to either," she said, "but I'm going anyway."

"I know it seems like she's made a big fuss over this," Lucille said. "And I hope it hasn't spoiled your trip."

I said it hadn't and touched my gold locket with the picture of Ronnie Martinez inside, felt the card with his address in my pocket.

"Don't feel too hard toward her." Lucille reached over and touched my arm. "You've never had to do without like she has,

Patsy. During the war you couldn't get so many things and she hasn't ever forgotten, I guess. Stockings were prized so highly you wouldn't believe it. They could have been gold instead of silk and she still refuses to wear any but silk stockings. Everyone has something that having a lot of, makes them feel wealthy, secure, whatever—be stockings—or gold."

Grandma held tight her suitcase, slid it on the train herself, into our seats, and popped her feet on it fast.

Aunt Lucille hugged and kissed us. "Don't wait so long to come back," she said.

"I'll see you next summer." I winked.

Grandma said, "Now you take care and write more than you been."

Lucille waved from the platform.

The porter came by, motioned to Grandma. "You'll have more room if we put that overhead."

"I'll thank you not to touch my things," she snapped.

"Yes ma'am." He touched his cap. "Yes, ma'am. "

"I'm going to tell Daddy you sassed somebody," I sang.

"Watch out, young lady." Grandma settled her purse in her lap flat as a book. "I know more than a few things that could get you sent to your room for a month."

I settled back in my seat, watched the backs of buildings, warehouses, and auto junkyards roll past.

"I hope I see whoever hires and fires people on this railroad," Grandma mumbled, looking around. "I'll tell him he can't do much of a business with thieves for help."

"Grandma"—I patted her hand—"that's all behind us now. Let's don't talk about it again."

I felt very grown-up, sixteen at least. Or twenty. Traveled and celebrated…and kind.

The train slid through cities and the green fields of Virginia, tobacco fields and the open blue skies of North Carolina. I breathed deep, cleaned my lungs, and shouted inside my head, "I'm home, I'm home."

*Ruth Moose*

When we neared the station, I saw in a dizzy sea of faces someone that looked like Mama and Daddy beside her and my little brother, Robbie.

Grandma got off first, pushed her suitcase at them and told Daddy to take it and not let go for a minute. He looked puzzled.

Everybody hugged us and began a second round. Robbie smelled like damp hair, soap, and popcorn. "Did you bring me a baseball pennant from Yankee Stadium?" he asked.

"Wait and see," I said. The only thing I had brought him was a T-shirt that said Atlantic City and a Confederate Flag beach towel.

I started talking about the Rockettes and Atlantic City and Daddy almost hit the car in front of us. "Hold on." He turned around. "Do you hear her? She's been gone two weeks and come back talking just like a Yankee. I got a good notion to send her back where they talk such stuff."

"You'll do no such thing." Mama reached an arm back and pushed my bangs off my forehead. "That's an awful thing to say about your own flesh and blood."

"My flesh and blood don't talk Yankee." Daddy slammed on brakes for a stop sign.

I didn't say anything else, except in whispers to Robbie. At supper I asked Mama to pass the butter for my corn on the cob and Daddy gave me a hard look with the corner of his eye. Robbie giggled.

When I unpacked I couldn't find the beach towel I bought for Robbie.

I leaned in the door of Grandma's room. "Did I put Robbie's towel in your suitcase?"

She stood at her round old oak dresser with the black teardrop pulls. She turned with a white look and something in her hand.

"It was like a flag," I said.

*Ruth Moose*

She tried to push the colored packages in her hand back into the small drawer that hung half-open.

"Those look like—" I started.

"Well, they're not," Grandma said. "I had them in that back pocket in my suitcase. They were the last thing I put in and—never mind."

I didn't know what to say.

"Nobody's perfect," Grandma said. She straightened the crocheted scarf on her dresser, rearranged her jars and bottles, the velvet pincushion. "Nobody in this world ever got through life without making a mistake."

I kissed her powdered and violet-smelling neck and tiptoed out.

She died the year I was eighteen and I wonder often what she would have said about my husband, Carlos. Whatever, she would adore our little Rosita Ann.

Ruth Moose

# He Holds a Black Umbrella
# At my door

TWO SCRUBBED ALL-AMERICAN boys, white shirts, ties, wire-rimmed glasses, crew-cut hair the color of wheatfield stubble. They bow, smile as if waiting for a camera to click. Elder Jones and Elder Richardson at your service, ma'am. Elder? I think Younger. Tweedledum and Tweedledee. Dum has a black tooth and smiles crookedly to try to cover. I wonder how they let him in the Order of the Church of Yesterday's Saints with so obvious a flaw? Elder Jones asks if they can come in, give me God's Message For Today. They have a card with a picture of Jesus ascending. White clouds, gold halo. Blue Sky. A memento of the visit. A weather chart. The card sky is blue today. When it turns pink there is a chance of rain. The charts really work and are nice to hang on your wall, Elder Jones says. Elder Richardson admires his fine shined shoes, pats four fingers on his Bible, impatient to be on with The Word. May they come in for a moment? I am busy, it has been a rough morning. The dishwasher stuck, but its pump did not. Flooded the floor. My tile may buckle. Too bad, they say, to be too busy to take time to hear the Scriptures. My child has eased out the door and reaches for the weather chart/Jesus card. They hold it away from his sticky hand. The card can only be left after a visit. They walk across my yard, leave a wake of bent grass, a brushed path. Next door I hear the other Elder take his turn. Good day, ma'am. Good luck. Next door lives the World's Champion Bitch. I take my child into his room,

*Ruth Moose*

give him crayons, an index card, tell him to make a weather chart.

It is raining my husband is reading Walden, Thoreau's Words for Today. He reads aloud. I am reading Can This Marriage Be Saved. Sometimes in bed he reads Walden aloud. This is his third reading. Thoreau is not good in bed. The children are asleep. The stereo plays An Evening with Bach Harpsichord and Cello. The record finishes, flips, and Johnny Cash moans he is so lonesome he could die. My husband does not look up from Walden, but his eyebrow does. Variety, I say, is the herb and sinew of life. I decide to make coffee, perked coffee, let it smell good long. Tease my senses. Like sex, half the enjoyment is in the anticipation. The doorbell rings and out my rainy porthole I see night, a wash of street lights and empty streets. I open the door to a child. A girl of perhaps nine or ten. Her dark hair is matted, limp across the soiled imitation-fur collar of a too-short coat. She holds a used paper bag, both hands tight around its neck as though it is alive and might try to escape. I think of drawings of street urchins, round-eyed children, stray kittens, and want to let her in. She reaches inside her bag, hands me a torn slip of paper. My Father, she says, wants you to read this. Against the rain and Johnny Cash, her voice is a whisper. Has there been an accident? Her father injured and she has come to my house for help? I unfold the slip of lined paper and read the dark pencil scrawl, "For God so loved the world, He gave His only begotten Son." I read it twice, ask where her father is. Out there. She points down the street. I step onto the porch. Cold dampness makes me shiver, wrap myself with my arms. I see nothing. Can you come in? He won't let me, she says. My Father wouldn't like it. What would he say? He tells people about Jesus' Love and how he came to save the world. My Father is a Preacher. I have to go now. She snatches the paper back, runs down the street. Under a misting globe, I see a man. He holds a black umbrella.

*Ruth Moose*

In the Safeway supermarket a woman in a blue smock imprinted We Care stocks the dairy case. I reach for cottage cheese. She hands me a carton. I thank her. We discuss the price of meat, the state of the world. She says she has quit going to church. Last week was her last time. Preachers, she says, do not bless our boys in service anymore. They do not pray for them in their Sunday prayers. Just because there is not a war on does not mean our boys do not need praying for. I take a box of margarine and say the special on real butter is real good. At the register line, I unload the grocery cart; lettuce, carrots, a can of peas. Onions, potatoes, a potted plant, a package of pantyhose, Moonlight Petite One Size Fits All. My child reaches from his cart seat and takes a small red book from a bird feeder display. The New Gospel in Miniature. Free. Take One. He chews. Red drips down his chin, onto his shirt, stains his hands. I put the book back and buy him candy. A small line under the Free says $1 donations will be accepted for the Continuing Ministry and appreciated. I wonder if the red will wash out, if the dye is safe, if my son will be sick? Stopped for a traffic light, the yellow pickup truck in front has an empty gun rack across its rear window, is driven by a vanilla-haired lady. Her left bumper sticker says God Is Not Dead I Talked to Him This Morning. Her right bumper sticker says Prayer Is the Answer. My son hits the horn. In her mirror, the driver gives me a peace sign, a faceful of black exhaust. Even God cannot breathe. At home I open the cottage cheese and see green fuzz mold. The freshness date guarantees next week. I feed it to the dog, tell him penicillin is made from mold and he will never have an infection, live forever.

Having lunch with a friend she blesses our tuna fish sandwiches. I haven't read the papers today and wonder if tuna is the latest ban. God is great. She folds her hands like the picture in a child's prayer book. God is good. There is a dog hair, stiff as a bristle, in my sandwich. Under the table Mollie the Collie bumps my feet, clicks her teeth as she bites fleas. God we thank him for this food. She shows me a cookbook put out by the Ladies Church Circle. $4.50. Did it themselves, even turned the mimeo by hand. There are recipes for Black Pepper Cake, Radish Pie, Celery Pudding. I dread dessert. By his hands.

After the fifth phone call I accept the invitation. Dinner for two. Free. No charge to you as Guests of the Great American Land Developers Association. We wear our sales resistance armor. The male Cheerleader at my elbow tries. He has scored with the other couple at our table. Newlyweds. Six months, already the owners of a Piece of Paradise. She wears a yellow floral corsage. Mr. Cheerleader makes a great show of pinning it to her chest. I feel left out of the May Court, flowerless. The newlyweds rent an apartment, lease furniture, but have been thinking toward retirement, put their down payment on Florida Forests Forever. During dinner they talk golf. Mr. Cheerleader asks if we play. No, my husband says. Sail? No again. Swim? Boat? Fish? Three more nos. Then he asks exactly what my husband does do. He reads, I say. Reads! Cheerleader is astonished. Reads, he repeats. Reads. He meets all kinds of nuts in this business but this is a new one. During dinner the new bride snaps at her husband because he got catsup on his tie. He snips back. I wonder who gets payments on Paradise in a divorce settlement? The attraction of the evening is unveiled. The Head Cheerleader gyrates with his roving microphone. Hip hip hooray. They show slides of Paradise. Grass, birds, trees and breeze. The GALDA made the waters and firmaments and found they were good and have not rested. Let's hear it for payments of $83.09 a week for the rest of your life. The giant green kidney of a map is cheered. We can buy a square as big as a Chiclet beside the golf course, adjoining the country club, on the lake, across the canal. We have a Chapel, says Cheerleader, for all faiths. A different door for each.

*Ruth Moose*

Jewish, Catholic, Protestant. Which are you? Waldenites, I say, and Cheerleader says we have that too. There are many unmarked doors in Paradise. Invest, he urges, double, triple, googolplex your money. Send your son to college. Why, my husband asks. He can already read. We leave without a tip and the waitress blocks Cheerleader's stride after us. On the way home, a billboard proclaims in sparkle letters the Second Coming of Christ. Everyone is invited, but only ticket holders will be admitted. Underneath is a picture of Billy Graham, and the dates May 20-25.

*Ruth Moose*

# Cows, Coathangers, and the K-Mart Kid

**The Voice**
EACH NEIGHBORHOOD MUST have a single voice. One nobody would claim. A sound you'd hear if you put your ear to the ground in the middle of the night. A chatty, busybody, gossipy, snippy sort of barnyard voice that is heard when people live too close and pick, pick, pick into each other's lives.

The Green Pastures That Became Ashwood Heights Subdivisions are all alike. Call them Merry Hope Runs, or Cricket Hops, or Hobble Horse Hills, they're pretty standard. Planned and priced to the square inch, brick, boards, trees, and turf. Models of American Pie. The people too are pretty much the same. Salt, pure salt of the earth. But this story is about grass, the folding green, mowing green, fertilizing and airing green of suburban kind. And what salt does to grass. And one house in a neighborhood. You've seen those houses. Black sheep in a family, ill-fated from the first, the unusual, the pieces that don't fit in the Norman Rockwell picture puzzle.

In Ashwood Heights the kids call it "the bad house." It was the last to be sold and stood empty almost a year after the others became curtained and mailboxed and fenced, with petunias in their identical planters. The bad house's yard went to seed. Its shrubs died. Its one stick tree got broken off even with the ground. It was a disgrace. Bettye Cobb, who lived on one side, and Sally Zimmer, who lived on

*Ruth Moose*

the other, worried that this house contaminated the whole neighborhood. They looked and talked about it as if bricks and boards could spread some contagious disease to their own dear yards and loved ones. Bettye and Sally spent mornings and afternoons while their babies napped drinking coffee in each other's kitchens. If their husbands were out of town, they often slipped over with some sewing or embroidery, going back every fifteen minutes to check on Stevie or Susie, deep asleep in their cribs. The bad house between them was an eyesore, a pox. Their dozen trips daily across its yard packed it hard, wore a path in the pale, thin grass. Both said the house was an absolute disgrace and the city should do something. The developer should do something. Somebody had to do something.

**The Farmer's Wife**

When someone learned that the bad house had been sold, excitement went around the neighborhood like a twenty-four-hour virus. In a day or two a truck backed up, started to unload. A small car from some unknown country, the color of a stray cat, parked in front. It had a cracked windshield on the passenger side and the rear window was broken, replaced by a cardboard that read "Kotex" in four places. Sally was over with her Good Neighbor pot of coffee and some fresh, home-baked sweet rolls, "last year's winner in the Bake-Off" recipe. Before the car doors shut, the family pooch, a cross between collie and German shepherd, marked the front door.

"Those people," she said to Bettye, "those people…I don't know how to say it…but they're hicks. Pure hicks. God knows where they came from and what they're doing here—in our neighborhood. I wouldn't think they've got enough sense, much less money, to sign a mortgage agreement."

Bettye sniffed with one nostril. "I think we may have been better with the house empty." She had never thought she'd say those words.

Moving boxes stayed in the yard two months. Kids flattened them to slide the slope in the front yard. No sooner than a garbage man would cart one off, aided by Sally or Bettye who took turns stealing out in the dark of midnight to stack them on the curb and pray from their windows for early pickup, than the kids pulled out more. They spent hours sliding and squealing down the brown slopes. If they had toys, no one ever saw them. They played with things like brooms, mops, pans, spoons, curtains, sheets, and old furniture. Sofas and chairs sat in the yard like old people with sagging stomachs. Cotton and packing hung out like intestines. In the yard the furniture was rained upon, left to rot. Bettye and Sally almost gagged every time they looked at it. "Isn't there a law against stuff like that? "Surely there is." There must be."

Jack and Jill, the two oldest Farmer children—yes, their name was Farmer—looked like twins. Lottie Farmer told Sally they were ten months and two weeks apart. "Don't let anyone tell you that you can't get pregnant when you're nursing. Because I'm the living proof."

"Oh, I wouldn't," said Sally. "I wouldn't for anything."

She put her hands in the air. Her eyes were dark as nipples.

The Farmer baby, called Boo, was a year younger than Jack. If she had another name, no one ever heard it. They were always called Jack and Jill and Boo like a nursery rhyme that was wrong.

All three children, like Lottie, were thin as rags. They had frog eyes the color of pond water and Saran Wrap-like hair. Their noses continually ran and they coughed constantly, not hack-hack coughs, but deep, retching, dark-colored adult coughs. Bettye and Sally kept their babies, who were just learning to walk, in freshly polished high-top white shoes, ironed cotton zippered jumpsuits, and carefully buttoned pink and blue sweaters with a row of embroidered ducks on the chest. They immediately dashed into their houses, babies swooped under their arms like shoplifted food, if they saw a Farmer child look as if he or she even thought about coming close. Farmer children never wore sweaters, coats, or caps. Sally swore once Jill appeared at her door, teeth chattering, bare legs purple as a sparrow's, asking to borrow a cup of sugar. "I sent her home in one of my sweaters," Sally said, "and with a bottle of Stevie's cough syrup and told her to tell her mother the name of the pediatrician on the label."

The kids caused a rash of gossip around the neighborhood—and their coughs a fence of hard feelings between Lottie and Sally-and-Bettye. It seems either Sally or Bettye or both for good measure called the county health department. There was a case of whooping cough in Ashwood Heights. The county nurse could not get out fast enough to investigate. After she left, Lottie went from house to house on three streets, her children clinging to her like possums. "If my children were sick and needed a doctor, I can afford to take them," she said. "They got allergies. Nobody had to go and call the county. My kids got allergies. They ain't nothing contagious."

Another call went to a different county department when Lottie made the statement she wished she had a cow. Her back yard was big enough for one, there was enough grass, and the fresh milk would better and cheaper for the kids.

"A cow!" Sally rolled her eyes when she heard. "A cow? Out here? Next door?"

Bettye echoed her. Both saw Stevie and Susie in high-top, white polished shoes, stepping, stepping. They had a city official check zoning and restrictions, call Lottie Farmer. Lottie said she never actually planned to get a cow, only that it would be real nice, what with her kids drinking milk like it come from a faucet and all. And prices going up, up, all the time.

*Ruth Moose*

Lottie was never included in Sally and Bettye's coffee klatches, but they couldn't help talking to her when they watched their babies in the back yard sandboxes or at the swingset.

No one could ever understand how or why Lottie called on them to act as her private CIA. She must have been desperate and they must have been driven with curiosity. Lottie didn't drive, so either Sally or Bettye drove her and all the kids on her spying missions.

Lottie's husband was called Wink. She pronounced it "Wank" with a long, very flat a. Wink drove a city bus. He had a swinging sack of a stomach that must have leaned into the steering wheel and helped pull the tons of bus around curves. His forehead was marked in half by a pale streak from the bill of his cap and he was bald in an oval patch that almost met, but not quite, his pale streak. Lottie giggled a lot when she was around him, said things like "Ain't Wink the cut-up though? Ain't he the stuff?"

What she said to Sally and Bettye when they drove her behind him on his bus route was a different story. Somehow, somewhere, Lottie had gotten wind that Wink had a girlfriend on the side. She wanted to catch him "redhanded," have it out "once and for all."

"Lord, I nearly went crazy," Sally said later. "That bus stops at every corner and there was Lottie saying every woman who boarded that must be Her. 'That's Her. I know that's the one.' And the kids were in the back seat fighting or crying over a sucker stick one of them found under the seat."

Finally Lottie hired a taxi for her spying. Where or when she caught Wink no one ever knew—only that she had a moving van to the door and was gone in a day's time. Wink came home to the cleanest house he'd ever seen, walked in, looked around, stood on the porch a few minutes, reached into the outdoor light, unscrewed the bulb, shoved it in his pocket, and left.

*Ruth Moose*

A few years later, somebody on Maplewood Lane told Sally, who told Bettye, they had seen Lottie in a nightclub in Atlanta. They said they would never have known her if she hadn't spoken first, introduced herself and her new husband. "He was a good fifteen years younger than Lottie," they said, "and she was dressed up like a doll. Long skirt, eyeshadow, hair dyed dark as night and piled on top of her head like a queen. Nobody in a million years would have known her. She's done all right for herself."

**A Second Crop**

The house was empty almost a year the second time. Grass, where the Farmer kids had not stamped it out completely, grew in clumps as tall as shrubbery.

Several neighbors snickered it was too bad the Farmers never got that cow.

Everybody complained but nobody did anything, until one day Sally's son brought in a green snake, held out his hand, and said, "Look, Mama." Sally broke a Pyrex dish getting out of the house and over to Bettye's to call Ring, the developer of Ashwood Heights. That afternoon the yard was mowed. Then mercifully it was the hottest, driest August and September on record. Then winter. The stubble was brown, maybe dead, or so Sally hoped.

Next spring, Lottie's yard, everyone still called it that, had weeds high as windows. "Ticks breed in places like that," Bettye said. "And Rocky Mountain spotted fever—there've been two cases reported this year already." She called Ring again. His secretary said the house had been sold and it was up to the new owners to take care of the "grounds."

Six weeks later the new owners moved in. Not during the day, but at night, all night. Several trucks backed in, out, unloaded. Each truck had a bad muffler. And backing seemed to strain both the motors and mufflers, for there was also a lot of yelling. "This way, Charlie. Hold it right there." And odd noises. Toward dawn things got quiet, and Sally said, "I finally closed my eyes and next thing I knew somebody was peeking in my window. He was gone the minute I screamed. I know I didn't dream it …and Bob out of town. My God, I was scared out of my mind."

She had to have a third cup of Bettye's good coffee before she could go into the closet to get dressed.

"What kind of people are they?" Sally asked. "With all that noise I expected a circus, tent, elephant, and all."

It took six men with a lawnmower, a scythe, and several rakes to whip the yard into shape.

## The Case of the Curious Coathanger

Lisa Miller turned out to be a tall blonde with a fondness for dressing gowns until noon, large diamonds, and a fulltime maid. She enjoyed coffee all day and stayed tuned to the latest in gossip. Sally and Bettye took turns entertaining Lisa, defended her when others asked, "What's Lisa Miller with all her diamonds and a maid doing in Ashwood Heights?" Sally said Lisa said it was only until they could find something else. They had to have a place while, she looked. Lisa went out looking a lot of afternoons with either Sally or Bettye or both in tow, touring new homes in Rockwall Estates, or Stonebrook Glen. The three decorated for hours over pots of coffee, drew traffic patterns and wall arrangements.

Lisa had to make sure she bought the "right" house. They planned to do quite a bit of entertaining. Her husband's business demanded it. Floy Miller ran a television repair service. "F&S, We Fix the Best, Leave the Rest." Lisa said, one hand holding a cigarette in a teakwood holder, "and you know how much money television people make."

She loved to emphasize that Floy was an independent businessman. The panel trucks and vans with various names and designs spent a lot of trips in and out of the Miller drive.

Lisa told Sally that Floy owned ten trucks. They hadn't had time to repaint them, but all the drivers worked for him.

"Why are they in and out so much?" Sally asked. She inwardly shuddered at any of the men near six feet tall, remembered the one who had looked in her window that night.

"Floy sends them," Lisa said, "to get things."

"He forgets an awful lot of things," Sally told Bettye.

## The Millers' Three

Lisa and Floy Miller had three children. A thin, tall gawk of a teenaged boy who wore glasses thick as the bottoms of Coke bottles. Ricky. He smiled when anyone said his name, but was never known to speak a complete sentence. Deena, a five-year-old, was blonde and dimpled. Petula was a darkhaired baby of five months. The maid carried Petula on her hip like a sack most of the time, even home at night. "She's my treasure," Lisa said loudly when the maid was in the room. "My right hand." She also told Sally and Bettye when Petula was born the doctor found a tumor the size of a grapefruit on her left ovary and one the size of an orange on her right. That she was not supposed to do a thing—not even lift a finger.

When panel trucks and vans were not moving in and out of the Millers' drive, delivery trucks were. Lisa bought a canopy crib for Petula. "This is my last baby and my last chance to get the kind of crib I always wanted for Deena." Sally held her breath at all the eyelet ruffles around the crib's canopy. She said it looked like the one in Better Homes and Gardens' May issue. Like a storybook.

Bettye said it would get limp and the first time it was washed would draw up. That it was nothing but a dust catcher and she wouldn't want one in her house.

Deena's room was painted lavender and Lisa bought layers of lace, ruffles, purple and pink shag carpet. Her lamp was a ballerina who spun on her toes to "Lara's Theme." Then when the light came on she glowed lavender and green.

Bettye said if this house was only temporary, why were they so busy fixing it up?

Sally said the house was so awful Lisa couldn't stand it the way it was another minute. And fixing it up would help the resale.

Lisa gave a neighborhood cookout with drinks first at her new upholstered bar in the living room. She had a new, specially made, white sectional sofa, glass tables, and two stereo units, plus plastic plants and hanging baskets. "We're using them for display ideas," Lisa said. "Floy can bring home customers to see how everything looks in actual use. Besides"—she clinked her ring against a glass—"it's tax deductible."

"So are abortions," Bettye muttered, but only Sally heard her. Lisa had told them she'd done hers herself. Sally, who saw a gynecologist four times a year (five last year, if you counted the time in January she was two days late and panicked) was horrified. She opened her mouth, but no sound came out.

"How?" Bettye asked, her pale eyes large.

"It's easy," Lisa said. "You just take a coathanger, honey. Any kind will do, bend it and—"

"Stop," said Sally. "I can't stand to hear any more. I'm not feeling too well."

**The Grand Opening**

Lisa earned a red carnation corsage when she became the tenth person to enter the new K-Mart store on Dogwood Boulevard, three blocks south of Ashwood Heights. She also bought one of almost everything in the store. "I opened their first charge account," she said, "and they gave me an umbrella. See." She twirled it around like a flower, tried to tap dance like Debbie Reynolds in Singing in the Rain.

*Ruth Moose*

"Don't," Bettye said. "That's bad luck." "I don't believe in it." Lisa kept twirling.

She had also hung so many strands of plastic fruit lanterns across her yard it looked like the hot dog stand at a drive-in movie. She bought shelves for every corner of every room, filled them with china dogs and cats, vases, revolving lights. She cut carpet to fit her bath and bought color-coordinated accessories, plush paper, mat and bowl brush to match. She bought a wading pool for each child—so they wouldn't fuss. Ricky sailed boats in his and tried to drown a couple of cats from the next block. Lisa swore if he got cat scratch fever from the awful claw marks she was going to sue.

"The cats or the owners?" Bettye said from the corner of her mouth.

Lisa made at least one trip a day to K-Mart, sometimes two. She had been known to go three times and once five, if you counted the trip for sno-cones. "I love new things," she said. She especially liked new clothes. She wore things once, gave them to the maid. Ricky's, Deena's, and Petula's too.

Floy wore gray uniforms the maid washed and ironed. His name was embroidered in red thread above the front pocket and "F&S" across the back.

"Does Floy Miller make that kind of money?" Bettye asked. Floy was an angry man who chewed stumpy cigars, slammed doors on trucks, cars, and houses, raced motors, and cussed in what Bettye said sounded like an original language.

"He has to be in something illegal," Bettye's husband said. "Nobody makes TV house calls at 2:00 a.m."

## The K-Mart Kid

Ricky tried to hold not only the neighborhood cats underwater but also Stevie, Sally's son. "Ricky had been so sweet to come over, offer to watch Stevie, to share his pool. I tried to think I didn't see what I saw from my kitchen window. Thank God I ran out in time."

The next time Lisa told the story of Ricky's brilliant school career and how the teacher sent him home because he was two grades ahead of the other children and "there was nothing she could teach him," Sally excused herself from the room.

According to Lisa, Ricky had read every book in the county they moved from and the librarian just adored him.

Bettye cleared her throat at that, looked out the window, made another pot of coffee.

When Lisa rang their doorbells one night at 2:35 a.m., asking if they'd seen Ricky, neither got upset nor went with her to call the police nor drive around Ashwood Heights looking for him. "Where's Floy?" Sally said. "Maybe Ricky's with him." She went back to bed and woke up with a migraine.

Lisa had three police cars in her drive the next morning. They stayed until noon. Ricky had been found at K-Mart.

He'd gone to buy a goldfish for his pool and waited all night for the store to open. He slept in the Ride-Um Rocket and nobody saw him until some kid came up to ride and Ricky wouldn't let him in.

Several people from the Juvenile Authorities inquired around the neighborhood. Sally assured them Lisa was an excellent mother and Ricky an unusual child.

Bettye said there was something funny going on over there and she didn't know if it was all legal and not to mention her name in connection with anything.

Lisa started helping Floy "at the office." She left every morning before seven in a green Plymouth that was ten years old and had four dented fenders with rusty holes like lace. She didn't get in until after ten at night.

Ricky was sent to a special school in another state—or that's what Lisa told someone. Deena went to live with her grandparents in Florida and the maid took Petula. Floy told Sam, Sally's husband, that Petula was not his child and never had been.

Several months passed and no one entered the Miller house. Floy saw Sam once in the bowling alley and said that Lisa had left him for a keyboard player and was living in Nashville, if you could call that living. He didn't. That he was doing fine and had a cot in the back of his shop, took all his meals out.

Sally and Sam were transferred to Dallas. Bettye gave her a going-away coffee. She polished the silver service she had saved thirty-two books of stamps for four years to get. She baked a carrot cake and bought some green mints from the drugstore and said if that wasn't good enough for Miss Gotrocks, she didn't care. She didn't keep Lisa's baby while she packed, nor waved when the van left, nor get her forwarding address.

She told her husband that she hoped the real estate agent was a decent one and would be picky about who he showed the house to.

Meanwhile she planted a hedge of thorny limes, put in a birdbath, bought two pink plastic flamingos, and ordered a flagpole. At an auction she bought a black iron washpot, had it hauled home, and planted it by her front door. By June, purple-striped petunias tumbled their heads out.

The Miller house was emptied. Mostly by creditors. One took the furniture, another the stereo stuff. Others came to Bettye's door asking questions. "I only met them a few times," she said. "I don't know anything."

Two empty houses in the middle of the street affected the entire neighborhood, Bettye thought. They looked like castoff clothes, faded, scruffy, weak at the seams.

She and several others complained to Ring, the developer. Then they passed around a petition and got sixty-three signatures. Ring took over the Miller house, painted, wallpapered, glassed in the back porch, seeded and landscaped the yard. He hired a decorator who made it into a "Model Home for the Modest Budget," and it was featured in full color on the front of the Sunday newspaper. Bettye burned. The nerve of him. Making the rest of them look like fools with his money.

The house sold to a retired couple from Newark who planned to put a greenhouse in the back yard. They also announced they didn't like children and preferred privacy.

Sally's house sold to blacks. Bettye and her husband panicked, put a sign out overnight. They took a five thousand-dollar loss and said they were lucky at that, in trade for a split-level in Merry Hope Run.

Martha White, the black who bought Sally's place, became block chairman for the first neighborhood picnic. The streets were blocked off, everyone brought a covered dish, and there was music and dancing, beer and wine until the wee hours.

Someone said they thought they saw Floy Miller dancing with Lottie Farmer, but no one could be sure. It was that kind of party.

*Ruth Moose*

# The Blue Bonnet Bug

THE SOUND WAKES me. Someone is opening gifts. Opening and opening and opening. It seems like the middle of night or just before dawn. I think the tissue paper will never stop. They will never get to the gift. Hurry. I am pulling at the sheet, wadding the blanket. It is dark and I can't think where there is tissue in my bedroom. The sounds come from the closet. Someone is opening gifts in my closet?

I nudge Brian. "Listen."

"Huh?" He wakes slow, mud-headed.

I nudge harder, this time with my knee.

"Huh, huh, huh…what is it?" He half wakes, lifts his leaden head. I see the fine line of his chin in the dark.

"Listen."

"I don't hear anything."

"In the closet. Listen."

He listens. I see his forehead concentrate.

"Mice," he says disgustedly, pounds his pillow, sinks back to sleep.

I lie rigid. Awake in every cell. Scared. Mice. Mice are almost rats and the last time I knew rats I was five, Mother and I alone in a rented house. "It's all I could find," she says. We live in two rooms. Another family on the other side. A wide, dark hall between us. I hear people knock on their door. Voices. Cabbage and onion odors. Voices. I ride a school bus to a building crowded with strangers. At night I listen to the cream-colored radio on the table in our kitchen, my face

*Ruth Moose*

warm against the tubes and lights. Ozzie and Harriet, Jack Benny, Dagwood and Blondie.

At night Mother and I hear feet overhead. Hundreds of feet, running, thumping, jumping. A parade, a city, an upper world. "Rats," Mother says, and holds me close. "They won't come down here." I wondered how she knew, how she could be sure. I saw one rat in the yard once. He was large as a cat, with hard, bright eyes and teeth sharp as a trap. The rat glowered at me, parted the weeds and left like a shot.

Mother bought traps, baited them with gold cubes of the cheese I loved. "Don't dare touch them," she said. "Rats carry diseases."

"What kind?" I asked, thinking of measles and chicken pox.

"The bubonic plague," she said.

I shuddered.

She sets traps carefully around the rooms. I am afraid to walk at night, to go to the bathroom, lie holding myself full and hot. Sometimes in the dark I hear traps click in loud, red whacks. In the mornings, they are always empty. No rats, no cheese.

"I'm only feeding the things," Mother said.

We find small black curds in our kitchen drawers, in our underwear. Mother scrubs things, boils them, cleans, shakes things, cries. I cry. Rats, awful rats.

We keep writing letters to my father. At last he comes.

Mother runs to him, ducks her face into his arms. His sleeve in a uniform the color of dead grass scratches my face. Buttons brush my cheek as he lifts me up. "It's terrible," Mother says. ''We have rats.''

My father helps us get our things. We move to a hotel until he leaves. Then we ride a bus to my grandmother's in Mississippi, her clean house with curtains and starch and quiet ceilings.

*Ruth Moose*

Brian and I have quiet ceilings. They peak to a point with glass and overlook a lake, meadow and fields beyond. There are houses on each side of us, on the other streets, with more to be built on the meadow across the lake.

"Mice are not rats," Brian says at breakfast. He pours milk over cereal. "These are tiny field mice. They won't hurt you."

At work, I tell Ellie about the mice. "I can't sleep."

She stops opening mail, letter knife in her hand. "What you need is Amanda."

"Is she a mouser?" I wonder that Mother never thought of a cat. A cat would have been so much nicer than gray, flapping traps and disease all around.

I stop by Ellie's after work, bring Amanda home. In her travel cage she rides like a trapped beast, a yellow tiger. She howls, she paces, she is my protector. O Amanda—I stroke her through the bars—we will slay the mice.

Amanda, out of the cage, backs into the corner with the ficus. I catch and carry her to the bedroom, petting and talking all the way. She sniffs the closet, shoots back to the living room.

"Don't let the cat out," I yell. Brian blocks the door with the mail, his briefcase.

"What cat?"

Amanda slides between his legs. I dash after. "Amanda!" A yellow blur flicks through the hedge. "Kitty, kitty, here kitty."

I run six blocks, through yards, around fences, across budding border beds. I am wild in my chase—and unfruitful.

Later Brian drives the car and I call with cupped hands, "Amanda, here kitty."

What to tell Ellie? She's had the cat nine years, feeds her only the best. I should never have borrowed her. Never brought her home. Is she so afraid of mice that even the scent sent her running?

I wait until after dinner, hope against hope that somehow Amanda will reappear. Decide to return to her job, help me with my battle.

At nine-thirty, Ellie calls. "What happened? I heard a scratch at the door and there rubbed Amanda."

The cat has traveled several miles and some superexpressways. How in the world—? Fear can do strange things. Now that Amanda is safe I scoff. Coward.

Brian discovers how the mice have gotten in the house. A large opening around the water cutoff in my closet. Whoever put a water cutoff in a closet?

"At least we know where it is," Brian says. He finds a board and nails it tight. No more mice. Ah Brian, my protector. Who needs a cat?

It is wonderful in bed and I sleep until sometime in the almost light I hear the gift opening again. "Mice!"

I wake Brian.

"We must have trapped them in the house. They can't get back out."

At lunch I buy three mousetraps in a hardware store that smells of oil and sawdust and seeds. Traps with metal clamps and little clickety, gossipy tongues. They rattle, tattle in the bag as I walk to work, lie in my desk drawer like accusations.

After dinner Brian plays with them, hooking nutmeats, perfect pecan and walnut halves, into place. I argue for cheese and we settle for baiting one with cheese, two with nuts.

I carry the set traps as carefully as decorated hors d'oeuvres, to the bedroom, hall, kitchen.

Sometime in the night, I hear a clack, a whap, a final whamp. I snuggle closer to Brian. There are no screams. No mice death protests. All is quiet. I am a contented coward in the dark, dreaming of blackberry thickets and picking with my mother. Briars pull me, tangles of wire and bare feet. I wake thirsty, dry-throated.

Before Brian is up, I swirl into a robe and check my traps. String of a tail, finger of fur, one small, gray mouse. His tiny teeth stopped on the cheese. He is small. Not like a rat at all, but some novelty for a key chain, a woodland creature with a mushroom for an umbrella, a caricature for a child's picture book. And I killed him. Very dead. I feel terrible, have an urge I ought to send flowers, hang a wreath. In Miceville are they passing the news? John is gone. Martha a widow. Are there five mouse children made fatherless? I lean closer and touch him with my bare toe. He is soft, still, and so very small. I touch him again.

"You did it." Brian clamps a warm hand on my shoulder. I jump.

"You caught him." He looks at my mouse as if it were a trophy. A beast I have bagged ready to be stuffed and mounted. I see a row of them for my wall, a den of conquests.

In the hall we find the second dead mouse, quiet in his trap. And in the kitchen is a third. I pull my robe tighter, walk a half-circle to the sink.

"Take them out," I tell Brian.

"Not me." He makes toast, goes to the cabinet for grape jelly. "I didn't do it."

"Please." I'm clutching the edge of the counter now.

He eats his toast at the table like a small boy, gets jelly on his cheek.

How can he eat with a house full of dead mice?

"They didn't bother me alive," he says, brushing crumbs into his hand. "No big deal…couple of mice."

He goes to shower and I watch him carefully walk far around the mouse. As though he is afraid of it. I hear him whistling in the hall, bedroom, until he is past and the noise of his razor comforts him.

*Ruth Moose*

He was afraid and wouldn't admit it. Big hero, big protector. Big deal. And now he's afraid to empty the traps.

I grab a wastebasket and scoop the kitchen mouse and trap into it, then the hall one, then my poor dead Johnny Mouse. They tumble in the crumpled papers, lie there as if they are covered with flowers.

I clamp on the lid and dash to the house, wash my hands in hottest water, shower until my skin tingles almost raw.

Then hum as I dress. Ha, Brian, ha. I know your secret, you. big, cool fake. Afraid of mice. I touched one!

At the office, Ellie and I swim through end-of-the-month reports. We come up long enough for some soup and a salad brought in at three. At four I feel feverish, nauseated, chilled. Probably a touch of something, Ellie says. I know different. It is the bubonic plague. The blue bonnet disease, I used to call it. It strikes fast. In my mind I hear Mother's voice saying, "It killed thousands." Big, brave, foolish me—touching the mouse.

Ellie offers to finish up if I want to go home.

I cower on the living room sofa, bundled in a white afghan my grandmother crocheted. Shells and ripples that make me dizzy but warm.

Brian lets himself in, sees me.and is surprised. He feels my forehead. "No fever."

"I have chills."

He takes my temperature. Normal. These are the chills before the fever, I know that. Warnings, before the real stuff sets in.

Brian tucks the afghan in tight around me, kisses the top of my head. He brings me hot tea and toast on a tray, builds a fire in the fireplace. Feeling much better, I slide the afghan down and stretch.

Brian rubs my feet with his hands, kisses one of my ankles. "It was probably just a touch of a bug," he says.

"Yes," I murmur, "I'm sure that's what it was."

*Ruth Moose*

# Judas at the Table

MAREN NEVER KNOWS how many she'll have for Thanksgiving dinner until they walk through the door, but she isn't worried. It's covered-dish, and covered-dish always works out. There are always leftovers. The Asheville part of the Deal family has written they're bringing ham. Maren could have predicted that. Aunt Stella brings the turkey. Each year she worries, will it be tender? Will it be dry? It is never either, but she worries. Maren's mother calls to say she'll bring cranberry salad, sweet potatoes, pumpkin pie. It wouldn't be Thanksgiving without pumpkin pie. Maren hates it. Her two brothers and their current wives are coming. Then Ted's father, Frank; his brother, Tommy; and Tommy's wife, Lynda. With Ted and Maren, that makes thirteen, but who's counting? She doesn't set the table until everyone arrives.

Out-of-towners arrive first: Uncle Al and Aunt Lillian, the Asheville Deals, at the touch of twelve. Maren meets them at the car. Ted is still in the shower. He raked leaves until fifteen minutes ago—a job Maren has asked him to do for the last two weeks.

"Here you are," Aunt Lillian says. "Look at you." Aunt Lillian was a family therapist until she retired five years ago.

Uncle Al is retired from the post office. "How's my favorite niece?"

Maren kisses his cool cheek, which smells faintly lime.

*Ruth Moose*

"Your only niece," she says, "but I'm glad you like me."

"You wouldn't be my favorite if I didn't." He laughs, takes off a brown pancake of a cap. He's seventy, Maren thought, and his hair dark as ever. Maybe darker. He touches it up, she's sure, but that's okay. Aunt Lillian told her once how they'd met. During the war, at a USO dance. "I saw him across the room and thought he was the handsomest man I'd ever seen." She paused, then added in a softer tone, "I still do." Cornell Wilde, Maren thought. Yes, that's who her uncle looked like. She remembered a huge picture of Cornell Wilde that hung in the lobby of a local theater when she was growing up. Then forty-nine years into their marriage, Maren heard the story, realized who her uncle looks like.

She hugs her aunt, who is powdery and light. Maren smells mothballs and can't imagine why. Aunt Lillian has dressed entirely in black the last twenty years, ever since the double mastectomy. Today she wears a black pantsuit, black blouse with tiny sprigs of red. She carries the ham from the car, her shoulder bag, but no Thermos. Maren looks for the Thermos. Aunt Lillian never goes anywhere without coffee, not even to another room. It's been the family joke as long as Maren can remember that Aunt Lillian is a "coffee head," a "coffee junkie." Today she has only the ham rocking in its dish, spilling juices down her leg.

"It's wonderful to see you." Maren carries a cake in its see-through plastic keeper. "You made this?"

"With a little help from Sara Lee." Aunt Lillian grins.

"I've never known a Thanksgiving to be so warm," says Uncle Al. He wears a tan windbreaker. "There's snow in the Midwest. They can have it."

"We'll all be sick," Aunt Stella says. She arrived with Maren's mother and "the bird," twenty pounds of brown that glows on a tray like it's been waxed. The picture of Thanksgiving. "Look at this bird," she says. Aunt Stella is a gray wisp of a woman who never married and is proud of it. "I had my chances," she likes to say, "and made my choices. I never missed a thing." She wears a red bow in her hair that matches her lace-trimmed apron.

Maren has been up since six. She made a broccoli casserole, creamed onions, and a brandied pound cake. She feels slightly damp, hot, and tired. Wilted. She spent time on a fresh flower centerpiece and candles, but is waiting to set the table. Last night she polished the silver. Last night after Kellie called. "Mama, I'm not coming home," she said. "There's a bunch of kids here and we're going to Connecticut to ski. You don't mind, do you?"

Mind? Of course Maren minds. She minds a hell of a lot.

"It's only two weeks until Christmas vacation and I'll be home then," Kellie said. "It's silly to come home for only the weekend."

Sure, Maren thought. Sure, the whole Thanksgiving thing is silly to you. Family is silly. Parents are silly. Parents who spend themselves silly to send you to that fancy school because you failed two others.

"What's this?" Maren's brother Jim says, hands on her waist, lifting her a little. "One of those Pick-Me-Up Bouquets?"

"No," she says. "It's one of those I-Made-It-Myself in the green tissue from Food World." Jim and Susie have just arrived with a casserole and her cat, Toot, an overgrown gray tabby with a red rhinestone collar. Toot immediately fled under the living room sofa. "She'll come out when she smells the turkey," Susie says. "And that's when we'll have to watch her."

"It's lovely," Aunt Lillian says.

Does she mean the table or the cat or Jim and Susie? Maren wonders. Aunt Lillian calls Jim by his brother's name and she's given up on wives. That's what she said last year.

*Ruth Moose*

She can't keep track of these on-again-off-again new kinds of marriages. She pulls open an end-table drawer, muttering. The drawer is where Maren keeps the only ashtray in the house. Aunt Lillian shuts the drawer as though she suddenly realizes she doesn't need it. This is one of the few times Maren has seen her aunt without a cup of coffee or cigarette in her hands, or both. However, lately, her aunt has been taking her cigarettes outside to smoke, saying, "No one can say I inflict my bad habits on them." So this is "cold turkey," Maren thinks, and not like Lillian at all. She looks strained, her wrinkles deeper, complexion paler, almost transparent. And this time she didn't get her hair rinse right. Instead of the usual auburn, she got bright pink in places. Cotton candy pink. Lillian wanders around the table muttering, as though looking for a cigarette or match…something. Anything.

Meanwhile, in the kitchen, Aunt Stella and Maren's mother have the casseroles under control, rolls out of wrappers, gravy and dressing warming in the microwave.

Maren counts placemats. With Tommy and Lynda there will be thirteen. She gets out napkins, silver. There's space for twelve at the table with the leaves in. She sets another place at one end. That makes thirteen. She lights the candles, stands back. The table does look good and Maren doesn't feel so tired for a minute.

Tommy and Lynda arrive last, bringing Ted's father, Frank. Widowed a year ago, Frank still seems dazed, lost, a little confused. Lynda carries a little girl of about two, who hugs a blue Care Bear.

"Oh," Aunt Lillian says, "you got it already."

"No, no," says Lynda, "she isn't ours. We don't have ours yet. This is Stacy. Her mama's a friend and I said I'd take her for the day." Stacy has hair the color of frost and eyes blue as plastic.

"Set another place," Aunt Stella hisses to Maren, wiping her hands on her red apron. "I'm so relieved we have an-other person. Thank goodness." Before Maren can get another placemat, Aunt Stella has pulled one from the drawer, laid it on the table. "Thank goodness," she says, and rushes back to the kitchen.

"She can eat at the counter," Lynda says. "Put a place here."

"No, no," says Aunt Stella. "I've already got it set and you just leave it. Bring a kitchen stool for her."

Maren has fixed iced tea. If anyone wants anything else right now she's not offering it. Tea now, coffee later, except she hasn't made coffee yet. She made tea with the coffeemaker and you can't do both at the same time. She can't believe Aunt Lillian has been in the house longer than thirty minutes and not had a cup of coffee. She isn't Aunt Lillian without coffee and cigarettes.

Uncle Al carves the turkey, white and dark meat piling evenly in layers on the platter.

"I hope it's tender." Aunt Stella hovers at his elbow. "I hope it's not dry."

"It's tender," says Uncle Al. "Falling off the knife. I could have cut it with a string."

Ted tastes a piece. "If it was any more tender, we'd have to eat it with a spoon." He has grumbled so much about doing anything in the yard lately that Maren is ready to sell the 3,500 square feet on eight acres and buy a condo in town. Something with a concrete yard. How would he like that? The eight acres are woods and he couldn't get enough of them when they bought out here fifteen years ago. A year after they were married and Kellie a baby. There were no neighbors for miles. If Maren hadn't gone to work in Kellie's school as the secretary she would have lost her mind. Ted only has to mow or rake a postage stamp-sized strip around the house. It doesn't take him half an hour, but he growls for hours before and weeks afterwards. Maren is tired of his attitude lately. His attitude toward everything.

Frank says the blessing. He's fast and mumbles through "Thankyouforwhatweareabouttoreceiveandblessusaswegothroughthecomingyearamen." They file past the buffet, filling plates, stacking rolls atop servings of casserole, salad, sweet potatoes. "I hope the turkey's good," Aunt Stella says.

"All this good food," says Aunt Lillian, "and it goes right to my hips. I've got to quit. Just quit." Lillian always diets, eats carrot strips like popcorn, lives on celery, and seems to look always the same. Not thin, not chubby, somewhere in between. "Long ago I quit telling people what to do," she says, forking a cranberry. Lillian still has a small home practice in family therapy, with a dozen or so patients. "But sometimes I have to comment."

"You can comment," Maren teases. "We'll let you."

"Just this strange thing. Our good friend, Lewis Cormon, died. You met the Cormons."

Maren remembers them. They've been Al and Lillian's neighbors for forty years. In fact the whole neighborhood is people who've been there forty years or so. Lillian has described it as the "next thing to a retirement village with the only difference being they all own their own homes and have lived there forever."

"Lew died last week," Aunt Lillian continues, "and they had the strangest service. No funeral. Just a memorial." She shakes her head. "Six people stood up and talked about Lew. Even death isn't sacred any more."

Maren says, "It sounds very contemporary to me. Did you see The Big Chill?" Then realizes her aunt and uncle don't go to movies, don't get HBO. In fact they don't go out at night at all. Or any place they can help it. Today is a rare visit.

"It was awful," Aunt Lillian shudders. "The son spoke of going into bars with his father, taking him home after. Only the daughter gave a touching tribute."

"Did they say anything that wasn't true?" Ted asks.

*Ruth Moose*

"No," Lillian says.

"Anything you didn't know already?"

She shakes her head, doesn't seem to be listening."The only thing they didn't mention was other women. They spared us that, thank goodness."

"But you all knew?" Maren asks.

"Yes, everybody knew."

"So it's okay to know something as long as nobody talks about it openly, honestly. Is that it?" Ted says.

"It's the way the whole thing was done." Lillian seems far away, not eating now, but moving food around in circles on her plate. "I still can't get over it. I'm sorry I went."

At the other end of the table, Aunt Stella is talking of Lisa. "She's separated."

"When?" Lillian asks. "When did this happen?"

Lisa is a cousin, daughter of Al and Stella's oldest sister, Sally.

"Quite a while ago." Stella holds her mouth in a firm, disapproving line. "They just didn't tell it. Not after all that wedding and Sally bragging what a good catch he was."

"Well, I want my twenty-five dollars back." Lillian lifts herself a slice of lemon chess pie from the plate being passed. "Does anyone know why?" She takes a slice of pecan now, then chocolate meringue.

"Money," says Stella. "That's all he thought about. She said they always had good communications. The whole time. They never had trouble with that. Just money. He couldn't get enough."

Lillian sighs. "Long-term marriages are a matter of luck. I came to that conclusion a long time ago."

Before Maren can say what she has on the tip of her mind, Uncle Al says, "Did I ever tell you about the Deal who signed the Declaration of Independence? He was the one who raised the money for Washington's troops to cross the Delaware." .

*Ruth Moose*

Maren laughs. "The Deals could do it. We got the whatever-it-takes-to-get-the-job-done." She adds that she ought to trace the Deals back so she could join the DAR. "It might be fun."

Her brother Tim, loaded spoonful of banana pudding paused on the way to his mouth, says, "Maren, next thing you know, you'll be tracing us back to the NAACP."

Everyone at the table laughs and Maren pokes her tongue at him.

"Papa said once," Uncle Al continues, "some people from Philadelphia came to see him trying to trace Deals about an inheritance. If we could have proved our line direct, we could have inherited a lot of money. But we never could. Courthouse in Union burned and all the records with it."

"Makes it awfully convenient," Ted says, and Maren knees him under the table.

"A lot of courthouses in the South burned," she says.

"Deals are something else," Lillian says. "Al isn't manic depressive, paranoid, schizophrenic, any of the above. And my family has it all. We divided it up evenly among us."

"The Deals were too poor," says Maren. "All they had was farms and hard work staring them in the face. They didn't have time to be neurotic."

"When we got married," Uncle Al says, "I told Lillian there was going to be some stepping on toes. She was going to step on mine and I was going to step on hers."

"And you have," Aunt Lillian says quickly. She looks around as if a cigarette is going to descend upon her from the air.

"You know what happens when toes get stepped on? They get sore. And when a sore toe gets stepped on too much, you yell. So I say you better yell before your toes get sore."

"Communicate," Maren says, and looks at Ted, who is eating more turkey, dressing, gravy. "You had the answer before all the marriage counselors. Fifty years before."

*Ruth Moose*

Aunt Lillian gives her a gray little look. "Long-term marriages are a matter of luck—pure and simple."

"No," says Maren. "It's not that simple. You can't call it chance, like a card game. It's damn hard work."

Ted takes his plate and tea glass, goes to the kitchen.

The child Tommy and Lynda brought has ringed her plate with food, eaten little. Now she pats her marshmallow salad with the back of her spoon. "I'm going to bash somebody's head in," she says loudly to everybody and nobody. "I'm going to take my spoon and bash some heads in."

Lynda takes Stacy's spoon from her, puts food back in her plate. "I'll be glad when we get ours." She doesn't look at Stacy or anyone. Only the table. "I can't wait."

"I'm so glad you brought her," Aunt Stella says. "Thirteen at the table is bad luck. Haven't you always heard that? I've heard it all my life. Some people won't eat at a table if there's thirteen. They take their plate and go someplace else."

"Why?" Maren asks. She's never heard this before.

"Judas," Stella says. "Nobody wants to be Judas."

*Ruth Moose*

# Even the Bees in Denmark

LATER HE WOULD talk at great length about the nude beaches and she never added to it, never interrupted, only smiled and held in her mind a scene he missed, he'd never know because she'd never tell him. Talk about the nude beaches was a sure attention-getter and he gloried in the risque spotlight he created for himself among friends, family, delighting when their Baptist faces dropped, their Methodist minds fastened on him. "A car would pull up," he'd say, "and the whole family would jump out stark naked. Not a stitch among them. They'd make a mad dash for the water." He told of badminton games played on the Danish beaches, all players naked. Bridge games on blankets, each hand held by men and women in the buff. "No one thought anything about it," he'd add, "like it was the normal way to be."

He'd watch looks on faces and when he saw the question blossoming, he'd head it off. "Of course, we weren't nude. We wore bathing suits—such as they were—borrowed from our friends. But we changed behind the dunes. I tell you that was really something." He'd poke an elbow in her ribs. That was what she remembered. That he elbowed her every time they saw someone nude. At least he hadn't embarrassed her then. He hadn't said anything in front of the Jorgensens. Frankly it wasn't that big a deal. Everyone seemed to be enjoying the beach, acted so absolutely normal, she forgot most of them wore no clothes. She did remember noticing one heavily

*Ruth Moose*

bearded bald fellow who strolled along with only a towel hung over his shoulders. He smoked the biggest cigar she'd ever seen. In fact it was bigger than anything else he carried.

She remembered the fine, white sand on the dunes. How it dusted off like sugar. They used the dunes for shelter from the sharp wind, had coffee and pastries with chocolate. They drove leisurely back and she loved the countryside, cows, fields of blooming heather, wildflowers. Curt Jorgensen even stopped to let her pick wildflowers. She thumped a fat, lazy bee off one purple flower. They laughed the bee hadn't protested, merely droned on to the next flower. "Even the bees are happy in Denmark," Curt said. Kristen translated for them and they batted the phrase around in various ways in the days that followed.

A week later they were in Copenhagen and she still had jet lag. She'd wake at 2:00 a.m., unable to go back to sleep, then was terribly tired in the afternoons. Several times she got up, sat on the patio or in the garden, and waited for the rest of the world to awake. He didn't like her to do that. Didn't like to wake up and find her bed empty. Couldn't understand what bothered her, why she couldn't sleep at night, wanted to nap in the afternoons. There were things to do in the afternoons, places to go, museums, shops, tours. They had only three days left. She could nap at home. He didn't care, but for God's sake, while they were here, he sure as hell wanted to get his money's worth. Everything wasn't exactly cheap over here no matter where the dollar was and the rate of exchange. She got so tired trying to figure out kroner, dollars and cents. He carried the calculator, got annoyed if she asked to use it. Next time she'd bring her own. Next time. Already she wanted to come back. There was too much and she missed the one thing she really wanted to see, the Little Mermaid.

"It's not on the beaten track," he said. "It's out in the harbor and it's not all that big. You'll be disappointed after you see it."

She didn't care. It was the idea. She'd grown up on Hans Christian Andersen's stories, almost memorized them at one point in her life.

"You've seen the museum, his bedroom—all that junk. It was nothing but a bookstore. Weren't you disappointed?" he badgered. "Tell me the truth."

"I wasn't disappointed. It doesn't matter his birthplace was turned into a museum and bookstore. I liked just being there."

"Was the ground holy or something?" he said.

"Maybe. Something like that." It wasn't what he wanted to hear and she did really want to see the Little Mermaid.

"You'd have to take a tour and that's expensive," he said.

"Not that expensive. We could check."

"It would take time and we don't have that."

True. They had narrowed down museums and castles to ones close that could be done in a day or half-day. The castle outside Copenhagen was where his camera jammed and he spent an hour in the courtyard cussing, trying to pry it open. She told him they could go to a camera shop. There had to be a number of them around and someone would speak English, she was sure. He said the camera had jammed before. He'd always fixed it. He'd fix it now if he could get to a darkroom.

"A camera shop would have one," she said. "Let's find one."

"They'll ruin the film," he said. "I'll do it myself. I've done it before. Besides, they'd charge you an arm and a leg."

He refused to buy slides, saying he'd fix the camera, they'd come back in the afternoon. Their tickets were good all day. There were things he wanted pictures of, too.

She slept on the grass alongside the moat. For an hour. A delicious hour in sun the color of marigolds. She slept on the all-weather coat he insisted they carry. They hadn't seen rain

*Ruth Moose*

in almost two weeks, but the guidebooks said all-weather coats were essential.

When she woke in the shadow of the castle, the castle with spires like lances, he was not in sight. She stretched, felt wonderful. Funny how she couldn't shake what the light did to her. She knew now why Danes love sun. Before she left the States, a friend had taken her aside, said, "Don't be surprised at anything you see in Denmark." Lucy waited, wondered what she meant. "I just want you to be prepared," Ann had said.

"For what?" Lucy asked.

"Danes love the sun," Ann said. "Don't be surprised if you see someone sitting on a park bench suddenly remove her blouse, sit there bare-breasted soaking up the sun."

Lucy laughed, thanked Ann. Was that all? The idea didn't bother Lucy a bit. If someone wanted to take off everything and sit in the sun awhile it was okay with Lucy. She didn't think she'd do it but there was nothing wrong with what someone else chose to do. After her nap on the grass, Lucy understood. She would have removed her blouse if she could capture and keep some of that sun. That and the grass, her nap, made her feel like a child, rested, warm, and hungry. They'd missed lunch. The castle tearoom closed while he was working on his camera.

He came now from the other side of a black marble statue of a pawing, prancing, nostril-snorting bull. She hadn't seen it before.

"Did you think I'd left you?" he said, broken camera still on a strap around his neck. "Serve you right if I did. Let you find your way back by yourself."

She resolved to start dropping mental breadcrumbs, marking directions. Somehow it didn't bother her. She'd ask until she found someone who spoke English.

It made him angry when he had to check his camera with the guard at the Royal Doulton showrooms. It wasn't one of the places he'd wanted to visit, but there it was on the main street, and she was inside before he realized where they were. She sank in carpet almost to her knees and was dazzled by displays of glass and mirrors. When the uniformed guard stepped forward to take his camera, Allen stepped back, held it close, started to leave.

"It's policy," she said. "For goodness' sakes let him have it."

"It's an expensive camera," Allen said.

"So," she said, "and broken. Maybe he can fix it."

"Ha," Allen said.

She wanted to buy something, anything, here. "I love this place," she said. They watched women in identical blue and white smocks paint flesh-colored plates, cups, bowls. He tugged her away, but they had to go through the salesroom to reach the elevator. She lingered with plaques of the four seasons, bisque, bas-relief. "You'll break it," he said. "You don't have room in your suitcase."

"I'll carry it," she said, and settled on "Night," which showed an angel with a child under each arm, owls and bats overhead.

"It's too expensive, he said. "Maybe you'll see it someplace else cheaper."

"No," she said," this is the factory. It's cheaper."

"You don't know when we'll get to a bank."

"We haven't touched the traveler's checks." She hugged her plaque.

"You don't know how much it will cost to fix the camera."

"We'll put it on credit cards."

"You don't know that," he said. "You can't Visa everywhere in the world no matter what you think."

She figured out the exchange rate, didn't ask for the calculator. Twenty-eight dollars. The plaque would be triple that at home. She'd never buy it at home. Here, she wanted it with all her heart. In the end she charged it. Of course they had Visa. They were delighted to charge it.

He didn't say a word. The traveler's checks were still untouched. They'd be home in three days. For two weeks he had worried about every cent they spent. He was still doing it. To make her miserable? Frighten her? She'd be penniless in a foreign country. She was sure there would be Traveler's Aid, an embassy; they could borrow from the Sorensens.

There was a restaurant through double glass doors, tables under white umbrellas in a garden beside a wall where water spilled down, splashed musically below. Geraniums and impatiens tumbled in pinks, reds, whites from every available container. It looked delightful. She opened the doors, smelled water, coffee, and the warm wafts of something crisp and sugary baking.

"Wait." He pulled her back. "This place will charge three prices for everything."

"How much can coffee cost?" she said. "For goodness sakes?"

They hadn't had lunch and she was starved. "I'll check the menu and if it's too much, we'll just get coffee."

"I'm hungry and I don't want to waste my time and my money on an expensive cup of coffee. There are other places. Let's go."

They reclaimed the camera. "Didn't fix it," he mumbled, and pointed out what he said was a new scratch on the case.

She didn't know how he could tell. He'd had the camera five years, she knew. The case was already worn. It was the worst-looking camera the guard took from a row of them beside the entrance. She almost laughed, instead cradled her package close, followed him out.

She thought they walked forever and still hadn't found a shop where he would eat. Her feet felt heavy and numb. Like bricks, except bricks didn't have blisters and she was sure she had blisters.

*Ruth Moose*

Finally, one shop had nothing but pastries and breads in their window. Every shape, every size. Every price probably, she thought.

"Isn't this better?" Allen said. "You can see what you're getting. Pick what you want."

The shop was packed with people. She tried to read the prices .5 and .7, 1.5—and stay in line. Finally she pointed to a torte delicate as lace, rich in chocolate and creams as truffles, and looked for the cashier. Her pastry was passed down a line like a cafeteria toward a beverages worker. Allen chose something that looked greasy, stale, like a flat doughnut. Lucy hoped it would be good.

"I want something cold to drink," he said. "Order a soda for me."

"I can't," she said. "I don't know the word."

"Order it," he said.

"You order it," she called over her shoulder as the line of people surged forward.

"You're first in line. Order for both of us."

When the line moved past the woman catching cups of coffee from a steaming urn, calling, "Kafe? Kafe? You like kafe?" Lucy hesitated, said, "Soda. Cold soda."

"Kafe?" the woman chanted. "Kafe?" She pushed a cup onto the tray with Lucy's torte. "Kafe?" She pointed to Allen, ran another steaming cup, rocked it on the tray. "Kafe?" she said to the next person. "Kafe?"

The small space was packed with tables, people, shopping bags. Lucy eased her way between them, toward the one empty table in the back corner, put her tray down. Her knees felt weak and she had a dull throb in both temples.

"I didn't want coffee," Allen said, gritted his teeth. "I told you I didn't want coffee." He had sloshed his :into the saucer, onto the tray. "I wanted a soft drink. Soda. I would have taken any kind. Anything cold."

Their table was beneath a mural. A faded garden painted

*Ruth Moose*

onto the wall, like a window with a view instead of a flat wall. It was effective from a distance. Lucy had thought at first glance the shop opened onto a small walled garden.

She brushed crumbs from the last patron into her hand, dusted them into the ashtray full of twisted brown cigarettes. Her coffee was too hot to drink. Much too hot. Steam circled and swirled, rose like a genie. How did they get coffee so hot in this country?

The whole place was too warm, sugary smelling, air heavy as syrup. The kind of place bees would gather. In fact there was a buzz about the room—the hum and buzz of blended conversations, and none of them in English. Lucy listened, felt strange.

Allen pushed his pastry aside. "It's stale," he said. "And this damn coffee. I told you I wanted soda."

"Why didn't you tell the waitress?" she said. Her pastry was wonderful, rich, creamy…everything it looked. She took tiny bites, let them melt on her tongue. The torte had whipped cream, hazelnuts, a slight rum flavor.

"Why don't you get another pastry?" she said. "Get one of these. It's really good. Want a taste?"

"It looks gooey," he said, "and I'm not about to get back in that line. I'd be crushed."

"You could try to get a soda."

"I asked you to get me a soda," he said, "the first time. That's what I wanted." "I tried," she said.

"You didn't try very hard." His words had edges sharp as knives. "You don't give a damn whether I get anything to eat or drink or not, do you?" His voice was loud, getting louder. Two women at the next table turned around. They had been speaking Russian—probably they didn't know anything he said, only that he was angry at her. Lucy was embarrassed. "Please," she said. "Don't yell. It's only a pastry."

"But I told you. I told you I wanted something cold to drink and you order me this." His face was red. He held the coffee cup as though he meant to dash it in her face.

"I'm sorry," she said. "I tried." The women stared, talked to each other in low tones. Others in the shop glanced in their direction. Allen kept on, heaping every angry thing he could remember since they stepped off the plane.

All those women know is the tone of voice, Lucy thought. That he's upset. He could be screaming at me because I have a lover or I've overspent our checking account...a thousand things, and it's none of them. She was so tired. Her feet didn't ache now. They burned on the bottom. Felt scalded like the first sip of coffee on her tongue. She finished her torte, blew on her coffee. "How do they get it so hot?"

He glared at her, didn't answer. At least he was quiet. People in the shop had gone back to their own conversations, pastries. She felt like giggling. Did he know how ridiculous he had looked? Crazy Americans, they probably said, then shrugged their shoulders. Crazy.

Over the next few weeks, he repeated the insult of the coffee she'd gotten him when he had specifically asked her to get him a soda. She always let it drop. All she remembered was that he ruined a moment of small pleasure for her. That she had been both embarrassed and humiliated yet somehow able to step out of herself to see the humor in the whole damn thing.

Their last day in Denmark had been in the museum, his joy. He'd been bubbling before some of the paintings, excited, taking her hand like a child. "Come see this one. Marvelous craftsmanship. I'm overwhelmed." He could study a painting from twenty different angles, across the room, up close, over his shoulder. "Great composition. Look how he slants that light."

She looked at suits of armor, portraits of people who looked starched and stuffed with straw. All the rooms were beige with beige carpeting, beige-cushioned benches in the center. Some were near windows. She sat on those occasionally, packed her suitcases in her mind.

"What's wrong with you?" he said. "Can't you concentrate?" He took her shoulders, turned her to face him. "Can't we do one thing I'm interested in?"

She didn't answer. They walked to the next room and he lost himself in another painting. "God, I wish I had my camera. The one museum in the world that allows you to use cameras and I don't have mine. Damn."

His camera was still broken. They had passed a dozen camera shops since it jammed and he refused to go in, let them look it over. "I'd have to explain it to them," he said. "They wouldn't know what I was talking about."

"You could point," she said. "It's amazing how much you can explain with a smile, gestures, and patience."

He didn't have the smile very often and he certainly didn't have the patience. She stopped suggesting camera shops, that he try to get it repaired.

She stopped sitting on benches in the rooms of the museum, instead stood before windows and looked across the green lawn circled with trees whose branches seemed to float. On the lawn families walked babies in strollers, boys threw Frisbees that were caught by other boys. People walked dogs. One couple sat in folding chairs, read. There was another wide lawn behind the museum. People picnicked with spread-out cloths, bottles of wine, long loaves of bread they broke and dipped into bowls. In the center of the lawn lay a woman on a blanket. She wore a straw hat tied under her chin with a purple scarf, sunglasses and sandals. Otherwise she was nude. Completely naked. She had narrow hips, long legs, and very large breasts. She too was reading and looked completely comfortable where she was, as she was. No one paid any attention to her.

Allen called from across the room, "This guy was a genius. I've never seen such brushwork."

*Ruth Moose*

She walked away from the window. "Yes," she said, "that is a good painting. I like the light."

He put his arm around her. "I want to go back to several paintings again. Really spend some time with them before we catch the train. Do you mind?"

"Of course not."

"You can stay here or go with me. There's a museum shop on the bottom floor, a place to have coffee."

"I'll get some cards," she said, and followed the arrows to the stairs. If she stayed here, he'd see the nude woman, destroy the beauty, naturalness of the whole scene. He'd stare. He'd talk about it later. "Of all the nudes we saw, all those people naked on the beach, not a one of them had anything worth showing. Worth looking at." Then he'd say, "The best-looking one I saw was in downtown Copenhagen, broad daylight," laugh. at his pun, describe the scene, embellish all of it. Destroy it for her.

Later when he talked on and on of the nude beaches, she smiled, said nothing.

A camera shop at the airport fixed his camera, didn't charge him anything. All he did was fuss about the good photos he missed, the great shots. He fussed in the tone of voice of a small child who stamps his foot, a very spoiled child.

*Ruth Moose*

# Friends and Oranges

**Michelle and I**

TEEN ANGELS. WE lie to our mothers. We say we have to study. Algebra, history, awful biology. But she is a year older, Mother says, not in your class. She can help, I say. It is choir practice night. On Sundays we sing like angels. Our robes have wings. We lift and float over the rolling music to the pious sea. We like being almost bad. We like being so very, very good. Old ladies with saggy crepe arms pat our smooth and shiny heads. We wear thin dresses, tiny heels, straps of nothing shoes. When we sing, we arch our white throats sweet as song sparrows.

We have to practice, we have to study. We go to the movies. Miss Sadie Thompson with Rita Hayworth, Jose Ferrer. A cat cries in the alley. She is thin and white with clear green eyes. We hold her, stroke her, say kitty, kitty things. We have to hurry, take the cat along. Mikki buys the tickets. I hide the cat inside my sweater. It does not cry out, but kneads my skin with soft, firm paws.

In the movie the cat sleeps, takes turns on our laps. Afterwards, Mikki and I walk home, carry the cat. We name the cat "Sadie"; discuss the movie. Why was it called Rain? Why are men so mean? Mikki doesn't answer. Sadie, who was so light, is now all heavy legs and fur.

We sleep at Mikki's house. Her mother has changed the sheets and the four-poster bed is a summer hill. Under the window, the mock orange blooms and thorns. Its fingers

*Ruth Moose*

scratch the screen like a peeping tom. We open the window, reach out and pick the teasing oranges. My favorite smell in the whole world, says Mikki, tossing them up. That's all they're good for. Smell. She throws me one for under my pillow. It is mapped and green, fuzzy as a baby's head. The room is all citrus and flowers. We sleep in the top of a blossom tree, Mikki profile. Her nose and chin in the light are sharply drawn and beautiful. I prop on my elbow, watch her eyelids flutter as though she watches a movie. She moans and whimpers like a child; a three-year-old with bad dreams, half-asleep, afraid in the dark. I rub her hand and arms and finally sleep in the special scent of her.

Next morning, Sadie is gone. No one let her out, but she is nowhere we can find. Mikki and I look and call all the way to school, but the cat has disappeared.

## Girl Graduates

I help Mikki pack. Plaids and sweaters, pajamas and socks, panties for each day of the week; Saturday embroidered in red, Sunday crude blue on shining yellow. We hug, promise to write. I do, Mikki doesn't. A year later, I pack and go away to school, meet a hundred girls, gossip and pry, pick and giggle. Mikki is a mugging photo, a silly two pages in my annual, something pressed like flowers between rough paper and leather bound.

Once, home for Christmas, someone calls. It's me, she shouts, it's Mikki. I'm at Mother's. We talk old times. Friends and boys, clothes and parents, school, books and friends. We promise to write. I do. She doesn't. In the summer I go to work for a dentist, wear a uniform crisp as paper, say Yes Doctor, Of Course Doctor, Certainly Doctor. I hand him tools, smile all the time, feel good and clean and tired, tired, tired. Mikki goes out West with a friend. She writes a card picture of the desert. You ought to see the colors. You would not believe how brilliant. I am sending you some. Look out.

*Ruth Moose*

My second year I marry. An artist. He is tall and thin and full of dreams. He smokes a lot, waves his hands when he talks, lives in museums and galleries. He paints, goes to school at night. I work in a department store. Lingerie. You would not believe the styles and patterns. Old ladies gasp. Teens giggle. I cook and clean and scrub his paints off furniture, shirts, the bathroom sink. Titian, Umber, Cadmium, Venetian. The words ring in my head. He is so full of Eakins, Homer, Whistler, Wyeth, and Wyeth. I am a study for a still life without apples.

He graduates, goes to work for an agency where the heads snap and roll. He is regarded as eccentric, a genius, highly creative, an exceptional individual. I am regarded as the artist's wife who makes babies and marvelous pies. I am a commercial for all the well-known brands. I know which are best and fast and better priced. I recite them like an alphabet, a spelling bee, and win. How clever. All my friends are into Tupperware and Sara Coventry. I listen well, learn that language. What you can store where, in what and for how long. Miracles of Tutankhamen's tomb. What you wear with jade and pearls.

**Another Christmas**
Michelle marries. Mother sends me a clipping from the paper, Central News and Views. An announcement and paragraph of a shower her mother gave. Finger sandwiches, pastel mints, assorted nuts. There is nothing I can send Mikki but good wishes and a pot for tears. Who is Barton Francis Roberts III? Mikki's western friend? A few days after New Year's mother sends another clipping. Mikki on the front page of the News and Views. New Mother and Baby of the Year. Five hundred dollars in prizes. Mikki has a ribbon in her hair, a smile like Mona Lisa's sister. Her picture tells me nothing a stranger wouldn't know.

*Ruth Moose*

A year later, her mother sees my mother in the beauty shop. They each have standings. Mikki and Rob have moved to Texas. They are building a lovely home. Something on the order of Tara. They have horses, a pool.

They have another child. Someone sends me a clipping. Is it Mother? There is no note. The postmark is smeared.

My husband wins awards, frames and hangs them in the den. Soon he has the whole wall. He works nights, holidays, weekends. He is brilliant in design, grows a mustache, sings country/western in the shower.

What do you do, people ask at parties. I tell them I am an astronomer, a conchologist, a doctor, a lawyer, a princess, a tax collector and thief. They say how wonderfully talented you are. I do so many things well. My, we are a wonderful team. They haven't heard a word I said.

My husband plays the guitar, sings "The Wreck of the Edmund Fitzgerald." Everyone applauds. He hands me the case to carry. I bow. Thank you very much, I play better, but only at home.

In a class at the Y, I find a wheel, learn to spin. It takes me a year to center. I throw and throw, develop glazes, show my work. The rest of the time, I am my husband's wife, president of the PTA, carpool queen and Bear Cubs mother. Isn't this what you wanted, he says. All hours, wheels in my head turn the clay into forms.

One day Mikki calls. I'm here, she says. I'm in town. I'm coming to see you. I give her directions. Past the Golden Arches, the Kentucky Fried, the Innerbelt, the cemetery, the brick breezeway and lighted lanterns and third box on the left. We laugh and laugh. She sounds the same. I'm into clay, I tell her. She screams, I'm into fibers. You ought to see my work. It's good. It's different. I think it will sell. I wait with the coffeepot and hot brownies, clean hands and house. Mikki never comes. Did I dream her voice? Fibers? I told you, my husband says. She's always been like that. Unpredictable.

*Ruth Moose*

Unstable. What did you ever see in her? What kind of friend is she?

**Down on the Farm**

We buy some land, with house and barn, pastures, fences, sheep, cows, chickens and two large dogs. My husband wants to paint his greatest thing. He needs quiet. I take the children to school fifteen miles away, become the long distance carpool queen, shop the six stores in town, buy little, have sodas in a bitter-smelling, marble-cool drugstore. I see myself in the mirror behind the counter. My face above the oranges, limes, bananas waiting to be used, my dark eyes. I ask if anyone is in there. One eye waters and cries.

The sheep die, cows break fences, eat corn, wander away. Pigs get big and hard to discipline. The barn falls, fences sprawl, drag their wire bellies. There is a drought and our crops burn, savings melt. We have great green thunderstorms with lightning that zips open the sky, rains hard balls of hail. The roof leaks and we sleep in ruin until a panel truck ruts up the rocky drive. The roofer is a naked man in boots. He has an even tan, only works in good weather. I like his voice, his wide shoulders, his quick and fun hands. He whistles down the chimney, adjusts the gutters, smooths the hearth.

My husband paints. He paints an apple, a chicken, and finally a nude. Our neighbor poses. Her hair is long and blond and thin. It brushes her buttocks like a hand. She stands on a crop of far rocks in the pasture. My husband gets excited. Did you ever see such skin? The way the light reflects? He sits by the pond for water. I braid cattails by the creek, wade, pick wildflowers and watch. The work gets in a show and everyone asks did you pose? Of course, I answer. See my long blond hair, my lovely skin. He never asked. The artist's wife is always last. I am plain and brown, dusty as a wren. A mother mouse with her tail snapped in a trap.

*Ruth Moose*

Clay is all I know. I make flat things into something that holds and waits empty to hold again.

## I Take a Saturday Off

The kiln is emptied and cool. My wheel wiped clean as an after-dinner platter. The pots sit in rows on shelves of hope. All day Catherine and I lie in a field of red clover. The air is all lavender and thick honey. I could eat it and fly. We count birds, began the count that morning with a pair of pleated woodpeckers. We write them down. Bluebirds, flickers, redeyed vireos, kingbirds, doves. A red-tailed hawk. This is a dangerous sport, she says. Her binoculars are black and heavy against my chest. Field larks. She points, holds my eyes with her hand. Nine, she whispers. Last year we counted an even dozen in this spot. I watch the brown arrows dart and fan in the blue. I have never felt. so happy. Alive in every humming cell. The top of my head feels electric. If I reached out my hand, touched Cath, we'd both be illuminated. She stands, reaches down for me. We have to go now, she says. We have hungry husbands and children waiting. I never want to go but take her cool hand that still smells of fresh water where we swam in the creek, of willow and wet fern.

Did you have fun, my husband asks? Tweet, tweet. He has built a rock wall, piled stone upon stone upon stone. All the ones I liked best where they were. I knew them there. Now there are pock marks in the pasture, gaps in my daily wall. How dare he? How could he?

Someone had to stop the erosion, he shrugs. What is one wall against a mile? He is the Dutch boy with his finger in the dike. The whole damn wall.

## Michelle Again

It's me, she calls, I'm coming out. This time she does. All in black, like a widow, mourning. She wears a sheer black dress with sweeping balloon sleeves; long black gloves, a large black braided hat. Her hair is up and hidden. Her face opaque as a cloud, and her eyes are gray and full of hurt. She is all silver and black and sad. I got the children, she says. That's all. Would you believe? His boss's wife. I believe. She hooks her arm around my husband's waist. Tell me, she coos, are all artists sexy? She bats her eyes, pale lashes and transparent lids. Would you want to paint me nude she asks? Want a mortgage, I seethe. I know where there's a big one. It goes with him.

After she leaves, he says she is not his type. Too clingy, too much heavy perfume. Magnolia, I say, tons of magnolia. Oh, Mikki, how could you?

In my potting shed, I turn and turn. The clay is me. Raku and sawdust, fire and water. I glaze and etch, sand and salt and fire. The kids complain. You never cook. I burn and bake with life. Sometimes when I tuck them in, my hands are dry and rough. There is mud under my nails. They don't like the smell. It is all I have. I am the clay.

**Mikki Comes Again**

She is different this time. She is copper and red. Her nose is tipped, her smile recapped, she has diamonds in her eyes, on her hands, at her throat. William is in stocks. She met William at a Parents Without Partners meeting. Only William isn't a parent. Don't tell anyone, she cautions. He came to meet people and guess who he found? Tra-la…little ole me, she sings. Across the smoky room. William is so rich. He buys me everything. A condo, a car... a white MG. We're learning to fly, she says. Now he wants a plane.

What about your weaving, I ask. Who has time? She blows smoke at the ceiling. It is so dusty and full of lint and lonely. She wants a farm like ours. All the joys and charm of country life. But William won't live on a farm she says. Not in a thousand years, he only needs the write-off. You got the bright idea, my husband says.

*Ruth Moose*

The farm they buy is in the next county. Mikki says it has sixty cows, but not the milking kind. How do you know? William asks. He looks deep into her eyes. Mikki can't believe him. Isn't he cute? She says he is a prince. A man in his prime. He writes poetry. Brings her a poem a day with a vitamin like a rose. She can't believe he is real. He is everything she always wanted. Everything. She does not look at me when she says this. After she leaves, I look around. The poor farm, my husband with his paints, my filled potting shed…and God knows the kids. Who is kidding whom?

**I Go on the Road with a Green Chair**

The beanbag chair wears my husband's hat. Dumb, he says. But I am afraid to travel three hundred miles alone. I need a male companion. The green chair beside me has a thick neck, wears a pulled-down black felt hat. Little old man. Quiet fellow. I leave at 5:00 a.m. in the dark. A van chases me fifty miles through dense forest. All my doors are locked, the gas tank full, no one else on the road. I speed, hope for a ticket, listen for sirens, finally lose the van.

The beanbag chair slumps to the dash. I stop in a city for breakfast, cut my hand on a map, leave bloody prints, a trail for whoever has to look when I am kidnapped, raped, and killed. All day I sell my work. I can't price and wrap pots fast enough. That night I stay with friends. You work too hard, they say. Come have fun with us. I call home. Are you painting, I ask? It's too quiet, he says, come home. At the end of the week, I limp ragged home, rip off my ERA for Everyone sticker, and fall in the door. He wants to have fun, go out to eat and dance, drink wine, make love. I want to sleep and sleep and sleep. At least a hundred years. At least until the true prince wakes me up and someone has cleaned out the kingdom. The Agean world of the house.

My husband has learned to cook. He can read packages, measure, time, and taste. He can wash and dry, but not fold or find homes for the mingled crowd of clothes that hovers in the laundry room door. He has watered my plants and each one greets me like a favorite child.

The children have gone to live with friends. They never plan to return. They are sixteen and mature. Who needs adults? They have jobs, cars, school, friends. They have tennis and music, disco and pinball.

In my pottery shed, I throw mud against the world that never stops. It turns like time, a spinning clock that wears my face.

My husband's work does not sell. He says no one knows what great art really is. He refuses to paint birds or flowers, wildlife or friends. He hates buckets and wagons, old barns, wants to paint his message to the world, repent at leisure.

A piece of my pottery is accepted in a museum show. Porcelain pears in a lattice basket. They display it under glass. My husband asks, are you proud of that? That? Yes. It's an original. It's beautiful and I made it. He walks away. Ha. A museum guard stares. Are you the artist? Yes, I answer. The word seeks my husband, finds and taps him on the shoulder. He turns around. Come on, he says, let's get out of here.

He paints a weathered board with rusty nails and insect writing. It looks real, I tell him, really nice, really good. Behind the wood and through a hole, he paints his eye. A blue vision. Do you realize that is your eye? It is your self-portrait. Call it Self-Portait of the Artist as an I. He makes an ugly noise in his nose. I make a pot with the same name and nose, mustache and glasses. It sells to a collector and I pay the current bills. My husband never asks when the money comes, where it goes. Bills come to stay like aged relatives, grow cantankerous and ill, but never die.

He has another show. I help him pack and price and hang. I play good hostess with the cups of punch and good cheer. I circulate at the opening event. Isn't he great, people ask and reach for another glass. I know you are so proud. They say

*Ruth Moose*

all the right things, but don't buy his work. One day he takes his books, mustache cup, guitar, and leaves. At first I hear strange noises. The house seems large and I am Alice who drank the wrong bottle. Then I learn to play the radio loud, dance by myself in all the places I never knew before.

**Once Again the Cat**

Mikki calls. I'm here, she yells. It's me. It's Mikki. I'll be out to see you. She drives a small red car, the dogs wag and lick the sweet air around her. She is slender gold and silver. She brings mock oranges in a basket. Aren't they marvelous? She holds one to her nose, juggles others in her arms. There's nothing like them in the world. She heaps them high in my largest blue pottery bowl. The room is alive with citrus smell.

Remember the cat? Mikki says. Sadie the cat? I thought you died. I hug Mikki. Her bones are sharp as saws and she feels light as knitting. I did, she laughs, O God, I did. I died. She says she has been through hell and home. William left. His secretary—she rolls her green eyes. That old cliché. I should have known. The least suspected. Five psychiatrists pulled me through.

Why didn't you call? I ask. I couldn't talk, she says. All I did was cry. Not Mikki. I'm glad she didn't call. I wouldn't want to know, to see, to hear. Not Mikki.

But I won, she says. I won. You should have seen me on the stand. I was the perfect little wounded wife. The cast aside waif. The judge held my hand, cheered me up. O that judge was great. And I got the condo, the car, five thou a month for the rest of my life…and—she screams—I got the farm. All that grass and crazy cows and house and barn are mine. He fought like a fish, a big, big fish, but I won.

I pour red wine into new goblets still warm from the kiln. Their glaze is smooth as Mikki's skin. We finish the bottle and another, talk silly, then serious. We compare battle scars,

*Ruth Moose*

wounds from war. Mikki lost her breasts, I my uterus. The crocheted scar is pink from my crotch to my waist. What a waste, we lament and laugh. Then march like veterans in a no day parade. Mikki, I open my arms, welcome home. Her eyes are the same. Sadie the cat. O Sadie the cat.

*Ruth Moose*

Ruth Moose has published two other collections of short stories, *The Wreath Ribbon Quilt and Other Stories* (St. Andrews Press) and *Dreaming in Color* (August House). She is the author of three collections of poetry, *To Survive* (Book Mark Press, University of Missouri), *Finding Things in the Dark* (Briar Patch Press) and *Making the Bed* (Sandstone Publishing). Moose has published individual stories in *Atlantic Monthly*, *New Delta Review*, *South Carolina Review*, *St. Anthony Messenger* and other places. Her poems have appeared in *Yankee*, *New Mexico Humanities*, *The Nation*, *Christian Century* and several anthologies from Papier Mache Press.

Her books have been taught in classes on Southern Literature at the University of Denmark.

She received five PEN Awards for Syndicated Fiction, a Robert Ruark Award for Short Story, a North Carolina Writers Fellowship, a MacDowell Fellowship and the Oscar Arnold Young Award for Poetry.

Moose has been on the Creative Writing Faculty at UNC-Chapel Hill since 1996.

Moose has had work anthologized in textbooks, the most recent, Modern Fiction about School Teachers from Allyn and Bacon.